KASHMIR

Advanced Praise

In this powerful book, Gowhar Geelani recounts how Kashmiris are reclaiming their own narrative, which has for so long been told mainly by outsiders. Geelani's book is itself a landmark in that process. Here is one of the most articulate and well informed of Kashmiris giving voice to how Kashmiris feel, and what it's like to live in a pressure cooker...Geelani details the perils and pressures faced by the news media in Kashmir and looks for chinks of light which might lift the political gloom that has settled on the Valley that he loves. Let's hope this book is widely read.

—**Andrew Whitehead, former editor, BBC World Service,**
author and historian

Gowhar Geelani has written a brilliant book. It has three major qualities. First, it is informative, with the author revealing his and other ethnic Kashmiris' interesting, often distressing, on-the-ground experiences in Kashmir. Second, it is engaging—grippingly so, at times—as Geelani relates in a very readable style significant events endured by Kashmiris in recent times. Third, it is thought-provoking, with this reader now much better informed about Kashmiris' aspirations, intentions and experiences. This is one of the most informative and stimulating books that I have ever read about Kashmir.

—**Christopher Snedden, noted historian and author**

It takes courage to write about Kashmir, especially for a Kashmiri. In *Rage and Reason*, Gowhar Geelani writes with passion about the past, present and future of his homeland. As a journalist and coming from a generation of Kashmiris who have witnessed 'the horrors of violence', he combines his own experiences with those of others as well as citing from the prevailing literature, prose and poetry. 'Documenting pain can be a challenge', he writes. Yet, he has been forthright in undertaking that challenge. For anyone wishing to comprehend the complexities of anger, uncertainty, hope and despair, Geelani's well-sourced narrative provides an authentic window of understanding.

—**Victoria Schofield, acclaimed author, biographer and historian**

KASHMIR RAGE AND REASON

GOWHAR GEELANI

RUPA

Published by
Rupa Publications India Pvt. Ltd 2019
7/16, Ansari Road, Daryaganj
New Delhi 110002

Sales centres:
Allahabad Bengaluru Chennai
Hyderabad Jaipur Kathmandu
Kolkata Mumbai

ISBN: 978-93-5333-407-9

First impression 2019

10 9 8 7 6 5 4 3 2 1

The moral right of the author has been asserted.

Printed at Replika Press Pvt. Ltd, India

Primarily, I dedicate this book to my Mummy, who stood by me through thick and thin. More often than not, she backed my decisions, often silly, but at times, reasonable too. Without her blessings, I wouldn't be where I am today. She is no longer present amongst us in a physical sense, but I have never felt her absence in my life in a spiritual sense. I am sanguine that she would be smiling and feeling proud that her not-so-obedient son didn't let her down!

To my Daddy Jan from whose analytical mind and debating skills I learned a lot. He taught me lessons of life to make me appreciate the difference between a dream and reality.

To my granny, Boba, whose unconditional love for me can never be explained in words!

To Shabu and Muhi, my lifelines!

And to my three sisters, younger cousins and members of the extended paternal and maternal families.

CONTENTS

Preface / ix

1. Teenager to Rebel Icon / 1

2. Why Tral 'Bleeds Green' / 19

3. Homeland or Caliphate? / 46

4. A Nationalism of Multiple Identities / 88

5. Violence to Non-Violence: A Lost Opportunity? / 119

6. A New Language of Resistance / 146

7. Hell in Paradise / 179

8. Media Wars / 200

9. The Path Ahead / 223

10. A Leadership Crisis / 253

Acknowledgements / 287

PREFACE

'Jaago, jaago, subah hui,
fateh ka parcham lehraya'

(Wake up, wake up, the dawn has arrived,
Our victory's flag is flying high)

This is perhaps one of the first freedom songs I vividly remember by heart. Like the bedtime lullabies, these songs, which played either from the loudspeakers of the mosque or during the pro-azadi* demonstrations, became very much part of Kashmir's collective memory in the 1990s.

Before 1989, I, along with other kids of my age, would be hatching conspiracies to prepare tehri, a special dish of rice cooked with turmeric. It was a common practice among kids to steal mugs of rice from their house to half-cook it, by mixing haldi in it, in an earthen pot. We would pile up wooden sticks and surround these by bricks, and then set the tiny twigs on fire, using a matchstick and some stolen kerosene for smooth combustion. Then we would distribute this tehri amongst ourselves. Some kids would play as hosts while others acted as guests. It was great fun.

Another attention-grabbing childhood activity was to plan scrupulous attacks on apple and almond orchards, and pomegranate trees. I would often visit my matamaal (maternal home) for this reason alone. In Kashmir, the matamaal is a robust social institution that plays an important role in a child's upbringing and overall development. My extended maternal family owned beautiful orchards. All the kids would together organize 'Operation Apple and Almond Theft'. I was the laziest, for I loved

---

*'Azadi' means freedom.

to have apples without taking the risk of being caught by Nana, Nani, my mamas and my khalas*. In a way, however, I would be the strategist. Other kids followed my plans to execute them with perfection.

At the time, one hardly ever heard any sirens of ambulances or police vehicles. Mostly music around us children was produced by the plucking of apples from the branches and throwing stones at ripened almonds and walnuts. In the evenings, we would plan 'Operation Anar**'.

We would plan our four-course meal in the mornings itself—apples, walnuts, almonds and pomegranates. Life seemed wonderful.

During Kashmir's harsh winters, our plans, of course, needed some novelty. Therefore, our focus shifted to the making of concocted ice creams. I and my khalas would break the icicles hanging from the roof of the house and mix powdered milk and sugar with them to bluff ourselves to think that we had made ice cream. Another activity during the winters would include making a snowman. Charcoal pieces from our kangris were used to draw eyes, nose and eyebrows of our perfect snowman, which sometimes resembled Santa Claus.

Hence, the only tense moments in our life were to avoid the risk of being seen by our elders plucking apples or stealing things like mugs of rice, powdered milk or cookies from the kitchen.

I would also play cricket, a passion I continue to nurture even today. There was no dearth of playgrounds. We played in orchards with tree trunks as wickets or on the sides of the nearest graveyard. Older boys would bring their radio sets with them to listen to the live commentary of cricket matches from Radio Pakistan in chaste Urdu. This was my initiation into the world of commentary; it was lovely to listen to persuasive and fluent commentary in the language of elegance and grace.

---

*'Nana' and 'nani' mean maternal grandfather and maternal grandmother, respectively. Likewise, the term 'mama' means maternal uncle. 'Khala' means 'aunt'.
**'Anar' means pomegranate.

Besides this, it was very common for Kashmiri Pandits to have friends from the Kashmiri Muslim community and vice versa. Several women from both communities would visit famous astaans (sufi shrines) located in downtown Srinagar and Chrar-e-Sharief in central Kashmir's Budgam. They would tie ritualistic threads at the shrines when their children were to appear in examinations or competitive entrance tests with the aim to become engineers or doctors.

This was our small world.

One chilly morning in January, probably in 1990, an announcement was made through a mosque's public address system. I wanted to know why people were expected to pray one more time after the Fajr (pre-dawn) prayers in the unpleasantly cold season. (Not that I myself had been a regular at the mosque.) Soon, I realized it was not a call to prayer—azan—by the muezzin. The songs that the boys in my neighbourhood had been singing for some days were being played on the mosque's loudspeaker.

Earlier, the imam at our mosque would complain about people not saying the mandatory prayers, five times a day, on a regular basis. Especially on Fridays, his sermons would reprimand people like me for not visiting Allah's home on other days as well. As a child, I'd keep my head down and not meet the imam's eyes, probably because of the embarrassment caused by his hard-hitting words. Words can heal, but words can hurt too. Thus, one day, I decided to visit another mosque not far away from home, thinking the imam there would not be as 'brutal' and 'heartless'.

I was wrong.

It was Friday and the imam there was spewing fire. 'Why is the mosque houseful today, jam-packed? Is there a "No Entry" board displayed outside the masjid on other days?'

I began to develop a soft corner for the first imam now. I thought of him as a 'lesser evil'.

I did not mind visiting our neighbourhood mosque more regularly now. No, the imam's words had not done any magic or changed my heart. I would go there to listen to the tarana (song): '*Jaago jaago, subah hui/Fateh ka parcham lehraya.*'

Almost everyone knew this song by heart. It was about Kashmir's free will. The psychological ownership of this song was claimed by all those who loved and romanced the idea of azadi. Most Kashmiris identified with it.

'Azadi' is such a romantic word.

But now everything had changed. The music of bullets had replaced the sound of our recess bells in school. Armed resistance to New Delhi's rule had broken out in the Kashmir Valley in 1989, with some groups calling for independence and others calling for a union with Pakistan. School-going children of my generation learned new words and phrases: 'curfew', 'crackdown', 'cordon', 'custody killing', 'catch-and-kill', 'torture', 'interrogation', 'arrest', 'detention' and 'disappearance'.

Children of my age also got used to daily violence. It was natural for me or anyone else to feel angry at the people who marched on our streets with weapons held high. We were angry at the Armed Forces personnel who frisked us, asked us to prove our identity in our own land, threw our school bags away, ordered us to do push-ups as punishment, and hurled the choicest of invectives at us just because of who we were—Kashmiris. As we grew older, we learned more terms like 'fake encounter', 'extra-judicial killing', 'custodial disappearance' and 'mass graves'. Viktor E. Frankl, professor of neurology and psychiatry at the University of Vienna, who experienced the horrors of violence at Auschwitz and other concentration camps during World War II when Adolf Hitler's Nazi troops had wreaked havoc in Germany, wrote in his book, *Man's Search For Meaning*, 'An abnormal reaction to an abnormal situation is normal behaviour.'* This, then, became the new normal in Kashmir, and was to change our lives, stories and literature forever.

Nearly thirty years have passed since. And the Valley is in the throes of a new phase of rebellion. It is natural for kids to be affected by what is happening around them. The context for Kashmiri kids of this generation is different. They have not seen

---

*Frankl, V. E. (1985). *Man's Search for Meaning*. Simon and Schuster.

times of peace. They have no photo albums of shared memories of cultural confluence with members of the Pandit community. Similarly, the new generation of Pandits has no memories of living together with Kashmiri Muslims. This has widened the chasm between the two communities. Thankfully, on festivals like Maha Shivratri, many families continue to send special walnuts and nadrus (lotus stems) from Kashmir to several Pandit families known to them. But this mutual fondness and warmth is missing in the new crop from either community for the absence of the memories of living together.

The new generation has only witnessed oppression and violence. They will make their decisions in life based on their own experiences and context. Kashmir's generation born after the 1990s is fearless, conscious, educated and articulate.

In 2016, as many Kashmiri parents were confined to their homes, reading history books on their homeland, the children were asking questions: 'What is India? Who is Pandit Jawaharlal Nehru? What is a referendum? Why has India grabbed our land? When will we get independence?'

The year 2018 was the bloodiest in a decade. Has Kashmir become a slaughterhouse for their young? Is the Valley, known previously as the land of sufis and saints and alcoves of almonds and apples, fast turning into a valley of funerals of its young?

Defence analyst and author Pravin Sawhney argues that 'Incensed by India's high-handedness and with no political respite on the horizon, Kashmiris have become defiant.'*

This book contextualizes that defiance.

Kashmir is fast losing its precious human resource: its teenage boys. It can't afford to normalize this colossal humanitarian crisis. Mourning cannot be Kashmir's permanent politics. Funerals of young cannot be political events. This tragedy, indeed, is the outcome of the absence of meaningful, sincere and clean politics.

---

*Sawhney, P. (2018, December 2). The Real Googly: More than Imran, the Pakistan Army Wants Peace with India. Retrieved from https://thewire.in/diplomacy/the-real-googly-more-than-imran-the-pakistan-army-wants-peace-with-india

Killing of a human is not news anymore; it's a bloody routine. The dead are mere statistics. Everything abnormal has either been normalized or rationalized.

On 25 November 2018, as I was busy writing this, a nineteen-month-old baby girl, Hiba Nisar, was hit by lethal pellets fired by government forces in south Kashmir's Shopian district soon after protests broke out in her village.* Government forces had killed six local armed rebels there. She knew nothing about Srinagar, Delhi, Islamabad, stones, guns, freedom, protests, curfews, strikes, army or militants; neither could she raise her voice to protest anything. She is just a baby. Kashmir's circumstances changed her fate and gave her a new vocabulary. Perhaps for the rest of her life, it will be 'P for Pellets' for her.

Such tragedies are an inseparable part of the Kashmir story today, which is not known to many outsiders. This is perhaps why many non-Kashmiris often ask: 'Why is there so much of rage in Kashmir? What does Kashmir's angry generation want? What is the reason behind this rage?'

Kashmir: Rage and Reason attempts to answer these basic questions.

Gotthold Ephraim Lessing, a German writer, critic, dramatist and philosopher, once remarked that 'There are things which must cause you to lose your reason or you have none to lose.' The Kashmir Valley is angrier than before. It is not anger alone, though. It is a bold and expensive expression of political aspiration that most Kashmiris think is legitimate, that is deliberately being criminalized by the State, and that is delegitimized by vast sections of the corporate-owned media houses based in Noida, Delhi and Mumbai. The assertive generation of Kashmir is weaving its homegrown narrative to deconstruct the State's Kashmir plot, and its hypernationalist media's conventional and convenient savagery that cashes on falsehoods, propaganda and provocation. This new

---

*Kashmir Infant, Hit By Pellet in Eye, May Not Regain Full Vision: Doctors. (2018, November 27). Retrieved from https://www.ndtv.com/india-news/kashmir-infant-hiba-nisar-hit-by-pellet-in-eye-may-never-regain-full-vision-doctors-1954133

generation in Kashmir appears to be on a mission to challenge New Delhi on all fronts. More importantly, it seeks to counter the mighty State without Pakistan's 'moral, diplomatic, political or financial' assistance. It is Kashmir's indigenous narrative, which has unnerved the New Delhi establishment. That's why we are witnessing a renewed native rebellion on Kashmir's streets. This new upsurge is Kashmir's 'romantic rebellion', where an almost idealistic notion of freedom and love for the land is combined with combative, militaristic resistance.

This resistance found its poster boy in the late Burhan Wani. He did not come from an underprivileged background. His father, Muzaffar Wani, was a principal at a government school. He had all the comforts a teenager in Kashmir or anywhere else in the world could aspire for. Why did he then pick up a gun? Why did he challenge the State's monopoly over violence? Many in Kashmir perceive the very presence of government forces, the Army and paramilitary troopers as 'military occupation' of their homeland. The narrative in Kashmir is that New Delhi has no moral or political argument on Kashmir; it has the argument of power. On the contrary, Kashmiris feel they have the power of argument. The State did not respect a peaceful transition from a violent to nonviolent movement that occurred in 2008. Its brutal response to peaceful civilian uprisings in 2008 and 2010, after which the world also witnessed the Arab Spring, telegraphed a message to the dispossessed Kashmiris: 'You can't raise your voice. You can't protest. If you will, you will have to face bullets, pellets, and eventually death.' Another message that was conveyed was that 'Delhi will not bend.'

Such militaristic messages forced the present generation of Kashmir to do a rethink. A section of young boys in impressionable ages was also forced to reach a discomforting conclusion: Delhi neither understands nor respects nonviolent political movements or creative forms of protest. That's how Burhan was born. That's how he became the face of Kashmir's new age of rebellion and another reference point in Kashmir's recent history.

No matter what the hawks from both sides aspire for, peace

is in everyone's interest. And peace arrives when injustice ends. Kashmir deserves justice, a solution to the political problem and an end to political uncertainty, so that the coming generations do not have to face the same ordeal. But peace will remain elusive if the dispute remains unresolved.

The Kashmir story is now being told by Kashmir's young storytellers in various forms. It deserves the world's attention.

And the world *has* to listen!

1

TEENAGER TO REBEL ICON

Friday, the 8th of July.

Yes, Friday.

But it wasn't just any other Friday in Kashmir. Fridays are usually reserved for pro-azadi demonstrations and incidents of stone throwing (at government forces)—often likened to the Palestinian Intifada—in many parts of the Kashmir Valley. At Srinagar's historic Jamia Masjid, scores of masked youth engage government forces in ding-dong battles after Friday prayers because peaceful assembly is not allowed. It is the anger of the dispossessed. With a stone in one hand and a pro-azadi placard in the other, the youth raise vehement slogans and draw anti-India graffiti on the walls and roads.[1]

Government forces, usually outnumbered by local demonstrators but enjoying protection under the controversial Armed Forces (Special Powers) Act [AFSPA][2], react with lathis, tear gas shells, pellet-firing shotguns and, at times, bullets. However, even though the Indian Army is shielded by the AFSPA, the Jammu & Kashmir (J&K) police force is not.

Such scenes are part of the tapestry of everyday life in Kashmir. But on this particular Friday, 8 July, most people were either relaxing at home or visiting friends and relatives because of Eid-ul-Fitr, also known as Chhoti Eid. Kashmir had celebrated Eid on 6 July, after Pakistan's Markazi Ruet-e-Hilal Committee, the government department in charge of announcing the sighting of the new moon, declared that Eid would be celebrated on 6 July. Traditionally, Kashmiris observe Eid only when Pakistan announces it. It was no different this time either. The state's education department had also announced summer vacation in all government and private schools from 4 July to 17 July, for about a fortnight. Because of Eid and the brief summer vacation, most people were at home, glued to television screens, watching movies and sports shows, or visiting new cafes and restaurants with friends and family.

In this atmosphere of leisure and celebration, no one in Kashmir could have possibly anticipated that the Friday after Eid would bring with it another cycle of death and destruction. By Friday evening, unverified information about Burhan Wani's possible killing had begun circulating locally. Such rumours had erupted at other times as well.

This time, though, was different.

I received an urgent call from an editor who wanted to know whether I could file a detailed story about the incident along with Burhan's profile. I nodded in agreement. The first thing I did was to call a credible source in south Kashmir to confirm Burhan's death. He requested that I wait for five minutes or so but called back almost immediately, confirming the news.

'Yes, Burhan has been martyred.'

About an hour later, pictures of the bullet-ridden bodies of Burhan Wani and his two associates, Sartaj and Parvez, began to circulate on social networking sites. The news that the social-media-savvy commander of Hizbul Mujahideen (HM) had been killed in an 'encounter' with government forces in Bumdoor village in south Kashmir's Anantnag district, some 80 km from Srinagar, spread like wildfire. In a matter of hours, Kashmir erupted yet again. Mourners began to descend on the 'encounter site', which was swiftly accorded the status of a place of pilgrimage. Burhan had become a phenomenon, the glamorous hero of an almost romantic anti-State rebellion. Popularity creates its own authority, even in a place like Kashmir where modesty is appreciated. Burhan was empowered by the perception of his popularity.

Meanwhile, my source in Tral called again to inform me that thousands of people were out on the roads and marching towards Burhan's hometown. They were seen on the Srinagar-Jammu highway, and on the streets, lanes and bylanes of Tral, Awantipora, Pulwama, Pampore, Shopian, Kulgam, Kokernag, Anantnag, Qazigund, Srinagar, Sopore, Pattan, Baramulla, Hajin, Bandipore, Ganderbal, et al. Their common desire was to reach Tral to grieve over Burhan's shahadat (martyrdom) and pay khiraj-e-aqeedat (glowing tributes) to their hero.

South Kashmir was tense and angrier than it had been in recent times. People started protesting even in areas that had until then been considered 'protest-free zones' by the security establishment. The People's Democratic Party (PDP)-Bharatiya Janata Party (BJP) coalition government in J&K—which fell apart after the latter ended its alliance with the former on 19 June 2018—was caught unawares. The state's security grid grew nervous, unable to stop the swelling crowds that had rapidly formed a sea of protesters. They resorted to tried-and-tested tricks like firing bullets and pellets indiscriminately at unarmed protesters, hitting most of them above the waistline. News of the brutal crackdown further exacerbated an already tense situation. Kashmir was on the boil. The calm of Eid had vanished into thin air. The cycle of killings had resumed.

A seemingly clueless Chief Minister (CM) Mehbooba Mufti did exactly what her predecessor, Omar Abdullah, had done during the pro-azadi protests in 2010. Slogans from mosques' loudspeakers and sirens of speeding ambulances carrying the injured and the dead were the only sounds to break through the enforced silence that engulfed Kashmir. Predictably, the PDP-BJP government tried to hide its embarrassment by blocking cellular and Internet services as its first response to the crisis. The junior Abdullah had employed the same trick during his tenure from 2009 to 2014. It is one of the most common standard operating procedures in Kashmir. The data and mobile Internet has been blocked in Kashmir at least thirty-one times between 2012 and 2016[3], and sixty-two times until July 2018.[4] I could no longer access the Internet on my mobile phone.

The next morning, on 9 July, I called my photojournalist friend,

Javed Dar. He had made his way through pastures and meadows to reach Sharifabad in Tral to cover Burhan's funeral. Traversing a hilly route on his bike, he spoke to me, a little out of breath, about the people assembled at Tral. Those at Tral's Eidgah included men, women, children, young girls and boys, and elderly people. Waheed Mirza, another friend from Tral and a witness to Burhan's funeral, said that at least 300,000 people attended Burhan's janaza. Moderate estimates put the number of mourners at 250,000. Top police officers conceded, off the record, that the number of people was over 100,000, but would not mention the exact figure for obvious reasons. Young people, who hero-worshipped Burhan, put the figure at 500,000, which might be an exaggeration. A Tral resident might be overwhelmed by emotion, but a professional photojournalist would not stick his neck out unnecessarily; he will speak with a sense of responsibility. I will, therefore, place the figure of attendees at 200,000.[5]

Remarkably, many young Sikhs from the neighbourhood could also be seen at Burhan's funeral, raising slogans in favour of Kashmir's azadi. It had taken the death of a 'people's hero' to recharge the sentiment of azadi, it seemed. Women joined men and the old joined the young to raise slogans that rang out on the streets and were cried out from mosques.

'Hum kya chahate, azadi,
Hai haq hamara, azadi,
Burhan, tere khoon se, inquilab aayega'

('We want freedom,
freedom is our right,
Burhan, your blood will bring forth the revolution')

'Burhan bhai se rishta kya,
La ilaha illallah,
Tum kitne Burhan marogay?
Har ghar se Burhan niklega'

('Our bond with Burhan is the Kalima, article of faith,
How many Burhans will you kill?

A Burhan will emerge from every home')

Some protesters also chanted this slogan:

'*Burhan bhai ka kya farman:*
Kashmir banega Pakistan'

('What is the order of brother Burhan:
Kashmir will merge with Pakistan')

The slogans highlight the many fissures that have appeared among the people of Kashmir over the years. Pro-azadi and pro-Burhan slogans could be heard across north, south and central Kashmir and in the capital, Srinagar. At Burhan's funeral, his close associates, like Sabzar Bhat who was immediately nominated the slain commander's successor and was later briefly replaced by Zakir Rashid Bhat, appeared in Tral's Eidgah to offer a volley of gunshots as a mark of respect to their charismatic commander. Locals greeted the masked rebels with cheers and slogans, and a human chain was formed to protect them from a possible ambush until they left the scene. This overt and often exclusive expression of love for Kashmir's renewed militancy brought back memories of the early 1990s, when the people of Kashmir would greet and hail the militant Mujahideen. Almost everything was chillingly reminiscent of those times—the curfews, the slogans for azadi, the protests and the killings.

It was as if it was 1989 once more, the year when armed revolt against Delhi's rule erupted in full earnest. Spontaneous protests broke out on the day of Burhan's funeral and were stifled by government troops using indiscriminate force. In the cycle of protest and crackdown that followed, at least ninety civilians were killed and over 15,000 injured, including women, and children as young as between one to fourteen years. About 1,100 received injuries from pellets in their eyes, of which about 200 were on the verge of losing their vision temporarily or permanently.[6] The Srinagar-based English daily *Greater Kashmir* reported that over 7,000 people, mostly youth, were arrested while the police registered 2,300 first information reports (FIRs) as Kashmir completed hundred days of uprising post Burhan.[7] Why had the news of Burhan's killing inspired an uprising in Kashmir? Why had common people turned up to face bullets and pellets? Why did everyone feel as if they knew him on a first-name basis?

★

Against a picturesque backdrop of apple orchards and mountain peaks, Burhan, in combat fatigues, had posed with an AK-47 rifle along with ten of his associates. A video in which he could be seen playing cricket had made him an Internet sensation in 2015. Photos posted on Facebook were shared widely. There was an element of romance to his rebellion. Numerically, these eleven boys posed no threat to the Indian Army, one of the largest armies in the world. However, psychologically, these boys telegraphed a message that New Delhi can be challenged. Their rebellion was romantic; it was largely symbolic, too.

Almost two years before the floods that devastated large parts of Kashmir in September 2014, I heard murmurs about a young militant commander, Burhan Muzaffar Wani. But it was only after a sensational picture of him and his associates in combat gear, faces uncovered and holding AK-47 rifles, went viral in the summer of 2015 that Burhan acquired both notoriety and star status. Along with his band of ten, he became the talk of the town. After his pictures were posted on social media, Burhan also released a video statement with what could be considered a 'moderate' message. He appeared to take a sort of moral high ground by saying that though the police was harassing family members of the HM rebels, his outfit would not retaliate by penalizing family members of the 'guilty' police personnel.

This message came from a handsome twenty-one-year-old boy who, thanks to new-age technology, had become a rebel without a mask. He had lifted the veil. Everyone knew who this young boy was and where he came from. His courage and open defiance of authority as well as the moderate content of his first video message made him an instant hero among vast sections of

Kashmir's population.

In his second video message, which also went viral on the Internet, Burhan welcomed the return of Kashmiri Hindus (also known as Kashmiri Pandits) to their homes and supported the annual Hindu pilgrimage to the holy Amarnath cave in south Kashmir's Pahalgam area. Large sections of Kashmiris seemed to identify with Burhan's moderate ideology. Publicity on social media platforms was the currency Burhan was spending. His fame repaid him with fresh recruits and also donations. By September 2018, the number of armed militants in the Kashmir Valley had crossed 350, most of them from four districts of south Kashmir viz. Pulwama, Shopian, Anantnag and Kulgam.[8]

Soon, Burhan was being discussed at the dastarkhwan* in many Kashmiri homes. Using social media intelligently, and wielding the powerful tool to his advantage, Burhan attracted the youth and the elderly alike to his cause. His emergence revitalized the spirit of resistance against New Delhi's authority in Kashmir, which had become jaded partly because of a kind of disenchantment with the pro-freedom alliance, the All Parties Hurriyat Conference's (APHC) inability to deliver anything substantial, partly because of New Delhi's refusal to address the political dispute and partly because the former had few cards to play with. Burhan's coming out as an armed rebel appeared to have given fresh impetus to an otherwise waning militancy. His popularity as a young tech-savvy rebel commander had attracted new recruits, mostly youths from his home and surrounding districts of south Kashmir. In the aftermath of his killing, renewed attempts were made in the form of large-scale civilian protests and demonstrations to address the root cause of the Kashmir conflict.

In such an atmosphere of disillusionment and mistrust, when the leadership of Kashmir's resistance movement has, by and large,

---

*In Muslim culture, most people take lunch and dinner while sitting on the floor. During mealtimes, the dastarkhwan, which is a piece of (cotton) cloth/(plastic) sheet, is traditionally spread on the floor to facilitate everyone to sit around it and eat in peace.

shifted away from the old leadership, the youth are driven by a strong sentiment for azadi. Interestingly, the action of the youth on the ground is also shaping the position of leaders and public representatives. The fifth generation of Kashmiris since the anti-Dogra uprising in 1931 is sacrificing their lives and limbs for the dream of freedom—or rather, their romanticized idea of it. Burhan represented this generation in a unique way. Many Kashmiris admired his courage, conviction and defiance. The symbolic importance of Burhan in a place like Kashmir, which feels it has been wronged many times by New Delhi since 1947,[9] could not be underestimated by any stretch of the imagination. Burhan's decision to pose with weapons was equivalent to cocking a snook at one of the largest standing armies in the world. Why more than 200,000 common Kashmiris participated in his funeral on 9 July 2016, is a question New Delhi must ask itself and ponder over. Those who turned up to commemorate his memory did not see Burhan through New Delhi's myopic prism; for them, he was a heroic 'freedom fighter'. When it comes to Kashmir, New Delhi appears as a martyr to a constipation of ideas.

To understand the 'Burhan phenomenon', I travelled to 'Kashmir's Tora Bora'—Tral. Almost every second household had a story to narrate, and their pain to share. For them, Burhan had found a new way of fighting against the injustices towards Kashmir at a time when militancy was perhaps at its lowest ebb. He infused fresh life into an otherwise declining armed rebellion. His USP, as I understood it, was that he instigated Kashmiris to think beyond Pakistan. With his bravado, he effectively conveyed the powerful message that Kashmiris can rise against New Delhi without seeking Pakistan's 'diplomatic, political, moral or financial' support, thus renewing and reinvigorating the indigenous strain of Kashmir's rebellion. As a result of the Burhan phenomenon, for the first time in a long while, security officials began to admit that local rebel recruits outnumbered 'mehman mujahideen' (foreign militants). If one goes by official statistics, the total number of armed rebels in the Kashmir Valley is still less than 400. Three hundred and fifty odd guerrillas, most of them neither battle-hardened nor fully trained warriors, do not pose a threat to India's huge security presence in Kashmir. But the twenty-one-year-old Burhan did present a threat grave enough to warrant immediate elimination.

From the perspective of most Kashmiris, Burhan was neither a religious extremist nor considered to be on Pakistan's payroll. In Kashmir, the perception is that loyalty is often on sale and offered to the highest bidder. More potent than the gun in his hand were Burhan's images on Facebook and his videos on YouTube. What this means is that despite the conflict fatigue of the last twenty-nine years or so, a section of the youth in Kashmir refuses to give up or surrender. There is no denying the fact that the Indian Army, along with paramilitary forces and local police, has—in the last nearly three decades—broken the back of Pakistan-supported militancy in Kashmir. But, it is also a fact that a section of Kashmir's educated youth continues to romanticize the idea of picking up a gun against New Delhi's presence in Kashmir. Anti-India rebellion is a socially sanctioned reality in today's Kashmir, not necessarily driven by Islam, but not entirely devoid of it either. The very idea that Kashmir can challenge New Delhi with whatever little power it has is pretty significant, especially in an atmosphere where democratic spaces for dissent stand choked.[10]

For New Delhi, Burhan was a 'terrorist' who carried a bounty of ₹1 million (₹10 lakh) on his head. Some reports said that the bounty was ₹20 lakh. For most Kashmiris, Burhan was a new symbol of resistance. These are two conflicting and competing narratives about the same individual. This has often been the case since 1947, as the distance between New Delhi and Srinagar has only increased. New Delhi has always viewed Kashmir as a 'law and order' problem,[11] or at best, it has accused Pakistan of fishing in troubled waters. It has consistently followed a policy of managing different cycles of unrest and waves of anti-State protests to buy time, with the aim to impose so-called normalcy and peace in the region, even as it refuses to acknowledge the deeper political crisis in the state.

The people of Kashmir are today challenging the much parroted 'anger and alienation' narrative, and the very presence of government troops on their soil. Former CM of J&K, Omar Abdullah, in an interview with Karan Thapar in *India Today*'s programme, *Nothing But The Truth*, argued that the children injured by pellets and bullets in the mass uprising following Burhan Wani's death on 8 July were waiting for their wounds to heal so they could pick up a gun and join the ranks of militants.[12] India had been dishonest with the people of Kashmir, he said. This acknowledgment from someone who is part of pro-India mainstream politics in J&K and is a working president of the National Conference (NC) should have been an eye-opener for New Delhi. Even the state's new governor, Satya Pal Malik, appointed soon after the breakup of the BJP and PDP in June 2018, admitted that 'India has made mistakes, and its mistakes have, in the process, alienated itself' from the people of the Valley.[13]

When I met Burhan Wani's father, Muzaffar Wani, at his home in Sharifabad at the end of May 2016, Burhan was still alive. I was surprised to hear Mr Wani say that he was a proud father because many in Kashmir were naming their newborn babies after his son. A well-regarded teacher, he came across as moderate and civilized, and treated the guests and mourners who often descended upon his home with respect. As we chatted, he shared some personal details of Burhan's life, like his passion for cricket, and his fondness for mutton and chicken. For a moment, it felt as if we were talking about just another Kashmiri teenager and not a militant commander. Indeed, Burhan, he told me, was like any other teenager—particular about his appearance and fussy about his food. During summers, he would bathe twice a day and use hair gel to maintain his stylish hairstyle. He wouldn't eat if there was no chicken or mutton dish. His neighbourhood knew him as a handsome teenager, a talented cricketer and the child of an educated middle-class family.

Until recently, Muzaffar Wani, an MSc in Mathematics, was a father of three sons and a daughter. Now that he has already lost two sons, Khalid in April 2015 and Burhan in July 2016, he is left with his elderly parents; wife, Maimoona; daughter, Iram; and son, Naveed. Khalid was pursuing his post-graduation when he was killed in the forests of Tral by the Indian Army on the evening of 13 April 2015. Some reports suggested that he had cooked biryani for Burhan and wanted to have it with him and a group of common friends. Khalid left after telling his family that he was going for a picnic with his friends. The Army dubbed Khalid a militant and claimed that he had died in an encounter, one that was strongly refuted by his family and others in the area. Muzaffar Wani told me it was possible that Khalid died in custody because if he had been killed in an encounter, as claimed by the Indian Army, why did his body not have a single bullet wound? Tral residents claim that Khalid was tortured to death because his brother was a rebel commander.

When I met Muzaffar Wani, he was posted as the principal at a government secondary school in neighbouring Lorigam village in Tral. My first question to him was, why did Burhan, a teenager from a well-off family, choose to join the ranks of militants? Before he could respond, his father, Ghulam Ahmad Wani, intervened to say that unemployment was not a major problem in Kashmir. 'Kashmir is a political issue which craves a political solution,' the senior Wani said. He had been a government employee and had retired as assistant director, Department of Planning, in the state government. As he spoke about Khalid and Burhan, tears began rolling down his face. No father could be at peace, he said, when one of his sons has been killed and the other's body might reach home any moment. On noticing his father's distress, Muzaffar Wani gently told him that a guest had come to see him in another room.

When we were alone, Burhan's father told me that he sometimes wondered how his son, who would bathe and change a couple of times a day, would have adjusted to living in forests for the past six years. He thanked Allah and the people of Kashmir for keeping his son safe ever since he left home at the age of fifteen. He said that even though his son was a mujahid, he was himself not affiliated with the APHC or any other political or religious party. Even so, he clearly blamed New Delhi's continuing 'ziyadtiyaan' (atrocities) and troop presence for the renewal of violent militancy in the Valley.

Burhan was not the first Kashmiri to pick up a gun and neither will he be the last, he said. Burhan was not even born when anti-State armed rebellion first erupted in Kashmir in 1989. And, it is not only Burhan who wants azadi from India; tens of thousands of people who participate in a mujahid's janaza also raise the same slogan, 'Hum kya chahate—azadi!' It is not Burhan's struggle alone. It is a struggle that enjoys unparalleled popular support among the people of Kashmir. If people were not seeking freedom from India, they wouldn't gather in their thousands to commemorate the death of a mujahid, knowing fully well the consequences of such an act of defiance.

✻

The incident that prompted Burhan to leave home has been well documented. It was 2010. A wave of anti-State demonstrations had begun after it came to be known that the government forces had killed three young men in a fake encounter in Macchil in north Kashmir. The Indian Army later admitted to the fake encounter in 2014 and its northern command in September 2015 confirmed life terms to six Army personnel, including a former commanding officer, who were found guilty of killing three people in a staged encounter in 2010 and branding them as foreign militants for brass medals and cash rewards.[14]

It was a first in Kashmir's recent history that Army personnel found guilty were awarded life terms after a court martial. But in July 2017, the Indian Army's Armed Forces Tribunal, in a hugely controversial decision, suspended the life sentence of five of the Army personnel, including a colonel and a captain.[15]

Widespread protests against the Macchil fake encounter had thrown normal life out of gear in Kashmir. The state was under lockdown. According to Ghulam Ahmad Wani, Burhan, Khalid and their friend were out on a motorbike when some Special Operations Group (SOG) personnel stopped them and asked to get them cigarettes. After they did so, some members of the SOG pounced on Khalid and beat him up. Burhan was deeply hurt by this incident and was affected by a sense of dispossession and disgrace. He reportedly told the SOG men that he would avenge this ignominy. '*Ab main tumhe nahin chhodoonga*' ('Now, I will not spare you!') are the words he is said to have spoken then, and which have become almost apocryphal now.

Going by this account, it is clear that Burhan was not driven by any global jihadi ideology. In any case, he did not have a deep understanding of religion or the concept of jihad in Islam. According to his father, he was not regular with his prayers, like any other teenager. He had not studied any Islamic literature, and was not under the influence of any religious text or organization. It is almost incidental that his name was Burhan and that he was a Muslim. Burhan was a Kashmiri Muslim who felt humiliated after his brother was beaten up by members of an 'occupying force'. The circumstances he found himself in, especially in three successive years of 2008, 2009 and 2010, had influenced him. The incident in 2010 acted as a trigger. When he left home, he took refuge in the forests of Tral. He certainly did not cross the Line of Control (LoC) to receive arms training in Pakistan-administered Kashmir (PaK), Pakistan or Afghanistan.

In the initial phase of militancy that broke out in 1989, Ashfaq Majeed Wani, a young and educated commander-in-chief of the pro-independence Jammu Kashmir Liberation Front (JKLF), became a household name in Kashmir. Born in 1966, Ashfaq Wani was killed by government forces on 30 March 1990, when he was only twenty-four. A massive crowd had attended his funeral and vowed to carry forward Wani's mission, which he had defined as a struggle for the right to self-determination. Mohammad Yasin Malik, the current chief of the JKLF, often draws parallels between Ashfaq and Burhan. They were young, and extremely popular. The difference between them was that in its earlier phase, militancy in Kashmir was partly controlled, sponsored and hijacked by Pakistan; this time around, Burhan had made a difference of sorts.

Many in Kashmir, who may not choose the path that Burhan did, admire him and think of him as a role model in more ways than one, for standing up and speaking up, and by proving that Kashmiris have a choice to exist as free individuals who must have the freedom to make their own decisions. Like most Kashmiri youngsters of the early 1990s and post-2000, he had experienced, first-hand, the brutishness of the Armed Forces deployed in Kashmir. Every gun-toting soldier ruling the streets of Kashmir was and is a symbol of 'Indian military occupation' for the majority of Kashmiris. The formidable crowds at Burhan's funeral procession were raising a political demand, '*Hum kya chahate—azadi!*'. Their assembly was not merely symbolic. It was evidence of what Kashmiris think of the forces that killed Burhan, and why they showered love and accolades on someone who had chosen to fight those very government forces.

In my entire journalistic career, I have never witnessed an assembly at a militant leader's funeral quite of the same scale. One such funeral I can recall as a kid was that of Jamaat-e-Islami (JeI) leader Ghulam Nabi Nowshehri offering janaza at the funeral of Ajaz Dar in September 1988 at the hostel lawns of Sher-i-Kashmir Institute of Medical Sciences (SKIMS) in Soura, Srinagar. A few hundred people had attended the funeral and raised slogans that I do not remember clearly. I did not then know who Dar was and why he had been killed. It was much later that I came to know that he had died in a violent encounter with the police, and that a group of young Kashmiri youths, displeased by the farce of decades of professed democracy under New Delhi's rule, had decided to fight for Kashmir's independence. Although Dar was not the first Kashmiri to die fighting for Kashmir's tehreek-i-azadi (freedom struggle), his death did mark the beginning of the popular armed uprising of 1989.

Meanwhile, Khalid's gratuitous beating might have turned Burhan to armed rebellion, but that's not the complete story. It has an important context—the perception among the people of Kashmir that their homeland was under a military siege. In his death, Burhan became another reference point in Kashmir's history and gave Kashmir its next hero, after Maqbool Bhat and Ashfaq Wani. The former, JKLF's co-founder, was hanged in Tihar Jail in New Delhi on 11 February 1984. Five years later, Kashmir would witness the beginning of armed militancy.

Burhan's popularity among the locals, especially the youth, was astonishing, to say the least. On 9 July, people from the length and breadth of Kashmir defied curfew and crippling restrictions to catch a final glimpse of their swashbuckling rebel leader at his funeral. The crowds presented a sharp contrast to the meagre 3,000 who had gathered at Srinagar's Sher-i-Kashmir Cricket Stadium (SKCS) to participate in the funeral of Mufti Mohammad Sayeed, former CM, earlier that same year, in January 2016.[16] This was also a sort of referendum on who enjoys social sanctity and popularity in Kashmir, and a reiteration of the well-known fact that pro-India politicians will remain unloved. In April 2016, a hardcore pro-India politician in Kashmir told me that 'Delhi's treatment of Kashmiris has made people lose confidence in mainstream politics... As of today, an ordinary Kashmiri feels more alienated, humiliated and sidelined. Mainstream politics in Kashmir is at the precipice of complete irrelevance.'[17]

Another measure of the popularity of the young rebels was a local cricket tournament in Tral in 2016, where three teams out of a total of sixteen were named after popular militant commanders—Burhan Lions, Aabid Khan Qalandars and Khalid Aryans. It was a two-month-long tournament organized in the memory of Burhan's older brother, Khalid. Eventually, the Khalid Aryans lifted the trophy on 24 April, beating the United XI of Tral.

In death, Burhan Wani's popularity has only surged in Kashmir. In fact, if one goes by the kind of slogans that were raised in pro-azadi rallies after his death, it appears that his popularity had leapfrogged over other prominent resistance leaders of Kashmir. Seemingly, there is also a shift in Kashmir from a pro-APHC/JKLF sentiment to a pro-militant sentiment, which perhaps signals disenchantment with the political process. Mosques reverberated with songs like '*Soan Burhan, myoan Burhan, choan Burhan...*' ('Our Burhan, My Burhan, Your Burhan...'), eulogizing his struggle and sacrifice, for months after his killing. Slogans like '*Geelani-wali azadi*' ('Geelani's brand of freedom') are being replaced by '*Burhan-wali azadi*' ('Burhan's brand of freedom'), an explicit reference to Wani and evidence of his growing eminence as an icon of the popular sentiment of azadi in Kashmir.

NOTES, SOURCES AND REFERENCES

1. Kashmir Unrest: Youth paint anti-India, pro-freedom slogans on walls, roads. (2016, August 02). Retrieved from http://www.greaterkashmir.com/news/kashmir/story/224488.html

2. The AFSPA received the approval of the President of India on 10 September 1990. The Act, however, was deemed to have come into force on 5 July 1990. It grants certain powers to members of the Armed Forces in the disturbed areas of J&K. According to The Gazette of India, a disturbed area is 'an area which is for the time being declared by notification under section 3 to be a disturbed area.'

3. India: Kashmir social media ban criticised. (2017, April 28). Retrieved from http://www.bbc.com/news/world-asia-india-39741886

4. Source 1: Geelani, G. (2018, July 26). In Kashmir, ban on Pakistani TV channels raises questions – about those from Delhi (and Mumbai). Retrieved from https://scroll.in/article/887823/in-kashmir-ban-on-pakistani-tv-channels-raises-questions-about-those-from-delhi-and-mumbai Source 2:
    Source 2: Bhat, A. A. (2018, January 24). Kashmir's internet shutdowns hit schools and businesses but fail to quash dissent. Retrieved from https://www.alaraby.co.uk/english/indepth/2018/1/24/kashmirs-Internet-shutdowns-hit-schools-and-businesses-not-militants

5. Source 1: Kuchay, B. (2016, July 19). A Hero's Farewell. Retrieved from http://kindlemag.in/a-heros-farewell/
    Source 2: Qadri, A., & Shah, S. A. (2016, July 10). Two lakh across Valley attend Burhan Wani's funeral. Retrieved from http://www.tribuneindia.com/news/jammu-kashmir/two-lakh-across-valley-attend-burhan-wani-s-funeral/263661.html
    Source 3: Ashiq, P. (2016, September 18). Burhan's funeral: Dangerous writing on the wall. Retrieved from http://www.thehindu.com/news/national/other-states/burhans-funeral-dangerous-writing-on-the-wall/article8831559.ece

6. Source 1: Raafi, M. (2016, October 09). #Day93: Curfew Continues In Srinagar Parts As Kashmir Observes Complete Shutdown. Retrieved from http://www.kashmirlife.net/day93-curfew-continues-in-srinagar-parts-as-kashmir-observes-complete-shutdown-120289/
    Source 2: Nazir, T. (2016, August 12). 1-yr-old baby girl hit by pellets in father's

lap inside her home. Retrieved from http://kashmirreader.com/2016/08/12/1-yr-old-baby-girl-hit-by-pellets-in-fathers-lap-inside-her-home/

Source 3: Hussain, A. (2016, July 21). In Kashmir, pellet gun victims are as young as 4 years. Retrieved from http://www.hindustantimes.com/india-news/in-kashmir-pellet-gun-victims-are-as-young-as-4-years/story-1tMf1PBrubqxTw3f5V3IgL.html

Source 4: Editorial: Crushing dissent to construct perception. (2016, October 13). Retrieved from http://thekashmirwalla.com/2016/10/editorial-crushing-dissent-to-construct-perception/

7. Yusuf, S. (2016, October 07). Over 7000 arrested, 2300 FIRs registered. Retrieved from http://www.greaterkashmir.com/news/kashmir/over-7000-arrested-2300-firs-registered/230262.html

8. An informal chat with a top intelligence officer in Srinagar revealed that in the first nine months of 2018, at least 146 more recruits had joined the ranks of the armed rebels, thus taking the total number of active militants in the state of J&K to over 350. According to the officer, at least forty-five new recruits had joined militancy from Pulwama district alone.

9. The story of the gradual and perhaps systematic erosion of J&K's constitutional position and special status within the Indian Union is a tragic one. From Sheikh Mohammad Abdullah's arrest and removal as J&K's prime minister (PM) on 9 August 1953, to throwing the autonomy resolution passed by the J&K state legislative assembly in a dustbin in 2000, and the rigged elections of 1987, New Delhi has played many a political game on Kashmir's turf, thereby discrediting democratic processes, elected representatives and institutions.

10. There is a complete ban on student politics in universities in Kashmir, as well as on peaceful assembly and pro-freedom rallies.

11. Source 1: Noorani, A. G. (2015, July 27). India's failure in Kashmir. Retrieved from http://www.greaterkashmir.com/news/opinion/story/192659.html

Source 2: Ehsan, M. (2016, July 13). Kashmir protests: Centre handling of situation failure on state govt's part, says J&K Oppn. Retrieved from http://indianexpress.com/article/india/india-news-india/kashmir-protests-centre-handling-of-situation-failure-on-state-govts-part-says-jk-oppn-2909465/

Source 3: Congress backs Omar, says Kashmir unrest not a 'law and order' issue. (2016, August 21). Retrieved from http://www.business-standard.com/article/news-ani/congress-backs-omar-says-kashmir-unrest-not-a-law-and-order-issue-116082100104_1.html

Source 4: Noorani, A. G. (2018, April 24). It is a revolt. Retrieved from http://www.frontline.in/cover-story/it-is-a-revolt/article8932435.ece

Source 5: Bimal Prasad (Ed.), *Jayaprakash Narayan: Selected Works*; Vol. 7; Manohar; page 115.

Source 6: Bazaz, P. N. (1976). *The History of Struggle for Freedom in Kashmir: Cultural and Political, from the Earliest Times to the Present Day.* Islamabad: National Committee for Birth Centenary Celebrations of Quaid-i-Azam Mohammad Ali Jinnah, Ministry of Education, Govt. of Pakistan.

Source 7: Mitra, A. (2018, June 30). NO TIME FOR THE VALLEY— The Indian nation is alienated from Kashmir. Retrieved from https://www.telegraphindia.

com/opinion/no-time-for-the-valley-the-indian-nation-is-alienated-from-kashmir/cid/493680

Source 8: Haksar, N. (2015). *The Many Faces of Kashmiri Nationalism: From the Cold War to the Present Day*. New Delhi: Speaking Tiger.

12. India Today. (2016, July 23). Nothing But The Truth With Karan Thapar : Omar Abdullah On Kashmir Unrest. Retrieved June 07, 2019, from https://www.youtube.com/watch?v=6w2bBwXv7KQ&feature=share

13. Iqbal, N. (2018, October 04). J&K governor Satya Pal Malik: India's mistakes alienated state, my job is to make space for talks. Retrieved from https://indianexpress.com/article/india/jk-governor-satya-pal-malik-local-body-elections-hurriyat-pakistan-5385532/

14. Ehsan, M. (2015, September 07). Machil fake encounter case: Army confirms life sentences for its six army personnel. Retrieved from http://indianexpress.com/article/india/india-others/machil-fake-encounter-case-life-sentences-of-six-army-personnel-confirmed/)

15. Jaleel, M. (2017, July 26). Macchil killings: Tribunal suspends life sentence of five Army personnel. Retrieved from http://indianexpress.com/article/india/machil-fake-encounter-armed-forces-tribunal-suspends-life-imprisonment-of-five-armymen/

16. Source 1: Bhatt, S. (2016, August 02). Facing moral blindness in Kashmir. Retrieved from http://www.dawn.com/news/1274764

Source 2: Poor turnout at Mufti funeral worries PDP. (2016, September 22). Retrieved from https://www.thehindu.com/news/national/other-states/Poor-turnout-at-Mufti-funeral-worries-PDP/article14001925.ece

17. Geelani, G. (2017, April 21). The ones who pay for war: Is mainstream politics in Kashmir on the verge of complete irrelevance? Retrieved from http://www.catchnews.com/pov/the-ones-who-pay-for-war-is-mainstream-politics-in-kashmir-on-the-verge-of-complete-irrelevance-58407.html

2

WHY TRAL 'BLEEDS GREEN'

In the last week of humid May in 2016, I travelled to the picturesque town of Tral in south Kashmir, some 40 km from Srinagar. Tral is almost picture-perfect, surrounded by high mountains, green pastures, paddy fields and apple orchards. In the recent past, the place has earned sobriquets like 'Chhota Pakistan' and 'Kashmir's Tora Bora' because of its hilly terrain and its reputation for being the hotbed of renewed militancy. It is one of those 'liberated zones' of Kashmir where the love for Kashmir's azadi is unprecedented. It is considered relatively 'safe' for militants because some of them are from this region, they enjoy immense public support and the topography of the area is conducive for them to disappear in. The common people are unapologetic about where their loyalties lie. The widely held opinion of pro-freedom is proclaimed with a sense of pride.

My visit to Tral's Sharifabad, Burhan Wani's hometown, began with a local shopkeeper who had both English and Urdu newspapers and magazines prominently displayed at his shopfront. I asked him about circulation and subscription trends in the area that is reported to have one of the highest literacy rates in Kashmir. Global politics, Kashmir affairs and sports were topics of interest, he said. The people I know in Tral are avid readers and sports freaks. The shopkeeper soon got busy. I too felt it would be unfair to disturb him during peak business hours and so I moved on.

My earlier visits to Tral have left deep impressions on me about the people and their political awareness. It was a learning of sorts to know that here people, especially the youth, openly declare their love for Kashmir's struggle for 'self-determination'. They are unhappy with the status quo and favour a durable political solution to the Kashmir dispute. They do not use ifs and buts, and insist that they want azadi from India. Their candid arguments leave little room for ambiguity. They are aware that their straightforwardness can easily invite the wrath of the government and intelligence agencies, but they simply don't care. They say that they are ready to pay the cost for their political sentiments and aspirations for Kashmir's azadi; they say they are all 'Burhans (militants) without guns'.

Among the anti-India proponents, there are those who favour independence but do not necessarily support Kashmir's merger with Pakistan. But there are some villages, like Laribal and Lorigam, where pro-Pakistan sentiment is deep-rooted. This is true of the rest of the state as well. This sentiment is particularly heightened in parts of south Kashmir, like Shopian, Pulwama and Anantnag; in north Kashmir's Baramulla; and in parts of Srinagar. The JeI, a well-known sociopolitical and religious organization in the Valley, has a large following in parts of south Kashmir. JeI (J&K) was founded in 1942, and has a strong cadre base across the state. It is separate from JeI (Hind), and maintains that J&K is a disputed territory that seeks its resolution through a right to self-determination. The organization is very popular among people in the Kashmir Valley and draws its strength from the work that it does in imparting education and carrying out social reform and relief work, especially during natural calamities like earthquakes or floods.

India's Ministry of Home Affairs (MHA) imposed a ban on the JeI for a period of five years, beginning 28 February 2019. According to the MHA, the ban was imposed under Section 3 of the Unlawful Activities (Prevention) Act [UAPA]. The MHA accused the JeI of being 'involved in anti-national and subversive activities', a charge denied by the latter. Over 300 of its members, including its emir (chief) Dr Abdul Hameed Fayaz and chief spokesperson Advocate Zahid Ali, were arrested.[1] Earlier, the JeI had been banned twice, in the 1970s and the '90s.

One often comes across young people in this area who say they 'bleed green'. They are in love with Pakistan and their cricketers, television dramas, and so on. This reference is indicative of their ideology. To 'bleed green' means different things to different people. Whether pro-freedom or pro-Pakistan, they are unanimous in saying that they don't consider themselves 'Indian'. Like most Kashmiris, they openly support Pakistan's cricket team, which wears a green jersey in shorter versions of the game. They favour an armed rebellion because New Delhi disregards protests and creative forms of resistance. They seldom use the term 'militant', preferring the term 'mujahid', or holy warrior, instead. Any rebel who dies fighting government forces is a 'shaheed' (martyr) for them. They say that those who chose to fight and were 'martyred' in the process are far better than those who remain alive and do not speak up against oppression.

I could easily understand this statement. A top security officer of the J&K Police, who has had a long experience in counter-insurgency operations, told me that if he were to bring 100,000 AK-47 rifles to south Kashmir in the morning, there is every possibility that he would return home empty-handed in the evening. Weapons are not readily available in the Valley especially after the enhanced fencing along the LoC. Another senior police officer who served in north Kashmir's frontier district of Kupwara told me that smart fencing has made infiltration difficult, if not impossible. That's perhaps why there is a growing number of incidents where young boys snatch rifles from local police or paramilitary Central Reserve Police Force (CRPF) personnel as a precursor to joining the ranks of rebels.

Even some Special Police Officers (SPOs), employed on meagre salaries by the J&K Police as special security guards for VIPs, have indulged in weapon-snatching bids and later joined militancy in what has now become a signature style. In a recent development of such nature, SPO Adil Sheikh fled with at least seven assault rifles and a pistol from the guard room of a residence of a legislator at Jawahar Nagar in Srinagar city.[2] Sheikh was posted as SPO with PDP legislator Aijaz Ahmad Mir from Wachi constituency in south Kashmir. He was later seen with a group of HM militants along with the weapons. There are an estimated 30,000 SPOs in the entire state of J&K. The PDP legislator too was quizzed by the police. Later, in a tweet, he complained that he was abused by the munshi (policeman) of a local police station in Srinagar.[3] The legislator also alleged that the munshi was pressurizing his SPOs to speak against him in the weapon snatching case.

About the nature of militancy, the security officials have their own assessment based on intelligence inputs, on-the-ground research, media reports and so on, but it is a fact that the youth in Kashmir, in general, is not fascinated by any global terrorist movement like the Islamic State of Iraq and Syria (ISIS/ IS). Generally, they are aware enough to make a clear distinction between global terrorists and freedom fighters involved in an indigenous struggle to reclaim their homeland from perceived occupiers. But in the absence of meaningful political intervention, things could easily change; and such a situation—in which paranoia and fanaticism could occupy minds that are closed, disempowered, dispossessed, disadvantaged, vulnerable and impressionable—may not be far away. That is perhaps why Kashmir witnessed one of the deadliest suicide attacks in Lethpora, Pulwama, in south Kashmir, on a CRPF convoy on 14 February 2019. Forty CRPF soldiers were killed in this suicide car bomb attack, which the government forces believed was carried out by a local Kashmiri youth named Adil Ahmad Dar, alias 'Waqas Commando', a resident of Gundibagh hamlet in south Kashmir's Pulwama district. Jaish-e-Mohammad (JeM) claimed responsibility for the attack. In police records, Dar was listed as 'C category militant', which means very few cases of militancy were filed against him compared with those listed as 'A category militants'. This suicide bombing almost took two countries, India and Pakistan, to war. India launched an air strike on Balakot, Pakistan, on an alleged JeM training facility, which Pakistan flatly denied. Pakistan also crossed over the LoC to launch a similar air strike. One Indian Air Force (IAF) pilot, Abhinandan Varthaman, was captured and later released by Pakistan as a 'peace gesture'. Such are the dangers of an unresolved Kashmir dispute.

Even veteran resistance leader, Syed Ali Shah Geelani, who

is considered a hawk by New Delhi, has openly and vociferously spoken against the ISIS and termed its policies as un-Islamic. On 7 January 2016, he denounced the ISIS in a hard-hitting statement at a time when its flag was repeatedly displayed in Srinagar by a handful of masked youth, terming it a terrorist organization that does not represent Islam. According to a confidential report by J&K police's intelligence wing, the first time the ISIS flags were seen in the Valley were in 2014, after the devastating floods. A few masked youth appeared outside Jamia Masjid, Srinagar. According to the report, few arrests were made and it was found out that the suspects had little or no idea about what the ISIS stood for. Geelani also declared Tehreek-i-Taliban Pakistan (TTP) and Daesh (acronym of the Arabic name of ISIS) to be terrorist organizations. This statement was widely reported by Kashmir's regional media and sections of Indian media based in Noida, Delhi and Mumbai.[4]

In several interviews with me, Mirwaiz Umar Farooq, the Srinagar-based head priest and chairman of a faction of the APHC, echoed the same view and said that some boys wave ISIS flags during routine Friday demonstrations only to irritate and annoy India. He too was firm in his belief that the ideology of the IS had no takers in the Kashmir Valley.

Nonetheless, there is a tiny group of armed youth in Kashmir that claims its allegiance to the Islamic State of Kashmir and Ansar Ghazwat-ul-Hind (AGH). A few journalists have described this occurrence as a 'shift' in Kashmir's new age of militancy. That said, the IS ideology does not enjoy popular support on Kashmir's turf. Many Kashmiris have taken to social media and described a handful of IS-sympathizers as 'hooligans'. According to a top-ranking police officer, there are no weapons, support system or infrastructure available for the ISIS in Kashmir.[5]

Therefore, armed resistance against Delhi's rule in Kashmir has to be seen in the context of Kashmir alone. There are proponents of the argument that mass mobilization after Burhan's death is proof of the people's approval for the path chosen by Burhan and possibly others like him in the future, but one must not lose sight of the fact that the number of people to have joined the ranks of rebels remains small and largely symbolic. Emotional scenes of people carrying militant commanders on their shoulders during pro-azadi rallies in the aftermath of Burhan's killing were indeed a throwback to the early 1990s, when large sections of Kashmir's population endorsed armed revolt en masse, unaware of the entire gamut of its ramifications. This time around, there exists the history of the last twenty-nine years. This overt support for azadi and militants like Burhan tells us a story that New Delhi perhaps does not want to listen to, because it would like to remain in denial mode.

The public backing of this renewed armed rebellion should have provoked New Delhi to do a rethink on its tried, tested and failed strategies of managing the conflict over different waves of agitations in Kashmir. But, New Delhi chose to look the other way, in what can only be described as willful self-deception. Though New Delhi made statements and a joint parliamentary committee visited the Valley, these were largely perceived as firefighting measures and a denial of ground reality.

The uprisings of 2008–10 should have forced Delhi to do some soul-searching and adopt a judicious approach in dealing with widespread anger in the Valley. Unfortunately, it has again, and wrongly so, taken refuge in a blame game involving Pakistan, which boomeranged on multiple fronts. All attempts to paint Kashmir's indigenous movement as 'Pakistan-sponsored unrest' have proven to be counterproductive. New Delhi and its representatives in Kashmir lack respect and sanctity among the common people. As vast sections of the Indian media, especially electronic media, indulge in populist 'Pakistan bashing', a greater number of Kashmiris than ever before raise slogans like, '*Pakistan se rishta kya La illaha illallah*' ('Our bond with Pakistan is the Kalima, article of faith').

Perhaps Delhi needs to discredit Kashmir's indigenous mass uprising and make an argument at international forums that it is a victim of 'Pakistan-sponsored terrorism' in Kashmir. However, facts on the ground in 2016 tell a different story. Going by official statistics, there were less than 250 militants in Kashmir, which was a testimony to the fact that these boys—most of them neither battle-hardened nor well-trained in guerrilla tactics—had chosen the path for symbolic reasons. In Kashmir, many are of the view that even militancy is a political statement. If Kashmir were a jihadi hotspot, Kashmiris would have embraced the armed guerrilla movement in droves, but the numbers suggested otherwise. These young men enjoyed popular support because they were mostly locals, and people respected the choices they had made in fighting Delhi's rule. People may not prefer joining the ranks of armed rebels themselves, but they also do not want to take away the agency from those who do become militants out of their volition. The fact that they did not usually target civilians and limited their actions only to armed forces and the police also gave them credibility as 'freedom fighters'.

Any assertion linking Kashmir's struggle with forces of global jihad has no factual evidence to back it. Rebels in Kashmir do not blow themselves up in the manner of the recruits of ISIS, Al-Qaeda, or even the Taliban, in markets and public/religious places to cause civilian casualties. There are no suicide bombings that target common people. That's one more factor behind the immense popularity of these rebels among the locals. Militants in Kashmir mostly target Indian Army patrol parties, convoys and military installations to make their presence felt from time to time. HM continues to be Kashmir's largest homegrown rebel outfit. Pakistan does support Lashkar-e-Taiba (LeT), JeM and Al-Badr, and makes infiltration bids to send their new recruits to Kashmir, but their numbers are far less today than HM's local rebels. Analysts in Kashmir often insist about making a clear distinction between political radicalization and religious radicalization/violent extremism.

As I tried to make sense of the deep-seated pro-azadi sentiment in Tral along with its religious underpinnings, I met a retired seventy-year-old government school principal, Abdul Gaffar Khan. He had retired as in-charge principal at a school located in Panzgam in south Kashmir's Pulwama district. He now runs a hardware shop in Tral. The elderly man's eyes speak as if they're witness to many historical events. For, he has lost two sons, Maseehullah and Rizwanullah, in encounters with government forces. Maseehullah died fighting government soldiers in September 2010 while Rizwanullah, according to his family, was killed in a suspected encounter at Panthal in south Kashmir, close to the Srinagar-Jammu highway. Though Khan is clear about Maseehullah's direct involvement in Kashmir's armed rebellion, he told me that Rizwanullah, a graduate and an expert mobile phone repairer, was killed by government forces and falsely declared a 'militant sympathizer' in police records.

Abdul Gaffar Khan told me that all land and territories belong to Allah, and what belongs to Allah should be governed by His laws alone. That implied the implementation of shariah law in Kashmir, but he was quick to add, though, that this was a call that only leaders, Islamic scholars of various schools of thought in Islamic jurisprudence and learned people could take.

Maseehullah was working as a mechanical engineer at Jalandhar in Punjab, Khan told me. He returned home in 2009, saying that he had come to Kashmir for a holiday. Maseehullah was well-versed in Islamic teachings and had completed several rounds of tafseer (interpretation and translation) of the Quran, despite his young age. He was sensitive and influenced by Islamic history and literature. With a sense of pride, his father told me that he himself had taught his son. Apart from the father-son relationship, there was also a teacher-pupil bond between the two.

On his return from Jalandhar, Maseehullah began to preach at a local mosque. On noticing this, his father asked him whether he had sought permission from the mosque's management to deliver sermons. Maseehullah had already done so. Maseehullah's fiery discourses on jihad granted him instant popularity and also made his father nervous. He had also come under the radar of the local police and intelligence sleuths. Anxious, his father tried to enquire why his son was not returning to his job in Jalandhar, but got no straight answers.

Khan says he tried his best to reason with his son, saying that the people of Kashmir, or even Tral, were still not 'mentally ready' for the kind of teachings he was imparting in the mosque. One cannot invoke jihad when the leaders of Kashmir's freedom struggle have not come to a decision on the issue, Khan would often argue. However, his father's suggestions could not stop Maseehullah from treading a path he obviously felt was right for him. Due to his oratorial skills, Maseehullah's popularity grew with each passing day. For the Khan family, there was more to see, more to follow and more to endure. Maseehullah's mother intervened. She tried to reason with her son that the head of the family was not happy with his preaching jihad in the mosque because people's minds were not 'fertile' enough for such a change. It was then that Maseehullah revealed to his mother that he had seen the Prophet of Islam, Hazrat Muhammad (PBUH), in his dream, and the Prophet had asked him, 'If you know so much about jihad, why do you not do anything about it?'

That dream was a turning point in Maseehullah's life. In July 2009, he left his family quietly to join the ranks of the HM to wage jihad. 'Jihad' is an Arabic word that essentially means 'struggle'. It can be interpreted as a struggle to feed one's family, or for justice; to help the needy and poor; or against oppression and a perceived enemy.

There are enough people in Kashmir who think they are in a state of war with New Delhi,[6] and feel that India treats Kashmir as 'enemy territory', to be grabbed for its land, even if it means oppressing its people. Some of them say they are militants sans weapons.

For young men like Maseehullah, the Indian State is the real 'enemy' against whom they believe they are waging a religiously sanctioned and righteous jihad. Maseehullah, once a mechanical engineer, became a mujahid and eventually, HM's area commander. The life expectancy of a militant in any conflict zone is said to be between two and three years. Government forces zeroed in on him in September 2010, and he was killed in a gunfight in Posh Pathri village in Tral. Upon noticing that he had been surrounded, Maseehullah offered special midnight prayers, tahajjud, and raised slogans of freedom and Islam. He was finally killed along with three associates. For Khan and many other Kashmiris, Maseehullah had achieved martyrdom. *'Jaam-e-shahadat nosh kar gaya'* ('He tasted martyrdom'), his father said to me, proud of the 'sacrifice' his son had offered for a cause.

In Maseehullah's rebellious story, religion played a part. That was not the only reason for choosing the path that he did, though. There had been a wave of mass protests in the summer of 2008, when Kashmir and Jammu had been deeply divided along religious and regional lines. In the summer of that year, the infamous Amarnath land transfer dispute had raged for about two months in the Muslim-majority Kashmir Valley and Hindu-dominated Jammu city. The grant of 99 acres of forest land in Baltal to the Shri Amarnath Ji Shrine Board—a temple trust headed by the governor of the state, via an agreement between the state government and the Government of India—triggered protests because it was perceived as an attempt to change the demographic of the Muslim-majority region. Kashmir faced an economic blockade. Several Kashmiri truck drivers were beaten up in Jammu. The situation in the Valley was tense. As a response to the uprising, government forces showered bullets on protesters, killing more than sixty civilians, most of them in their teens.

During this time, the PDP had formed a coalition with the Congress in the state, and Congress leader Ghulam Nabi Azad was the CM. Fearing the consequences of being seen as a partner in crime, the PDP withdrew its support from the state government. All PDP ministers submitted their resignations to the then governor, Narinder Nath Vohra. PDP President Mehbooba Mufti, who was at that time building her career as a grass-roots pro-Kashmir politician, regularly visited families of slain rebels to express her condolences. With this gesture, she created a niche for herself as a 'soft-separatist' who favoured 'self-rule' for J&K. It is another matter that her party ended up forging a partnership with the Right-wing BJP in March 2015, the same ideologically antithetical political force about which she had famously said in her 2014 poll campaign, 'Kashmiris won't sell their zameer (conscience) by voting for the BJP.'[7] In an interview with NDTV

24x7, she accused the Hindu nationalist BJP of spreading its 'communal' and 'sectarian' agenda while categorically ruling out any partnership with it.[8]

After losing her post as CM in the aftermath of the breakup of the PDP-BJP partnership in June 2018, she, in an interview with me at her official residence at the fortified Fair View at Gupkar, asked for people's forgiveness for the civilian killings that took place during her tenure: 'All I can say is, please forgive me... if you can. I was the chief minister when the killings happened, and it does not matter why and how it happened.'[9] She also regretted making some statements that she said had 'hurt the sentiment of the people.' In a moment of anger and frustration, she had been both reckless and insensitive with her language and ended up blaming the teenage youths and protesters for their killings at the hands of government forces in 2016 during the post-Burhan, three-month-long civilian agitation. She had asked questions like 'Why had the youth gone out of their homes to protest? Were they out to fetch milk, buy toffees?'

Political commentators and key Kashmir watchers had described the PDP-BJP partnership as an 'unholy alliance' and predicted that joining hands with the BJP was no less than 'political suicide' for the PDP. On its part, the PDP seemed focused on assuming power and, thus, compromised on its principles and ideology to partner with a party they had denounced till then, and which was not popular with the people of the state because of its allegiance to Right-wing Hindutva ideology and the Hindutva project. The alliance, forged by the late Mufti Mohammad Sayeed in March 2015 against the popular mood, seemed yet another step towards Delhi's politics of invasion in Kashmir. The feeling that the identity of Kashmiris, especially Kashmiri Muslims, was under severe attack got cemented further, because of a series of nationalistic Hindu pilgrimages like the Abhinav Gupt Yatra, proposals for setting up composite townships for migrant Kashmiri Pandits, construction of separate Sainik colonies for former soldiers, among others.

The Amarnath land transfer agitation of 2008 had sharply

polarized opinion in the Kashmir Valley and in Jammu like never before, as if the battle was between Kashmiri Muslims and Jammu's Hindus. The government's brutal response to peaceful protests forced a new generation of Kashmiris to do a rethink on their conscious transition from the gun to street protests. Delhi's militaristic crushing of Kashmir's popular agitation actually paved the way for passing the 'baton of freedom' on to the fifth generation since 1931, which young boys like Maseehullah and later Burhan Wani became a part of.

In 2008, the message that Delhi ended up conveying to the young generation in Kashmir was that even peaceful dissent will not be tolerated. This rigidity and lack of empathy by the State sowed the seeds of a renewed rebellion in the hearts and minds of Kashmir's new generation with a new vocabulary and a new idiom. Delhi's continuing policies of oppression never helped it win the 'hearts and minds' of Kashmiris. A section of Kashmir's educated youth in impressionable and vulnerable ages concluded that since Delhi only speaks to Kashmiris with violence,[10] it will only understand the language of violence as a response. It was a conclusion that shaped the then thirteen-year-old Burhan Wani as much as it did the twenty-two-year-old Maseehullah.

According to Gaffar Khan, Maseehullah was repeatedly called in for interrogation by the local police for his sermons on jihad. Raids were periodically conducted on his house until he was killed. Maseehullah was declared an HM rebel. In police records, Khan's other son, Rizwanullah, was recorded as an over-ground worker (OGW) and a 'militant sympathizer' accused of 'supplying arms to militants', justifying his killing at the hands of government forces.

The absence of his sons has created a void in Khan's life that cannot be filled. '*Sajdoun main bhi beytoun ka khayal aata hai*' ('My two sons appear before my eyes even when I say my prayers'), he told me, tears rolling down his cheeks. He also wanted to say that in the absence of an intelligent and honest leadership, nations do not fight wars. Those who have sown the seeds of resistance against New Delhi have forgotten about their role and responsibility, he maintained. Emphasizing that there is no linguistic, cultural, religious or geographical connection between Srinagar and Delhi, Khan made a case for Allah's laws being implemented in a Muslim-majority region. He also explained how his son had been influenced by the JeI's literature, reading books like *Jihad Fi Sabeelillah* (Holy War in the Name of Allah) written by JeI founder, Maulana Abul A'la Maududi. Khan led me to Tariq Ahmad Naik, a JeI khateeb (sermonizer) in Tral. Naik claimed to have been Maseehullah's mentor and guide, but said he was surprised when the latter decided to join the armed resistance when he could have rendered his services more effectively in the cause of Islam as a public orator and religious scholar. In a long conversation with Naik, I asked him about the perception held by some that JeI's literature or sermons inspire young boys to take up arms. Naik argued otherwise. There was no connection between the two, he reasoned, because the JeI only teaches the basic tenets of Islam, helps people learn Arabic to understand the Quran and hadith (sayings of the Prophet of Islam), and encourages Muslims to read translations and interpretations of the Quran. Naik's main contention was that the JeI could not be blamed if someone chose to fight injustice of his or her own volition. There is no link between Kashmir's armed movement and the JeI, he asserted.

Naik is a JeI sympathizer and works as nazim halqa Tral (in charge of the segment of Tral). His role is to deliver Islamic sermons on Fridays. Naik, about forty-seven years old, believes that police atrocities, arrests and continuous harassment might have forced his student, Maseehullah, to pick up arms. He described the latter as an obedient and loyal student who could have served Islam as a preacher. Preaching Islam as a religion, as a way of life, has no direct or indirect link with Kashmir's armed movement against Delhi, he maintained, and that anti-Islam forces across the globe were conspiring to vilify Islam for their own vested interests. From his perspective, Kashmiris are fighting for genuine rights and it is up to every individual to contribute the best way they can.

Naik's statement that 'JeI literature and militancy are not

linked' kept ringing in my ears as I moved on to meet others in Tral. I made a conscious decision not to meet parents of militants or Islamic preachers. So, I met a young government school teacher, who I will not identity for obvious reasons, for a relatively neutral perspective. The young teacher told me that the people of Tral were proud that HM commander Burhan Wani was from their area. Like others, he too was convinced that Burhan was on the right path in challenging Delhi's rule in Kashmir, with limited resources and no foreign support. He felt that New Delhi is unnerved because Kashmiris have risen to the occasion to start an indigenous uprising, challenging its rule and control on multiple fronts. 'Thanks to Almighty Allah, Burhan and other rebels from our neighbourhood have brought glory to Tral through their acts of bravery,' he said. According to him, the people of Kashmir have endured enough, and do not want injustices and military siege to continue. They want to see the sun of freedom rising in Kashmir.

Apart from the desire for Kashmir's azadi, the continued atrocities by government forces and huge presence of soldiers in civilian areas also force young and impressionable minds to pick up the gun as a last resort, the teacher said. Freedom comes at a cost, and if we want it, we have to offer sacrifices and struggle to achieve our goal, he added. The teacher then quoted a hadith, that there are three options available for a Muslim to fight injustice: one, to take the oppressor head-on; two, through writing and speeches; and three, by having utter disdain and contempt for the oppressor inside one's heart. People take their decisions according to their mental and physical strengths. According to his assessment, most people in Tral are 'Islampasand' (strict followers of Islam). Delhi's presence in Kashmir does not have any moral or legal justification for them, a fact that is exacerbated by the military siege inflicted upon them and the routine humiliation they face at the hands of government forces.

In June 2018, the United Nation's Office of the High Commissioner for Human Rights issued its first-ever forty-nine-page report on Kashmir. The damning report accused Indian security forces stationed in Kashmir of using 'excessive force' against civilian protesters that led to 'unlawful killings' and a very high number of injuries during widespread anti-State demonstrations in the Kashmir region.[11] Though the UN report detailed human rights abuses and violations in both parts of Kashmir divided by the LoC, its main focus was the human rights situation in the Indian-administered part of J&K from July 2016—when large and unprecedented demonstrations erupted after government forces killed Burhan Wani—to April 2018. Citing civil society estimates that up to 145 civilians were killed by the security forces between mid-July 2016 and the end of March 2018, the UN report described the pellet-firing shotgun as 'one of the most dangerous weapons' used against protesters in 2016, which is still being employed by government forces. Besides this, the UN body laid out recommendations for both India and Pakistan and asked India to 'respect the self-determination of the people of Kashmir'. The then UN human rights body chief, Zeid Ra'ad Al Hussein, called for an investigation into 'all civilian killings since July 2016' and also into 'the excessive use of force by security forces, including serious injuries caused by the use of pellet guns immediately'. In its official response, the Indian foreign ministry dismissed the UN report saying it was 'fallacious and motivated'.[12]

Meanwhile, the school teacher concurred with Tariq Naik's assertion that the JeI only propagates the understanding of Islam and how to be a good Muslim, and does not motivate or indoctrinate people to endorse or join the homegrown armed rebellion. He, however, admitted that the JeI had made some mistakes in the past. He did not elaborate on this further, but hinted at the JeI's endorsement of HM's armed wing in the early 1990s. By the late '90s, it had withdrawn its political and moral support for the largest Kashmiri rebel outfit. A friend of this teacher interrupted our conversation to say that if someone provides weapons, 'our boys' will happily pick them up to fight New Delhi's rule in Kashmir. On that note, we ended our conversation and decided to meet another family in Laribal.

I reached the beautiful hamlet, some 6 km from Tral town, to meet Mohammad Ismael Parray, father of slain HM militant,

Ishaq Parray, popularly known by his alias, Ishaq 'Newton'. Upon entering his house, I saw Ismael Parray reading a book, *Daee Ke Ausaaf* (Traits of the one who invites people to Islam). Another book caught my eye, *Mohsin-e-Insaniyat* (Benefactor of Humanity), written by a renowned Pakistani Islamic scholar, Maulana Naeem Siddiqui, who was among the founder-members of the JeI and a close associate of Maulana Abul A'la Maududi. Ismael, who I discovered is a member of the JeI, retired as a veterinary assistant in J&K's Animal Husbandry Department. Although associated with the JeI since 1982, he became its permanent rukn (member) only in 2000. Talking about his son, Ishaq, he told me that in December 2011, when the annual matriculation results were declared by the J&K Board of School Education, Ishaq had obtained 492 marks out of 500, an impressive 98.4 per cent. It is this performance that inspired the nickname, 'Newton'. Two years later, in 2013, he scored 85 per cent marks in his Class XII exams.

How did Ishaq, a school topper, become a militant? Although his family members say that Ishaq, a voracious reader, was fond of Islamic literature, they would not, even in their wildest of dreams, have imagined that he would pick up a gun to fight the State at such a tender age. He would occasionally attend religious gatherings known as Ijtima, where children are usually sent by parents to learn the fundamentals of religion and to get accustomed to pray regularly. According to Ismael, Ishaq left home on 16 March 2015, telling his parents that he had to submit a fee of ₹1,000 for his new Computer course.

Ismael vividly recalls that cold March morning when there were snowflakes all around. 'Snow was falling. After inquiring about his computer course, I opened my cupboard and handed Ishaq the 1,000 rupees he needed for his fee.' Soon after, Ishaq took an umbrella from his sister, Shakeela, a postgraduate in Chemistry, and left home. Family members insist that Ishaq would never lie to his family. Indeed, he did submit his fee as he had said he would. But he never returned home, until his encounter with government forces a year later. Members of his family had tried calling him on his mobile phone. It had been switched off.

After a tireless search, the family finally gave up when they were informed that Ishaq had joined the ranks of local HM militants. An Army officer stationed in a nearby camp visited their house to inform them that Ishaq had joined hands with Burhan Wani. Ismael's son-in-law, who works with the local police, also confirmed the news to the family. 'Newton' was in the woods with Burhan, both bright boys from Tral. On the same evening, Shakeela said she tried to send messages to Ishaq on Facebook and WhatsApp, but it had been too late. Both accounts had been deactivated. The inevitable had happened.

According to Masood, his younger brother Ishaq would religiously follow the news through the papers. He was influenced by the protests in 2009, when two women, Asiya and Neelofar, had died and it was alleged that the Indian Army had killed them after abducting and raping them. This case is known in Kashmir as the alleged 'Shopian double rape and murder case.'[13] Asiya and Neelofar were sisters-in-law who went missing from their orchard on their way home on 29 May 2009. The next day, their bodies were found 1 km apart. The official version was that they had died by drowning—a version that the people of the village refused to buy. Shopian observed a protest strike that lasted for months. Authorities led by the then CM Omar Abdullah imposed a curfew-like restriction for forty-seven days. In the end, the NC-Congress coalition government was forced to appoint Justice Muzaffar Jan as an inquiry officer in a judicial probe, as people did not have faith in the local police's ability to investigate the case. Simultaneously, the Shopian Bar Association also formed a six-member fact-finding committee. The Justice Jan-led inquiry commission submitted a 300-page interim report to Omar Abdullah, confirming the rape and murder of Asiya and Neelofar. The report also accused the civil administration of negligence, and police and doctors of mishandling the case, leading to the destruction of vital evidence.

Ishaq minutely followed the case. A year later, the wave of the 2010 azadi protests engulfed the entire Valley. Then, on 9 February 2013, Mohammad Afzal Guru, convicted in the attack on India's Parliament, was hanged in Delhi's Tihar Jail. The Guru episode also left a deep impression on the young and sensitive Ishaq, Masood told me. These incidents convinced Ishaq that Delhi was oppressing Kashmiris and inflicting deep wounds on their psyche, which ultimately led him to join Burhan Wani's militant group.

Government forces claimed to have killed Ishaq in an encounter on 3 March 2016 in Mir Mohalla, Dadsara, in Tral. He had survived a little over a year in his life as a militant. I asked Shakeela what she thought of Ishaq's decision to join Burhan's ranks. She responded with a sense of authority that she was proud of her brother. 'I'm a proud sister. My brother preferred a martyr's death over a life of servitude.'

Rahati Begum, Ishaq's mother, joined our conversation to say that her son faced no financial stress or any other problem. 'Everyone loved him—family and friends, relatives and neighbours. He was a darling at school. Everyone respected him when he was alive. Everyone respects him after his shahadat, when he is not present among us in a physical sense anymore.'

There was only pride in the eyes of Ishaq's family, not tears. Ismael said he does not regret his son's martyrdom because he had raised his voice against tyranny and oppression. '*Uss ne azadi baraie Islam ke liye apne jaan ka nazrana paish kiya*' ('He sacrificed his life for freedom so that Islam prospers'). The only complaint that the Parray family has is that the media did not report that Ishaq's body was charred after he was killed in an encounter. Ismael said that his son was a militant. He fired bullets, and received bullets in return. 'But even after killing my son, his arm was burnt and an eye gouged out. What kind of justice is this?'

The stories narrated by Abdul Gaffar Khan, Tariq Naik and Mohammad Ismael Parray would give one the impression that there could be a JeI link behind Maseehullah and Ishaq becoming armed rebels. How far is this perception true that Kashmir's young boys may have been influenced by Islamic literature? At Rathsuna, another village in Tral, another narrative emerged. There is little or no influence of the JeI in Rathsuna, where I met the family of an eighteen-year-old militant, Shakir.

Ghulam Hassan Dar, Shakir's father, is a carpenter by profession but can no longer work because of his poor health. His eldest son, Noor Mohammad Dar, runs a small provisional store just outside their home. The family lives in an incomplete two-room house that cannot be called a proper home. They are influenced by Mushtaq Veeri, a firebrand speaker of the Jamiat-e-Ahle-Hadith (JAH), a religious group that believes in a puritanical form of Islam and usually speaks against those who pray at shrines. The JAH group is deeply influenced by the Wahhabis—the creed-bound sect that predominates in Saudi Arabia—who condemn the veneration of tombs. After they occupied Jeddah, the Wahhabis knocked down the supposed tomb of Eve in 1928, and today it is a typical Wahhabi graveyard, with long rows of featureless, unmarked graves, like unplanted flower beds.[14]

Soon after the crackdown against the JeI, government forces also arrested Mushtaq Veeri, vice president of JAH, who hails from south Kashmir's Bijbehara district, in a place called Veeri. He was first arrested on 22 February 2019, and slapped with the Public Safety Act (PSA), which allows imprisonment without charge and trial for six months, on 14 March 2019. Then he was shifted to Kot Balwal Jail, Jammu.[15] On 3 June 2019, however, the J&K high court quashed the PSA detention of Veeri.

Noor Mohammad, a graduate in Islamic Studies, intensely feels the pain of Shakir's separation. 'He's just a young boy. He (Shakir) left his home a year ago and hasn't returned. And we are in deep distress,' he said. Like Burhan, he was too young to be called a radicalized Islamist. How did he become a militant, then?

Shakir left home on 14 April 2015, to attend the funeral procession of Khalid Muzaffar Wani, Burhan's elder brother, who had been killed by government forces. Like everyone else in the neighbourhood, Shakir too had arrived at Tral's martyr's graveyard at Eidgah. He did not return home that evening. At the funeral, he had decided it was time to fight the 'enemy'.

After Shakir joined the ranks of local militants, his family became a soft target for the police. The first thing that they did was to seize Noor Mohammad's mobile phone to see if Shakir would contact his elder brother. But Shakir made no calls. Noor Mohammad told me that Shakir was good at sports and would talk only if necessary. His mother, Rafiqa, sat in one corner of her room and didn't speak much. The only time she broke her silence was to say, '*Khodayas chu hawale*' ('May God be with him').

It was unclear what exactly had motivated Shakir to become a militant. Was it the passionate sloganeering at Khalid's funeral? Was it the perception that government forces were indiscriminately killing Kashmir's youngsters? Was it a sense of dispossession as a Kashmiri Muslim? Was it the anger of the dispossessed? Shakir Hassan Dar was eventually killed in Hafoo, a village in Tral, in a gunfight with government forces in November 2018. It was believed that he was close to Zakir alias Musa, and part of the tiny armed group, AGH.

On the day of Khalid's funeral, Shakir was not the only one who had left his home. Just a few hundred metres away, another boy, Sabzar Ahmad Bhat, from Rathsuna Nai village, Tral, also attended Khalid's janaza and did not return home. People in their thousands had decided to participate in the funeral; they said they did not believe he was a militant.[16] His only possible crime was that he was Burhan's brother. There was a collective sense of injustice. An estimated 40,000 people participated in Khalid's funeral.

Until then, Sabzar had been the lone bread earner of his family. After helping his father in the fields as a farmer, he also worked at a café in Awantipora in south Kashmir, on the Srinagar-Jammu highway. With his hard-earned money, he had constructed a new house for his family. The poverty-stricken family dared to dream of good days ahead because Sabzar, nicknamed 'Soaba', was their hope. The word 'sabzar' when roughly translated into English, means 'greenery', and Sabzar had provided that hope of a better future to his family. He would work hard and do everything possible to keep his family cheerful. And when he constructed a new house, the family members thought they would live happily together. His family friends told me that he had fallen in love with a girl from a distant village, whom he wanted to marry. The family was elated at the prospect of their son's impending wedding.

Ghulam Hassan Bhat, Sabzar's father, told me that his son had joked with him about getting one of his favourite mutton dishes from the girl's family, whom he would be visiting the next day to finalize the date of the nikah. Ghulam Hassan was busy making arrangements to visit his son's would-be bride's family. Until late evening, the father-son duo was busy chatting about the imminent visit. Next morning, when his father was about to leave, Sabzar stopped him with moist eyes. When his family asked him for an explanation, he just wept. Sabzar's life had changed. Khalid had been killed. After participating in Khalid's janaza, Sabzar disappeared. Some people say that Sabzar snatched a rifle from a cop and fled along with Shakir to join Burhan in the woods.

★

In August 2016, Zakir Rashid Bhat, another Tral resident, was immediately declared Burhan's successor. Zakir, twenty-five, was also an educated young man who was pursuing a degree in civil engineering at the Ram Devi Jindal College at Lalru in Punjab's Mohali (SAS Nagar) district, a suburb of Chandigarh, in 2013. He had come for a holiday in Kashmir along with his friends from Punjab, but dropped out in the third year of his BTech.[17]

Before Zakir, Sabzar had been nominated as Burhan Wani's successor. In the manner of Burhan, Sabzar—popularly known by his alias 'Mehmood Ghaznavi'—appeared with his associates in a short high-definition video. The video starts with the camera focused on Sabzar, who is in combat fatigues and waving towards the camera. Two associates are busy on their mobile phones. One of the associates, probably a new entrant, handles his assault rifle and smiles at the camera. Afterwards, both Sabzar and the apparent new recruit turn their gaze towards the mobile phone of Burhan's close comrade and new rebel commander, Zakir. The chirping of birds can be heard in the background. Then, the camera moves away from Sabzar to focus on the two other rebels who are seen lying on the ground at a distance from the trio. Both of them also have mobile phones in their hands. One of them briefly waves to the camera and smiles. There is no verbal message in the video. Sabzar was also known as Burhan's close friend. Although it is unclear whether his proximity to Burhan had contributed in any way to his ascendancy or his progression as commander in the HM ranks, both he and Zakir are immensely popular among the locals. Though it is not clear why the HM replaced Sabzar with Zakir, my guess is that it might have been because Zakir was more educated. It could also have been a ploy to confuse intelligence agencies. Immediately after this, Zakir parted ways with the HM and formed his own group, the AGH.

Jana Begum, Sabzar's mother, is heartbroken. She likens her son's separation from her to cancer. She feels as if her back is broken and her hopes dashed. His father says that he would have counseled his son to return home if he ever visited the house again. His older brother, Mohammad Younus Bhat, says Sabzar was influenced by Tablighi Jamaat, a religious organization that seldom discusses politics or global affairs. He adds that Sabzar never discussed politics at home. 'He wouldn't have constructed a new house for us if his dream was to become a rebel,' he says.

Eventually, Sabzar was trapped in a house in Saimoh village, in his hometown Tral, on the evening of 26 May 2017 and killed in a gunfight with government forces the very next morning along with Adil and Faizan, his two close associates. Sabzar had ultimately replaced Zakir, who had fallen out with HM after overtly declaring his love for establishing the Caliphate and 'Islamic State' in Kashmir. Zakir threatened to behead the APHC leaders if they continued describing Kashmir as a mere political dispute. In an audio message, he announced that he will sacrifice his life only for the sake of Islam, never for politics.[18]

HM's top leadership strongly dismissed Zakir's statement, declaring that forces like Al-Qaeda or ISIS have no role in Kashmir. This snub forced Zakir to distance himself from the rebel outfit. On 27 July 2017, an exclusive report by Michael Safi for the UK-based newspaper *The Guardian* claimed that an Al-Qaeda-affiliated propaganda channel announced Zakir 'as the head of a newly created cell in the disputed Himalayan territory'.[19] Eventually, the formation of a new movement of jihad in Kashmir, AGH, was declared. Zakir was eventually killed in a brief encounter in Dadsara village in his hometown Tral, on 23 May 2019. J&K's then director general of police, Shesh Paul Vaid told reporters that 'so far there is no evidence of Al-Qaeda's advent in Kashmir'.[20] The police chief described the thought of Al-Qaeda as 'inimical to Kashmir's culture'. Then what made Sabzar pick up a gun? Is it the collective sense of dispossession among Kashmiris that they are being forced to accept what they do not want to? Are they seeking the redressal of their grievances? Or, are they seeking a new order; a new compact? Many Kashmiri youths think they have employed all peaceful options and creative forms of resistance to demand their basic political and human rights, but New Delhi has not responded in like. They say they did try to wage a peaceful struggle in 2008–10. In 2008, about a million Kashmiris had even marched peacefully from Srinagar's Eidgah to the Tourist Reception Centre (TRC) grounds.[21] There was no violence. There was no stone-pelting either. But instead of engaging with them, the government responded with the same old tactics of imposing long curfews and firing indiscriminately at protesters.

The fifth generation of Kashmir firmly believes that Delhi is in denial that the Kashmir dispute needs a political solution. That's why some also make a decision to pick up a gun, knowing fully well that their symbolic defiance may not be enough to defeat India. But there is a romantic notion attached to this act of defiance—that, at least, they fought the oppression and did not choose silence. Their struggle, they say, is not driven by hatred. It is driven by a passion that they can challenge the Indian State morally. They are aware that their armed resistance will eventually lead them to death, but they have no regrets. They are at peace with their own decision to fight, and that their people have fully endorsed them and their act of defiance and sacrifice. At the same time, there is a genuine concern that Kashmir is losing its precious human resource in the form of young and educated boys.

Since many such boys in Tral told me almost the same thing

over and over, I asked a few that if the result of their acts of defiance was certain death, wasn't there a need to think of other means? The reply was astonishing: those who have sacrificed their lives as mujahideen for Kashmir's bright political future are successful at an individual level.

★

After returning from Laribal and Rathsuna, I had reached Sharifabad's Eidgah. Accompanied by a couple of friends and colleagues, I entered the Mazar-e-Shohada (local martyrs' graveyard). Little boys were playing cricket and a group of youth was trying their hand at volleyball. As we were about to step in, some boys yelled at us, 'First take off your shoes.' Tombstones of slain militants are like shrines in Kashmir and people consider a visit to martyrs' graves no less than a pilgrimage. Such is the veneration people have for them. After taking off our shoes, we took pictures of the graves, tombstones and epitaphs of Mohammad Ishaq Parray alias Ishaq 'Newton', Younus Ahmad Ganai alias Umair, Muzaffar Ahmad Malla alias Gohar and Khalid Muzaffar Wani—the last, without a code name.

I began chatting with the boys who had asked us to take off our shoes earlier. They said that the armed rebels were their real heroes and role models. One of them said that the rebels are the chosen ones, and not everyone can be as brave as them to challenge one of the world's largest armies. One of them, an engineering student, said that at a collective level, Kashmir may have been defeated militarily, but Delhi has lost a psychological war and has no moral case in Kashmir. He said that Kashmir's educated boys, and even school toppers from well-off families have sacrificed their comfortable lifestyles to become rebels, knowing well that death is imminent. That's why they are heroes in people's eyes. Another boy, a student of English literature, said that Kashmiri mujahideen are not a bunch of illiterate people; they are not facing problems of unemployment either. They have picked up arms to resolve the political dispute over Kashmir.

This conversation with the boys at Tral was enough to

understand why the area is considered a cradle of Kashmir's new age of militancy. Public endorsement of armed rebellion in Kashmir has been frustrating for government forces. In April 2016, Voice of America reported public announcements from the minarets of various mosques in the village of Lelhar, asking women and men to beat back government troops with a hail of rocks.[22] Clashes erupted and the armed forces had to leave, allowing three militants who had been hiding, to flee to safety. Officials have estimated that there are less than 400 armed rebels in the restive Himalayan Valley; no comparison to the 20,000 believed to have waged the armed revolt in 1989.

Indian Army officers are worried because locals are forming human chains and women are singing songs to eulogize local rebels and offering a safe passage to them. Lieutenant General (retired) Deependra Singh Hooda, who had taken over as the Northern Army Commander in June 2014 in Udhampur, admitted on record that it was getting increasingly difficult for the Army to conduct anti-militant operations. He said that the Armed Forces had little hope of competing with the local militants for sympathy, and confessed that the Indian Army was losing the battle for a narrative in Kashmir. 'Frankly speaking, I'm not comfortable anymore conducting operations if large crowds are around. Militarily, there's not much more to do than we already have done. We're losing the battle for a narrative.'[23]

NOTES, SOURCES AND REFERENCES

1. Masood, B. (2019, March 01). Jamaat-e-Islami (J&K) is banned, Govt says it is in close touch with militants. Retrieved from https://indianexpress.com/article/india/jamaat-e-islami-jk-banned-militants-home-ministry-5605844/
2. Cop Posted at PDP MLA's Residence Flees with 10 Weapons, Alert Sounded in Kashmir. (2018, September 29). Retrieved from https://www.news18.com/news/india/spo-posted-at-pdp-mlas-residence-in-srinagar-flees-with-10-weapons-1892743.html
3. @MirAijaz894. (2018, October 04). Is this a policing? How can a Munshi (policeman), of Rajbagh police station, abuse a legislator in front of dozens of other policemen? And then went on levelling serious allegations, accusations against his family as well.@MehboobaMufti @OmarAbdullah. https://mobile.

twitter.com/MirAijaz89/status/1047787862798651393
4. Hardline Hurriyat leader Syed Ali Shah Geelani slams ISIS. (2016, January 07). Retrieved from http://www.dnaindia.com/india/report-hardline-hurriyat-leader-syed-ali-shah-geelani-slams-isis-2163405
5. From the author's interaction with a top-ranking police officer in Srinagar.
6. Subramanian, N. (2016, April 21). Mentally, we are militants: That's the angry youth chorus in South Kashmir. Retrieved from http://indianexpress.com/article/india/india-news-india/handwara-kupwara-violence-valley-heats-up-mentally-we-are-militants-thats-the-angry-youth-chorus-in-south-kashmir-2762954/
7. Kashmiri voter manhandled for refusing to vote for BJP, alleges Mehbooba Mufti. (2019, April 11). Retrieved from https://www.indiatoday.in/elections/lok-sabha-2019/video/kashmiri-voter-manhandled-for-refusing-to-vote-for-bjp-alleges-mehbooba-mufti-1499442-2019-04-11 8.
9. Geelani, G. (2018, August 31). Mehbooba Mufti interview: 'Upholding Indian flag in Kashmir will be tough if Article 35A is diluted'. Retrieved from https://scroll.in/article/892416/mehbooba-mufti-interview-upholding-indian-flag-in-kashmir-will-be-tough-if-article-35a-is-diluted
10. Guha, R. (2016, October 22). Valley on the boil: Why no one has clean hands in Kashmir. Retrieved from http://www.hindustantimes.com/columns/why-no-one-has-clean-hands-in-kashmir/story-cQpbbwprW19kmE4vtaBPiP.html
11. First-ever UN human rights report on Kashmir calls for international inquiry into multiple violations. (2018, June 14). Retrieved from https://www.ohchr.org/EN/NewsEvents/Pages/DisplayNews.aspx?NewsID=23198&LangID=E
12. Razdan, N., & Ghosh, D. (2018, June 14). India Rejects UN Report On Jammu and Kashmir As "Fallacious, Motivated". Retrieved from https://www.ndtv.com/india-news/government-rejects-un-rights-body-report-on-jammu-and-kashmir-calls-it-fallacious-tendentious-and-mo-186743213. http://indianexpress.com/about/shopian-double-rape-and-murder-case/
14. Wright, L. (2018). *The Looming Tower: Al-Qaeda and the Road to 9/11*. New York: Vintage Books, a division of Random House. p. 71
15. Kashmir cleric Mushtaq Veeri booked under PSA, shifted to Kot Balwal jail Jammu. (2019, March 14). Retrieved from https://www.greaterkashmir.com/(X(1)S(c1g3iovjyqh1hj55h0ik4dve))/news/kashmir/kashmir-cleric-mushtaq-veeri-booked-under-psa-shifted-to-kot-balwal-jail-jammu/316176.html
16. Source 1: Masood, B. (2015, April 14). 'If my son was killed in encounter why his body didn't bear a bullet wound?' Retrieved from http://indianexpress.com/article/india/india-others/if-my-son-was-killed-in-encounter-why-his-body-didnt-bear-a-bullet-wound/
    Source 2: Mohammad, M. (2017, January 03). Has the Kashmir government contradicted army's claims about Burhan Wani's brother? Retrieved from https://scroll.in/article/824014/kashmir-government-announces-compensation-for-burhan-wanis-elder-brother-killed-by-the-army
17. Mufti, I. (2016, August 18). Burhan Wani's successor studied engg in Punjab: 'Tech-savvy, talkative'. Retrieved from http://www.hindustantimes.com/punjab/when-hizb-commander-burhan-wani-s-kashmir-successor-zakir-studied-engg-in-punjab-eager-to-mingle-tech-savvy/story-xbCO1eFCoZ7K8f1ZXN4S9I.html

18. Rashid, T. (2017, May 12). Hizbul threatens to behead Hurriyat leaders over Kashmir statement. Retrieved from http://www.hindustantimes.com/india-news/top-hizbul-mujahideen-leader-threatens-to-behead-separatist-hurriyat-leaders-for-calling-kashmir-struggle-political/story-JaQImZP05WVAUHtbk802wK.html

19. Safi, M. (2017, July 27). Kashmir militant leader announced as head of new al-Qaida-linked cell. Retrieved from https://www.theguardian.com/world/2017/jul/27/kashmir-militant-leader-announced-as-head-of-new-al-qaida-linked-cell-zakir-musa

20. Bashir, A. (2017, August 11). Militants have 2 options—return home or get killed: DGP. Retrieved from http://www.greaterkashmir.com/news/front-page/militants-have-2-options-return-home-or-get-killed-dgp/257248.html

21. Source 1: Post-Egypt, Kashmir may put Centre in a spot | India News - Times of India. (2011, February 23). Retrieved from http://timesofindia.indiatimes.com/india/Post-Egypt-Kashmir-may-put-Centre-in-a-spot/articleshow/7554862.cms?referral=PM

    Source 2: Vij, S. (2011, March 18). A Million March in Kashmir?: Suvaid Yaseen. Retrieved from https://kafila.online/2011/03/19/a-million-march-kashmir-egypt-india-democracy-revolution-suvaid-yaseen/

22. Kashmir Villagers Rise Up, Foil Rebel-hunting Indian Troops. (2016, June 03). Retrieved from https://www.voanews.com/a/ap-kashmir-villagers-rise-up-foil-rebel-hunting-indian-troops/3360064.html

23. Shah, F. (2016, June 23). Kashmir Is Slipping Away From India. Retrieved from http://thediplomat.com/2016/06/kashmir-is-slipping-away-from-india/

3

HOMELAND OR CALIPHATE?

I s Kashmir's tehreek-e-azadi a political movement or an Islamist movement? Or, is it essentially a political struggle with ethno-religious undertones, much like the Irish conflict? Or, is it a struggle for political, human and economic rights, drawing strength from multiple sources and multiple identities that include Kashmiri ethnicity, Kashmir's distinct culture, and, at times, also Kashmiri nationalism and/or its geographical proximity with Pakistan?

Questions like these have been asked in the past. Some of these had also been asked in 2016—the year of Burhan. And such questions will perhaps be asked in the future, too. Academic Happymon Jacob argued that 'The reality is that neither do Indian Muslims have anything to do with what happens in Kashmir nor is the "azadi" struggle in Kashmir a purely Islamic movement.'[1]

Are Kashmir's armed rebels somehow inspired by the networks of global jihad? Do they want to establish the law of shariah in J&K? What is the role of Islam in the azadi movement? What are the dominant slogans raised by ordinary Kashmiris seeking Azadi? Is it conceivable that an independent J&K might become a jihadist hotspot, or Balkanize into smaller units based on allegiances to different sects within Islam? Does Kashmir's armed rebellion draw inspiration from concepts like the Muslim ummah or caliphate, or is it limited to fighting Delhi's control in Kashmir? What has been the role of multiple identities in mobilizing public opinion and shaping the various political struggles since 1931?

In October 1995, *Outlook* magazine had commissioned a survey in the Kashmir Valley.[2] The Outlook-MODE poll had found that 'the quest for freedom in Kashmir remains undiminished.' It had established beyond doubt that the yearning for azadi was as intense as before. It had said that a whopping 77 per cent Kashmiri respondents were firm in their belief that a solution to the Kashmir problem did not lie within the framework of the Indian Constitution, and 72 per cent had said categorically that it was independence alone, which could bring peace in the violence-driven Valley.Meanwhile, at least 19 per cent respondents had favoured J&K's merger with Pakistan. Another survey titled 'Kashmir: Paths to Peace', conducted in many districts of both parts of Kashmir divided by the LoC, and released in May 2010 by the London-based Chatham House, established that for 80 per cent of Kashmiris 'the dispute is very important to them personally.'[3]

The struggle of Kashmiris for political and economic rights, justice and dignity predates the birth of India and Pakistan as separate nation states. Though the hostilities between Israel and Palestinians actually began in 1948, with the establishment of the State of Israel, the roots of inter-communal violence in the Himalayan region can be traced to 1920. Internationally, Kashmir's struggle is much older than the Palestinian struggle for freedom and justice against the Israeli occupation. The Soviet-Afghan War started in 1979 and lasted over nine years. An estimated 8,50,000–1.5 million civilians died as a result of this occupation while millions were forced to migrate. The Soviet Union's military intervention in Afghanistan began in December 1979, two years after the ascendancy of military ruler Zia-ul-Haq to power in Pakistan. With support from Washington D.C., Islamabad decided to increase its support to the mujahideen fighting the Soviets. The Taliban emerged in the early 1990s in northern Pakistan, following the withdrawal of Soviet troops from Afghanistan in February 1988. The Iranian Revolution, also known as the Islamic Revolution or the 1979 Revolution, resulted in the overthrowing of the Pahlavi dynasty under Mohammad Reza Shah Pahlavi, who was supported by the United States, and its eventual replacement with an Islamic republic under Ayatollah Ruhollah Khomeini. According to the BBC, the Al-Qaeda was created in 1988 after the withdrawal of Soviet troops from Afghanistan. Osama bin Laden was its founder. The Islamic State of Iraq and the Levant, also known as the Islamic State of Iraq and Syria and often shortened to Islamic State, was founded in 1999 by Abu Musab al-Zarqawi. Afghanistan's resistance against Soviet occupation is a recent phenomenon; so is the Iranian Revolution. The birth of the Taliban, Al-Qaeda and IS are all recent too. Kashmiris were fighting for their basic rights against the Dogra ruler Maharaja Hari Singh before 1947, and have continued after the momentous year that gave the subcontinent freedom and simultaneously partitioned it too. The earlier struggles, though not organized, were waged when the Mughals, Afghans, Sikhs and Dogras ruled Kashmir, in that order.

'Historically, Kashmir has seen three major religions gaining ascendancy in this tiny country. It is a tale of conflict and confluence among Hinduism, Buddhism and Islam', Kashmiri author and historian Khalid Bashir Ahmad notes in his exhaustive book, *Kashmir: Exposing the Myth Behind the Narrative.*[4] After the decline of Shaivism in Kashmir, the period of the Salatin-e-Kashmir began in 1339, with Shah Mir as Kashmir's first Muslim ruler. The sixth ruler of the Shah Mir dynasty, Sultan Sikandar Shah, is credited for introducing shariah in governance and also hailed for establishing schools, constructing mosques and laying the foundation for Srinagar's Aali Masjid, at Eidgah. Having ascended the throne at the age of eight, Sikandar was a devout Muslim, abstaining from wine and not listening to music on religious grounds. Several historians, though, have accused him of the reckless destruction of Hindu temples and the maltreatment of his Hindu subjects. Bashir takes a sympathetic view of the sultan and argues that the amount of disapproval Sikandar has received at the hands of successive historians makes Aurangzeb, the seventeenth-century Mughal ruler of India, look like a saint.[5] The eighth sultan of Kashmir was the popular Zain-ul-Abidin, who was known to his subjects as 'Bud Shah' (the Great King). He maintained a liberal outlook towards non-Muslims and reversed many of Sikandar's oppressive policies. One of the last native rulers of independent Kashmir was Yousuf Shah Chak, who ruled from 1579 to 1586. His wife was the renowned poet and ascetic, Zoon, known post her marriage as 'Habba Khatoon'. Yousuf Chak was captured by troops of the Mughal emperor, Akbar. He is believed to have been taken first to Bengal and later to Bihar, where he passed away and was buried.

As pointed out by Bashir, the transformation of Kashmir from a Hindu to a Muslim society more than 600 years ago, gave birth to a narrative according to which the Muslim rulers forcibly converted and evicted Hindus from Kashmir and destroyed their religious places, symbols and icons. According to the author, this narrative is 'a fairy tale' and actually almost entirely based on the observations of a chronicler, Jonaraja, who lived during the early years of Islam in the Kashmir Valley.[6]

It is important to contextualize and historicize the struggle of Kashmiris for independence, which can be traced to the sixteenth century, when it was taken over by the Mughals.

It is often contended that a section of youth in Kashmir is radicalized and can be seen waving Pakistani flags while raising pro-Pakistan and anti-India slogans, and a few masked boys displaying the IS flags while talking about the Caliphate, especially on Fridays. India routinely blames Pakistan for fuelling unrest in Kashmir and sponsoring militancy in the region. Sections of the Indian media often show pictures of militant commanders of LeT and HM being cheered, greeted and welcomed by Kashmiri crowds at anti-India protest rallies. The more recent examples are videos and pictures of Burhan's funeral on 9 July 2016, in which the slain commander's close associates surfaced, and offered a volley of gunshots as a mark of respect.

On 31 July, a massive pro-azadi rally was organized in south Kashmir's Kareemabad area in Pulwama.[7] Local media reported that people from different parts of Kashmir, like Tral, Pulwama, Shopian, Pampore, Awantipora and Budgam gathered at the town's Eidgah. People defied curfew at the call given by the elderly people of the area (it had almost become a routine for village elders to organize massive public gatherings called 'Ittihad-e-Millat', to show that different Islamic sects stand united for the goal of Azadi). Many protesters were seen carrying Pakistani flags and raising pro-HM, pro-LeT, pro-Burhan and pro-azadi slogans at the 31 July rally. Family members of slain local militants like Naseer Pandit—who was part of Burhan's group and photographed in combat fatigues in 2015—were also present at the rally.

Religious leaders from different sects of Islam (like the Sunnis [consisting of the Hanafis and the Salafis]; the followers of Ahl-e-Hadith; the Wahhabis; and the Shias, among others) and social representatives addressed the rally to urge Kashmiris to rise above sectarian affiliations to achieve the 'cherished goal of freedom'. Reportedly, three masked militants, brandishing weapons, also surfaced at the venue. Purportedly, one among them was the late Abu Dujana, the then Lashkar commander in Kashmir, while the two accompanying him were apparently local militants.

Another group of masked militants arrived at a massive public rally organized at Arwani, Bijbehara, in south Kashmir, also the hometown of former CM and president of the PDP, Mehbooba Mufti. They briefly addressed the rally and reportedly asked people to follow the APHC leadership's protest calendar. After armed militants appeared in at least half a dozen rallies in south Kashmir alone, following Burhan's killing, Syed Salahuddin—chief of HM and the Muzaffarabad-based United Jihad Council (UJC), an alliance of various armed groups—issued a statement through news agencies in which he directed local armed militants to stay away from public rallies.

Local militants, mostly masked, have appeared in Arwani and Bijbehara in Anantnag, Kaimoh in Kulgam and Kareemabad in south Kashmir's Pulwama district.[8] The frequency of this routine of armed militants appearing at the funeral sites of their fallen associates to offer gun salutes has amplified.

Is this a worrying trend? Has this happened for the first time in Kashmir? In 1989 and the early 1990s, a majority of Kashmiris openly supported armed rebellion against Delhi's rule. The reason why people continue to support local militants is because most Kashmiris feel oppressed, dispossessed and disempowered on multiple fronts, as spaces for democratic dissent stand choked in the restive region. There is a ban on peaceful assembly, and student politics in universities is not allowed either. While New Delhi continues to ask questions like, 'why do the Kashmiris side with the militants and see them as saviours and heroes?' and 'why do they look at government soldiers with contempt and disdain?', the fact is that the militants have come to symbolize defiance and resistance towards the State and New Delhi for the ordinary Kashmiri.

In November 2018, Bharat Bhushan, a veteran editor/journalist based in New Delhi, wrote in his piece in *Business Standard* that to understand developments in J&K, a good mental exercise would be to imagine that the region exists in two parallel universes, both of which are inhabited by real people, and there is a perceptual disconnect between the two parallel universes.[9]

> In one, the people are angry, frustrated and helpless. They think they lack effective political representation and have no faith in what passes for democracy. They find themselves at the receiving end of state violence with child protesters maimed and blinded by pellet guns or killed when they try to counter the violence of the State by picking up guns. They cannot understand why any State would treat them the way they are treated.

In a parallel universe, he contended, everything is normal: elections are held; people vote, even if in a very small number; mayors are appointed to cities and towns and local bodies are manned by people's representatives. In the same write-up, the author argued, 'In this alternative reality, law and order prevails and every problem is a nail for which there is a hammer handy. It is run by the security establishment and a coterie accountable to their masters in Delhi.' He concluded by saying that everyone in the real world can see that 'the emperor has no clothes.'

Indeed, a section of Kashmir's population unambiguously

favours Kashmir's merger with Pakistan and believes that Kashmir is the unfinished business of the subcontinent's partition.[10] Their argument in support of such a merger includes Kashmir's geographical proximity with Pakistan, and a shared religion: Islam. This view is shared by the JeI and one of Kashmir's most respected and followed resistance leaders, Syed Ali Shah Geelani. Inarguably, Geelani has been one of the most popular pro-Pakistan Kashmiri leaders and his followers admire him for his unwavering stand against Delhi. However, some who adore him as an individual, do not necessarily subscribe to his political stand that 'Kashmir is a natural part of Pakistan'. Referred to as 'Qaid-e-Inquilab' (Leader of the Revolution) with respect, the hugely popular octogenarian is often compared to the Libyan revolutionary, Omar Mukhtar. His detractors criticize him for what they describe 'prolonged monologues' and his 'desire to die as a martyr'.

In my several exclusive interviews with Geelani, I have asked him a hypothetical question: 'What if, in case of a referendum, the people do not vote for merger with Pakistan, and opt either for independence or India?' With a smile on his face, Geelani said that he was sure that people would choose Pakistan, but in case they did not, he would respect the people's democratic verdict. 'Even if they choose India, in a referendum held under international supervision and guarantees?' I asked. Yes, even then, he would respect the people's choice. He concluded by reiterating his stand that 'Kashmir is a natural part of Pakistan and that the state's independence is not a viable option for political, economic and strategic reasons.'[11]

Geelani is a defendant of Kashmir's armed resistance, and compares it with the path chosen by India's celebrated freedom fighters like Subhash Chandra Bose and Bhagat Singh. They fought against the British Empire and are today glorified by their countrymen as heroes.

In the first week of August 2016, the then Indian home minister Rajnath Singh visited Pakistan's capital, Islamabad, to attend the Home Ministers' meeting of the South Asian Association for Regional Cooperation (SAARC) countries, where he condemned terrorism in all forms and manifestations. However, the massive protests that were held in Islamabad, Lahore and Rawalpindi against Mr Singh's visit, prompted him to return home at least four hours earlier than scheduled. There were different versions about his hasty return that led to his skipping the official luncheon there. India accused Pakistan of showing disrespect to its home minister and not following diplomatic protocol. But the Pakistan media had a different story to narrate. It said that Rajnath Singh had no answers when he was cornered about India's alleged excessive use of force against unarmed Kashmiri protestors in the Valley, following the death of Burhan Wani on 8 July.[12] Singh told the Indian Parliament that one country's terrorist cannot be a freedom fighter for another country. Many in Kashmir reacted to this statement, arguing that by Mr Singh's logic, Bhagat Singh would be a terrorist!

Syed Ali Shah Geelani is convinced that the Kashmiris fighting Delhi's rule in the state are 'mujahideen'. In November 2015, Geelani, in an interview with English daily, *Rising Kashmir*, endorsed the role of the gun as the only option available for Kashmiri youth under the prevailing circumstances.[13] In the same interview, he said that the people of Kashmir had failed the resistance movement's leadership. His statement triggered a passionate debate on Kashmir's hotly contested political turf. He was referring to the people's participation in assembly polls— an act that, according to him, was detrimental to the anti-India movement. At the same time, he condemned the mindless violence perpetrated by international Islamist organizations like Daesh, Boko Haram, Al-Qaeda and TTP, though he had once led the funeral prayers in absentia in Srinagar for Osama bin Laden when the Al-Qaeda chief was slain by American forces at Abbottabad in Pakistan in 2011. He justified his act by saying that since bin Laden was unarmed when he was killed, he was a 'martyr'. About the stray incidents of IS flags being displayed in Kashmir every now and then, Geelani said that a tiny group of youth was probably doing this to 'irritate' India.

As mentioned earlier, even top officers in J&K police share this view that the ISIS ideology has no takers in Kashmir, for there is neither infrastructure available nor sympathy, and the people in general do not subscribe to the IS world view. Police sources have revealed that 'a tiny group of boys, less than fifteen in number, [with access to social media] could be IS-inspired', but the ISIS, in itself, does not exist in the Kashmir Valley.

In an exclusive interview with me in June 2013 for *Dawn*, Geelani argued that Pakistan's stability was of utmost importance to the people of Kashmir. He urged Pakistan's then PM, Nawaz Sharif, to lend support to Kashmir's genuine cause morally, diplomatically and politically.[14] Prior to founding his party, Tehreek-i-Hurriyat Jammu & Kashmir (THJK), Geelani was a member of the JeI and fought the Assembly elections several times. Before 1989, Geelani, as a JeI candidate, had won the Assembly elections in 1972 and 1977 from his home constituency, Sopore. In 1987, he was instrumental in bringing together the JeI and several other influential Valley-based socio-religious organizations under the umbrella of the Muslim United Front (MUF), known in Kashmir as 'Muslim Muttahida Mahaz'. The MUF fought the elections in 1987, which were widely believed to have been rigged.[15] The MUF's election symbol, a pen and inkpot, was later adopted by the PDP to hoodwink the masses for electoral gains.

Geelani's experience as a three-time legislator contributes to his phenomenal popularity among the general masses, for he has been involved with both electoral as well as resistance politics in Kashmir. In the first innings of his political career, he had been a Unionist, while in the second part, he was perceived as a revolutionary. Hence, the demand by many Indian politicians that Geelani prove his popularity by participating in elections does not make sense to him or his supporters, since he has already proved his popularity both within and outside the electoral fold. Having achieved a hat-trick of election victories (1972, 1977 and 1987), combined with his ability to pull a half-million-strong crowd makes him one of Kashmir's most popular leaders at the moment.

Geelani joined the APHC—an amalgam of political, social and religious parties, trade bodies and civil society and lawyers' groups; and also known as the Kul Jama'tei Hurriyat Conference—in 1993. Other prominent pro-freedom politicians, like the late Khawaja Abdul Ghani Lone, Mirwaiz Umar Farooq, Shabir Shah, and Professor Abdul Ghani Bhat were part of the APHC. It was formed on 31 July 1993 as a political platform for the azadi movement. In a way, it was an extension of the MUF, which had come together to contest the Assembly elections of 1987 against a regional pro-autonomy NC and its alliance partner, the Congress. The APHC, though an amalgam of contrasting ideologies (some pro-Pakistan and others pro-independence), was held together by their common position that J&K was 'under military occupation', and the collective demand that 'the wishes and aspirations of the people of J&K should be ascertained for a final resolution of the dispute'.

In the early 1990s, the APHC emerged as the political face of the anti-Delhi armed movement. It also claimed to represent the wishes and aspirations of a majority of the population of Kashmir. Moreover, it brought together two ideologies that till then had remained divergent: those who sought independence from both Pakistan and India and believed in the formation of J&K as a sovereign, secular and independent entity; and those who favoured J&K's complete merger with Pakistan. The APHC conglomerate split into two factions when Geelani initiated a 'tatheeri amal' (purification process), leveling accusations that a constituent of the APHC had fielded proxies in the 2002 Assembly elections. He was pointing at the People's Conference headed by Sajad Gani Lone, a former pro-independence leader who had allegedly fielded a proxy candidate in the 2002 Assembly elections; he now supports the 'Hindu nationalist' BJP. There was a war of words between Geelani and Lone. Later, Geelani formed a separate political party, THJK. Besides heading a faction of the APHC, Geelani also serves as a spiritual hero, resistance leader and religious guide to many, while his close friend and pro-Pakistan leader Mohammad Ashraf Sehrai has now taken over as chairman of the THJK.

The Urdu word 'hurriyat' means 'freedom' or 'liberty'. The APHC was formed to spearhead Kashmir's struggle for freedom from Delhi's rule. It was tasked with negotiating Kashmir's future with both India and Pakistan, through a trilateral dialogue process. It often invokes the UN Security Council (UNSC) resolutions to settle the Kashmir dispute, but also favours a negotiated settlement with Islamabad and New Delhi. APHC leaders maintain that Kashmiri Pandits and Sikhs are an inseparable part of Kashmir and without them, the state's society is incomplete. Geelani once told me in an interview that Kashmiri Pandits are like essential body parts without which the body cannot function properly. Senior pro-India leaders in Kashmir have told me in private conversations that Geelani is crucial to maintaining the sanity and balance of Kashmir's social fabric. The Indian media describes Geelani as a 'hawk' for his pro-Pakistan views, largely ignoring his moderate messages on vital issues that matter in Kashmir's polity and society.

A strong perception among most Kashmiri Muslims in the Valley is that 'Brahmanical Hindu India' has occupied them. This perception has existed for a while, but has been cemented since the PDP-BJP alliance came to power in March 2015. To fight 'Hindu India', they appear to draw strength from their multiple identities as ethnic Kashmiris and as Muslims. The struggle in Kashmir, in some ways, has ethno-religious undercurrents. Kashmiris take pride in being Kashmiris, and of their distinct culture, which they say is different from both Pakistan's and India's. Their religious and political identity inspires them to fight Delhi, while their ethnicity and unique culture doesn't encourage many to merge with Pakistan either. Islam helps mobilize people in the Muslim-majority Kashmir Valley, and it also enables Pakistan to find common cause with Kashmir.

On the contrary, a strong view exists in New Delhi that Kashmir has changed in the last decade or so and become more 'radicalized' than before. 'Yes, Kashmir has changed,' Professor Siddiq Wahid Radhu, a Srinagar-based historian, author, academic and political commentator, told me in a telephonic interview.[16] 'Because India has changed,' he insisted. As India is perceived to be heading towards a muscular, militaristic and radical Hindu nationalism, it is but natural for Kashmir to react with something that it is already nervous about—swamping* nationalism, for instance. After the ascent of Narendra Modi as India's PM in May 2014, there has been a substantial change in India's social atmosphere. Noted English weekly magazine *India Today,* in its editorial dated 24 July 2017, noted that 'India has recently seen a spate of horrific lynchings accompanied, quite disturbingly, by prolonged silences from those in power, at the Centre and in the states.'[17]

In recent times, concern has been voiced that religion appears to have dislodged or dominated politics in public discourse in Kashmir. This apparent trend has to be seen in larger regional and global contexts, though. When the late Mufti Mohammad Sayeed, who had also served as India's Home Minister in the past, forged a power-sharing deal with the ideologically antithetical BJP in the state in early 2015, a large section of the Kashmiri population sensed an attack on its identity as Kashmiri Muslims. Sections of the Indian media described the PDP-BJP alliance as a 'wedlock between Kashmiri Muslim "soft-separatists" and Hindu hyper-nationalists'. Analysts and key Kashmir watchers observed that it was an 'unholy alliance' and possibly 'political suicide' for the regional PDP.[18]

The domestic ascension of the BJP to power in New Delhi in May 2014, followed by its coalition with the PDP in J&K, made most Kashmiris exceedingly anxious. The BJP's aggressive stand on scrapping Article 370 that grants special status to J&K within the Indian Union, its proposals to resettle migrant Kashmiri Pandits in 'separate townships', and its move to construct 'Sainik Colonies' for former soldiers, contributed to growing apprehensions of an impending demographic change in Kashmir.

In an interview with *Kashmir Ink,* a senior and well-known Kashmiri lawyer, Zafar Shah noted:[19]

> ...it was a bolt out of the blue when the Supreme Court issued notice to the Union and State governments on J&K's

---

*'Ethnic swamping' is the process of introducing a population into a disputed area. Sekulić, D. (2015). Ethnic Cleansing and Ethnic Swamping. *The Wiley Blackwell Encyclopedia of Race, Ethnicity, and Nationalism,* 1-3.

special status on Aug 21, 2015 and set the alarm bells ringing in the restive Valley. The direction was issued in response to a writ petition filed by an NGO 'We the Citizens', seeking scrapping of Article 35A. The move was read a clear judicial onslaught on J&K's special status as the article defines special privileges enjoyed by J&K's permanent residents in matters related to employment, acquisition of immovable property, settlements and scholarships.

Like many civil society actors, politicians and rights defenders, Mr Shah also feared that 'J&K may lose its special status'.

Sayeed, patriarch of the pro-self-rule PDP, had told me in an exclusive interview in February 2015 in Jammu that he was going to put a final stamp on the power-sharing deal to form a coalition government with the Hindu nationalist BJP.[20] He always described himself as an 'Indian by conviction' and defended his decision to forge a partnership with the BJP by saying that it will be a 'paradigm shift' in the state's political history.

He was wrong—terribly so.

Sayeed had often been reckless with his language and always careless with the bottle. He would make controversial and contradictory statements and later go on to justify his contradictions with ease and nonchalance. Some also saw in him an astute politician who was not only difficult to understand but also the one whose unpredictability with decision-making never came as a major surprise. In early 2000, Sayeed had famously and controversially said, 'Kashmiri militants don't need guns anymore because their representatives are now in the Assembly.'[21] In 2002, Sayeed's PDP entered into a partnership with the Congress to form a coalition government on a three-year-rotation basis. From 2002–05, Sayeed acted as the CM, while from 2005–08, senior Congress leader Ghulam Nabi Azad took over as the CM.

In the 2014 Assembly polls, Sayeed's PDP emerged as the single largest party, grabbing twenty-eight seats, most of these from the Muslim-majority Kashmir Valley, while the BJP won all its twenty-five seats from the Hindu-majority areas of Jammu.

Despite their bitter election campaigns against each other, the BJP and PDP embraced each other to form an unpopular coalition government. After hectic parleys that lasted for over two months, from mid-December 2014 to end-February 2015, the two parties agreed on a common minimum programme and named the alliance document 'Agenda of Alliance'. It included commonly agreed-upon issues like good governance and development, and contentious ones like reconciliation with Pakistan, dialogue with the APHC and maintaining the status of the state as per Article 370 of the Indian Constitution.

Both sides appeared to have made compromises on their respective positions to form the coalition government. While the BJP did not press for the abrogation of Article 370 and agreed to maintain the state's constitutional status, the PDP did not include its vision of self-rule and joint mechanism for J&K in the alliance document. Sayeed's decision to ally with the BJP came as a shock to his own supporters. They could not comprehend why Sayeed would join hands with the Narendra Modi-led BJP.

It had been the first time in the history of J&K's electoral politics that BJP, in March 2015, had become part of any coalition government. This had been unacceptable to a majority of people of the state because of the BJP's anti-Muslim track record.[22]

In his defence, Sayeed had argued that the BJP had got twenty-five seats from Jammu and therefore, it was important to respect the people's mandate and form a government that was inclusive and took into account the interests of all three distinct regions of the state—Kashmir, Jammu and Ladakh. He had called it electoral arithmetic and argued that the partnership with the BJP was an opportunity to reconnect the people of Jammu, Kashmir and Ladakh with each other, and help reduce regional tensions as well. Internationally, he had said the PDP-BJP alliance would give a message of 'India's diversity'.

He told me that Kashmiris had suffered as a result of wars between India and Pakistan (in 1947, 1965, 1971 and the Kargil confrontation in the late 1990s) and were the victims of the Indus Waters Treaty (1960). Because of this treaty, he said, injustice had been done to Kashmiris. He blamed Dr Farooq Abdullah, former CM of J&K, for handing over all power projects to Delhi. He said that the PDP-BJP alliance document mentions in detail that Kashmir should have the control of all its power projects and the state should be compensated for the losses incurred because of the controversial Indus Waters Treaty. The PDP believed in its economic and aspirational agenda, which combined self-rule and economic independence by assuming control of hydropower projects, he said. But Sayeed's words proved nothing more than political rhetoric, as tensions between Srinagar and Delhi only kept growing.

Mehbooba Mufti, Sayeed's daughter and also former CM, during her party's election campaign in an interview with NDTV Hindi, accused BJP of 'dividing Kashmiris on sectarian and communal lines' while ruling out any alliance with the Hindu rightwing party.[23] The rest, as they say, is history. In an exclusive interview with me in August 2018, Mufti acknowledged that the decision to stitch a partnership with the BJP was 'something very wrong' and 'very sad' as 'I was the one fighting to keep the BJP at bay, but the mandate of the people was such that we tried to make the best of it.'[24]

The 2016 uprising was not an outcome of the PDP's decision to join hands with the BJP, however. The sentiment for azadi is deep-rooted in ordinary Kashmiris who refuse to identify with the idea of India. For Delhi, from their perspective, 'it is a matter of holding on to the territory no matter what', as Arun Jaitley told Sagarika Ghosh of CNN-IBN during the 2010 mass agitation, when the NC-Congress government in J&K was conspicuous by its absence on the ground.[25] Events like Burhan Wani's killing in July 2016, the PDP-BJP partnership in March 2015, proposals like the construction of Sainik colonies for former soldiers, separate townships for migrant Pandits, handing over land to the Amarnath Shrine Board in 2008, or paving the way for new Hindu pilgrimages like Abhinav Gupt, and so on, acted as triggers to mobilize the people at different junctures to push for their collective political demand.

Reviving certain Hindu pilgrimages and creating new ones is a recent phenomenon. For instance, traditionally, Pandits would travel to Kausar Nag, a high-altitude lake in south Kashmir's Kulgam district in the Pir Panjal Range. This pilgrimage has been restarted in recent years. Another yatra was proposed in the name of Abhinav Gupt, a renowned philosopher and mystic from Kashmir who lived in 950–1016 CE, in Beerwah in central Kashmir's Budgam district, by a New Delhi-based organization, Acharya Abhinav Gupt Samaroh Samiti.[26]

In a situation where Kashmiri Muslims feel they are cornered from all sides in the presence of a 600,000-strong military, they seek some strength and inspiration from religious sources. That is why you hear slogans like '*Narai-e-Takbeer, Allah-o-Akbar*' ('Allah is great is the greatest slogan'). Such slogans do not make Kashmir's movement Islamist in character. Rather, it is an assertion of their multiple identities as Kashmiris and also as Kashmiri Muslims.

Similarly, a slogan like the following does not seek to establish the Caliphate in Kashmir, '*Yahan kya chalega, Nizam-e-Mustafa*' ('The Prophet of Islam's system of governance will prevail').

Rather, it is an articulation by the Muslims of Kashmir that they will not accept either the military invasion or the cultural aggression of a perceived 'Brahmanical Hindu India'. Not a single anti-minority (Hindus, Sikhs, Christians) slogan has ever been chanted in Kashmir by the civilian protesters. Even during the worst crises, an estimated 300,000 workers comprising carpenters, masons, painters, barbers and daily-wage labourers from Uttar Pradesh, Bihar, West Bengal, Rajasthan and other states of India have remained unharmed in Kashmir. Likewise, nearly half-a-million pilgrims come to south Kashmir annually to visit the holy cave at Amarnath. Kashmiri Muslims have welcomed them and continue to do so. Tourists from all corners of India and the world visit Kashmir in summer and winter, and they are not targeted by the local population. This is evidence of the tolerance that is ingrained in Kashmir's composite culture.

True, this composite culture has come under threat in the recent past. There had been audacious attempts by some forces like a rebel group named 'Allah Tigers', to impose a certain code of conduct and thrust a particular lifestyle on Kashmiris, as if Kashmiris face a crisis of faith and need to decide about their social conduct and lifestyle. The Allah Tigers's chief, Air Marshal Noor Khan, on 18 August 1989, announced a ban on cinemas and bars through local newspapers. The stated aim was to shut these popular public hangouts and create an atmosphere of 'jihad' against Delhi's rule. This, obviously, did not work, for the society refused to accept a new code of conduct that was being dictated to by a lesser-known armed group. In fact, Yasin Malik of JKLF told me that their group was surprised by the Allah Tigers, and the JKLF boy kidnapped Noor Khan and discovered that he did not even have a pistol; he was just acting as a maverick and issuing statements to the press. The Allah Tigers as an organization disappeared from the scene as quickly as it had appeared. Quite contrary to his earlier avatar, Noor Khan then sold stamp papers in the Srinagar High Court for some time.

The slogan from the 1979 Iranian Revolution, '*La Sharakeya Wala Garabeya, Islamia, Islamia*' ('Neither West nor East; only Islam is the best') became the banner of the uprising, which many in Kashmir believe was inspired by the fall of the Soviet Union, a key ally of India, and the earlier formation of the Islamic Republic of Iran.[27] These dictats amounted to an imposition of a kind of Islam that was at variance with the homegrown version practised in Kashmir for nearly six centuries now.

Coming back to Allah Tigers, when, in 1989–90, armed members of the group launched a vociferous campaign against the sale and consumption of alcohol, the operation of cinema halls, video libraries, and so on, most liquor shops in Srinagar and other towns of the Valley closed down, fearing reprisals. Kashmiri cinema halls included Firdous Cinema, Shiraz and Khayam in downtown Srinagar, and Regal, Palladium, Neelam, Naaz and Shah in and around the city centre Lal Chowk. Two others include Broadway, which was just outside the sensitive Srinagar-based Indian Army's 15 Corps at Sonwar, and Samad Talkies, which was in north Kashmir's Sopore town. In the late 1990s, Neelam and Broadway were opened under fortified security arrangements, but most of these were turned into paramilitary camps or torture centres[28] soon after. Today, most of Kashmir's cinema halls are in ruins and some have been converted into shopping centres. In the end, only two had been functional under heavy security cover, but fearing attacks on government troops by the militants, people stopped visiting them.

A few militant groups had disallowed the screening of Bollywood and Hollywood movies in Kashmir. In the mid-1980s— only a few years before the eruption of armed struggle in 1989— the Anthony Quinn-starrer *Lion of the Desert* was screened at Regal cinema in Srinagar. It was an action film based on the life of the Libyan revolutionary, Omar Mukhtar, a Bedouin leader who fought the colonial Italian Army in the years leading up to World War II. Its screening in Kashmir had inspired the people to protest against Delhi and widespread demonstrations were witnessed in Srinagar. As a result, it was banned.

Everything had changed by early 1990. Cinema halls could not survive the onslaught of those times either. Apart from banning films and alcohol, some radical groups also wanted to enforce a dress code on women. Some women were harassed and forced to wear burqas, abayas and headscarves. This move did not go down well with the common masses.

Kashmir, by and large, is a conservative society, but it does not follow a puritanical form of Islam. Most Kashmiri Muslims, both women and men, visit shrines as part of their spiritual journey and faith and largely believe in the values of Sufi spirituality. In fact, before the migration of Pandits in January 1990, several Muslims and Hindus would visit dargahs and astaans together. Apart from a spiritual journey, a visit to a Sufi shrine was also considered a cathartic experience as well as an act of cultural confluence.

Kashmir has traditionally been known as a cradle of Sufis and saints, the 'Pir Waer' in Kashmiri language. Shrines dedicated to them are an intrinsic part of Kashmir's culture, social fabric and vibrant tradition of communal harmony. The first Sufi Muslim saint from Central Asia to have visited Kashmir was Hazrat

Syed Sharif-ud-Din Abdur Rehman. Zareef Ahmad Zareef, a well-known humourist-poet and historian based in Kashmir, told me that the Sufi Abdur Rehman became popular as 'Bulbul Shah'. A Kashmiri myth about Hazrat Abdur Rehman is that he was so absorbed and engrossed in meditation that a nightingale (bulbul) would sit on his head undisturbed. This is perhaps how he came to be called 'Bulbul Shah'. He arrived in Kashmir during the reign of Ranchan Shah, a Buddhist ruler who had converted to Islam. Abdur Rehman—believed to have travelled all the way from Turkistan—settled in Kashmir around 725 AH (1324 CE). His shrine is located in Srinagar at a place called Bulbul Langar (now 'Bulbul Lankar').

Many saints from Central Asia and Persia (now Iran) have visited Kashmir over the centuries. Born in Hamadan in Iran, many historians say, Hazrat Mir Syed Ali Hamadani played a significant role in spreading Islam and spirituality in Kashmir. Historians agree that Hamadani, a Persian Sufi of the Kubrawi order, also known as Shah-i-Hamadan, visited Kashmir on three different occasions between 774–785 AH (roughly 1373–84 CE) and moved here along with 700 followers and companions, referred to as 'saadat'. According to Zareef, apart from his role in spreading Sufism in Kashmir, Hamadani was also instrumental in refining the region's art and craft.[29] Many in Kashmir in those days would earn their livelihood through the art of stone carving. After mass conversion to Islam, a delegation of such skilled workers and artisans is believed to have approached Hamadani to suggest alternative work for them, as they had abandoned 'but-tarashi' (the carving of idols) after embracing Islam. The saint suggested that they make mosque pulpits, carve the ninety-nine names of Allah around the mimbar, and design the interior architecture of places of religious worship. This prominent Muslim scholar and Sufi was buried in Khatlon, Tajikistan.

For the past six centuries, people in Kashmir have regularly visited shrines, while Sufi disciples, as per the teachings of their spiritual masters, recite the 'Wazaif', the prescribed verses to seek forgiveness, blessings and favours from Allah. Perhaps it is because of this, that most Kashmiris did not feel comfortable with the kind of orthodox Islamic lifestyle that was being thrust upon them by certain forces. The early years of armed militancy in the 1990s were, therefore, frustrating for the people of Kashmir. On the one hand, government soldiers would humiliate common people in the name of frisking, ordering them to deboard local buses for identification parades and making them walk long distances before they could take their respective seats in the buses again; elderly people, too, were not spared. On the other hand, some militants would conduct their own random checks in public buses and private vehicles to ensure that women covered their faces adequately with niqabs or burqas!

The militant groups that were trying to enforce a particular dress code for women soon retracted from such undemocratic practices because of the lack of social acceptability and social sanction for the same.

Besides, when eight Amarnath pilgrims were killed in a suspected Lashkar attack in south Kashmir's Anantnag district on 10 July 2017, there was massive outrage in the Valley. In fact, the attack on Amarnath yatris evoked a robust response from Kashmir's vibrant civil society formations, for there is a lack of social approval regarding attacks on civilians, unarmed policemen, tourists and pilgrims. Despite rainy conditions on 11 July, many members of Kashmir's civil society coalitions, human rights bodies, business fraternity, academia, historians, social activists, poets, journalists and students gathered at Srinagar's Pratap Park to register their strong protest against the attack on Hindu pilgrims.[30] In their unequivocal condemnation, they demanded an independent probe into the attack to identify the perpetrators.

Authorities blamed LeT for the attack on pilgrims. In a detailed telephone conversation with me for *India Today*, Kashmir's then Inspector General of Police, Muneer Khan, claimed that a Pakistani national, Ismael, had 'planned and orchestrated the attack on yatris'. Weeks later, Ismael was killed in an encounter. Even the UJC, in a statement to CNS, deplored the attack on

Amarnath pilgrims.[31] LeT also denied its involvement and described the attack on pilgrims 'a highly reprehensible act.'[32] 'Islam does not allow violence against innocent civilians of any faith. India wants to defame and sabotage the freedom struggle of Kashmiris and therefore it uses such attacks to fulfil its agenda,' the UJC statement said.[33]

It often gets very difficult in Kashmir to establish truth, as there are many versions and many layers to truth in a conflict zone.

Meanwhile, the pro-independence JKLF was the main face of the armed movement in the early 1990s. A guerrilla outfit led by its chief commander Mohammad Yasin Malik, it announced a unilateral ceasefire on 21 May 1994, to pursue its struggle politically through peaceful means. Around the same time, on 31 August 1994, the Irish Republican Army announced complete cessation of military operations against the UK in Northern Ireland. Yasin Malik's decision to launch a non-violent struggle based on Gandhian principles became controversial, and his group started losing its popularity among the people of the state. Malik says that Delhi did not respect his offer and alleges that at least 500 JKLF men were killed by government forces after the unilateral ceasefire was announced by him.

Soon after, HM emerged as a pro-Pakistan rebel outfit and a rival to the JKLF's ideology, which favoured independence. Informally, the JeI extended its unstinted support to HM. Initially, HM was seen as the JeI's 'fouji bazu' (sword arm), but JeI had to retract its support in the mid-1990s. Undoubtedly, the JeI organized one of the best social reformist, religious and political movements. Though not as old as the NC, the JeI is known for its efficient cadre, organizational skills and reach. The group has a massive cadre base spread all across the Kashmir Valley, parts of Chenab and also the Pir Panjal in Jammu province. Syed Ali Geelani has been a JeI supporter for most of his life. Although, of late, he had developed some differences with the JeI, he continues to shower flowery appreciation on it as a socio-politico-religious organization. The Government of India imposed a ban on the JeI and authorities arrested over 350 of its members.[34]

Other well-known militant organizations of the 1990s were the Jammu and Kashmir Students Liberation Front, Jamiat-ul-Mujahideen, Harkat ul-Ansar, Tehreek-ul-Mujahideen, Al-Umar Mujahideen, Al-Badr, Muslim Janbaz Force, Al-Jihad, Allah Tigers and a lesser-known outfit like Hizb-ul-Momineen, though HM was, and continues to be, the largest and most popular because almost all its recruits have been native Kashmiris.

The ideological differences between HM and JKLF came to the fore when they executed violent campaigns against each other in which the former ultimately prevailed because of its superior muscle power. Many militants were killed as a result of this inter-group rivalry. HM and Harkat-ul-Ansar also clashed with each other. Eventually, this infighting led to the birth of a government-sponsored renegade group, Ikhwan-ul-Muslimoon. Those associated with this group were mostly former rebels who came to be called 'Ikhwani' (or 'Nawabadis'). This group, at times, settled personal scores by helping government soldiers go after armed militants. The Ikhwanis mostly targeted pro-Pakistan groups like HM. Led by a Kashmiri folk singer known for his melodious voice, Mohammad Yusuf Parray, later known as 'Kuka Parray', the renegade group unleashed a reign of terror. Parray became notorious and was accused of killing innocent people, kidnappings, torture and extortion.[35] He was helped and encouraged by the government to become a Member of the Legislative Assembly (MLA). Parray, a singer-turned-militant, surrendered before government forces in 1995, formed his own political party and became a lawmaker in the J&K Assembly. Eventually Parray founded his own political outfit, the Jammu and Kashmir Awami League.

On 13 September 2003, militants, believed to be from the JeM, laid an ambush with the aim to kill Parray when he was on his way to inaugurate a cricket tournament in Hajin Sonawari, his hometown and a major town in north Kashmir's Bandipore district, which, in the mid-1990s, had earned notoriety for being the headquarters of the dreaded pro-India Ikhwan militia led by Parray. They opened fire on his car and his bullet-ridden body was rushed to Srinagar's SKIMS hospital, though he had died en route. J&K's then CM, late Mufti Mohammad Sayeed, described Parray's killing as a 'setback to the peace process'. It was an interesting statement in the context of Parray's past, and the fact that he was a government-sponsored renegade and a gunman accused of horrific crimes.

★

When the armed uprising began in Kashmir, the JeI played a significant role in mobilizing support for the same, through its powerful cadres and an impressive support base. In the beginning, the JeI did unofficially invoke religion and Tehreek-e-Islami, the global Muslim movement for supremacy of Islam as envisioned by two Egyptians—Hasan al-Banna, the Supreme Guide of the Society of the Muslim Brothers; and Sayyid Qutb, a well-known educator, academic and writer—with the aim to rally the masses for Kashmir's political struggle against New Delhi. Lawrence Wright argues in *Looming Tower: Al-Qaeda's Road to 9/11*, that it was Sayyid Qutb who had lit the spark of political (radical) Islam way back in 1948.[36]

The JeI in Kashmir is one of the sister organizations operating with the same name in different parts of the subcontinent. Originally, it was a part of, and functioned as a branch of, the erstwhile Jamaat-i-Islami Hind of undivided India.[37] In fact, Pir Saad-ud-Din, Maulana Ghulam Ahmad Ahrar, Qari Saif-u-Din, Dr Ghulam Rasool Abdullah and Syed Mohammad Shafi participated in the All India Ijtima held in 1941 at Lahore, that became instrumental in the formation of the JeI.[38] Abul A'la Maududi, the well-known theologian and an ideologue of political Islam, founded the JeI Hind in August 1941 (some historians say it was founded in 1940) to promote moral values and Islamic practices. He was elected JeI's first ameer (commander) and remained so till 1972, when he withdrew from the responsibility, citing reasons of health. From Aurangabad (in the former princely state of Hyderabad and now in Maharashtra), Maududi migrated to Pakistan in August 1947 and concentrated his efforts on establishing an Islamic State and society in that country.

According to a Kashmiri researcher Younus Rashid, who works as assistant professor in the Department of History at the University of Kashmir, the JeI in J&K unofficially began working in the pre-partition state of J&K in the 1940s itself. The organization, as an independent entity in the shape of JeI's J&K chapter, drafted its separate constitution in the 1950s.[39] The Jamaat-e-Islami Jammu and Kashmir (JIJK), as a separate entity, was founded in 1952 after two of its senior and committed members, Maulana Ahrar and Ghulam Rasul Abdullah, drafted the party's separate constitution, which was accepted and passed by its members in November 1953.

Eleven months later, in October 1954, the late Sa'ad-ud-Din (Tarabali) was elected as the JeI president. Though its activities had started in the Kashmir Valley in the mid-1940s itself, with its first ijtima, a large congregation held in Srinagar, which was attended by traders, government employees and youth, JIJK began establishing schools and expanding religious and social activities in the mosques. Key JIJK leaders would distribute Maududi's literature at religious places and also at social gatherings. Apart from its founder, the party also drew some inspiration from Sayyid Qutb. In November 1948, Qutb, as an individual, was experiencing a different world on his visit to New York while the JIJK leaders in Kashmir were busy expanding their base in the Valley and talking about the welfare of Muslims. As the armed uprising erupted in Kashmir in 1989, the JeI workers and sympathizers, besides distributing an assemblage of Maududi's khutbaat (sermons) and works of Islamic literature, would also talk about Qutb's manifesto called 'Milestones' ('Ma'alim fi al-Tariq' in Arabic, and 'Naqoosh-e-Rah' in Urdu). At a later stage, Qutb's ideas would give birth to what would be called Islamic fundamentalism.[40]

On Kashmir's turf, the JIJK leaders and preachers would often talk about a new social order and reach out to the general masses via school education, public contact programmes using the mosque pulpit, and also its ijtimas, seminars and other conferences. Unofficially, soon after the outbreak of armed struggle in Kashmir in 1989, this socio-religious party also advocated Kashmir's merger with Pakistan.

As mentioned earlier, when HM was launched as an armed outfit in the early 1990s, the JeI first appropriated it as its 'fauji baazu', but soon distanced itself from it, inviting scathing criticism for its flip-flop. It was at that point that Syed Ali Shah Geelani began developing differences with the JeI. Geelani has, all along, been a strong votary of armed resistance. In the third volume of his autobiography, *Wular Kinaray* (On the banks of the Wular), he has also questioned the former JeI ameer, Ghulam Mohammad Bhat, for calling Kashmir a mere 'political issue'. Geelani's contention is that young Kashmiris embraced armed rebellion to pressurize New Delhi to accept that J&K is a disputed territory.

The JeI's influence on Kashmir's polity cannot be understated by any stretch of the imagination. Its founder, Maududi, had written specifically about the Kashmir dispute and how it can be resolved, in a book titled *Masla-e-Kashmir aur iska hul* (The Kashmir issue and its solution). It is a compilation of his lectures and pamphlets on Kashmir. In the first part, Maududi talks about the historical context of the Kashmir dispute, the India-Pakistan Partition, and the official stands of both countries. He then explains his party's stand on Kashmir, and discusses the right to self-determination; Kashmir and Muslim ummah; Kashmir and Pakistan; the ways and means to achieve Kashmir's liberation; and how jihad is the only viable option to achieve the desired results. Maududi believes that negotiations with India will always prove meaningless, for the country knows that its control of Kashmir is 'illegal and illegitimate' but still has the audacity to claim Kashmir as its 'integral part'. One cannot have a result-oriented dialogue with a country that believes in deception while negating history and ground reality, he contends.[41]

In the book, Maududi also describes in detail how reliance on UN's resolutions is mere stupidity. He writes that the UN has lost its moral standing and there is the absence of honesty in its efforts to resolve Kashmir. He argues that, like India, there is no point in relying on the UN. He also does not see any benefit in the intervention of other nations like the UK and calls any such expectation an exercise in 'self-deception'. Finally, Maududi talks about his 'wahid hal' (only solution) and that, according to him, is liberating Kashmir through jihad. He writes that, as a last resort, we have to rely on Allah and use our 'daste bazu' (hands and arms) to resolve Kashmir; there is no other solution. He also explains that in war, people generally talk about numbers, but when it is a question of honour, one should not think about numerical strength. It is a question of choosing between honour and humiliation, dignity and disgrace. He says that even the legitimacy of Pakistan as a Muslim nation state will largely depend on whether it chooses to fight for Kashmir or not.

Conversely though, all leaders of prominent militant outfits as well as political organizations active on Kashmir's complex political landscape always invoke the UN resolutions on Kashmir, and make appeals to the international community, the European Union and other Western institutions as well as global human rights bodies like the Human Rights Watch (HRW) and Amnesty International to play their role vis-à-vis Kashmir.

On Kashmir's political turf, the JeI as an organization is facing a crisis of a different kind. In the past, the party has demonstrated flexibility and participated in the Assembly elections until the controversial and rigged elections of 1987. After the eruption of armed struggle in 1989, it has either fully or partially supported the gun or talked about Kashmir being a political dispute. Some in Kashmir accuse the JeI of 'doublespeak' and lack of courage to admit its contradictions displayed at various junctures. The larger reality, however, is that an overwhelming majority of Kashmiris, irrespective of their religious affiliations, sectarian preferences or socio-economic statuses, fully endorse and support Kashmir's struggle for the right to self-determination in various forms. In 1989, the armed resistance movement in Kashmir challenged J&K's constitutional relationship with the Indian Union and favoured either complete independence or a merger with Pakistan. As mentioned earlier, during the pro-freedom rallies of the early 1990s, attended by tens of thousands of Kashmiris, the oft-repeated slogans were: *'Narai-e-Takbeer, Allah-o-Akbar'*; *'La Illaha Illallah'*; *'Pakistan Se Rishta Kya, La Illaha Illallah'*; *'Yahan Kya Chalega, Nizam-e-Mustafa'*; *'Hum Kya Chahate—Azadi'*; *'Jis Kashmir Ko Khoon Se Seencha, Woh Kashmir Hamara Hai'* ('The Kashmir that we have irrigated with our blood, is ours'), and so on.

The *Outlook* survey of 1995 established that a majority in J&K prefers complete independence of the restive Himalayan region and favours a solution to the dispute outside the ambits of the Indian Constitution. Due to the absence of any empirical study to ascertain whether the inclination towards pro-independence is more dominant in Kashmir than that towards pro-Pakistan, the general impression is that most Kashmiris have a preference for independence, over a merger with Pakistan or even staying with India. What is unquestionable though is the fact that 'anti Delhi' remains the major ideology. However, in the absence of a credible referendum, attributing concrete figures to either perspective is difficult. For instance, it is well documented that, in the past, many Kashmiris in their wills have requested their children and grandchildren to hoist the Pakistani flag on their graves once the region merges with Pakistan. Some of the youth who died in the 2016 uprising or in the 2017 protests were buried wrapped in the Pakistani flag in place of the usual 'safed kafan' (white shrouds).

There is also no doubt that most Kashmiris feel they bond over a shared religion and geographical proximity with Pakistan. In February 2016, I sought the view of Kashmir's veteran columnist, Ajaz-ul-Haque, on this issue. In his emailed response to me, he wrote that the pro-Pakistan sentiment in Kashmir is neither dead nor diminished; it's suppressed and the reasons are rooted in the conditions created since the 1990s. Moreover, the worsening situation in Pakistan is creating a negative feeling among Kashmiris and that is perhaps one of the reasons why people don't display their pro-Pakistan emotions as openly as they used to or would like to.

In my observation, many in Kashmir continue to express their love for Pakistan overtly through symbolic gestures like cheering for its cricket team, waving or hoisting Pakistan's flag in pro-azadi rallies, setting Pakistan's national anthem as the ringtone on their mobile phones and attending funerals of militants of Pakistani descent in colossal numbers. For example, when Indian forces, in October 2015, claimed a 'major success' in the killing of top LeT commander, Abdur Rehman alias Abu Qasim, accused of masterminding the Udhampur attack, at least 20,000[42] people participated in his janaza. He was killed in an overnight encounter in south Kashmir's Kulgam district of J&K. The thirty-year-old Qasim was from Bahawalpur in Pakistan and was accused of some of the major attacks on government forces in Kashmir. It was alleged that Qasim had masterminded the attack on an Indian Army convoy in Hyderpora on the outskirts of Srinagar in June 2013, which had resulted in the killing of nine Army personnel. He carried a bounty of ₹2 million (₹20 lakh) on his head.

In the eyes of some Kashmiris, Pakistan's inconsistent and wavering policy on Kashmir has been a cause for concern, as has been an increase in Taliban violence in that country. But people make a distinction between the Pakistani State and its people. Khurram Parvez, coordinator of Jammu and Kashmir Coalition of Civil Society (JKCCS), admitted that Pakistan's policy vis-à-vis Kashmir has been 'problematic' and that there was no dearth of people in Kashmir who feel frustrated with what Parvez calls Islamabad's 'inconsistent Kashmir policy'. The government in J&K seldom allows the APHC leadership to hold public rallies, but whenever that happens, one can clearly hear loud pro-Pakistan slogans like *'Jeeve jeeve Pakistan'* ('Long live Pakistan') alongside the dominant slogan *'Hum Kya Chahate—Azadi'*. A section of people in Kashmir continues to showcase its love for Pakistan openly, even in a suppressed environment and at the cost of paying heavily for it. This overt expression, Parvez argues, does not necessarily indicate they are in favour of Kashmir's merger with Pakistan, though for many Kashmiris, a visit to Pakistan is no less than an 'emotional pilgrimage.'[43]

Socio-politico-religious organizations like JeI, and armed outfits like HM, at best favour Kashmir's merger with Pakistan but do not talk of establishing the 'Khilafat' (Caliphate) in Kashmir. Except the Zakir Musa-led splinter group, AGH, and a tiny and lesser-known IS-inspired group, Islamic State of Jammu and Kashmir (ISJK), which does not have more than ten to fifteen members, hardly any rebel group fighting in Kashmir has ever linked Kashmir with other global conflicts, though parallels are often drawn with the Israeli occupation of Palestine for argument's sake. Though it is true that Burhan Wani did once casually mention 'Khilafat' in a video statement, he did not elaborate what he meant by it and HM has not officially linked its armed struggle with the establishment of a Caliphate. Barring slain militants Zakir Musa of AGH and Mohammad Eisa Fazili of ISJK, all armed groups and political alliances and groups like the APHC and JKLF[44] only talk about Kashmir in terms of a political dispute.

At the same time, it will be naïve to ignore the perils of a possible ideological drift in the Kashmiri armed movement narrative (not in the political struggle), especially the impact of the Internet and social media. After a gap of seventeen long years, a Kashmir boy was involved in a suicide attack on government forces. On 31 December 2017, Fardeen Khanday, the sixteen-year-old boy from Nazneenpora village in Burhan's hometown, Tral, led a suicide attack on a camp of the CRPF at Lethpora on the Srinagar-Jammu national highway, which also housed a training facility and residential quarters. Fardeen and two of his accomplices—Manzoor Ahmed Baba, another local Kashmiri; and Muhammad Shakoor from Pakistan—were part of a JeM suicide squad, which targeted the camp on New Year's Eve. At least four CRPF personnel died in the attack, and one died of cardiac arrest during the attack.[45] Prior to this suicide attack, Afaq Ahmed Shah, a JeM militant from Khanyar in Srinagar, in 2000 tried to ram an explosive-laden car into the Indian Army's 15 Corps headquarters at Badami Bagh in Srinagar.

The involvement of two Kashmiri boys in the 2017 suicide mission had alarmed Indian intelligence agencies. Fardeen, of the JeM, had recorded his video just before he prepared himself for the attack on the CRPF camp. In the video, Fardeen is seen sitting cross-legged, wearing a traditional Kashmiri woolen cloak called pheran and a kaffiyeh, in front of a stash of grenades and an AK-47 rifle, and explaining in Urdu why he had become a fidayeen.[46] Similarly, before carrying out the 14 February 2019 suicide attack in Pulwama, the twenty-year-old Adil Ahmad Dar, a local Kashmiri boy from Gundibagh village in south Kashmir's Pulwama district, had recorded a video message: 'By the time this video reaches you, I will be enjoying in heaven... This is my last message for the people of Kashmir... Jaish has kept the flame alive and stayed put in adverse circumstances. Come, join the group and prepare for one last fight.'[47] The question is, how did Kashmir reach this point? How did a Kashmiri boy decide to become a human bomb? What changed so abruptly?

On 13 August 2016, a senior PDP leader and Member of the Indian Parliament, Muzaffar Baig, who had attended the all-party meeting on Kashmir in New Delhi the previous day, in an interview[48] remarked that there was a danger that the Taliban experiment could be replicated in Kashmir. He argued that after the emergence of the ISIS ideology, which he said is spreading across the globe, there are chances that Kashmir could also be affected if a solution to the political dispute is not found soon. To counter such a possibility, he suggested that the real battle in Kashmir is to win the hearts of the youth, which cannot be done by excessive use of force, pellet-firing shotguns, bullets and curfews. Baig said he was all for weaving a new narrative for Kashmir's youth in order to win their hearts and minds. But he failed to suggest any solid evidence to back his claim that Kashmir's youth were vulnerable to the IS/Taliban ideology. In an interview to NDTV on 15 August 2016, he also articulated that Afghanistan's youth became vulnerable during the war between Russian communism and American capitalism. He was obviously referring to the emergence of the Taliban during the Cold War. This was interesting, especially in the context of Kashmir's struggle against the Dogra Maharaja in the 1930s, when Left-wing intellectuals had thought of Kashmir as 'a laboratory for testing Socialist ideals'.

Eight decades later, a pro-India Kashmiri politician argued that 'the Taliban experiment could be simulated in Kashmir.'[49] That is why Muzaffar Baig's statement was not well received by Kashmiris; even the pro-autonomy NC rejected his contentious remarks. Omar Abdullah slammed Baig[50] for his statement and held the PDP responsible for what he termed New Delhi's 'shocking and hawkish' stand on the situation in Kashmir. Abdullah's official statement, issued on 13 August 2016, slammed Baig for the latter's 'perverse anti-Kashmir tirade and stereotypical Muslim bashing'.

The junior Abdullah said in his statement as reported by the local media:

> PDP was the only political party from J&K that was present in the All Party Meet—allegedly held on the Kashmir situation. It is therefore extremely disappointing that the party chose to ridicule and vilify the people of Kashmir and went to the extent of saying there should be no agitation by political parties against excessive use of force and pellet guns. Not only did PDP choose to tacitly support the use of excessive force in the Valley it also stooped to the extent of deriding those voices of empathy and solidarity...

On 30 August 2016, HM released a 10.43-minute-long video statement that was emailed to news agencies from an anonymous email ID. A young man in combat fatigues, sporting a small beard and wearing a pair of spectacles starts the message by reciting verses from the Quran followed by a few revolutionary couplets. He is, purportedly, Riyaz. He goes on to talk about various issues, which include the 'martyrdom' of Burhan Wani, the migration and return of Kashmiri Pandits, local policemen and the Indian government's Kashmir policy. In the background, one can see a big green flag on which a couplet of famous poet, Dr Allama Iqbal, is inscribed, along with a picture of Burhan. Riyaz speaks in both Urdu and English.

First, he explains, 'Kashmiri boys did not pick up the gun to become terrorists but only after India did not leave them any option but to choose the path of violence.' After reciting the verses, he pays tributes to Burhan with these words: *'Sab se pehle hum shaheed Burhan Wani (Rehmatullah-e-Alaih) ko dil ki umeeq gehraiyou'n se khiraj e tahseen pesh karte hain'* ('To begin with, let's pay glowing tributes to our martyr Burhan Wani from the depths of our heart'). He then urges the people of Millat-e-Islamia, especially of the Kashmir Valley, to not mourn Burhan's death because, in his words, 'a true Mumin [Muslim] does not mourn the martyrdom of a martyr, but carries a burning desire in his heart to achieve martyrdom'. He credits Burhan for providing fresh impetus to Kashmir's tehreek-e-azadi and demonstrating before the global community that 'we are not terrorists, but freedom fighters involved in a just struggle for Kashmir's freedom'. He says that the number of people that attended Burhan's funeral made it obvious to the world that he was a freedom fighter who enjoyed the massive backing from his people, while the thin attendance at the funeral of J&K's former CM, Mufti Mohammad Sayeed, indicated the exact opposite:

> If Burhan was a terrorist, why did 5 lakh people participate in his janaza? Why did the Indian government impose a ban on the Internet and use of social media on the death of a 'terrorist'? Why did the people of Kashmir come out on the roads to offer sacrifices and blood for Kashmir's freedom? India wants to suppress our voice by imposing a strict ban on social media and not allow our voice to reach different countries of the world.

He goes on to say that Kashmiri Pandits were driven out of Kashmir by the notorious governor, Jagmohan, in 1990, but those who stayed back in Kashmir are living with the majority community as brothers and sisters. He also showers praise on the minority Sikh community, saying that they never left the Valley and were not harmed by the mujahideen. In an emotional moment, the spokesperson says that his eyes became moist when he watched the six-year-old daughter of Pramod Kumar—the Commanding Officer of the 49 battalion who died after sustaining a bullet injury to the head on 15 August 2016 in a militant strike in Nowhatta, Srinagar—on television, mourning her father's death. He says that Kashmiri mujahideen had not gone to Kumar's home to kill him, but it was he who had come to Kashmir to 'occupy and suppress us'. Then he urges Pramod Kumar's widow to consider Kashmir's thousands of yateem (orphans) whose parents have been killed by the government's armed forces. He warns local policemen not to target Kashmiri mujahideen, and urges them to stay indoors like other government employees who were following the APHC's protest calendar after Burhan's assassination.

On the other hand, Zakir alias Musa, chief of AGH, in no uncertain terms, linked Kashmir's struggle with the larger struggle of Muslim ummah and overtly talked about establishing the Caliphate.

One of Kashmir's many realities is that social media has become a new battleground for competing and conflicting ideologies and narratives, and for testing various ideals. In a first, an emotionally broken father and school principal, Naeem Fazili, utilized his Facebook account to make a passionate call to his son Mohammad Eisa Fazili, who had joined the ranks of armed rebels, to return to the family. Along with posting a picture of Eisa, Naeem wrote a message on Eid in September 2017 with the aim of convincing his son to come home:

> Eisa, your innocence is being exploited by some vested interests. You are being used as a pawn or a poster boy. I swear you are not on the right track in the light of Quran and Sunnah (practices of the Prophet). Please don't play with fire. Return as early as possible. Your mum is wandering hither and thither with your belongings in hands. Mind it one can never succeed in (the) absence of prayers of his parents.

Naeem later removed his post. Eisa was an engineering student who had left his studies to join the ranks of an extremist militant group. Police suspected that Eisa may have joined the AGH. Later it turned out that he had joined ISJK.

On 12 March 2018, Eisa was killed in an encounter with government forces along with two of his associates—one of them, Syed Owais Shafi of south Kashmir's Kokernag, in the Hakoora area of Anantnag district. Shafi had completed his BTech in Electronics and Communications from Baba Ghulam Shah Badshah University in Rajouri district of the Chenab valley region. There, he met Eisa.

Naeem again used Facebook to share the news about the killing of his son. 'As per reliable sources, my son Eisa Fazili has left for heavenly abode,' he wrote. Soon after, he added: 'It is for the information of all nears and dears (sic) that Nimaaz-e-Jinaaza of my son Mohammad Eisa Fazili... will be held at 3 pm sharp near his residence at Sharjah Ground, 90 Feet Road, Ahmednagar, Srinagar.'

Eisa was a resident of Shadab colony in Soura, Srinagar. He went missing from his hostel room in Baba Ghulam Shah Badshah University on 17 August 2017. A few days before Eid-ul-Azha, he passionately talked about jihad while quoting specific verses from the holy book in an 8.24-minute-long video.

In the video, Eisa, sporting a beard and wearing a white-coloured skullcap, was seen with an assault rifle. He began his video message by reciting Quranic verses (38 and 39) from Surah At-Tawbah in Arabic. When roughly translated into English, the verses mean this: 'Believers! What is amiss with you that when it is said to you: "March forth in the cause of Allah," you cling heavily to the earth. Do you prefer the worldly life to the hereafter? Know well that all the enjoyment of this world, in comparison with the hereafter, is trivial.' After Arabic, Eisa switched to Urdu to read: '*Maslihat ki niqaabein utaaro bhi ab, kufr ko kufr kehkar pukaro bhi ab*' ('Remove the masks of expediency, to describe infidelity as infidelity'). Using his oratory skills, the new militant recruit further declared that 'jihad in Kashmir is only for the sake of Allah and dominance of Allah's religion (Islam); nothing else.' This, he said, could only be achieved through 'jihad fee sabeelillah' (the holy struggle for Allah's sake). In a possible shift in Kashmir's twenty-nine-year-old armed militancy, Eisa—like Zakir—talked about problems faced by Muslims in Iraq, Yemen, Syria, Palestine, Pakistan, Kashmir and Myanmar (formerly Burma). 'Only over the last three days, nearly three thousand Muslims have been mercilessly martyred in Burma,' Eisa said, while highlighting the plight of Muslims around the globe. 'I appeal to the young Muslims, irrespective of their professions as engineers or doctors, to play a constructive role to help the Burmese (Rohingya) Muslims,' he added.[51]

In the later part of his video message, he explained the reasons behind his becoming an armed rebel:

I know what is happening in Kashmir, what happened in Kunan Poshpora, the Pathribal 'fake' encounter and many such incidents like in India's Muzaffarnagar and Gujarat. I felt as if sisters of my Ummah were calling for my help to come forward to protect their honour... I was not fed up with society, worldly affairs or my engineering studies in the college. Only after seeing the abject condition of Muslim Ummah did I choose to tread the path of jihad in the name of Allah for Allah's sake.

He concluded with a message of Zarqawi about how to celebrate Eid.

In the absence of a sincere, credible and meaningful dialogue to resolve the political dispute of Kashmir, these dangers are real. If the political vacuum continues and Delhi continues to see Kashmir through a myopic law-and-order prism, more and more educated Kashmiri boys could spread across Kashmir to plant the seeds of a possible Islamic insurgence.

In January 2018, a well-known PhD scholar Manan Bashir Wani from Takipora hamlet in Lolab in north Kashmir's Kupwara district, joined HM after he had gone missing a few days earlier. Wani had completed his research studies at the prestigious Aligarh Muslim University (AMU) situated in the state of Uttar Pradesh in northern India.[52] A picture of him wielding an AK-47 rifle had gone viral, and on the morning of 11 October 2018, this research scholar-turned armed-militant commander was trapped in a house along with his associate in the Shatgund hamlet of north Kashmir's Handwara district. Hours later, around afternoon, the local authorities and J&K Police confirmed that the highly educated twenty-nine-year-old gun-wielding rebel Manan Wani was killed in a brief firefight with government forces. Hailing from a well-to-do family, Wani had remained busy with his studies at AMU from 2011, and had completed his MPhil followed by a PhD in geology. Even after joining militancy, Wani wrote two long letters explaining his unanticipated decision to take the path that he did while sacrificing his career ambitions. Both of his letters had gone viral on social media.

Wani was among a stream of educated youths from Kashmir to have joined the new age of armed rebellion since the 2016 civilian uprising intensified in the Himalayan Valley following the killing of Burhan. Few months before Manan Wani's killing, Mohammad Rafi Bhat was killed in a gunfight with government forces in the month of May. Bhat, a young assistant professor at the University of Kashmir, was one among the five armed militants killed in an encounter in a remote hamlet in south Kashmir's Shopian district, about 45 km from Srinagar. Bhat, a resident of Chundina area of central Kashmir's Ganderbal district, which is 25 km from Srinagar, was working on a contractual basis in the sociology department of the university. He had joined the ranks of armed rebels only thirty-six hours before getting killed in a deadly encounter, the likes of which have become a routine in the restive region for over three decades now.

Barring Burhan Wani, who survived for nearly six years after joining militancy, others like Manan, Rafi and Eisa could not even survive for six months. These killings in 2018 stirred a debate in the Kashmir Valley about a possible trend of highly educated young men getting attracted to Kashmir's new age of militancy, which comprises mostly of local recruits than fighters from PaK or mainland Pakistan. According to informed sources in the local police's Intelligence department, there are between 325 and 350 armed rebels currently active in various parts of the

region, of which over 210 are native boys from varying socio-
economic backgrounds. For some years now, local militants have
outnumbered foreign fighters in Kashmir. From January until
August 2018, at least 146 local boys joined various militant outfits
in J&K. Fresh recruits mostly belong to south Kashmir's volatile
districts of Pulwama, Shopian, Anantnag and Kulgam.[53]

Politicians representing competing ideological strands—pro-
independence, pro-Pakistan or pro-India—in Kashmir also differ
on why the educated youth are attracted to the idea of taking up
the gun than joining the political struggle for a peaceful conflict
resolution process in Kashmir.

Mehbooba Mufti believes that the 'circumstance around us
act as a catalyst' and sees 'the othering of Muslims across India'
as one of the reasons behind the worrying trend. She told me:

> Basically it is the political nature of (the) Kashmir problem,
> its internal and external dimension(s)—a fact that is being
> denied (by Delhi). The circumstances around us play the
> role of a catalyst. The othering of Muslims in India and
> a strident Hindutva assertion instigates a reaction and a
> sense of insecurity and hopelessness within the system...
> The global atmosphere of political radicalisation and wrong
> interpretation of jihad also contributes to it (the youth taking
> up arms).

On the other hand, the Srinagar-based influential head priest and
chairman of a moderate faction of pro-independence amalgam,
the APHC, Mirwaiz Umar Farooq is of the view that 'the intensity
of Delhi's repression pushes educated Kashmiri youth to the wall.'

However, the top-ranked officers of J&K Police (Kashmir
Range) opine that for militants in Kashmir, 'publicity is the
currency they thrive upon.' They believe that there is an instrument
of propaganda in all of this. This propaganda, they say, has the
capacity to influence young and impressionable minds by using
social media to good effect. They are of the view that not even
10 per cent of militants in Kashmir are highly educated. In any
case, the police force does not see local militants—200 odd boys

who are not battle-hardened or fully trained in combat—as a 'major challenge.'[54]

On 23 March 2018, which fell on a Friday, another young man went missing in Srinagar, soon after the noon prayers. Hours later, it was public knowledge that he had joined HM. The man was twenty-six-year-old Junaid Ashraf Sehrai, an MBA from the University of Kashmir and the son of senior pro-Pakistan leader Mohammad Ashraf Sehrai. The junior Sehrai too announced joining militancy in the signature style of Kashmir's renewed armed rebellion. The gun-toting new entrants publicize their joining by posting their pictures and videos on social media with their original names, aliases and educational qualification. His joining of militancy came at the same time as Eisa Fazili joining the ISJK. In early November 2018, another educated youth, Ehtisham Bilal from Srinagar's Khanyar locality announced his joining the same group that had attracted Fazili to militancy.

Interestingly, Muzaffar Wani, Burhan's father, told me at his home in Tral in May that he was a proud Kashmiri who does not differentiate between a Muslim and a non-Muslim. With tears in his eyes, he said that he often dreamt about his Kashmiri Pandit classmates and shed tears even when asleep. He recalled his childhood days when he and his Pandit friends would live, study and play together. Once, he along with three other friends, visited Jammu with the sole aim of looking for their four Pandit classmates. He said that their search took them one full day. They felt some contentment only after they found their childhood friends. 'I see my Kashmir Pandit friends in my dreams, and cry. This is our love. And see, what this country (India) does to us?'[55]

NOTES, SOURCES AND REFERENCES

1.   Jacob, H. (2016, August 29). Kashmir and the clash of symbolisms. Retrieved from http://www.thehindu.com/todays-paper/tp-opinion/Kashmir-and-the-clash-of-symbolisms/article14595970.ece
2.   Till Freedom Come. (1995, October 17). Retrieved from https://www.outlookindia.

com/magazine/story/till-freedom-come/200005
3. Bradnock, R. W., & Schofield, R. (2010). *Kashmir: Paths to Peace*. London: Chatham House. Retrieved from https://www.chathamhouse.org/sites/default/files/public/Research/Asia/0510pp_kashmir.pdf
4. Ahmad, K. B. (2017). *Kashmir: Exposing the Myth behind the Narrative*. New Delhi, India: SAGE Publications India Pvt.
5. Ibid.
6. Ibid.
7. Gul, K. (2016, August 01). Thousands march to Kareemabad, 'LeT chief Abu Dujana surfaces in rally'. Retrieved from http://www.greaterkashmir.com/news/front-page/thousands-march-to-kareemabad-let-chief-abu-dujana-surfaces-in-rally/224414.html
8. Militants appear at rallies. (2016, August 06). Retrieved from http://www.tribuneindia.com/news/jammu-kashmir/militants-appear-at-rallies/276607.html)
9. Bhushan, B. (2018, November 19). Jammu & Kashmir's parallel-universe conundrum, and the need to end it. Retrieved from https://www.business-standard.com/article/opinion/jammu-kashmir-s-parallel-universe-conundrum-and-the-need-to-end-it-118111900114_1.html
10. Geelani, G. (2016, February 05). Is pro-Pakistan sentiment in Kashmir still alive? Retrieved from https://www.dawn.com/news/1237193
11. Source 1: Geelani, G. (2013, June 24). Interview: 'Pakistan's stability is of utmost importance to Kashmiris'. Retrieved from https://www.dawn.com/news/1020464
Source 2: Masarat Alam by side, Pakistan flags in crowd, Syed Geelani steps out. (2015, April 16). Retrieved from http://indianexpress.com/article/india/india-others/srinagar-supporters-wave-pak-flag-as-syed-geelani-holds-rally-after-5-yrs/
12. Khan, I. A. (2016, August 05). Rajnath leaves SAARC meeting abruptly amid bitterness. Retrieved from https://www.dawn.com/news/1275551
13. Bukhari, S., & Yaseen, F. (2015, November 28). People have failed leadership: Geelani. Retrieved from http://www.risingkashmir.com/news/people-have-failed-leadership-geelani
14. Geelani, G. (2013, June 24). Interview: 'Pakistan's stability is of utmost importance to Kashmiris'. Retrieved from https://www.dawn.com/news/1020464
15. Guha, R. (2017, April 22). The darkness deepens in Kashmir with the rising tide of jingoism. Retrieved from http://www.hindustantimes.com/columns/the-darkness-deepens-in-kashmir-with-the-rising-tide-of-jingoism/story-QExLY9upW1CWxCTmWCawYM.html
16. Geelani, G. (2017, August 10). Battle of Perceptions. Retrieved from http://www.kashmirink.in/news/perspective/battle-of-perceptions/ 420.html
17. Editorial. (2017, July 24). Retrieved from https://www.pressreader.com/india/india-today/20170724/281479276460183
18. Hyper-Nationalism Weds Soft Separatism: Watershed Day in Jammu and Kashmir? (2015, March 01). Retrieved from http://www.ndtv.com/video/news/we-the-people/hyper-nationalism-weds-soft-separatism-watershed-day-in-jammu-and-kashmir-358436
19. Handoo, B. (2017, August 8). 'State Subject Law may go. We need to worry'.

Retrieved from http://www.kashmirink.in/news/coverstory/-j-k-may-lose-its-special-status/418.html

20. Geelani, G. (2015, February 27). PDP-BJP alliance could be a 'paradigm shift' in Kashmir's history: Mufti. Retrieved from http://www.dawn.com/news/1166271

21. Masoodi, N. (2015, January 02). Blog: PDP-BJP Alliance Could Create Dangerous Vacuum. Retrieved from http://www.ndtv.com/blog/pdp-bjp-alliance-could-create-dangerous-vacuum-721405

22. Jaffrelot, C. (2010). *Religion, Caste, and Politics in India*. Primus Books.

23. NDTV. (2014, November 19). BJP trying to create sectarianism including among Muslims of Kashmir: Mehbooba Mufti. Retrieved from https://www.youtube.com/watch?v=aekqsN8cuAo

24. Geelani, G. (2018, August 31). Mehbooba Mufti interview: 'Upholding Indian flag in Kashmir will be tough if Article 35A is diluted'. Retrieved from https://scroll.in/article/892416/mehbooba-mufti-interview-upholding-indian-flag-in-kashmir-will-be-tough-if-article-35a-is-diluted

25. Source 1: Bharatiya Janata Party. (2010, September 27). Part 1: Kashmir Situation: Shri Arun Jaitley: Sept 2010 :. Retrieved from https://www.youtube.com/watch?v=cI8da8XPIEo
Source 2: Bharatiya Janata Party. (2010, September 27). Part 2: Kashmir Situation: Shri Arun Jaitley: Sept 2010. Retrieved from https://www.youtube.com/watch?v=g3Q7xq4E2yw

26. Ganai, N. (2016, June 11). BJP blames separatists for opposing Abhinav Gupt yatra, says ban indicates narrow mindset. Retrieved from http://indiatoday.intoday.in/story/bjp-blames-separatists-for-opposing-yatra-says-ban-indicates-narrow-mindset/1/689408.html

27. Mir, N. (2012, April 29). Forgotten, Forbidden Cinema Culture Of Kashmir. Retrieved from http://www.jammu-kashmir.com/archives/archives2012/kashmir20120429d.html

28. Source 1: Ganai, N. (2012, February 19). Makeover for Sringar's dreadful interrogation centres. Retrieved from http://www.dailymail.co.uk/indiahome/indianews/article-2103469/Makeover-Sringars-dreadful-interrogation-centres.html
Source 2: Hamid, P. A. (2007, September). Kashmir's tortured past and present. Retrieved from http://old.himalmag.com/component/content/article/1284-kashmirs-tortured-past-and-present.html
Source 3: McGirk, T. (2011, October 22). Kashmiri student tells of torture: Tim McGirk in Srinagar reports on. Retrieved from http://www.independent.co.uk/news/world/kashmiri-student-tells-of-torture-tim-mcgirk-in-srinagar-reports-on-the-increasing-evidence-of-2325054.html

29. Gowhar Geelani's interview with satirist-poet Zareef Ahmad Zareef at his residence in Srinagar, July 2013.

30. Kanjwal, H. (2017, July 12). Kashmiris do not need to prove their humanity. India needs to prove its own. Retrieved from https://www.washingtonpost.com/news/global-opinions/wp/2017/07/12/kashmiris-do-not-need-to-prove-their-humanity-india-needs-to-prove-its-own/?noredirect=on&utm_term=.da6f3de5c58c

31. J&K Police Blame LeT For Amarnath Attack, Group Denies Any Role. (2017, July 11). Retrieved from https://www.news18.com/news/india/jk-police-blames-let-for-amarnath-attack-group-denies-any-role-1457859.html

32. UJC calls Yatri attack barbaric, blames India. (2017, July 12). Retrieved from https://kashmirreader.com/2017/07/12/ujc-calls-yatri-attack-barbaric-blames-india/

33. UJC condemns attack on Amarnath pilgrims. (2017, July 11). Retrieved from http://www.knskashmir.com/UJC-condemns-attack-on-Amarnath-pilgrims--18087

34. Govt bans Jamaat-i-Islami Jammu and Kashmir. (2019, February 28). Retrieved from https://thekashmirwalla.com/2019/02/govt-bans-jamaat-i-islami-jammu-and-kashmir/

35. Hajin: The Kashmir town that is a 'militant hub'. (2017, November 28). Retrieved from http://www.bbc.com/news/world-asia-india-42062192

36. Wright, L. (2011). *The Looming Tower: Al-Qaedas road to 9/11*. London: Penguin Books.

37. Unpublished MPhil dissertation by Ghulam Nabi Lone, 1993: 'The Role of Jamaat-i-Islami In The Politics of Jammu and Kashmir 1972-1989', Department of Political Science, University of Kashmir, p44.

38. Ibid.

39. Conversations with a Kashmiri researcher, Younus Rashid, who works as assistant professor in the history department at the University of Kashmir and is writing on the foundation of the JeI in J&K.

40. Wright, L. (2011). *The Looming Tower: Al-Qaedas road to 9/11*. London: Penguin Books, p.10

41. Maududi, A. (1988). *Masla-e-Kashmir aur iska hul*. Al Ansar Publications, Delhi.

42. Devadas, D. (2015, October 31). LeT commander Abu Qasim's killing: Police claim big victory, but attendance at funeral reflects sobering reality. Retrieved from http://www.firstpost.com/india/let-leader-abu-qasims-killing-cops-claim-big-victory-but-attendance-at-funeral-reflects-sobering-reality-2489990.html

43. Geelani, G. (2016, February 05). Is pro-Pakistan sentiment in Kashmir still alive? Retrieved from http://www.dawn.com/news/1237193

44. Bose, S. (2011, August 02). The evolution of Kashmiri resistance. Retrieved from http://www.aljazeera.com/indepth/spotlight/kashmirtheforgottenconflict/2011/07/2011715143415277754.html

45. Bhat, T. (2018, January 21). Old embers, young fire. Retrieved from http://www.theweek.in/theweek/cover/jem-militant-groups-teenage-terrorists-in-kashmir.html

46. Profile of Pulwama suicide bomber: 'Don't fall in love'. (2019, February 16). Retrieved from https://economictimes.indiatimes.com/news/politics-and-nation/profile-of-pulwama-suicide-bomber-dont-fall-in-love/articleshow/68006566.cms?from=mdr&utm_source=contentofinterest&utm_medium=text&utm_campaign=cppst

47. Youth can't be won by force: Muzaffar Baig. (2016, August 14). Retrieved from https://www.greaterkashmir.com/news/front-page/youth-can-t-be-won-by-force-muzaffar-baig/225655.html

48. Ibid.

49. Bhat, T. (2018, January 21). Old embers, young fire. Retrieved from http://www. theweek.in/theweek/cover/jem-militant-groups-teenage-terrorists-in-kashmir. html

50. Yusuf, S. I., & Gul, K. (2016, August 14). Unprecedented clampdown; Another youth succumbs, toll 51. Retrieved from http://epaper.greaterkashmir.com/ epapermain.aspx?queryed=9&eddate=08/14/2016

52. Kashmir: A father-son duo take to social media; one for jihad and another for a call to return home. (2017, September 5). Retrieved from http://www.catchnews. com/india-news/kashmir-a-father-son-duo-take-to-social-media-one-for-jihad-and-another-for-a-call-to-return-home-80310.html

53. PhD scholar 'joins Hizb', photos wielding AK-47 go viral. (2018, January 08). Retrieved from https://kashmirreader.com/2018/01/08/phd-scholar-joins-hizb-photos-wielding-ak-47-go-viral/

54. Geelani, G. (2018, December 04). The rise of educated young Kashmir militants: Propaganda or unpalatable truth? Retrieved from https://thedefensepost. com/2018/11/30/kashmir-educated-young-militants-propaganda-unpalatable-truth/

55. Gowhar Geelani's interview with a top police officer, who wished to remain anonymous, in Srinagar.

56. Gowhar Geelani's interview with Muzaffar Wani, Burhan's father, in Tral, south Kashmir, in 2016.

4

A NATIONALISM OF MULTIPLE IDENTITIES

During my annual visits from Bonn to Srinagar, in 2006–10 and again in 2014–15, I'd find myself in the misery, pain and hardship that I remembered from my growing-up years. In 2008–10, the entire Valley was on the boil. It was terrible in 2016, post Burhan. My entire time in Kashmir was spent under strict curfew, amid massive pro-freedom protests and a rash of civilian killings. These visits gave me the opportunity to draw parallels between life in Kashmir and the outside world. It begins the moment I land at New Delhi's international airport, where I get the first intimation of what is to follow.

In 2008, a dashing young officer at the immigration counter at the airport asked me a strange question while examining my travel documents: 'Are you a relative of that firebrand Kashmiri separatist leader, Syed Ali Shah Geelani, who's seeking freedom from India?' For a moment, I was speechless. How does one respond to such a query? Soon, though, I saw its funny side. 'I'm related to Syed Ali Shah Geelani in the same way as India's off-spinner Harbhajan Singh is related to the (then) Indian Prime Minister, Dr Manmohan Singh,' I replied with a sarcastic smile. The young officer smiled back, eventually; the matter ended on a cordial note.

This is what a Kashmiri faces on a daily basis. You are a suspect, your credentials are questioned and you are judged. It doesn't matter how many times you stand up and say, 'I'm Kashmiri, I'm also a Muslim, and I'm not a terrorist. But I do have legitimate political aspirations!'

A Kashmiri living and working in Delhi or anywhere else

in India has to often prove who he/she is and who he/she is related to. A Kashmiri living in Kashmir is forced to prove his/her identity every day to an outsider. That's how one grows up. This problem got magnified after the Pulwama suicide attack. Several Kashmiri students, traders and professionals were attacked by Right-wing mobs in various parts of India, forcing many to return home. Hate and revenge attacks against Kashmiris took place in northern, southern and eastern parts of India.

Outside India, one carries multiple identities within him/herself: an individual whose mother tongue is Kashmiri, loves his/her culture, is proud of his/her traditions, and who could be a Muslim, Sikh or Hindu.

Kashmiris born in and after the 1980s have dealt with the overwhelming presence of Armed Forces in civilian areas. They are brought up under the shadow of the gun in an overwhelmingly militarized zone. For a majority in Kashmir, government troops are equivalent to an invading force. There is, however, a deeper issue related to the politics of identity that goes back to 1931, when J&K was a princely state under the Dogra Maharaja's tyrannical rule. Before I come to that, it is important to realize that the political movement in Kashmir involves people of multiple political orientations.

Since the early 1930s, multiple identities have played a role in rallying public opinion in J&K. The first significant political mobilization of Kashmiri Muslims against Dogra rule is said to have happened in 1931. Earlier agitations against the Dogra ruler, Maharaja Hari Singh, were not politically centred. The first such recorded instance is when a group of Kashmiris gathered at Khanqah-e-Molla in downtown Srinagar. A young man called Abdul Qadeer is believed to have delivered a fiery speech against Dogra rule, which predictably resulted in his immediate arrest on the charge of 'sedition'. Public outcry forced the judge to hold Qadeer's trial within the premises of the jail on 11 July 1931.

On 13 July, it was rumoured that Qadeer's case would be heard before a magistrate at the Central Jail. In solidarity, hordes began marching towards it. Historians say that, faced with the crowds, the sessions judge ordered people to disperse, but they made a request to be allowed to offer prayers first. The police arrested some of those assembled, which infuriated the crowd. One of them is said to have recited the call to azan loudly. He was shot dead by a policeman. This resulted in angry reactions and stone pelting.[1] The Dogra forces got unnerved and opened fire, resulting in the killing of twenty-two civilians. Scores were injured.[2] Ever since, 13 July has been observed as Martyrs' Day in Kashmir. The victims of 13 July are also claimed as martyrs by both pro-India and pro-azadi leaders.

A previous agitation by Kashmir's silk weavers, shalbafs (shawl weavers) and artisans, demanding better wages and humane treatment, had been crushed by Dogra soldiers in 1924. Dr Allama Iqbal, renowned philosopher and poet, during a visit to Kashmir in June 1921, had observed and reflected on Kashmir's sociopolitical conditions and abject state of economy. He described the miserable condition of workers in Srinagar's silk factory in a Persian poem, 'Saqi Nama', written at the Nishat Bagh, in which he calls for a sociopolitical awakening in Kashmir. In the first half of the poem, the conventional imagery associated with Kashmir is beautifully rendered. In the second half, the Kashmiri is portrayed as one who is used to servitude and unaware of his selfhood. Besides showering immense praise on the majestic beauty of the Nishat and Shalimar gardens, the last lines of the poem describe the misfortune of Kashmiris, their economic dispossession, the Dogra oppression and the exploitation of silk weavers by the tyrant ruler. This poem lit a spark that would soon grow into a raging fire.

Three years after 'Saqi Nama' was written, the Kashmir Valley witnessed a rebellion of sorts against Dogra rule at the silk factory in Srinagar. This crisis marked another important stage in the evolution of political resistance against the Maharaja's rule. The workers launched an agitation and organized a strike against their low wages. An earlier strike, in 1917, had been brutally crushed. The second uprising, too, was suppressed, but it had set the stage for the economic awakening among the common people of Kashmir. Political awakening would follow soon after.

In October 1932, Kashmir's first political party, the All Jammu and Kashmir Muslim Conference (AJKMC), was formed. At this time, Left-wing intellectuals were also reasonably influential in the state. A young Sheikh Mohammed Abdullah was emerging as an educated leader. Born in December 1905, he had shot to instant fame for spearheading the agitation against Maharaja Hari Singh's rule, which was perceived as repressive by the majority. In April 1932, the Glancy Commission, appointed by the Maharaja, presented a report acknowledging the existence of grievances among common people in the state.

Headed by B.J. Glancy, an officer at the Foreign Affairs Ministry of British India, the commission was probably appointed under pressure from the British. Its significant recommendations included the formation of political parties and adequate representation of Muslims in state services. The Pandits felt that its recommendations were not favourable to their interests, and launched an agitation called The Bread Movement against the Glancy Commission's recommendations on 22 March 1932.

One of the fallouts of the Glancy Commission's recommendations was that Sheikh Abdullah, in association with Chaudhry Ghulam Abbas, a lawyer and an influential Muslim leader of the time, Mirwaiz Yusuf Shah and Khwaja Ghulam Nabi Gilkar, besides other Kashmiri leaders, formed the AJKMC to provide a political platform to the Muslim citizens of the state. For all practical purposes, the party was an assertion of Kashmiri Muslim identity.

Some Pandit authors like Motilal Kemmu wrote that the AJKMC, as the state's first political party, would often discuss the alleged economic and political dominance of Kashmiri Pandits, a minority community, in the state. Members of the Pandit community were, at times, spoken of as enemies of Kashmiri Muslims. Later, too, the influential Abdullah family blamed many of their problems on Kashmiri Pandits, who allegedly held disproportionately powerful positions in the government under Jawaharlal Nehru and Indira Gandhi. The Abdullahs were convinced that some of them acted as 'informers' who carried tales back to Delhi, and therefore could not be trusted.[3] Pandits considered close to state bureaucracy under Delhi's rule in J&K have often been described as 'fifth columnists', especially by Sheikh Abdullah in his autobiography *Aatish-e-Chinar* (Blazes of Chinar).

Historian Khalid Bashir Ahmad, in his book *Kashmir: Exposing the Myth Behind the Narrative*, quotes from *Aatish-e-Chinar*, in which the Sheikh described Kashmiri Pandits as 'the fifth columnists' and 'the instruments of tyranny'.[4] I personally liked Ahmad's strong rebuttal of this sweeping portrayal of a community from a person who stands accused of having handed over Kashmir to New Delhi on a platter. The author rightly names celebrated mystic poetess Lalleshwari, philosopher Abhinavagupta, poet Dinanath Nadim and others, to talk about the Pandit community's success and contribution in different walks of life, which include education, media and bureaucracy. He also says that members of the minority community (then 4 per cent) were quick in learning the languages of rulers, for example Sanskrit and Persian.

Even though Muslims formed an overwhelming 85 per cent of the state's population then, Sheikh Abdullah decided to change the party's nomenclature, apparently to strengthen its secular credentials. In his presidential address at the party's sixth annual session on 26 March 1938, the Sheikh said,[5]

> 'Like us, a majority of Hindus and Sikhs in the state have immensely suffered at the hands of the irresponsible government...The main problem, therefore, now is to organize joint action and a united front against the forces that stand in our way in the achievement of our goal. This will require rechristening our organization as a non-communal political body...'.

The AJKMC was renamed National Conference soon after a historic session of the party at Pathar Masjid in Srinagar, on 11 June 1939. This was a conscious attempt to accommodate the minority viewpoint. Prem Nath Bazaz—then president of the Sanatan Dharam Yuvak Sabha, which represented Kashmiri Pandit interests to the Dogra rulers—was considered to be close to Sheikh Abdullah and was thought to have played a crucial role in convincing Abdullah about the name change.

Prior to 1932, Left-wing intellectuals had formed the Reading Room Party (RRP) in 1930, which was not a formal political group. Rather, it was established to discuss the French and Russian revolutions and the way forward for the state. Historians say that the RRP of the 1930s played a role in shaping Kashmir's political future. Lawyer-activist Nandita Haksar argues in her book, *The Many Faces of Kashmiri Nationalism*, that Sheikh Abdullah had received the Communists well and counted many of them as friends, including M.D. Taseer, a Punjabi Marxist from Lahore, who served as the principal at Srinagar's Shri Pratap (S.P.) College.[6]

What the RRP meant for Kashmir's sociopolitical awakening then, and how it is relevant to the current discourse when the Internet, technological advancements, the digital revolution, smartphones and the social media have drastically altered Kashmir's sociopolitical narrative on its hotly contested landscape, is an important question. Srinagar-based veteran columnist and author, Zahid Ghulam Muhammad, told me that he had interviewed Khwaja Ahmad Abbas, noted Indian film director, novelist and journalist, in Bombay in 1984 during which the latter said that in the decades of the 1930s and '40s, Kashmir was considered a 'laboratory for testing Socialist ideals.'[7] Kashmir, many believe, continues to be a laboratory for testing political projects even now.

The 1930s onwards, the Communists occupied some intellectual space in J&K for about two decades. Bazaz is said to have convinced Sheikh Abdullah that his dream of 'empowering Kashmiri Muslims and awakening them politically' would not translate into reality unless Maharaja Hari Singh's rule was replaced by a responsible secular government. The Sheikh was easily persuaded, but was also sceptical about the Muslim-dominated Kashmir Valley accepting a secular political movement. Bazaz then proposed that the Sheikh raise public awareness through an Urdu weekly, *Hamdard*. The party's flag was bright red with a white plough in the middle, designed to appeal to the vast majority of peasants who lived in extreme poverty. Haksar writes in her book:

'The colours and symbol of the flag reflected the influence of Communist ideas and ideals: the Russian Revolution had taken place barely twenty-three years earlier and the proximity of the Soviet Asian Republics to Kashmir was a source of inspiration to young Kashmiris who yearned to liberate themselves from an oppressive monarchical system.'

Zahid Ghulam Muhammad accuses Left-wing intellectuals and Communists of Kashmir of owing greater allegiance to the Soviet Union and sabotaging a plebiscite later, after India and Pakistan became independent nation states in 1947 and the fate of J&K remained undecided. Although there is a consensus that leftist intellectuals did associate with Kashmir's struggle against the Maharaja's autocracy, they had influence within the Sheikh-led NC. Muhammad argues that the leftist constituency later served India's interests in Kashmir, as the Communists had convinced Pandit Jawaharlal Nehru that Kashmir was a 'laboratory for testing Socialist ideals'. Some historians say that Sheikh Abdullah was approached by the RRP. Besides discussing revolutions, they would read Urdu and English newspapers and explore the possibilities of finding reasonable jobs for themselves.

Anwar Ashai, a retired engineer based in Srinagar, claims that his father, Ghulam Ahmad Ashai, was instrumental in establishing the RRP in Srinagar. 'Ashai Sahab, my father, was an educated Muslim who had graduated from Punjab University in 1915. He started working as (the) deputy inspector of schools. The autocratic ruler, Maharaja Hari Singh, dismissed him from his services because of religious prejudice,' Ashai told me in a telephonic interview. He added that his father set up the RRP in Srinagar in 1929. However, most historians believe that the RRP was formally established on 8 May 1930, while some, like Kashmir's celebrated satirist-poet, Zareef Ahmad Zareef, who lives in Srinagar, claim the date to be 12 April 1930. Zareef told me in an interview that the group would assemble in a house owned by Mohammad Sikander, the post and telegraph master, who had voluntarily reserved a portion of his house in Mohalla Syed Ali

Akbar for them. According to Zareef, Khwaja Ghulam Nabi Gilkar, Molvi Bashir Ahmad and Mohammad Rajab were instrumental in establishing the RRP. Members of the RRP would write articles under their own names or pseudonyms to highlight problems of the educated youth, their socio-economic and political issues, and also make recommendations to bring about a change. There was a place near the old Court Road in Srinagar, owned by the family of the late politician Ghulam Mohiuddin Karra, where many Kashmiri communists like B.N. Bazaz, P.N. Jalali, Gayasuddin and G.M. Sadiq would often meet to discuss contemporary issues. That place, according to Zareef, was also referred to as the 'study circle.' He claims that the progressive writer, poet and Communist Party member, Faiz Ahmad Faiz, had also visited it. Besides Bazaz, Jalali and Gayasuddin, people like Sajad Haider and some of his followers, two former PMs of J&K Bakshi Ghulam Mohammad and G.M. Sadiq, D.P. Dhar, Somnath Zutshi, Pran Kishore, and others were impressed and influenced by the Communist takeover of Russia. Sajad Haider and his comrades had unfurled a red flag near Palladium cinema located in the city centre, later renamed Lal Chowk, says Zareef.[8]

Interestingly, the city centre was named Lal Chowk inspired by Moscow's Red Square. According to local columnist and historian Mohammad Ashraf, the actual spot that came to be known as 'Lal Chowk' was in front of the Palladium cinema. It used to have a circular podium with a flag post, which no longer exists. Sikh leftist intellectual, Baba Pyare Lal Bedi, is credited by some for christening Lal Chowk, while Nandita Haksar claims that it was Sheikh Abdullah who was responsible for it when he became J&K's PM in 1948. She argues that even though Abdullah was attracted to Communist ideals, he never questioned the tenets of his religion (Islam).[9]

Abdullah, known as 'Sher-i-Kashmir' (Lion of Kashmir), was the first president of the AJKMC, which he formed to unite Kashmir's Muslims on one platform. With the aim to mobilize public opinion against the Maharaja's rule, Sheikh Abdullah would commence his public speeches with verses from the Quran in a melodious voice. Significantly, Abdullah, in his presidential address to the members, claimed that his party had come into existence to struggle for the rights of all oppressed sections of Kashmiri society, and not Muslims alone, and that the AJKMC was not a communal party. Paradoxically, Abdullah also spearheaded a vigorous campaign to convert the Muslim Conference into the National Conference to give his party a secular face and accommodative profile for a wider reach.

This conversion, according to the late Khwaja Sanaullah Bhat's account, *Ahad Nama-i-Kashmir*, led to disunity and fissures among its leadership. Many of Abdullah's friends and admirers deserted him and joined a revived faction of the AJKMC led by a popular Muslim cleric and Srinagar-based head priest, Mirwaiz Moulana Mohammed Yusuf Shah. Mirwaiz Yusuf had gone to Pakistan to meet Mohammad Ali Jinnah, founder of Pakistan, to discuss Kashmir's future before the Partition. He, however, was not allowed to return to the Indian-administered part of Kashmir. He stayed in Pakistan and went on to become the third president of PaK in December, 1951.[10]

As the Quit India Movement gained momentum in India in 1942, Abdullah and his NC launched a parallel Quit Kashmir movement against Maharaja Hari Singh's autocratic rule in Kashmir in 1946. Their aim was to restore the party's image among the masses, which had been dented by the rechristening of the AJKMC. Some accounts, like that of Khwaja Sanaullah Bhat, claim that the Sheikh was tremendously influenced by the Indian National Congress (INC). Even after forming the NC, Abdullah continued to begin his public rallies with verses from the Quran. This annoyed Kashmiri Pandits like Bazaz, who eventually left the NC after developing differences with the Sheikh on this issue.

The Quit Kashmir movement led to Abdullah's arrest on charges of sedition. A popular slogan of the time was:

'Bainama Amritsar tod do,
Kashmir chhod do'

('Terminate the Treaty of Amritsar and leave Kashmir')

It referred to the British East India Company's treaty in 1846 with Maharaja Gulab Singh, where the latter bought the Kashmir Valley, comprising:

All the hilly or mountainous country with its dependencies situated to the eastward of the River Indus and the westward of the River Ravi including Chamba and excluding Lahul, being part of the territories ceded to the British Government by the Lahore State according to the provisions of Article IV of the Treaty of Lahore, dated 9th March, 1846.

The Dogra ruler got hold of Kashmir for a sum of 7,50,000 Nanak Shahi rupees (currency of the Sikh empire). The signing of the Treaty of Amritsar after the first Anglo-Sikh war marked the beginning of the Dogra Maharaja's rule in the state.

Arrested on the charge of sedition, Sheikh Abdullah was detained at the Badami Bagh cantonment in Srinagar. The INC sent advocates to provide legal aid to the Sheikh. Abdullah, according to Khwaja Sanaullah Bhat's account, retracted the Quit Kashmir movement and argued in court that he was only demanding a responsible government under the Maharaja's supervision. In a volte-face, he refused to take responsibility for the fiery speeches he had made against the Dogra regime, which included saying that Kashmiris were ready to pay back 7,50,000 Nanak Shahi rupees to the Maharaja with interest, but would not accept any government under the command of the Dogra ruler.

In his article, 'The People's Militia: Communists and Kashmiri Nationalists in the 1940s', author, historian and former BBC journalist, Andrew Whitehead, notes that the well-known British communist, Rajani Palme Dutt, had met Sheikh Abdullah in court and showered accolades on the Kashmiri leader.[11] In the summer of 1946, Dutt had declared that the people's movement in Kashmir 'is the strongest and most militant of any Indian state...Its leader, Sheikh Abdullah (sic), impressed me as one of the most honest, courageous and able political leaders I had the pleasure of seeing in India.' Dutt had been personally invited by the Sheikh.[12]

Abdullah's NC, the main political force at the time, represented early Kashmiri nationalism. However, Abdullah's flip-flops, first in 1946–47, and then most notably in 1975, resulted in his party's image being seriously dented. Moreover, his popularity nosedived so much in later years that his tombstone at Hazratbal in Srinagar today requires a round-the-clock security vigil. After the retraction of his statements against the Maharaja's rule in 1946, he first opposed Kashmir's accession to both Pakistan and India in 1947, and then came to the Maharaja's rescue to bat for a conditional and provisional accession of the state of J&K to India. Mirza Afzal Beg, Abdullah's trusted companion, later described their twenty-two-year-long political struggle as 'siyasi awaragardi' (political meandering). In 1975, Abdullah finally agreed to form a government as CM, not PM—the position mandated by the state's constitution. This change in portfolio is seen as one of the main assaults on J&K's regional autonomy. Many more assaults would follow soon.

Sheikh Abdullah had shone on Kashmir's brutalized landscape as a bright star, who many people had hoped would revolutionize the state's body politic and guide them from darkness towards enlightenment. He did so briefly, but that he ended up falling in both Delhi's trap as well as lap, is the prevalent perception that the common Kashmiri has about him. A veteran Kashmir watcher describes the Sheikh as only tall in terms of height, not in terms of stature.

He was first seen as the architect of Kashmir's sociopolitical awakening when he spearheaded the Plebiscite Movement under the banner of the Mahaz-i-Rai Shumari (All Jammu and Kashmir Plebiscite Front). It was a platform established by Mirza Afzal Beg, Abdullah's companion, in 1955, soon after his release from prison. It is said that the Plebiscite Front had no Kashmiri Pandits as its members. The Sheikh was still under arrest when the Plebiscite Front was formed, and never joined it. It demanded a referendum in J&K so that the people would get a chance to decide their political future: whether to join Pakistan or India, or become an independent and sovereign state. The Front's second demand was for Sheikh Abdullah's unconditional release from prison.

The Plebiscite Front was an alternative to the NC. Anyone associated with the Front was targeted by PM Bakshi Ghulam Mohammad's government. Bakshi had deserted Sheikh in 1953 when the former was installed as the PM and the latter was unceremoniously dismissed from the post and arrested. Many workers, activists and sympathizers of the Plebiscite Front were harassed. Some served long prison sentences. The Front eventually merged with the NC in 1975, when Sheikh Abdullah finally gave up his struggle and then Indian PM Indira Gandhi welcomed his 'change of thinking'.

In January 1949, Abdullah had 'visualized the possibility of an independent Kashmir' in his interviews to two foreign correspondents, Davidson and Ward Price, in Srinagar, as recorded by B.N. Mullik, then chief of India's Intelligence Bureau (IB). Mullik mentions this in detail in his memoir, *My Years With Nehru*.[13] The Communist Party of India (CPI) had been legalized in 1942. This ensured that Communist literature was available in the Kashmir Valley, too. It is believed that members and sympathizers of the CPI worked through the NC's platform and played a role in the Abdullah-led NC's social and economic programmes. Many Communists and Socialists supported Abdullah in his fight against the Dogra regime. Abdullah had also requested some of his Communist friends to put forward a political and economic vision for the future of J&K in 1944. A document called 'Naya Kashmir' became the new manifesto for Kashmir's social and economic awakening. It is said that many Communists, especially Baba Pyare Lal Bedi and his wife, Freda Bedi, were instrumental in drafting the 'Naya Kashmir' document. Khwaja Ahmad Abbas is also believed to have played a role in drafting the new manifesto that visualized Kashmir along the lines of a Soviet Central Asian republic. In 1944, the Abdullah-led NC adopted the document as its manifesto at a session in Sopore, after presenting it to Maharaja Hari Singh.

Pro-India legislator Yusuf Tarigami, state secretary of the CPI (Marxist) and former member of J&K's Legislative Assembly from south Kashmir's Kulgam constituency (now a militant hotbed), believes that the 'Naya Kashmir' document is relevant even today. Tarigami, perhaps the lone visible Communist political figure in the Valley today, says, 'The "Naya Kashmir" vision document in itself is a reflection of Communist ideology. It is relevant even today, especially with the rollback of the welfare state, even as the gap between the haves and the have-nots is only growing.' He believes that rather than Left-wing intellectuals, it was leftist ideology that played a critical role in the Quit Kashmir movement of 1946. According to Tarigami, the revolutionary 'land to tiller' reform introduced by the Sheikh was also inspired by Communist ideals. Even after the collapse of the erstwhile Union of Soviet Socialist Republics, socialism has a chance to lead today's society. He agrees that the world has seen tremendous structural changes since, but if he were to choose between capitalism and socialism, he would not hesitate to opt for the latter.[14]

The 'Naya Kashmir' plan has separate charters for peasants' rights, workers' rights and women's rights, which include economic, legal, educational, social and cultural rights. The document was presented to Maharaja Hari Singh as a future constitution of the state of J&K. It described the citizenship of the state, and the rights and duties of citizens, as well as a National Economic Plan. Article 1 of the 'Naya Kashmir' document declares:

> All persons residing in Jammu, Kashmir, Ladakh, Frontier areas, and areas falling under Poonch and Chenini will solely be the residents of the State. In all spheres of National activities, Economic, Political, Cultural or Social, the equality of all citizens irrespective of their colour, race, religion or heredity would be considered a fundamental and inalienable right of the citizens of this State. Imposing any bar on these rights by direct or indirect means or granting any special privileges to any one citizen or body of citizens on the basis of their descent, family relationship, race or religion as well as demanding special treatment on the basis of heredity, race or religion as well as spreading discord and hatred among the citizens (on abovementioned grounds) would be held to be a punishable criminal offence...

In 1946, Sheikh Abdullah was lodged in Bhaderwah Jail. At the time of the Partition in 1947, the Maharaja was aware of how closely the people of the state were linked with Pakistan, in terms of trade, travel and culture. It was, therefore, highly unlikely that the people would favour joining India. On 14 August, Pakistani flags were hoisted atop post offices and telegram offices in Kashmir. Khwaja Sanaullah Bhat records in *Ahad Nama-i-Kashmir* that the Maharaja overlooked these fundamental facts and the people's aspirations, to start secret negotiations with Delhi.[15] Lord Louis Mountbatten, the last Viceroy of British India and the first Governor-General of independent India, had visited Srinagar twice to persuade Maharaja Hari Singh to join the Indian Dominion. When Mahatma Gandhi came to Kashmir for the first and last time on 1 August 1947, on a three-day visit, he too met the Maharaja and his wife, Maharani Tara Devi, at their palace, Gulab Bhawan, to influence them to join the Indian Dominion.[16]

In his book *Being The Other*, journalist and author Saeed Naqvi writes that 'rumours had been reaching Delhi since July 1947 that Maharaja Hari Singh was looking for an opportunity to accede to India although his subjects were overwhelmingly Muslim'. Quoting the late Ved Bhasin, editor of Jammu-based English daily *Kashmir Times*, Naqvi writes:[17]

> After the 3 June Plan, there was pressure on Maharaja Hari Singh to accede to India or Pakistan from both the Congress and Muslim League Leaders... In this backdrop, Gandhiji (M.K. Gandhi) visited Srinagar on August 1 and met the Maharaja. Though Gandhi declared that his mission was not political and he was only fulfilling an old promise to the Maharaja to visit Kashmir, there were clear indications that he had advised him to join the Indian Union. Gandhiji returned to New Delhi via Jammu where he arrived on June 3.

From Bhaderwah Jail, Sheikh Abdullah was brought to Srinagar to hold talks with the emissaries of the Maharaja. After his release in September that year, the Sheikh said, 'If the forty lakh people living in J&K are bypassed and the State declares accession to

India or Pakistan, I shall raise the banner of revolt and we face a struggle.'

An anti-Maharaja Hari Singh rebellion in Poonch had already begun, which led to communal tension and a massacre of Muslims in Jammu province. The respected Muslim leader, Mirwaiz Yusuf Shah, travelled to Lahore to discuss the issue of accession, where an interim government of J&K was announced on 4 October 1947. Ghulam Nabi Gilkar was appointed president. Only two weeks later, tribal raiders backed by Pakistan began marching towards Srinagar via Muzaffarabad. The news unnerved Maharaja Hari Singh who sought India's help after hastily signing the contentious Instrument of Accession (IoA) on 26 October 1947. Indian troops were airlifted to Srinagar on 27 October 1947.

After the creation of India and Pakistan as two independent nations in 1947, the fate of J&K had remained undecided. This was primarily because of the indecision of Maharaja Hari Singh, who was unable to make up his mind. An impending invasion by Pakistani raiders with the aim to 'forcibly' merge Kashmir with Pakistan forced the Maharaja to come to a decision. The IoA he signed with India has remained fiercely contested ever since.

India has claimed that Pakistan was the first aggressor at the time, however recent revisionist historians have argued otherwise. The Australian historian, Christopher Snedden, in his book, *Kashmir: The Unwritten History*, offers a new perspective on 'who actually started the dispute over the international status of J&K.' Snedden writes in the book's introduction:[18]

> After Partition in 1947, Jammuites engaged in three significant actions. The first was a Muslim uprising in the Poonch area of western Jammu Province against the unpopular Hindu ruler, Maharaja Hari Singh. The second was serious inter-religious violence throughout the province that killed or displaced a large number of people from all religious communities. The third was the creation of Azad (Free) J&K in the area of western Jammu Province that the "rebels" had "freed" or liberated. These significant actions took place before the Maharaja acceded to India on 26 October 1947.

Today, regional and religious divides between the Kashmir Valley and Jammu appear to have widened, as they had in Jammu in 1947, when a large number of Muslims were killed by soldiers of Maharaja Hari Singh. According to a report dated 10 August 1948, published in *The Times*, London, at least '2,37,000 Muslims were systematically exterminated—unless they escaped to Pakistan along the border—by the forces of the Dogra State headed by the Maharaja in person and aided by Hindus and Sikhs. This happened in October 1947, five days before the Pathan invasion and nine days before the Maharaja's accession to India.' There is also an article by writer and Quaker, Horace Alexander, on 16 January 1948, in *The Spectator*, where Alexander put the number of Muslims killed in Jammu at 200,000. In 1941, Muslims formed a 61 per cent majority in Jammu, which was reduced to 38 per cent after the massacre. Alexander wrote that the massacre had 'the tacit consent of State authority.' Zafar Chaudhary, a Jammu-based author and political commentator, in an article titled 'Being Muslim in Jammu', wrote, 'There was hardly any family in the region which escaped... (Those) events permanently changed the way the Muslims of Jammu would live or think.'[19]

Kashmiris challenged the Maharaja's decision to accede to the Union of India, arguing that the Dogra ruler was not in control of J&K since Partition. There existed a popular people's movement and therefore the Maharaja had no moral and political authority or right, to take a decision about Kashmir's political future on his own volition, while disregarding the aspirations of Kashmiris. Also, at the time of Partition, all the princely states had been given an option to join either of the two dominions—India or Pakistan— while taking into account a majority of their populace. Some princely states that had a Muslim majority, like J&K, were ruled by a non-Muslim, while some states that had a Hindu majority were ruled by a Muslim leader. Muslim-majority princely states were to accede to Pakistan and Hindu-majority states would join India. This standard, too, was not followed vis-à-vis J&K.

Soon after the Maharaja's conditional and provisional accession to the Union of India on 26 October, independent

India's first PM, Jawaharlal Nehru, pledged before the people of
Kashmir and the international community, that India will hold
a plebiscite to ascertain whether the people of the state of J&K
wanted to accede to Pakistan or India. It is New Delhi's reneging
on this promise of holding a free and fair plebiscite that fuelled
a new era of Kashmiri nationalism.

In the past, Kashmiri nationalism coupled with religious
beliefs and socialist and communist ideals had been used to fight
against the Maharaja's regime. In the decades of the 1930s and
'40s, Kashmiri Muslims and Pandits, irrespective of religion, had
played a role in the anti-autocratic and pro-democracy movement.
On 14 August 1947, J&K was one of the 562 princely states,
under the suzerainty of the British Crown, which were not a part
of British India. However, on the lapse of paramountcy on the
transfer of power, J&K became independent and was free to accede
to either of the two dominions—Pakistan or India—or to remain
independent.[20] Eminent advocate and constitutional expert,
A.G. Noorani, explains this meticulously in his well-researched
book, *The Kashmir Dispute, 1947–2012*. He argues that under
Section 7(1)(b) of the Indian Independence Act 1947, the
suzerainty of the British Crown over the Indian states lapsed
and with it all treaties and agreements in force between them.

J&K's accession to India was both provisional and conditional.
In a discussion on Kashmir on 12 August 2016, Dr Karan Singh,
Maharaja Hari Singh's son and J&K's former Sadr-e-Riyasat (SeR),
or the head of state, as had been known in J&K, in his speech
in Rajya Sabha, said:

> We say J&K is an integral part of India. Of course it is.
> The day my father signed the IoA, it became an integral
> part of India. On 27th October 1947, I was in my room,
> in my house. However, please remember something more.
> My father acceded for three subjects only, which included
> defence, communication and foreign affairs. He signed the
> same along with other princely states, but all other states
> subsequently merged. But J&K did not merge with India.

Dr Singh further said that J&K's relation with the rest of India is guided by Article 370 and its own State Constitution, which he signed into law. The fact remains that the state never merged with the Union of India. Veteran Kashmiri columnist and historian, Zahir-ud-Din, writes that J&K was an independent state from 14 August 1947 to 26 October 1947. Referring to an important case of 1953, Magher Singh v/s state of J&K, which was heard by a division bench of the State High Court, the author writes that the bench comprising Janki Nath Wazir and Justice M.A. Shahmiri delivered a 'landmark judgment.' 'The bench laid down that J&K was an independent state from August 14 to October 26, 1947.'[21] This judgment was widely debated by legal experts, some of whom claim that it had a bearing on the IoA signed by Maharaja Hari Singh.

On 2 November 1947, Nehru said in a broadcast on All India Radio,[22]

> Let me make it clear that it has been our policy all along that where there is a dispute about the accession of a State to either Dominion, the decision must be made by the people of that State. It was in accordance with this policy that we added a proviso to the Instrument of Accession of Kashmir... We have declared that the fate of Kashmir has ultimately to be decided by the people. That pledge we have given, not only to the people of Kashmir but to the world. We will not, and cannot, back out of it. We are prepared when peace and law and order have been established, to have a referendum held under international auspices like the United Nations. We want it to be fair and just reference to the people, and we shall accept their verdict.

This promise remains unfulfilled to this day. And it appears that peace in J&K has also remained elusive ever since. In a telegram to the then PM of Pakistan, Liaquat Ali Khan, Nehru referred to his broadcast the previous evening, 'I further stated that we have agreed to an impartial agency like the United Nations supervising any referendum. This principle we are prepared to apply to any

State where there is a dispute about accession.'[23]

Soon after Maharaja Hari Singh signed the controversial IoA in October 1947, Sheikh Abdullah was made chief administrator under the Maharaja's supervision in November to give a Kashmiri face to the new administration. Mehr Chand Mahajan became the state's first PM and remained in office for about 142 days, from 15 October 1947 to 5 March 1948, which was when Sheikh Abdullah succeeded him as PM. Bakshi Ghulam Mohammad was chosen as Abdullah's deputy and made in charge of internal home affairs. Mirza Afzal Beg and Ghulam Mohiuddin Karra were not included in the cabinet because of their role in the Quit Kashmir movement against Maharaja Hari Singh. The decision to elevate Bakshi and ignore Beg upset the latter.

Soon, though, the NC government went after some of its own comrades, and leaders of a revived faction of the AJKMC. This dented the party's image in the eyes of the people. Those arrested by the NC government included AJKMC's general secretary, Agha Showkat Ali; Mirwaiz Yusuf Shah's cousin, Moulana Mohammad Noor-ud-Din; Khwaja Ghulam Nabi Gilkar; and Mirwaiz Mohammad Abdullah Shopiani from south Kashmir's Shopian. After being kept in prison for some time, they were sent into exile to Pakistan via the Jammu border.[24]

This was also the time when the relationship between Nehru and Abdullah, who were known to be good friends, started to fall apart. The Sheikh would pay for this in August 1953. The first major blow to the constitutional autonomy the state enjoyed by virtue of its provisional and conditional accession to India and Article 370 that granted it special status, was the unconstitutional arrest and unceremonious dismissal of Sheikh Abdullah as PM on 9 August 1953. In *The Kashmir Dispute, 1947–2012*, A.G. Noorani quotes a letter dated 31 July 1953, written by Nehru, in which he issued instructions for Sheikh Abdullah's dismissal and arrest, recorded by his private secretary, M.O. Mathai,[25]

It will be desirable not to allow any marked lapse of time between the demand for resignation and the formation of the new Government. The Head of the State (Sadr-e-Riyasat,

Karan Singh) should send for all members of Government and inform them of his decision and ask for their resignations. If the resignations are not forthcoming, he should have an order ready for the dismissal of the Government because it cannot fulfil its functions properly. Immediately, he should entrust the formation of the new Government to the other person...

The 'other person' was Bakshi Ghulam Mohammad.

At the time, Sheikh Abdullah and his wife Akbar Jehan—known to Kashmiris as 'Madar-i-Meharban' (Compassionate Mother)—were in Gulmarg, a tourist resort in north Kashmir. On the intervening night of 8 and 9 August 1953, they were woken up by loud, incessant knocks on their door. It was his secretary, R.C. Raina, who broke the news that the Sheikh could not even have imagined in his wildest dreams. The tourist hut had been surrounded by soldiers of the Indian Army. Laxman Das Thakur, superintendent of J&K Police, was waiting outside the hut to arrest the man who had until recently been his PM.

Thakur had an official order of the Sheikh's arrest, signed by the SeR. He entered the hut along with an official of the SeR. The order dismissing his government was handed to him. It is recorded that the Sheikh was handed another envelope, which carried a memorandum to the SeR, signed by Abdullah's close associate and deputy PM, Bakshi Ghulam Muhammad, and two ministers—a Kashmiri Pandit, Shyamlal Saraf; and a Hindu Dogra from Jammu, Girdhari Lal Dogra. They had expressed 'no confidence' in Abdullah's government. S.P. Thakur displayed the arrest warrant and told the Sheikh that he had been ordered to arrest him.

Abdullah could not believe his eyes and ears. But a news broadcast by All India Radio confirmed the inevitable to him at 8 a.m. on the morning of 9 August 1953. Soon after, he was driven to Udhampur and imprisoned at the Tara Niwas Palace. Along with twenty-two members of his NC, Abdullah was charged with conspiracy and treason against the Indian State. In 1958, one of the allegations levelled against the Sheikh, Mirza Afzal Beg and twenty-two others in the Kashmir Conspiracy Case was that he was taking money from Pakistan.[26] This is how New Delhi treated J&K's popular leader and PM for visualizing an independent Kashmir and raising the slogan for Kashmir's independence. However, noted historian Ramachandra Guha, in his article titled 'A Fateful Arrest', claims that the real reasons behind Abdullah's sudden arrest remains unknown because the papers relating to this period have not been made accessible to the public.[27] Most Kashmiris believe it was a well-planned conspiracy. As it turned out, it marked a tragic beginning of New Delhi's treatment of Kashmir with a mixture of democracy (to attract and mollify) and martial law (to suppress and stamp out).

While in prison, Sheikh Abdullah and Mirza Afzal Beg decided to launch a new political party. It is said that the name 'Plebiscite Front (Mahaz-e-Rai Shumari)' was suggested by the Sheikh himself, but he did not officially become its member. Abdullah complained that Kashmir had been corrupted because Delhi was bribing certain people to retain power in Kashmir. This was an obvious reference to the likes of Bakshi Ghulam Muhammad. 'Thus, since Sheikh Sahib's time, anybody who's been on the right side of Delhi has been getting money from Delhi. It's as simple as that', writes A.S. Dulat, former chief of India's spy agency, Research and Analysis Wing (RAW), in his memoir, *Kashmir: The Vajpayee Years*.[28] Unfortunately, there has been no change in this policy since then.

Meanwhile, Bakshi Ghulam Mohammad remained in power for a decade as PM, from August 1953 to August 1963, when he too was dismissed. His cabinet colleague, Khwaja Shamsuddin, was installed as the new PM from 12 October 1963 till 29 February 1964. Subsequently, Ghulam Mohammad Sadiq was the PM from 29 February 1964 to 30 March 1965. The offices of the PM (Wazir-e-Azam) and president (SeR) remained in force till 30 March 1965, which is when they were abolished.

After two years of imprisonment, Mirza Afzal Beg was released in September 1955. Soon after, he formally launched the Plebiscite Front after consulting with the Sheikh's sympathizers and well-wishers. Beg became its first president. After the Sheikh's arrest in 1953, thousands of his supporters had come out on the streets in protest. Bakshi Ghulam Mohammad's government responded with a brutal crackdown on the protestors. This was an important moment in Kashmir's history. The people felt betrayed and their pride was deeply wounded. This was the first instance of Delhi's betrayal of Kashmiris, which would regrettably be followed by many more.

Abdullah's old and once-trusted comrade, Bakshi Ghulam Mohammad, who was also a founding member of the AJKMC, deserted him at a critical juncture. During his decade-long rule, corruption and nepotism flourished. He was seen as a 'gaddaar' (traitor) by most Kashmiris, especially those who supported and admired the Sheikh. Thousands of people had protested the Sheikh's dismissal and arrest. Government forces cracked down hard on them. It is not known how many people were actually killed at the time. Thereafter, resentment in the Valley against New Delhi's undemocratic interventions seemed to grow by the day.

Though Hindus, and to an extent Buddhists from Ladakh, had played a part in shaping Kashmir's nationalism, after the Sheikh's arrest, the NC descended into factionalism. Nineteen members left the party because of the corruption and bullying that had crept in by 1957, and formed another political party, the Democratic National Conference.

PM Bakshi earned notoriety for not tolerating any dissent, suppressing his opponents and going after activists and sympathizers of the Plebiscite Front. The Bakshi family earned a disreputable sobriquet: 'BBC', short for the 'Bakshi Brothers Corporation'.[29] During Bakshi's rule, a group of notorious musclemen, ironically named the 'Peace Brigade', were institutionalized and patronized.[30] This so-called Peace Brigade was a loose conglomeration of shady characters ready to do the bidding of their master without any regret. Their job was to keep an eye on all 'troublemakers' and to give them a thrashing with the aim to make them fall in line. In some cases, even their ration cards would be confiscated to starve their families as retribution. The members of the Peace Brigade would, in turn, be under the command of some strongmen of the localities, called 'Goggas.'[31] The members of this Bakshi government-sponsored force were called 'Khoftan Faqir' (late night beggars ['khoftan' is a Kashmiri word for 'night prayer']) or 'Kuntreh-Pandeh' ('29-15' in local parlance [they were paid ₹30 per month, and out of the sixteen annas of a rupee then, one anna was deducted as government stamp duty, reducing their pay to ₹29 and fifteen annas, which gave them the label of '29-15']). In the absence of weapons at that time, the members of the Peace Brigade would use muscle power.

In the decade of the 1990s, the state government under Governor Jagmohan Malhotra also patronized a band of notorious armed renegades, known as 'Ikhwanis', as a counter-militancy force.

In 1963, a disastrous event once again shone a spotlight on the fractures in Kashmir's society. Moi-e-Muqaddas, the sacred hair strand of the Prophet Mohammad, which was believed to have been brought to the Kashmir Valley in 1700, had been kept in a glass tube at the Hazratbal Shrine and was brought out for devotees on special religious occasions. This relic was reported stolen on 28 December 1963. As soon as news of the theft spread, common people in their thousands took to the streets to protest despite freezing temperatures and snowfall. Rumours began doing the rounds—some blamed Bakshi Ghulam Mohammad for it, while others saw a greater conspiracy.

On 6 January 1964, Laxman Das Thakur, the inspector general of J&K Police, who had arrested Sheikh Abdullah from Gulmarg in 1953 as superintendent of Police, claimed that the relic had been found. B.N. Mullick, chief of IB, had also been in Srinagar to solve the crisis. Moulana Mohammad Sayeed Masoodi, an Islamic cleric considered to be close to Sheikh Abdullah, provided assurances to the protestors about the authenticity of the relic. It was only after his assurance that the agitation died down. Till date, it remains a mystery how the holy relic was 'stolen' and 'found'.

Some historians are of the view that Moulana Masoodi bailed Delhi out after 'secret' negotiations. However, Khwaja Sanaullah

Bhat notes in *Ahad Nama-i-Kashmir*, that Moulana Masoodi and his associates got nothing in return for their 'favours' to New Delhi. Soon, G.M. Sadiq was installed as the new PM and Khwaja Shamsuddin removed clandestinely from the top post.

Many years later, on 13 December 1990, militants of the armed outfit, Hizbullah, gunned down the eighty-seven-year-old Moulana Masoodi at point-blank range at his home in Ganderbal, north-west Srinagar. He was declared a 'traitor' to the Kashmiri Muslim community, mainly because it was thought that he had misidentified the holy relic allegedly at New Delhi's behest to sabotage the people's agitation. The Hizbullah claimed responsibility for killing Masoodi in a press statement.[32]

Meanwhile, G.M. Sadiq's government, on New Delhi's directions, dropped the Kashmir Conspiracy Case against Sheikh Abdullah and ordered his unconditional release from jail to pave the way for his return to active politics. Upon his release on 16 April 1964, an estimated half a million people greeted the Sheikh in Srinagar and raised passionate slogans in favour of the referendum and the right to self-determination. On 18 April, Nehru sent an invitation to Abdullah to come to Delhi for talks. They met in the first week of May, after which Abdullah went to Pakistan at the invitation of Mohammed Ayub Khan, the then president of Pakistan and field marshal of Pakistan's Army. However, things would soon go from bad to worse for Kashmir. Later in the month, on 27 May, Nehru passed away in Delhi. After addressing a rally in Muzaffarabad, Abdullah returned to Delhi to participate in Nehru's last rites. Upon his return to Kashmir, he and his sympathizers were rearrested.

The relationship between Sheikh Abdullah and Nehru had shown signs of improvement after both tried to reconcile and put the ugly episode of 1953 behind them. Nehru had allowed Abdullah to visit Pakistan to see if a solution to Kashmir was possible. His demise at that point was a serious setback to the process that had been set in motion. Some believe that the time was ripe for negotiations on Kashmir in the early 1960s, referring to a theory in international relations called Ripeness Theory.

After his arrest for the second time, New Delhi sensed that Abdullah might be willing to show flexibility in his stance on Kashmir. On his release, Abdullah held discussions with members of the Kashmiri Pandit and Dogra communities to develop a consensus on the Kashmir issue. He declared his willingness to participate in the Assembly elections of 1967, but was advised by Delhi to rechristen the Plebiscite Front, which was demanding a referendum on Kashmir under the auspices of the United Nations (UN). He was told in no uncertain terms that he could not contest under the banner of the Plebiscite Front. Abdullah knew equally well that he would get people's support and votes only if he espoused their aspirations for a referendum. He could not make up his mind. Again, New Delhi did what it knows best. Weeks before the Assembly elections, Sheikh was detained at a bungalow in New Delhi, which had been provided to him for his stay. Many of his supporters were also put behind bars.[33]

After 1962, one more rigged election took place in 1967 in which G.M. Sadiq was declared the winner. Of a total of seventy-five seats, the Congress was declared victorious in sixty, of which in thirty-nine seats it won unopposed. This was another brazen instance of rigging after the rigged elections, electoral frauds and malpractices during the first and second Assembly elections in 1957 and 1962, when Bakshi Ghulam Mohammad (declared winner on sixty-nine and sixty-eigth seats respectively) won forty-seven and thirty-three seats unopposed respectively. This obvious rigging prompted Nehru to write directly to Bakshi on 4 March 1962: 'In fact, it would strengthen your position much more if you lost a few seats to bonafide opponents.'[34] Thus, Kashmir's democracy was orchestrated by New Delhi. In his piece, Noorani describes J&K as a 'godforsaken State' and talks at length about electoral frauds and rigging in elections. 'Three of them (elections) were lauded by the great democrat Jawaharlal Nehru; the one conducted by Sheikh Abdullah in 1951 and the ones of 1957 and 1962 conducted by Bakshi Ghulam Mohammad'. Bakshi had infamously said, '*Vote aap denge; ginenge to hum*' ('You will cast the votes; it is we who will count them').[35]

Meanwhile, the Sheikh and his sympathizers were released again in 1972. By then, he had probably undergone a profound change. G.M. Sadiq had passed away and Syed Mir Qasim, a Congressman, was the new CM. He served from 1972 to 1975. The Sheikh's Plebiscite Front was formally banned by the government. In 1971, India and Pakistan went to war, as a result of which, East Pakistan emerged as an independent nation. Abdullah finally caved in and signed the Sheikh-Indira Accord to return to power as the CM in February 1975. He gave up his political struggle for plebiscite and self-determination. India's then PM, Indira Gandhi, welcomed Abdullah's 'change of thinking'. There were widespread malpractices and frauds in the 1972 elections as well, during which the Congress won fifty-eight of seventy-five seats. Fresh elections were held in 1977, largely said to be the first-ever 'free and fair' elections in J&K. The Abdullah-led NC won forty-seven seats while the Congress got only eleven. Elections were held in 1982, but Farooq Abdullah's government was toppled by Delhi in 1984 when Ghulam Mohammad Shah, his brother-in-law, was installed as the new CM.

There was blatant rigging in the 1987 elections as well, orchestrated by the NC to stay in power and to thwart the rise of the MUF, a political alliance of like-minded Muslim groups. Only fourteen years after Abdullah signed the 'infamous' Sheikh-Indira Accord, an armed uprising fully backed by the majority community erupted in 1989. Due to the alleged rigging in the Assembly elections of 1987, many popular candidates of the MUF were mysteriously declared unsuccessful. The armed movement that erupted in the Valley in the following years drew its strength from Kashmiri nationalism and ethnicity, Islam and its solidarity with Pakistan. It challenged the state's constitutional relationship with the Indian Union and favoured either complete independence or a merger with Pakistan.

Many Indian authors, analysts and journalists often erroneously see the rise of armed resistance in 1989 in the backdrop of the rigged elections of 1987. That simplistic and naïve understanding of the conflict amounts to a denial of all the previous anti-Delhi movements since 1947. It also disregards Sheikh Abdullah's vision of an independent Kashmir, the twenty-two-year-long movement led by the Plebiscite Front demanding a UN-organized referendum, and the deep-rooted pro-independence and pro-resolution sentiment in J&K.

Such an unsophisticated analysis of the Kashmir dispute also does not take into account the formation of groups like al-Fateh, a rebel organization that came into existence in the 1960s, soon after the agitation over the theft of the holy relic. Cadres of al-Fateh crossed over to PaK to receive arms training. In 1965, two prominent leaders, Maqbool Bhat and Amanullah Khan, co-founded the pro-independence JKLF. Journalist Barkha Dutt wrongly mentions in her book, *This Unquiet Land,* that the JKLF was founded after the rigged elections of 1987 by Yasin Malik and Javed Mir.[36]

Maqbool Bhat, co-founder of JKLF, came from Trehgam village in north Kashmir's frontier district of Kupwara. Born on 18 February 1938, Bhat had master's degrees in history, political science and Urdu literature. He was hanged in Delhi's Tihar Jail on 11 February 1984, on charges of killing a Kashmiri Pandit named Amar Chand, an inspector of the regional CID.

Bhat ran a vigorous campaign for Kashmir's independence under the banner of JKLF and termed political representatives in PaK 'puppets of Pakistan'. His idea of independence for the whole of J&K made him an instant hero among the masses. In 1966, militants, including Bhat, ambushed a police convoy, of which Chand was a part. In retaliatory fire, a militant named Aurangzeb was also believed to have been killed. Bhat was arrested, and in 1968, was charged with being an 'enemy agent' for his alleged involvement in the shootout. After he was found guilty of killing Amar Chand, Bhat was sentenced to death by a Kashmiri Pandit judge, Neelkanth Ganjoo. Interestingly, Muzaffar Hussain Beg, co-founder of the PDP and a former member of the Indian Parliament, was Bhat's defence lawyer.

In the same year, Bhat and his associates escaped through a tunnel they had dug inside their prison in Srinagar and fled to

Pakistan. He was arrested there as well in 1971. In 1974, he was able to sneak back into the Valley clandestinely, but his freedom was short-lived. The authorities rearrested him from Langate area in north Kashmir.[37]

On 4 February 1984, JKLF men shot dead an Indian diplomat in the United Kingdom. Farooq Abdullah, who was now CM of the state, signed the black warrant against Bhat within three days of the incident. Bhat was hanged inside Delhi's Tihar Jail on 11 February and his mortal remains were not returned to his family. To avenge Bhat's hanging, JKLF men assassinated Neelkanth Ganjoo on 4 November 1989.

In Maqbool Bhat, Kashmiris had found a young nationalist leader and an inspirational hero. Minutes before his hanging, he is believed to have said, 'I love my people. I have loved my life and today I'll embrace my death with gladness and contentment'.

★

Sir Walter Roper Lawrence, the first settlement commissioner of J&K State, mentions in his 1895 book, *The Valley of Kashmir*, that the commonest Kashmiri can communicate intelligently on most subjects, and most Kashmiris have a great aptitude for sarcasm.[38] This is one of the reasons why Kashmiris often discuss their administrators, government officials and leaders in a shrewd, though tongue-in-cheek, manner. Lawrence noted that every governor of the state had a nickname. It struck him as odd that governors reputed to be unkind were given complimentary nicknames. Wazir Punnu, the most powerful figure in then Maharaja of Kashmir Ranbir Singh's council, and who had done a lot of good work, was loathed for his sternness. It was said about him: '*Wazir tsalith, Kashmir bali*' ('When the Wazir goes, Kashmir will prosper').

After 1947, the resistance on multiple fronts in Kashmir has been a conscious political response to Delhi's rule, which is largely considered to be 'foreign'. Unsympathetic nicknames have been given to rulers perceived as corrupt, unjust, anti-people and pro-Delhi. In the past, Kashmiris had invented invectives against

foreign rulers—from Mughals, Afghans and Sikhs to the Dogras—
some of which are now being used and hurled at representatives
of New Delhi in Kashmir. After giving up his demand for a
referendum, Sheikh Abdullah earned a nickname, 'Abla Gaade'.[39]
Critics of his son, Farooq Abdullah, refer to the latter as 'Byenuel
Daand' (a bull who can cause an earthquake). Omar Abdullah, the
Sheikh's grandson and also a former CM, has two nicknames—
'Omar Singh' (which disparages him for marrying a Sikh woman,
Payal [now separated]) and 'Twitter Baby' (which mocks him for
being 'active' online and 'absent' from the ground). Other pro-India
politicians, considered Delhi's representatives in Kashmir, are also
christened accordingly. Some people call senior Congress leader
Ghulam Nabi Azad 'Nabe Tulip', a reference to his having thrown
open Kashmir's Tulip Garden to tourists during his stint as CM
after 2005. It was a move that was seen by critics as an attempt to
whitewash the conflict and sell tourism in Kashmir as a symbol of
'normalcy'. Mufti Mohammad Sayeed was called 'Mufti Whiskey'
by his critics, because of him being careless with the bottle and
especially for his fondness for whiskey. His daughter, Mehbooba
Mufti, is called 'Rudaali', for shedding tears at funerals of slain
militants, which critics say were never genuine, before assuming
power. Another CM, Ghulam Mohammed Shah, brother-in-law of
Farooq Abdullah, is remembered as 'Gul-e-Curfew', for enforcing
long and strict curfews during his stint from July 1984 to March
1986. He had defected from the NC along with twelve MLAs to
join hands with the Congress to form the government. He founded
his own party, the Awami National Conference, which contested
the Assembly elections in 2008.

The late G.M. Shah had toppled Farooq Abdullah's government
in 1984, in what was seen to be yet another undemocratic
intervention by New Delhi. The brazenly rigged elections of
1987 ensured that the people's worst fears about Delhi's version
of democracy in Kashmir were true. In 1987, a school teacher
named Mohammad Yusuf Shah, member of the JeI, contested

elections from Amirakadal in Srinagar on an MUF ticket. He was declared to have lost, when the trends and expectations had suggested otherwise. Other MUF candidates met a similar fate. The immensely popular Mohammad Yusuf Shah, now known as Syed Sallahuddin, chief of the HM and supreme commander of the UJC, an amalgam of various armed rebel outfits based in PaK, also contested the elections, only to find his opponent declared the winner. Mohammad Yasin Malik, the current chief of JKLF, and Javed Mir were young boys then, who acted as Sallahuddin's polling agents in 1987. Malik, Mir, and their like-minded comrades like Hamid Sheikh and Ashfaq Wani, were part of the famous HAJY (Hamid, Ashfaq, Javed and Yasin) rebel group that crossed the LoC to receive arms training in PaK. This was the beginning of an anti-Delhi armed rebellion, which was backed by most Kashmiris and sponsored by Pakistan.

NOTES, SOURCES AND REFERENCES

1. Haksar, N. (2015). *The Many Faces of Kashmiri Nationalism: From the Cold War to the Present Day*. New Delhi: Speaking Tiger.
2. Bhat, S. *Ahad Nama-i-Kashmir.*
3. Dulat, A. S., & Sinha, A. (2015). *Kashmir: The Vajpayee Years*. Noida, Uttar Pradesh, India: HarperCollins India.
4. Ahmad, K. B. (2017). *Kashmir: Exposing the Myth behind the Narrative*. New Delhi, India: SAGE Publications India Pvt.
5. Bazaz, P.N. (1976). *The History of Struggle for Freedom in Kashmir: Cultural and Political, from the Earliest Times to the Present Day*. Islamabad: National Committee for Birth Centenary Celebrations of Quaid-i-Azam Mohammad Ali Jinnah, Ministry of Education, Govt. of Pakistan.
6. Haksar, N. (2015). *The Many Faces of Kashmiri Nationalism: From the Cold War to the Present Day*. New Delhi: Speaking Tiger.
7. Telephonic conversation with author Zahid Ghulam Muhammad in Srinagar.
8. Personal interview with Zareef Ahmad Zareef in Srinagar.
9. Haksar, N. (2015). *The Many Faces of Kashmiri Nationalism: From the Cold War to the Present Day*. New Delhi: Speaking Tiger.
10. Bhat, S. *Ahad Nama-i-Kashmir.*
11. Whitehead, A. (2010). The People's Militia: Communists and Kashmiri nationalism in the 1940s. *Twentieth Century Communism*, 2(2), 141-168.
12. Ibid.
13. Mullik, B. N. (1971). *Kashmir: My Years with Nehru*. Bombay: Allied.
14. Interview with J&K Legislator, Muhammad Yusuf Tarigami in 2016.

15. Bhat, S. *Ahad Nama-i-Kashmir.*
16. Ibid.
17. Naqvi, S. (2016). *Being the Other: The Muslim in India.* New Delhi: Aleph.
18. Snedden, C. (2013). *Kashmir: The Unwritten History.* Noida, Uttar Pradesh, India: HarperCollins.
19. Choudhary, Z. (2008). Being Muslim in Jammu. *Economic and Political Weekly,* 11-14.
20. Noorani, A.G.A.M. (2013). *The Kashmir Dispute, 1947-2012.* Tulika Books.
21. Din, Z. (2016, August 19). A land mark judgement. Retrieved from http://www. greaterkashmir.com/news/opinion/story/226073.html
22. Government of India. (1948). White Paper on Jammu and Kashmir, p 53: Jawaharlal Nehru's speech broadcast on AIR.
23. Ibid: Nehru's telegram to then Prime Minister of Pakistan, Liaquat Ali Khan.
24. Khwaja Sanaullah Bhat's account.
25. Noorani, A.G.A.M. (2013). *The Kashmir Dispute, 1947-2012.* Tulika Books.
26. Dulat, A. S., & Sinha, A. (2017). *Kashmir: The Vajpayee Years.* HarperCollins Publishers India. Chapter 'Spy Vs. Spy', p. 161
27. Guha, R. (2008, August 03). A Fateful Arrest. *The Hindu.*
28. Dulat, A. S., & Sinha, A. (2017). *Kashmir: The Vajpayee Years.* HarperCollins Publishers India.
29. Haksar, N. (2015). *The Many Faces of Kashmiri Nationalism: From the Cold War to the Present Day.* Speaking Tiger, p. 37
30. Ashraf, M. (2013, February 28). The new "Peace Brigade"! Retrieved from http:// www.kashmirfirst.com/articles/politics/130228-the-new-peace-brigade.htm
31. Ibid.
32. From Newspaper archives: In a public statement, Hizbullah stated that Moulana Masoodi's life was full of black deeds and he was one of the worst traitors to the cause of Kashmir.
33. Bhat, S. *Ahad Nama-i-Kashmir.*
34. Noorani, A. G. (2011, November 19). Electoral fraud. *Frontline,* 28(24). Retrieved from http://www.frontline.in/static/html/fl2824/stories/20111202282408500.htm
35. Ibid.
36. Dutt, B. (2015). *This Unquiet Land.* Aleph Book Company. p. 150
37. Bhat, S. *Ahad Nama-i-Kashmir,* p. 153
38. Lawrence, W. R. (2005). *The Valley of Kashmir.* Asian Educational Services. p. 276
39. 'Abla' is short for Abdullah, like 'Steve' for Steven. 'Gaade', which means 'fish' in Kashmiri, is a reference to his ancestors as 'fishermen' or those associated with the trade. They are usually looked down upon because of caste biases and prejudices in the society. This was confirmed to the author by historian Saleem Beg, former director general of Tourism in the J&K government, and also by satirist-poet, Zareef Ahmad Zareef, who told the author that the Abdullah family lived in Soura, Srinagar, near the Anchar lake, where lotus stems, fish and 'singhade' (water chestnuts) were found in abundance, and Abdullah's ancestors had some connection with the trade.

5

....

VIOLENCE TO NON-VIOLENCE:
A LOST OPPORTUNITY?

I belong to a generation of Kashmiris that has witnessed the horrors of violence. There is no doubt in my mind that much of the violence that ravages Kashmir continues to emanate from New Delhi. Indeed, Pakistan keeps fishing in troubled waters whenever an opportunity presents itself. The painful memories of the grave wounds inflicted on Kashmir, especially after 1989, are impossible to erase. The very fact that Delhi talks about 'winning the hearts and minds' of Kashmiris after seven decades of controlling the state is a telling remark on its standing in Kashmir. Even after seventy-one years, the Hindu nationalist BJP accuses J&K's oldest pro-India political party, the NC, and another major regional force, the PDP, of working at the behest of Pakistan. On 22 November 2018, the PDP president Mehbooba Mufti staked her party's claim for government formation with the support of the Congress and the NC when the state's Legislative Assembly lay in suspended animation (the BJP had parted ways with the PDP in mid-June). Top BJP leaders including Ram Madhav, the party's national general secretary, and Kavinder Gupta, former speaker of the J&K Assembly, alleged that the PDP and the NC had boycotted the urban local bodies' polls and panchayat elections in J&K after receiving instructions from across the border (Pakistan) and probably had 'fresh instructions' from Pakistan to form the government now.[1] After a backlash on Twitter, Ram Madhav withdrew his comment.

The fourth and fifth generations of Kashmir since 1931 have

a new vocabulary, a new idiom. In the early 1990s, as school children, we quickly learned terms like 'curfew', 'crackdown', 'cordon', 'catch and kill', 'torture', 'interrogation', 'custody killing', 'arrest', 'detention', 'hartal', etc. When it was time for us to learn 'A for Apple', 'B for Ball', 'C for Chocolate', we learned 'A for Army', 'B for Bullet' and 'C for Curfew'! The circumstances we lived in were horrific. As we grew older, other terms nudged their way into our vocabulary, like 'fake encounter', 'extrajudicial killing', 'mistaken identity', 'custodial disappearance', 'mass graves', etc. Ours was a generation destined to learn a distinctive terminology.

Our literature was bloody. It was not our choice, though. Some choices are not our own. We hardly had any choices. Boys of my age were inured to daily doses of violence. Anger at those who marched in our streets with their weapons held high came naturally to us. We were angry at the government forces personnel who frisked us, asked us to prove our identity in our own land, threw our school bags away, ordered us to do push-ups and squats, and hurled the choicest invectives at us. This daily humiliation made fear a staple of our lives. For them, we were 'the other'. For them to exert control on Kashmir's streets and to exist as a dominant force, they *needed* an 'other'.

Documenting pain can be a challenge. For many Kashmiris belonging to the post-1989 generation, it is a battle between memory and forgetfulness. Memory should win, they hope. It is not easy to wipe memory clean, like a slate. That's what history tells us.

Nothing was in our hands. We couldn't do anything to bring about a change. We were children of conflict, born and raised in the shadow of the gun. Historian Ramachandra Guha in one of his columns for *Hindustan Times* wrote,[2]

> The Indian case in and for Kashmir was made fragile in the past by the rigging of elections. And it is made fragile in the present by the rising tide of jingoism, which insists that the government of India and the Indian Army have never made a mistake in Kashmir; indeed can never make a mistake in Kashmir.

Markandey Katju, former Judge at the Supreme Court of India and former chairman, Press Council of India, in one of his articles argued that 'there is a massive deployment of about 500,000 Indian Army, paramilitary and other armed forces in Kashmir. Thus, in theory, while there is a civilian government, the truth is that it is the Army and paramilitary forces (that) are the real power in Kashmir Valley.'[3]

As mentioned before, Walter Lawrence wrote in *The Valley of Kashmir* that 'in intellect, Kashmiris are perhaps the superior of the natives of India.'[4] Their aptitude for sarcasm and wit has helped them sail through difficult periods in their history. Making light of their tragedies comes easily to them. They can poke fun at themselves and laugh heartily when the going gets tough.

During childhood, I considered myself brave. While boys of my age were scared to roam on the streets without their student identity cards, I occasionally risked possible arrest by going out without it. Though in my heart, I knew I wasn't brave at all. Perhaps I just wanted to experience what would happen to me if I were caught. Perhaps I was just being stupid, but children have the right to be stupid at times. When I was twelve or thirteen, I remember passing by a security bunker at Soura in Srinagar. I was nervous. What if the soldiers stationed outside that ugly bunker asked to see my identity proof? What would I do? I remembered Tom Sawyer and his mischievous plans that got him out of tough situations with Aunt Polly. Very craftily, I made a plan, which I thought would work wonders for me. I greeted a paramilitary soldier with a broad smile. I thought he would return the favour. He did return something, but it wasn't a smile: '*Abey, sipahi kay saamney hansta hai?*' ('Hey, how dare you smile in front of a soldier?') The expression on my face changed pretty quickly. I looked at him in utter despair. The soldier shouted at me, '*Hey, mujhe ghoorta hai tu?*' ('Hey, are you staring at me?').

I didn't know what to say. He spewed fire. He spat venom. But his anger ensured that he forgot to check my identity card. He shoved me away. I had emerged triumphant!

I must confess that when I narrated the encounter to my

friends in the neighbourhood, I added some masala to it. I gave my expert opinion: if you're confident and keep smiling before Indian soldiers, they don't check your I-cards. Almost all of them praised my bravado, which only I knew was fake. Some were sceptical but did not voice their feelings.

Another day, another story. A few years later, I was returning home with my childhood friend, Samiullah Beigh. We were walking on the main road in Elahi Bagh, Srinagar, after participating in a local cricket tournament. The soldiers patrolling outside a notorious military camp there stopped us and demanded identity proof. Neither of us was carrying an I-card, because we weren't far from home and were playing cricket in an area we were familiar with. Sami, as we called Samiullah, told them that he was an engineering student and a potential cricketing talent. The dress Sami wore, however, was exceedingly simple, even by moderate Kashmiri standards. After scanning Sami from head to toe, the soldier was obviously unimpressed. '*Engineer aisey kapdey pehanta hai? Phainkta kyun hai?*' ('Would an engineer dress up like this? Why do you brag?'). Sami had no answer.

The soldier turned to me with a slightly lesser degree of suspicion. I seemed a harmless creature to him probably. Or so I thought. 'We're good, decent boys, and educated. We were here only to play a cricket match,' I said. At the beginning and end of every sentence, I ensured I added 'Sir'. Suddenly, we heard a loud whistle. Perhaps their commander had arrived in a Gypsy. '*Ab jao jaldi, bhago*' ('Go quickly, run'). We obeyed. There was no choice. On reaching home, we also hurled some 'polite' abuses at them in our hearts. As an aside, Samiullah Beigh is an assistant executive engineer, a gazetted officer and has been a part of the J&K cricket team at the Ranji Trophy competition for about a decade and a half. He also captained his side briefly.

Our education in violence began in 1989 and continued into the mid-1990s. Things went from bad to worse. It was the era of renegades, when the government's Armed Forces depended on government-sponsored gunmen who acted as informers and accompanied soldiers during raids, as 'cats'.

Late one evening in 1996, a search operation was launched to nab a top militant commander. Acting on a tip-off, our entire neighbourhood was cordoned off. After playing at a cricket tournament, I came home later than usual. I was tired that evening and went to bed early. Around midnight, I was woken up by a loud noise. Outside, I could see powerful searchlights that signalled they had cordoned off our area. My parents and younger sisters were frightened. All of us gathered in one room, mindful that we should not speak loudly. 'It appears like a crackdown. Or a military raid,' my father said. We were suspended in uncertainty. We didn't know how to react. Our curiosity grew with each passing minute. And then, all of a sudden, rifle butts began banging on our door, soon followed by fierce knocking and abusive language. With trembling hands, my parents opened the door.

Some twenty soldiers entered our home. They immediately wanted to know about our family's structure. Following their orders, we answered every single question politely. 'We're a family of six,' my father said. 'I, my wife, our son, and three daughters.' They asked him about his profession, how old his children were, what each family member did, and many other such questions, most of them irrelevant and some doltish ones too. How I wished I could have mirrored their questions and asked them about their families too! But, the oppressed have few choices.

On seeing my textbooks, famous novels and autobiographies, a collection of poetry and other books in my room, they perhaps realized they were at a wrong place. Their facial expressions too suggested that they had made an error of judgment. But seldom will soldiers admit their mistakes. It was much later that we discovered they were looking for a militant commander whose family structure resembled ours. He too was an only son, brother of three sisters.

Finally, the soldiers told me that I needed to accompany them to meet their officer, whom they only referred to as 'Praveen'. *'Lagta hai yeh woh nahin hai, lekin phir bhi Praveen sahab kay paas lay chalo'* ('It appears he's not the one we're looking for, but let's take him to Praveen sir nevertheless').

One soldier held my neck and took me along with him, asking me on the way whether I knew someone called 'Niaz', the commander of a guerrilla group. I replied in the negative. As he was about to hit me, some soldiers came running towards him and said, *'Praveen sahab nay kaha hai isko haath nahin lagana'* ('Praveen sir has ordered to not hit him').

Another soldier ordered me inside their vehicle, a Gypsy. I had no choice except to follow their instructions. Inside the vehicle, a soldier from a group other than the one that had raided my house, said, *'Abey, dus saal se tumhari talaash thi'* ('Hey, you're wanted for the past ten years'). Ten years before, I'd have been a small kid. But who'd have dared argue with them?

I didn't know in which direction the Gypsy was headed. Finally, it came to a stop. I was given clear instructions not to open my mouth before their officer about what I had heard inside their dreaded vehicle. I nodded in agreement. Praveen, their officer, calmed me down and ordered his juniors to bring me some water. 'It's too late now. I regret the inconvenience caused. Sadly, you'll have to spend the night here in the police station. I know you're innocent and a bright student. Don't worry, you'll be home by tomorrow morning,' the kind officer told me. During this time, I had no idea what was happening at home.

Next morning, I was told Praveen had gone out on an 'important mission'. He came back only by late afternoon. With a smile on his face, he said, 'It's time for you to go home.'

I had a severe pain in my chest and was feeling breathless. Thankfully, I wasn't beaten up or tortured physically, except for a slap by one soldier. Most of those who were picked up in similar raids were not as lucky.

I couldn't believe my eyes when I came out of the police station and saw my mother and other relatives eagerly waiting outside. Everybody hugged me. They had worked really hard to ensure my release. For my parents, it was as if I had been reborn. On reaching home, I found a huge crowd waiting for me, as if I was the president of the United States of Kashmir!

Such incidents happened with sickening regularity in the 1990s. The generation that grew up then was surrounded by violence. The only argument that prevailed was one of violence. We were forced to remain indoors for months together, caged in our own homes like criminals. The enforced imprisonment gave us time to read why this was happening to us. We read Kashmir's history, Kashmir's literature of conflict and its literature of resistance. We got to know of the string of broken promises by the likes of Pandit Jawaharlal Nehru to Atal Bihari Vajpayee. The erosion of democratic processes through a series of rigged elections. The toppling of governments at New Delhi's behest. The suppression of dissent with brute force. The politics of militarization. And Delhi's stick-and-carrot policy that was an appalling mix of 'democracy' and 'martial law'.

Ramachandra Guha in his book *Democrats and Dissenters* argues:[5]

> Ho Chi Minh is said to have remarked that had Mahatma Gandhi been fighting against the French, he would have given up non-violence within a week. By the same token, Indian arrogance towards Kashmiris, and Sinhala intolerance towards Tamils, have at times been so brutal and extreme as to make reasoned non-violent protest ineffective, and perhaps even impossible.

Yet another aspect of the times was the armed militancy. Rebel outfits would plan and execute deadly attacks not only against government forces, but also those they perceived as 'collaborators', 'mukhbir' (informers) or 'Indian spies'. Hapless citizens would often find themselves caught between two guns. In several attacks carried out by militants, some innocent lives too would be lost in the crossfire. The people of Kashmir had become 'cannon fodder' and 'collateral damage' for both the Armed Forces as well as armed guerillas. Hundreds would be injured in grenade attacks that would miss the intended target and explode at crowded places instead. In 1989 and 1990, militants targeted and killed both Muslims and Pandits who they thought were close to the ruling establishment, the state's bureaucracy, the Armed Forces, intelligence agencies, and so on. Anyone suspected of being a mukhbir by militants would have to face their bullets. And anyone seen as a sympathizer of the anti-State movement would be targeted by government forces. If the Armed Forces killed a civilian, they would call it 'collateral damage' and regret the killing. Sometimes, they would use terms like 'error of judgment', 'mistaken identity' or an 'aberration'. Militants, too, would regret civilian casualties in grenade attacks. Civilians could not say 'you're welcome' or 'thank you' to either the Armed Forces or the armed rebels. Those with guns enjoyed the 'azadi' to kill, and the civilians at the receiving end did not have the azadi to even mourn their death.

A.S. Dulat, in *Kashmir: The Vajpayee Years,* noted that India's intelligence network and infrastructure in Kashmir grew during Rajiv Gandhi's prime ministership.[6] According to him, 1989 onwards, armed militants were trying to destabilize J&K at Pakistan's behest. They would target pro-India Kashmiri Pandits and those working specifically for India's intelligence agencies. As recorded in the previous chapter, Neel Kanth Ganjoo, a Pandit judge who had sentenced Maqbool Bhat to death, was gunned down by the outfit in an act of revenge. Other Pandits killed by militants in 1989–90 included Lassa Koul, director of Doordarshan, a government broadcasting organization accused of anti-Kashmir and pro-Delhi propaganda. Dulat was then the station head of the IB in Kashmir and his colleague was shot dead by the JKLF on 3 January 1990. Dulat writes that most IB officers in Kashmir were Kashmiri Pandits. They lived among the people and made for easy targets.

Militants also targeted several Muslims who were members of the pro-India NC or worked for spy agencies and the Armed Forces. Clearly, their strategy was to create fear among anyone with a pro-India affiliation and convert them to their ideology. On 21 August 1989, JKLF militants killed Mohammed Yusuf Halwai, a staunch NC block president from downtown Srinagar. Moulana Masoodi, as mentioned in Chapter 4, was gunned down by Hizbullah militants. Dulat writes in his memoir that the first IB officer to be killed in Kashmir, in Anantnag district, was from Bihar, R.N.P Singh. Kishen Gopal was killed in central Kashmir's Budgam district on 9 January 1990, followed by M.L. Bhan in Nowgam on 15 January and T.K. Razdan in Srinagar on 12 February. These were all targeted killings that were ideology-driven and not religion-specific.

Some Kashmiri Pandits associated with Right-wing groups like Panun Kashmir and Roots in Kashmir claim that their community faced an 'ethnic cleansing' and 'genocide'. This is far from the truth. Far more Muslims were targeted by militants than Kashmiri Pandits. In March 2010, the J&K government said on the floor of the Legislative Assembly that 219 Kashmiri Pandits were killed by militants from 1989 to 2004 (in fifteen years). A total of 38,119 Kashmiri Pandit families were registered with the government, of which 24,202 migrated in January 1990. According to official figures, the total number of Pandits stood at 1.5 lakh at the time of migration. Pandits represented less than 5 per cent of the total population. At present, the government claims 60,452 families are registered with it, of which 808 families (3,500 people) continue to live in the Valley.

In 2010, Basharat Bukhari, senior NC leader and a former minister in the PDP-BJP coalition government in 2016, had asked a question regarding the status, migration and killings of Kashmiri Pandits to the then revenue minister, Raman Bhalla, in the Assembly. In response, Mr Bhalla said, '219 Pandits were killed in Kashmir from 1989 to 2004. From 2004, no killing of any person from the community [Kashmiri Pandits] took place till now.' Raman Bhalla also said that 808 Pandit families consisting of 3,445 people had never migrated and still lived in the Valley.

In stark contrast to government figures, Panun Kashmir exaggerates the number of Kashmiri Pandits killed in the Valley with the intention of branding Kashmir's political movement for self-determination as an ultra-radical Islamist movement. On its website, Panun Kashmir claims that over 1,000 Kashmiri Pandits were murdered,[7] which is factually incorrect. They also allege forced conversion to Islam, which is untrue. The radical organization has failed to back and substantiate its horrific claims with facts. This is not to say that the Kashmiri Pandit community did not suffer, which will be dealt with in some detail in a later chapter.

Growing up in Kashmir in the horror-filled 1990s was nightmarish. It was a battle for survival, as if a sword was constantly hanging over one's head. For a child, the constant sight of the gun, whether in the hands of Indian military personnel or Kashmiri militants, was a constant reminder of the harsh reality of the times. The sloganeering during massive anti-State demonstrations was tempting, but the bullets piercing human bodies and the wails of mothers, sisters and wives forced one to be pragmatic. Mourning had become a routine affair, as if it was Kashmir's destiny.

The pro-freedom songs had lured many young people to tread a path fraught with dangers and serious ramifications. Young men in their thousands had crossed the LoC to receive arms training in camps run by the Pakistani Army and its spy wing, Inter-Services Intelligence (ISI). I was too young to take such a life-turning decision then, of fighting the State with a gun in my hand. All my hands could handle well were a cricket ball and bat, as an off-spinning all-rounder, and a pen, which I hoped to put to good use in the years to come.

As mentioned before, in 1994, the JKLF decided to eschew armed militancy to pursue a path of non-violence, but New Delhi showed little or no respect for the outfit's declaration of a unilateral ceasefire, announced by Mohammad Yasin Malik. Malik has told me in several interviews that at least 500 JKLF men were killed by government forces despite the ceasefire. Unsurprisingly, this has made him a sceptic and fierce critic of New Delhi's policy on Kashmir. He refers to members of India's civil society and intelligentsia as 'fire-fighters' who visit Kashmir only with the aim to 'douse flames' and bail out the Indian State. New Delhi's rigid stand has discredited and failed the institution of dialogue, he feels, which is why most Kashmiris do not have faith in it any longer. New Delhi's arrogance and denial of the legitimate political aspirations of the state has often made hardliners relevant, and sidelined moderates.

In a strange decision, the Indian government under Narendra Modi's leadership imposed a ban on the JKLF under the anti-terror law, UAPA. The move came days after New Delhi banned JeI (J&K) under Section 3(1) of the UAPA.[8] On the call of Joint Resistance Leadership, a Valley-wide shutdown was observed on 24 March 2019 against the ban on JKLF.[9]

This ban imposed by MHA, India, was criticized by all pro-Delhi political leaders in J&K, which include Omar Abdullah, Mehbooba Mufti and Sajad Lone. On the ground, J&K's civil society coalitions saw the ban on JKLF as 'wiping away the middle ground in Kashmir and criminalizing peaceful dissent.'

★

On 24 July 2000, the HM announced a conditional unilateral ceasefire at a press conference in Srinagar. Addressing the media, Abdul Majid Dar, then HM's commander-in-chief (operations), said that the outfit would 'halt attacks' against Indian security forces during a three-month period. A.S. Dulat describes Majid Dar as 'a man of guts' and 'a good guy' in *Kashmir: The Vajpayee Years*, who wanted to end militancy in Kashmir. HM supremo Syed Sallahuddin backed the group's conditional ceasefire at a news conference held in Pakistan's capital, Islamabad. India also acknowledged and reciprocated with a three-month ceasefire. Hope was generated that something would happen to assuage people's suffering and perhaps pave the way to a resolution of the long-lasting Kashmir conflict. To build an atmosphere of trust, a friendly cricket match between Kashmir rebels and Indian Armed Forces personnel was organized in north Kashmir's Handwara district. Thousands of people gathered to watch this 'Mujahideen-Military' cricket game.[10]

On 3 August 2000, the then Home Secretary of India, Kamal Pandey, flew to Srinagar with some Home ministry officials to meet a group of HM militants that included Majid Dar, Abdul Hamid

Tantray and Farooq Mircha, at Srinagar's Nehru Guest House. The HM had nominated Fazl Haq Qureshi as its interlocutor. For about a fortnight, there were no major incidents of violence from either side. People were hoping for some significant headway having been made in the course of the talks. Nothing happened. This prompted Syed Sallahuddin to withdraw from the ceasefire on 8 August. His declaration made many suspicious that Majid Dar might have been influenced by Delhi. Dar and Fazl Haq Qureshi were rendered vulnerable due to Delhi's lack of intent to move forward through the dialogue.

In 2001, Dar's associate, Hamid Tantray, was assassinated by unknown assailants. The HM expelled Majid Dar along with two others, Asad Yazdani and Zafar Abdul Fateh, in May 2002. A year later, in March 2003, Dar was assassinated as he was coming out of his house in an area called Noor Bagh in Sopore, north Kashmir. No major militant group claimed responsibility. In fact, HM condemned Dar's killing.[11] Some suspected that the HM might have killed him while others thought that New Delhi was behind his elimination. Till date, no one knows who killed Dar and his associates.

In fact, two lesser-known and obscure outfits, namely the Save Kashmir Movement (SKM) and the Al Nasireen had claimed responsibility for Dar's killing. SKM labelled Dar as 'an informant of Indian agencies' and 'an enemy of the Kashmiri people'. Seperately, an Al Nasireen spokesperson, in a message to a local news agency, said that activists of the group killed Dar for 'anti-movement activities'. Both organizations do not exist on the ground.[12]

Syed Ali Shah Geelani termed the entire ceasefire episode as 'drama'. According to him, the HM ceasefire had surprised everyone in Pakistan, Delhi and Kashmir. In the third volume of his autobiography, *Wular Kinaray*, he says,[13]

This sudden announcement of ceasefire made people suspicious about its (Hizb's) motives. Why did the ceasefire happen? What were the factors involved? Whether the Hizb leadership across the border (based across the LoC, in PaK) was taken into confidence or not? What were the modalities and how would it have impacted the ongoing anti-India resistance? Like all other people, these important questions had made me restless and edgy, too.

Like Geelani, the then chief of JeI Pakistan, Qazi Hussain Ahmad, had expressed serious reservations about the HM's ceasefire. The JeI and Kashmir's armed militancy have a connection. Immediately after the flawed and rigged Assembly elections of 1987, many top JeI leaders were not in favour of armed struggle. One could call the socio-religious political party a 'reluctant fundamentalist'. It finally gave the go-ahead for the foundation of the HM in April 1990 (though unofficially). It was also tempted to declare the HM as its 'armed wing', as already explained in earlier chapters. Until then, the JeI had made a mark in Kashmir's society through education, social work and religious teachings. The group is respected for its contributions in various fields. The JeI workers, its sympathizers and volunteers also contributed in rescue, relief and rehabilitation works during the devastating earthquake of October 2005 and unprecedented floods of September 2014.

Master Ahsan Dar, a resident of north Kashmir, was declared the HM's first commander-in-chief. As government forces and government-sponsored renegades went after many JeI leaders in the mid-1990s, and many of its leaders, preachers and sympathizers were brutally killed, the JeI was forced to rethink its policy on armed struggle. It then decided to distance itself from the armed movement and retracted its earlier stance declaring the HM as its 'fouji bazu'. This change of tack annoyed many of its supporters and sympathizers, including Syed Ali Shah Geelani.

Geelani, a former JeI rukn, addressed this in detail in his memoirs. Although he lauds the JeI for the services and sacrifices offered by the party since its inception, he voices concern over some JeI leaders who concluded that the role of the gun was over in Kashmir. Compellingly, he says that Kashmir's boys did not pick up the gun for frivolous or recreational purposes. The youth was forced to join the armed revolution to make India accept that J&K is a disputed territory and the dispute ought to be resolved in accordance with the aspirations of the people of the state, keeping in mind its historical background. Geelani criticizes the JeI's statement about the role of the gun by saying it would make many speculate that it had perhaps made a 'U-turn', 'changed its stance' or 'felt helpless under the weight of circumstances.'[14] Unsurprisingly, Geelani does come to the JeI's rescue in this matter. He argues that the people who made such statements might not have intended to demean the armed resistance but only tried to express their desire that meaningful negotiations should begin to resolve Kashmir. He, however, does take a jibe at former JeI chief, Ghulam Mohammad Bhat, who had earlier said that 'Kashmir is only a political issue.'[15] The political dispute had turned into a full-fledged 'military occupation', says Geelani, because of which the entire Kashmiri nation has suffered over several decades. This issue is a matter of life and death for Kashmiris. It is the question of honour and dignity. It has also become a matter of faith and religion, he says, of protecting the identity of the majority, as Muslims. He says that if any person, without naming Bhat, after unprecedented injustices and oppression, martyrdom, sacrifices and destruction, says that Kashmir is only a political dispute, one would have to say that he is simply unaware of the true spirit of Islam.

Like Sayyid Qutb, the JeI members also believe that 'Islam is a complete system' with laws, social codes, economic rules and its own methods of government. Most of the JeI members are articulate and impressive as communicators. Stories about Kashmiri prisoners' sufferings in various Indian jails and continued killings of civilians in actions by government forces have formed a kind of passion play for them. Most of them firmly believe that politics and religion are inseparable.

Interestingly, when I met Muzaffar Wani, Burhan Wani's father, at his home in Sharifabad, we briefly discussed the JeI's role vis-a-vis armed resistance. When I mentioned the statement made by Tariq Ahmad Naik, a local JeI ideologue in Tral, that 'the JeI and Kashmir's armed revolt are not interconnected', Muzaffar Wani was infuriated. He said the JeI could possibly not say something like this.

'If the Jamaat thinks that armed resistance is not the way forward, they must issue a fatwa that we will pursue our cause only through political means', he said. In his youth, Muzaffar Wani had been inspired by the Tabhleegi Jamaat, popularly known in Kashmir as 'Allah Waley' (Allah's Men). The Tabhleegi Jamaat usually focuses on the fundamentals of Islam—how to say your prayers, perform ablutions, make the pilgrimage to Mecca, pay zakat to the poor and needy, fast during Ramzan, sacrifice animals on Eid-ul-Zuha, and so on. As a purely religious organization, it does not take a clear political stand on Kashmir. Unlike the JeI, the Tabhleegi Jamaat seemingly has no political ambitions on Kashmir's turf.

According to Muzaffar Wani, the JeI is replete with contradictions. 'If armed resistance is a wrong path, why do JeI leaders endorse it when they see a sea of people at martyrs' funerals?' he asked. If the JeI is simply a social, religious and political organization with no links to the armed resistance, Wani asks, then why are their leaders the first to take the microphone at a mujahid's janaza to hail his martyrdom by reading Quranic verses? Why do they pay glowing tributes to martyrs and deliver passionate sermons? Isn't this an endorsement? Wani finds it difficult to accept the change in JeI's stand in the mid-1990s, after approving of armed struggle in 1990. His son, Burhan, was born seven years after the eruption of the armed resistance movement. Many Burhans have come before his Burhan, he says, and many will come in the future, too. 'It is a struggle for our rights, existence and identity', he says. For Wani, losing Khalid or Burhan is not important, though it hurts and causes immeasurable pain. For a true Muslim, Allah comes first, the Prophet and the Quran next, and then family, he says.

After Burhan's killing on 8 July 2016, many pro-Burhan and pro-azadi rallies were organized in every nook of the Kashmir Valley, from south to north, in which tens of thousands of people participated. Burhan's father received many invitations to lead demonstrations, but he does not have any ambition to become a mass leader and would prefer to remain a retired school principal and a father.

In 2016, it might have appeared to anyone watching the situation that Kashmir had slipped back into the 1990s. There was no serious political dialogue happening. There was the absence of political will in both Delhi and Islamabad to resolve the Kashmir dispute. Armed resistance was again receiving popular endorsement and young armed rebels were becoming objects of veneration. Gigantic pro-freedom demonstrations and public uprisings after Burhan's killing had become a new rallying point in Kashmir's political history.

However, in 2003, it had seemed that a different reference point might emerge when Indian PM Atal Bihari Vajpayee extended a 'hand of friendship' to Pakistan, and Pakistan responded positively to the offer made. On 18 April 2003, Vajpayee scripted history on a two-day visit to Srinagar. He addressed a rally at Srinagar's SKCS, the first time in fifteen years that an Indian PM had done so. He famously said at the time, '*Insaaniyat ke daayare main baat hogi*' ('Talks will be held within the ambit of humanism') and that the gun was no solution to political issues. Mufti Mohammad Sayeed was heading a PDP-Congress coalition government after reasonably peaceful Assembly elections in 2002. After massive rigging in many previous elections (1962, 1967, 1972, 1987 and 1996, to cite a few), the 2002 elections were said to be 'free and fair' like the 1977 elections, when Sheikh Abdullah had made his political comeback.

On the Pakistan-India front, the years 1999–2002 had witnessed much drama and heightened tensions. The Kargil conflict in 1999, the failure of the Agra Summit in 2001 and a deadly attack on the Indian Parliament in December 2001 ensured that relations between the two nuclear neighbours remained tense. It was widely conjectured that the then US president, Bill Clinton, had persuaded Pakistan to withdraw its Army from Kargil in 1999 to de-escalate tensions between the two countries and pave the way for political engagement to resolve outstanding disputes, including Kashmir. In November 2003, both countries agreed to a ceasefire on the LoC and the working boundary. Tensions eased. There was something positive in the air. People living along the LoC and the working border breathed easy. In Kashmir, people felt a sense of security and hoped that a solution was finally in the offing. Vajpayee's message of peace and friendship was hailed by many, and suspected by some. People hoped that concrete confidence-building measures would set the tone for a resolution. It seemed as if there was political will on both sides and something would eventually happen.

The general election of 2004 in India brought the Congress-led United Progressive Alliance (UPA-I) to power, with Dr Manmohan Singh as the PM. The equation and chemistry that had developed between A.B. Vajpayee and Pervez Musharraf had been described as 'magnificent' by some. Now, a new beginning had to be made. On 7 April 2005, in a welcome development, the trans-Kashmir Srinagar-Muzaffarabad road was reopened after a gap of fifty-eight years. It was officially launched by Manmohan Singh in Srinagar. I was fortunate to be among the journalists who travelled from Srinagar to Salamabad Uri, the last stop at the LoC, on the same day, to witness the making of history.

The atmosphere was electric. I was tempted to touch the soil on the other side and bring mounds of it with me as a souvenir. People were out on the roads, seeing something that had seemed unimaginable until then—a passenger bus ferrying people from this side of Kashmir to the other, and vice-versa. To see a passenger bus service connecting Srinagar with Muzaffarabad—the respective capitals of Indian-administered Kashmir and PaK—was indeed a dream come true for the people of the Valley. The proposal had been under official consideration with both countries since 2003 and was, in a way, inspired by the success of the Delhi-Lahore bus service.

The launch of the Srinagar-Muzaffarabad bus was symbolic for most Kashmiris. Almost everyone was joyous. However, the APHC faction led by Syed Ali Geelani and some armed groups openly opposed the trans-Kashmir bus service, arguing that it could not be mistaken for a permanent solution to the Kashmir dispute. On 6 April 2005, two militants attacked the TRC in Srinagar, where passengers scheduled to travel by the inaugural

Srinagar-Muzaffarabad bus service on 7 April were provided accommodation. A dozen people were injured in the attack. The old wooden TRC building was gutted. It took years to construct a new building there.

Despite this attack, the bus service was not halted. The moderate faction of the APHC, led by Mirwaiz Umar Farooq, had welcomed the proposal. Common Kashmiris did not see the opening of the road and bus service as a resolution, but many felt it could be one of the means through which a settlement could be arrived at. It was no ordinary event. I remember my evocative conversations with Mohammad Amin Bhat, a theatre director, who told me that after nearly six decades, a historic road had been reopened and the irony was that some were still confused whether to welcome the event or oppose it.

The Srinagar-Muzaffarabad bus service across the LoC was likened to the fall of the Berlin Wall by many. Notwithstanding objections from the Geelani-led APHC faction and some militant and hardline elements in both Pakistan and India, an overwhelming majority were in favour of giving peace a chance and build an atmosphere where a solution to the Kashmir dispute could be found amicably.

Only a year after this historic event, which I exclusively reported for the Srinagar-based English daily, *Kashmir Images*, in April 2005, I moved to Germany. There, I witnessed the twentieth anniversary of the fall of the Berlin Wall on 9 November 2009, when the city was abuzz with parties and celebrations. Exactly twenty years earlier, the entire world had witnessed this historic fall, followed eleven months later, in October 1990, by the reunification of East and West Germany. As a Kashmiri, I hoped that in time, the LoC too would become irrelevant like the Berlin Wall.

In 2009, the then US secretary of state, Hillary Clinton, was in Berlin. The then French president, Nicolas Sarkozy, then British PM Gordon Brown, and then Russian president, Dmitry Medvedev, were among the dignitaries who attended events at Berlin's Brandenburg Gate, alongside the German Chancellor,

Angela Merkel. Such was the importance of the event that in her maiden speech in the US Congress in 2009, Merkel, who grew up in East Germany, thanked the US for its role in the fall of the Wall.

Many South Asians living and working in Germany at that time had also witnessed the historic fall. Some had watched it on television and others had heard the news on radio. Amjad Ali, a senior broadcaster and my former colleague, was among them. Ali, who is from Lahore, recalls watching the event in his apartment in Cologne. 'All I could utter was the word "unbelievable"!' he told me. Ali had come to Germany in 1982 to study. Before moving to Cologne, he had lived in West Berlin for many years. Like many other foreign visitors, the Wall had attracted him too. Recalling the pictures, paintings, slogans and messages inscribed on the Wall, he said, 'The slogans were mostly about the liberation movements of Africa, Latin America and Asia. Some paintings showed people from the East crossing over to the West, and vice-versa, through an imaginary hole in the Wall. Messages were mostly about the possible reunification of East and West.' He said that the Berlin Wall was a symbol of fear. For him, the pictures inscribed on the walls were unbelievable. He remembers seeing slogans about former Pakistani premier, late Zulfikar Ali Bhutto. After its fall, Ali had met many South Asians selling pieces of the same Wall near the Brandenburg Gate as souvenirs.

Modern-day Berlin bears few reminders of the concrete walls, barbed wire, observation posts, Checkpoint Charlie and the 'death strip' that had run through its centre until 1989. My visits to Berlin over the years have made me think why such an event could not be replicated in Kashmir. When it existed, Ali told me that nobody would believe that the Berlin Wall would eventually fall—but it did.

Arunava Chaudhuri, a German national of Indian descent, was thirteen at the time of the fall and studying in Kolkata. His parents broke the news to him on the phone. 'Even as a child, I was politically conscious. I made it a point to record the news of the Fall of the Iron Curtain in my school notebook,' he told me in

Bonn. He recalled the mood in Germany in 1990, and the prevalent feeling that Germans were united and invincible. 'East Germany: the evil brother. And then I hear the news about reunification and oneness. It was a great feeling for my parents who originally came from West Bengal. Bengal, too, had suffered greatly because of the pain of the Partition in 1947. My parents fully understood what separation and reunification meant,' he told me.

Kishwar Mustafa, a Pakistani journalist based in Germany and another of my former colleagues, said to me that though the physical wall and barrier do not exist anymore, the mental barrier remains intact. 'In West Berlin, many believe they are economically on a higher footing and intellectually richer, while in the East, many say they are deliberately being left out,' she told me.

In 1989, when the world saw the end of European Communism, the end of the Cold War, the fall of the Iron Curtain, and the vanishing of seemingly impenetrable barriers and borders, India-administered Kashmir witnessed the beginning of armed resistance. Twenty-nine years hence, not much appears to have changed. There are no celebrations in Kashmir. The LoC dividing it remains intact. Promises to make it 'irrelevant' and 'just a line on the map' were scuttled because of continuing hostilities between India and Pakistan. True, the trans-Kashmir Srinagar-Muzaffarabad road was reopened and the historic bus service commenced to ensure that divided families could meet, but the pace of the peace process tested the patience of the people and seemed to vindicate the stand taken by the hardliners. Not much has changed on the ground. Will the time ever come, when like the Berlin Wall, all curtains and barricades dividing a son from his mother, a brother from his sister, and a daughter from her father will vanish and become irrelevant to make this Valley free, peaceful and prosperous?

The 2003–05 bonhomie was frittered away, and India and Pakistan once again pushed Kashmiris to the wall, sending the message that during bouts of peace, Kashmir's core political dispute will be put on the backburner. Indeed, those years represent a lost opportunity. No one seemed to care and make use of these islands of deceptive peace.

Ever since the two neighbours acquired nuclear capability, the Kashmir conflict has been considered a 'nuclear flashpoint' between India and Pakistan. Kashmir's possible resolution or maintaining its status quo defines and determines the future of peace and stability in this volatile portion of South Asia. Pakistan's official position is that Kashmir is its 'jugular vein', while the Indian government's stated claim is that the entire state, including territory under Pakistan's control, is its 'integral part'. Pakistan also believes that,[16]

> Geographically, economically, culturally, and religiously, Kashmir is a part of Pakistan. The overwhelming Muslim character of its population, its strategic position in relation to Pakistan, the flow of its rivers, the direction of its roads, the channels of its trade, the continual intimate association which binds it to the people of Pakistan from time immemorial, link Kashmir indissolubly with Pakistan.

However, the majority in Kashmir contests both these narratives and is involved in a struggle that is as much political as it is a battle for their unique identity and existence. The dominant scholarly narrative is one that reduces the Kashmir conflict to a territorial dispute between India and Pakistan. However, Kashmiris have been involved in many political struggles in the past, and the Kashmiri political resistance draws upon a complex of identity. The rise of hypernationalism in mainland India has prevented the country from a meaningful resolution of the conflict in Kashmir, making it an intractable geopolitical dispute. What seemingly renders it so is Delhi's flat refusal of third-party mediation, and Islamabad's claim on the entire territory of Kashmir and its 'diplomatic, political and moral' support to the struggle of Kashmiris for self-determination in the part administered by India.

It must be remembered that the people of Kashmir did give peace a chance. They made a conscious transition from armed rebellion to peaceful and creative forms of resistance in 2008. They wanted to see the results of a peaceful revolution, especially after Atal Bihari Vajpayee's promise of a dialogue within the ambit of humanism, not the Indian Constitution. Every Kashmiri is a victim and has paid a heavy cost for a political conflict that remains unresolved. How fair is it to expect concessions from a victimized population? On the question of the right to self-determination, some sections of the Indian intelligentsia expect Kashmiris to not only take care of the social fabric of the entire Indian State and its global image as a democratic and secular country, but also the 'aspirations of the minority' within J&K. But why should the majority community in Kashmir be held hostage to the 'aspirations of the minority' within the State and the 'majority within India', when sacrifices to change the existing state of affairs are being offered by Kashmiris alone?

Today, there is a growing feeling in Kashmir that further fragmentation of the right to self-determination should not become another political tool or an obstacle in the resolution of the Kashmir dispute. The political manipulation of Kashmiris must stop in order to create a conducive atmosphere on the ground for a result-oriented, time-bound and sustained dialogue process aimed specifically at a resolution.

When the transition from an armed struggle to a peaceful movement was made—the objective of which was primarily the demand for the right to self-determination—Delhi's response was fierce. During the protest waves of 2008, 2009 and 2010, Kashmiris didn't fight with guns. They didn't have the 'argument of power', but they had 'power in their argument'. Unfortunately, the State continued with its oppressive policies even when the people had consciously made a transition from gun culture to a peaceful uprising in the form of massive protest demonstrations.

Of late, many renowned Indian civil society activists have acknowledged that 'if the resistance in Kashmir remains limited to Palestinian-style "intifada" tactics like stone pelting, the positive international attention for the movement is likely to grow and continue.'[17] In a Track-II conference on Kashmir in New Delhi in

December 2010, noted historian and parliamentarian, Professor Rajmohan Gandhi went on to add that if stone throwing too is dropped, and the resistance is displayed in more dramatic and innovative ways that do not physically injure human beings or destroy property, the 'impact of the movement of Kashmiris will probably be multiplied.' It is also articulated that the chances for the movement are bright if it succeeds in separating itself from other radical movements and formulates a clear ideological stand against religious extremism.

A former member of the Rajya Sabha, Rajmohan Gandhi, however, cautioned that the movement's prospects might be poor if it failed to separate itself from radical movements: '...the Kashmiri movement has bright prospects if it distinguishes and dissociates itself clearly from the fanatical movement, which so far has taken many more Muslim lives than non-Muslim ones.' It is indeed good to know that some elements within Indian civil society remain in favour of a political resolution of the Kashmir dispute. In an article in *The Indian Express* after Burhan Wani's killing, Rajmohan Gandhi urged Kashmiris to 'drop the stone' and use innovative and fresh methods of non-violent protests. 'What is the way out for spirited Kashmiris (or Tibetans and Palestinians)? Do not infuriate the Indian people (or the Chinese people, or the Israelis). Shame and embarrass them, instead.'[18]

The question remains, can a South Asian giant and emerging global market like India afford to allow the conflict in Kashmir to remain unresolved? In the Valley, civilians have been killed in fake encounters and later dubbed 'militants'. Many are arrested and subjected to physical harm. For Kashmiris, it is vital to remind themselves of the ill treatment of yesterday that continues to haunt their realities today. The everyday humiliation and mistreatment that an ordinary Kashmiri faces, and the lack of accountability of the state police, Army and the paramilitary CRPF continues to be a sad reality in Kashmir till this day.

Whenever a Kashmiri travels to any Indian State, 'peace' seems to be the buzzword that is bandied about the most. Almost everyone enjoys lecturing Kashmiris on peace and reconciliation, but few people want to talk about their pain, injustices and the fact that the onus for finding a resolution to this political dispute, which continues to claim innocent lives, is not just on Kashmiris. How can peace be achieved in an atmosphere of oppression? It is far easier to preach peace and reconciliation when someone else is the victim. Only those who live in Kashmir are aware of what has happened in Kashmir over the past twenty-nine years. They know how the State responds. It killed more than sixty civilians in 2008, including at least 120 persons—most of them teenagers and school-going boys—in the 2010 protest demonstrations. As I was writing these lines, in a span of hundred days, over ninety civilians were killed in Kashmir following the death of Burhan Wani.[19]

Most of the civilians killed in pro-azadi protests in 2016 received injuries from bullets, pellets, tear gas shells, and some, like thirty-year-old ad hoc lecturer and PhD scholar Shabir Ahmad Mangoo of Khrew, Pulwama, in south Kashmir, was beaten to death by the Indian Army on the intervening night of 18–19 August.[20] *Greater Kashmir* reported that holding guns, and brandishing knives and iron rods, government soldiers beat around a hundred people in Khrew during a nocturnal raid. Shabir Mangoo was one of those brutally tortured and killed. Similarly, a young Kashmiri principal at a local school, namely Rizwan Asad Pandit, was killed in police custody.[21] The family of the young school principal from Awantipora claimed on Thursday that the victim had torture marks all over his body. Preliminary post-mortem findings have suggested that 'profuse bleeding resulting from multiple injuries' could have caused the death that triggered massive protests in Kashmir. Pandit's family members staged a protest on the Srinagar-Jammu highway at Awantipora Chowk, demanding that the state authorities make public the postmortem report and book the accused who 'murdered our son'.

More than 15,000 civilians were injured,[22] while over 800 received pellet injuries in their eyes—some of them on the verge of losing their vision permanently in one or both eye(s).[23] Twenty-one-year-old Riyaz, a resident of downtown Srinagar, who worked as a guard at a local bank, was killed by CRPF as he was returning home after work on 2 August 2016.[24] More than 300 pellets were found in his body. An autopsy revealed the cause of death to be multiple pellets fired from a close range at his abdomen. The Indian Army regretted the killing of the lecturer[25] while the police registered an FIR against unknown security personnel in Riyaz's case. The then general officer commanding, of the Srinagar Army's sensitive 15 Corps, Lieutenant General Satish Dua, had termed Mangoo's death as 'regrettable' and assured that the Army would investigate the incident. 'It was a joint patrol of army, police and CRPF. We will thoroughly investigate the incident,' he had told reporters in Srinagar.[26]

In such an atmosphere, preaching peace to Kashmiris hurts them like an invective. It reminds me of the immortal words of Pakistani poet Habib Jalib, known for his courage and resistance, written during 1928–93:

'Zulm rahe aur aman bhi ho
Kya mumkin hai, tum hi kaho?'

('When oppression continues unabated,
How can peace be possible?')

NOTES, SOURCES AND REFERENCES

1. Probably PDP-NC had instructions from across the border to form govt, says Ram Madhav. (2018, November 22). Retrieved from https://economictimes.indiatimes. com/news/politics-and-nation/probably-pdp-nc-had-instructions-from-across-the-border-to-form-govt-says-ram-madhav/videoshow/66747138.cms

2. Guha, R. (2017, April 22). The darkness deepens in Kashmir with the rising tide of jingoism. Retrieved from https://www.hindustantimes.com/columns/the-darkness-deepens-in-kashmir-with-the-rising-tide-of-jingoism/story-QExLY9upW1CWxCTmWCawYM.html

3. Katju, M. (2018, November 23). Truth about Kashmir: How militants, Army, politicians cause state's undoing. Retrieved from https://www.theweek.in/news/india/2018/11/23/Truth-about-Kashmir-How-militants-Army-politicians-cause-state-undoing.html

4. Lawrence, W. R. (2017). *The Valley of Kashmir*. Srinagar, Kashmir, India: Gulshan Books Kashmir

5. Guha, R. (2017). *Democrats and Dissenters*. Penguin UK. p. 96

6. Dulat, A. S., & Sinha, A. (2015). *Kashmir: The Vajpayee Years*. Noida, Uttar Pradesh, India: HarperCollins India.

7. Islamic Fundamentalism in Kashmir, India Ethnic Cleansing of Kashmiri Pandits. (n.d.). Retrieved from http://www.panunkashmir.org/fundamentalism.html

8. Singh, V. (2019, March 22). Centre bans Yasin Malik-led JKLF under UAPA. Retrieved from https://www.thehindu.com/news/national/centre-bans-yasin-malik-led-jklf-under-uapa/article26609882.ece

9. Ashiq, P. (2019, March 24). Shutdown in Kashmir over JKLF ban. Retrieved from https://www.thehindu.com/news/national/other-states/shutdown-in-kashmir-over-jklf-ban/article26627636.ece

10. Geelani, S.A. (2015). *Wular Kinaray-III*.

11. Ibid: Chapter 'Hizbul Mujahideen Ki Jung Bandi' (The Truce By Hizbul-Mujahideen), p. 227

12. Lakshman, K. (2003, March 23). Shock And Outrage. Retrieved from https://www.outlookindia.com/website/story/shock-and-outrage/ 219532

13. Geelani, S.A. (2015). *Wular Kinaray-III*.

14. Ibid.

15. Ibid.

16. Speech by Liaquat Ali Khan in the Constituent Assembly (L), on 19 January 1950.

17. This was said by Indian parliamentarian Rajmohan Gandhi in a conference in Delhi in 2010, which was organized by the Centre for Dialogue and Reconciliation. The author was part of the conference.

18. Gandhi, R. (2016, August 29). Drop the stone... Retrieved from https://indianexpress.com/article/opinion/columns/kashmir-violence-unrest-drop-the-stone-3002958/

19. Source 1: Duschinski, H., & Hoffman, B. (2011). Everyday Violence, Institutional Denial and Struggles for Justice in Kashmir. *Race & Class*, 52(4), 44-70.
Source 2: Faheem, F. (2016). Three Generations of Kashmir's Azaadi: A Short History of Discontent. *Economic and Political Weekly*, *51*(35).
Source 3: Kashmir clashes over militant Burhan Wani leave 30 dead. (2016, July 11). Retrieved from https://www.bbc.com/news/world-asia-india-36761527
Source 4: *HUMAN RIGHTS REVIEW 2016* (Rep.). (2016). Srinagar, J&K: Jammu Kashmir Coalition of Civil Society. Retrieved from http://jkccs.net/wp-content/uploads/2018/03/2016-Human-Rights-Review-JKCCS.pdf
Source 5: 223 people killed in Kashmir unrests in 2008, 2010, 2016: Govt tells House. (2017, January 30). Retrieved from https://www.hindustantimes.com/india-news/223-peoplekilled-in-kashmir-unrests-in-2008-2010-2016-govt-tells-house/story-f835qWXDdfOcqAI4DsF2HO.html

20. DAY 41 | Toll 66: Army beats lecturer to death in Khrew. (2016, August 19). Retrieved from http://www.greaterkashmir.com/news/kashmir/story/226092.html

21. Ahmad, M. (2019, March 21). Kashmiri School Principal 'Brutally Tortured, Burnt' Before Custodial Death. Retrieved from https://thewire.in/rights/kashmiri-school-principal-brutally-tortured-burnt-before-custodial-death

22. Akmali, M. (2017, January 24). After 15000 injuries, Govt to train forces in pellet guns. Retrieved from https://www.greaterkashmir.com/news/front-page/after-15000-injuries-govt-to-train-forces-in-pellet-guns/239453.html

23. Indian pellet guns in occupied Kashmir kill, blind and enrage. (2018, November 30). Retrieved from https://www.thenews.com.pk/latest/400167-indian-pellet-guns-in-kashmir-kill-blind-and-enrage

24. Ehsan, M. (2016, August 03). Kashmir: 21-year-old killed by pellets, case registered against security personnel. Retrieved from http://indianexpress.com/article/india/india-news-india/kashmir-21-year-old-killed-by-pellets-case-registered-against-security-personnel-2951122/

25. Naqash, R. (2018, March 25). In Kashmir, the family of a lecturer killed in an Army raid in 2016 no longer hopes for justice. Retrieved from https://scroll.in/article/872572/in-kashmir-the-family-of-a-lecturer-killed-in-an-army-raid-in-2016-no-longer-hopes-for-justice

26. Shah, S. (2017, July 05). Nobody probes the lynching of Khrew lecturer. Retrieved from https://www.greaterkashmir.com/news/kashmir/nobody-probes-the-lynching-of-khrew-lecturer/253893.html

6

A NEW LANGUAGE OF RESISTANCE

I n 1989, when the world celebrated the fall of the Berlin Wall, a popular anti-State armed rebellion broke out in J&K, then backed by Pakistan. This was to change the lives, stories and literature of Kashmiris forever. The generation that grew up at the time was supposed to treat abnormal as 'normal'. Curfews, strikes, arrest sprees, torture and killings became part of our daily vocabulary, our sense of 'normalcy'. We were caught between the guns of the State and non-State actors. And people could not even talk about the state of their hearts and minds.

What happened in Kashmir in 1989 did not happen in isolation. There was a regional context and also a global framework. The decade in question was the 1990s and the event was the battle for Bosnia. At the start of the decade, Yugoslavia was crumbling into chaos and civil war. Germany witnessed the historic fall of the Berlin Wall. Kashmir too had its own context of various vibrant political movements (the Quit Kashmir Movement launched by the Sheikh in the early 1940s against the despotic Dogra regime; a transitory armed struggle, al-Fateh, after the Partition in 1947; and The Plebiscite Front from 1953 to 1975).

Along the way, there were many ruptures.

Kashmir's society has traditionally been politically very conscious. It continues to be so. Usually, the youths get their first lessons on global politics, the Kashmir conflict, and classic and modern literature at the 'waane pyaend' (shop fronts). Normally, at a young age, a Kashmiri is exposed to Johann Wolfgang von Goethe, Mirza Ghalib, George Orwell, Mevlana Rumi, Hafiz Shirazi, Sir Muhammad Iqbal, Friedrich

Nietzsche, Karl Marx, Saadat Hasan Manto, Albert Camus, Frantz Fanon, Faiz Ahmad Faiz, Orhan Pamuk, Ben Okri, Annemarie Schimmel, Haruki Murakami and scores of authors, poets, mystics and sportspersons during the lively and insightful discussions at the shop fronts in downtown Srinagar and in the suburbs and ruburbs of the Himalayan Valley.

Among other things, the onset of militancy and counter-insurgency negatively impacted this rich tradition of perceptive and passionate conversations on world affairs in the once vibrant social settings. But then, the conflict also taught one how to reclaim the lost intellectual and social spaces through creative means. In this situation of a choked social atmosphere and political uncertainty, Kashmiris are finding new and innovative ways to talk, to share tales of tragedies and triumphs, to construct a narrative, and to produce knowledge and literature with the aim to tell their story in their words and document history for posterity.

In the last few years, Kashmir appears to be developing a new culture of resistance, a new language of resistance—intellectual resistance; narrative resistance; something that Kashmiris hope can produce an Anne Frank to document their misery and resilience. It is an attempt in which the narrative of victimhood is not the main contention. The main contention remains Kashmir's memory and dignified resilience through creative forms of defiance. Despite the rich records of resistance—the romantic and mystic literature from the past (in Kashmiri language by Lalla Arifa (Lal Ded), Sheikh Noor-ud-Din aka Nund Reshi, Habba Khatoon, Abdul Ahad Azad, Mehjoor, Amin Kamil, Akhtar Mohiuddin, Rehman Rahi, Mushtaq Kashmiri, Basheer Dada, Zareef Ahmad Zareef and hundreds of other writers, poets and short story writers)—the Kashmir story is now being told by Kashmiris themselves in English and Urdu, besides the native Kashmiri language. This is a visible change. The generation of the 1990s, which lived in conflict, has grown up to tell its story to the world. In this endeavour, Kashmir's young writers, novelists, poets and chroniclers have produced riveting memoirs, novels, literary non-fiction, prison diaries and numerous poetry collections.

For some decades now, thinkers in Kashmir have been expressing their unhappiness over a narrative vacuum in English language. The Kashmir story has usually been told by outsiders. *The Valley of Kashmir* by Walter Lawrence, *Kashmir: A Disputed Legacy* by Alastair Lamb, *The Meadow* by Adrian Levy and Cathy Scott-Clark, *Kashmir: The Unwritten History* by Christopher Snedden, *Kashmir in Conflict* by Victoria Schofield and *The Vale of Kashmir* by John Isaac are some examples. This narrative vacuum has hurt the cause of Kashmir. However, there has been a significant shift in the last two decades or so. Now, some sincere and serious efforts are in full swing to fill this narrative vacuum— particularly the literature of resistance—though the Kashmir story in English language still remains a work in progress.

Given the angst of being constantly under surveillance by the State machinery and the different wings of its security apparatus, Kashmiri youths have found it extremely difficult to contribute adequately to conflict or resistance literature. As mentioned before, resistance in Kashmir is a conscious political response to Delhi's rule, which is largely considered 'foreign'. How do people make the transition from living in constant fear and a culture of silence and suppression, to visible forms of resistance against it? How rich is the literature of resistance in Kashmir? How effective are the different forms of resistance? Unfortunately, the answers to all these questions are not easy. Times are changing fast, as are the dynamics of resistance. Young Kashmir is intelligent and assertive. It refuses to rely on crafty and manipulative one-sided narratives from either New Delhi or Islamabad. It has begun narrating its own story, telling its own tale. It is shouting to the world, 'Listen to me; it is my story—experienced, felt and narrated by me. No one else.'

Srinagar-born Mirza Waheed has written three novels, *The Collaborator, The Book of Gold Leaves* and *Tell Her Everything*. Before him, Basharat Peer had written his memoir, *Curfewed Night*. These books have perhaps become trendsetters and possibly also lit the spark to motivate other Kashmiri youth to document their stories. Mir Khalid's *Jaffna Street* is another addition to Kashmir's conflict literature. Khalid, a surgeon by profession, appears deeply influenced by Western literature. In his work, he has made an attempt to put Kashmir in a larger global context. Dr Rumana Makhdoomi, a senior doctor at SKIMS, has written *White Man in Dark*, which documents the suffering of doctors and paramedics during the years of conflict. Nitasha Kaul, a Kashmiri Pandit economist, author and poet based in London, wrote a novel, *Residue*. There are several other novels, such as *The Half Mother* by Shahnaz Bashir and a short story collection, *Scattered Souls*, by the same author. Other young writers are Feroz Rather, Insha Malik, Shaheen Showket Dar, Huzaifa Pandit and others. Their writings bring out the different layers of the conflict to the fore. New Delhi-based senior journalist Iftikhar Gilani, who was briefly jailed under the Official Secrets Act (OSA) of 1923[1] and who is the son-in-law of Syed Ali Geelani, wrote his prison memoir, *My Days In Prison*, to document his time in Tihar Jail. Gilani's book has been translated in Urdu as *Tihar Main Mere Shab-o-Roz*. Another book, *Of Gardens and Graves*, by Suvir Kaul, a Kashmiri academic based in the US, thoughtfully examines the disruption of everyday life in Kashmir in the years following restive region's militarization in 1990. His investigative essays are a blend of political analysis, literary criticism, memoir and observation. A book named *Witness* by Sanjay Kak is a collection of the photographic documentation of troubled times, by nine Kashmiri photojournalists belonging to different generations.

Siddhartha Gigoo's books, *The Garden of Solitude* and *A Long Dream of Home* (co-written with Varad Sharma), and Rahul Pandita's *Our Moon Has Blood Clots* talked about Kashmir from the Pandits' perspective.

Furthermore, there's Nighat Sahiba and Heena Khan, Kashmir's two young rebel women poets and writers, who are breaking barriers, challenging stereotypes and busting many a myth by writing about womanhood, violence, resistance, resilience and romance. They also write about bullets and blood, pellets and blindness, militarization, custodial disappearances, mass graves and unknown graves, rapes, eve-teasing and stalking—basically, most things under the sun; even the sun itself! With a pen in hand, they are contributing towards rewriting Kashmir's literary history with creativity, courage and conviction.

Sahiba, a young poetess from south Kashmir's Anantnag district, writes in her mother tongue, Kashmiri, and also in Urdu. Her writings are mostly about resistance, conflict, rebellion, romance, feminism and existentialism—and, yes, the pain too. 'I collected my scattered parts to rise,' she told me in an exclusive interview.[2] Sahiba wrote the following verses on the issue of custodial disappearances of Kashmir's youth since the eruption of the armed struggle in 1989:

> *Tarakh royei ase'i shaman hawith tim koat gayi*
> *Anni gatei shahras dil toamblawith tim koat gayi*
> *Poshan hindie anhaar agar tim aangan tschay*
> *Yaadan hyeund barood bichawith tim koat gayi*
> *Goliv yim niey tim qabran maenz moujoodei*
> *Maajan yeim aeis lari tal sawith tim koat gayi*

('Revealing their star-faces, to us by the evenings—
where did they go?
Dazzling the hearts of this light-starved city—
where did they go?
Those snatched by the bullets, are safe in their graves;
Sleeping they were, by their mother's side—
where did they go?')

Outspoken Sahiba tells me that women in Kashmir, especially in the rural parts, hardly have a say in matters like their dress code, choice of food, education, career, relationship and marriage. 'There is no point in waiting for any divine intervention. Nobody will come as a saviour,' she says.

Heena, an engineer by profession, hails from Srinagar. She writes poetry in English and Kashmiri. Besides, she also loves translating other writers' works into the English language. Heena uses nom de guerre 'Rumuz'. One of her poems on militarization in Kashmir is as follows:

Every day while
going to school
the unknown voices
from the concrete bunker
would tease us with
the bollywood songs
and sordid sounds
Today when I,
my eyes, my bosom
my dreams, desires
and my entire being
are porous by their pellets
I spend my time
On a lonely hospital bed
Making some sense
of songs and sounds

And another one, on the continued bloodshed:

Paradise or some hoors
I didn't see any
when the impartial bullet
in a perfect symmetry
found its way through
my weak chest.
The only fear however
that gripped me was
that the tomatoes I had bought
from the market for home
were all smashed, when I fell
with a thud on the ground,
Tomatoes and the blood
it was all red,
mixed syncretically!
Now who would tell the mom
not to wait for tomatoes
and learn to eat without me?

For Rumuz, poetry is an act of rebellion. It is a language of rebellion. One of her poems, titled 'Your Violence Shall Become My Poem Someday', is poignant:

Your violence shall only become
my poem some day
Strange is my world, the world of mad-men
where
the roses bloom in barren lands
sunflowers crave for a moonlight bath
peacocks dance in snowstorms and
nightingales sing the songs of redemption

Your violence shall only become
my poem some day
we are all but Parts of that Whole
equal parts, powerless parts, ephemeral parts
no part can exert violence on any other part
violence is only forgetfulness of being a part
love is being mindful of that supreme Whole

Your violence shall become
my poem some day
don't fret me my dear
come, let's swirl
here none shall make fun of
our worn-out selves.

Here is another of Rumuz's poems:

We all become
each other some day
as if some established mafia
of wandering spirits
rent our bodies
temporarily
and then leave
to make way for another.

a lover's spirit
a beloved's spirit
a victim's, a tormentor's spirit
I was, what he is today
I am, what someone had been
No spirits allow
the remembrance
or the request
of other that had been
or the one that is to come
in the helpless body
the body is blindly in love
always,
with the resident spirit
which was yesterday
my enemy's tenant.
We all become
each other some day
All claims be cremated!

Kashmir's literary world has produced names like Naseem Shifai, Rukshana Jabeen, Deeba Nazir, Nighat Sahiba, Rumuz and Rafia Wali, besides others. Well-known Kashmiri women poets who write in the English language include London-based acclaimed novelist, poet and academic Dr Nitasha Kaul, US-based academic and researcher Ather Zia and cultural anthropologist Mona Bhan, and Srinagar-based lecturer Syeda Afshana. That said, a vacuum exists in Kashmiri poetry and short story writing by women. It should be a moment of collective introspection as to why Kashmir does not have many significant women post Lal Ded and Habba Khatoon in this regard.

In Urdu, many young Kashmiris have written memoirs, prison diaries, short stories, novels and poetry that bring to light various aspects of the conflict. Resistance leader Anjum Zamarud Habib has written two books: a prison memoir, *Prisoner No. 100: An Account Of My Nights And Days In An Indian Prison*, and her autobiography *Nigah-e-Anjum*. Nayeema Ahmad Mahjoor, former BBC broadcaster-turned-pro-Delhi politician and former chairperson of J&K State Commission for Women, wrote her debut novel, *Dehshat Zadi* in Urdu (the English translation is called *Lost in Terror*). Late journalist Maqbool Sahil and short story writer Ghulam Nabi Shahid also contributed to Kashmir's conflict literature with their prison memoirs and short story collections respectively. I'm tempted to share two short stories by Ghulam Nabi Shahid[3] here, which I have translated from Urdu to English.

'JAWAAB DO' ('ANSWER ME')

Heads lowered, in groups of two or three, they are holding placards and marching silently towards the park located in the heart of the city. They have assembled here on the 10th of every month for many years to protest. Right in the middle of the city, and between two bustling markets, this park is a centre of attraction for its beauty and romantic atmosphere, especially during summer. To one side, facing the main square, a hoarding was erected just near the Chinar tree, about three feet inside the park's iron fence. On it, as a backdrop, the Valley's charm, its beautiful hills, waterfalls, streams and lakes were etched with such deftness and dexterity that every passerby could not resist looking at the hoarding over and over again.

These people in small groups enter the park and assemble near the big Chinar tree facing the main square. With her fatigued eyes, Khadeeja too looks at it with a placard in her hand. To her, the shade of the Chinar appears like deep black smoke. Moving away from it, Khadeeja proceeds toward the hoarding; her back resting on one of its pillars. As the event begins, all the people assembled in the park pick up their respective placards to stage a demonstration. The pedestrians don't move an inch, their eyes fixed on the demonstrators. They look at them with a sense of dispossession and helplessness. The protests continue. Khadeeja looks at the people... She gathers some courage... Slowly, she stands up and lifts her placard towards the sky with her trembling hands...

The assembled crowds on the road fix their eyes on the upright hoarding, on which the following lines are inscribed:

'agar firdous barooye zameen ast
hameein ast o hameein ast o hameein ast'

(If there is paradise on earth
it is here, it is here, it is here)

Right below this verse, is Khadeeja's placard: '*Mera Firdous kahan hai?*' ('Where is my Firdous?').

[Firdous is the name of Khadeeja's son, which when translated into English means 'paradise']

BAAZYAAFT (DISCOVERY)

Since Asr prayers before dusk, there was a lot of activity inside Ahad Lone's house, situated close to a mosque in the mohalla. Neighbours were somewhat perplexed at the commotion. As the time for Maghrib (evening) prayers arrived, speculations over the new developments in Ahad Lone's home were rife.

Along with his neighbours, Ahad Lone came out of the mosque after offering mandatory Isha (late evening) prayers. On finding him somewhat contented and relaxed, they asked him, 'Ahad Lone, what's the matter? Did you get any news about Aslam?'

'Yes,' Ahad Lone said self-assuredly after a brief pause.

'Where is he, when is he coming, has he returned already?' asked one of the neighbours emotionally.

'No, Aslam is not returning,' said Ahad Lone, with the same poise. 'His grave has been discovered.'

These two stories touch on two important subjects: custodial disappearances and the discovery of mass graves in Kashmir. For hundreds of families whose relatives—mostly male—have fallen prey to custodial disappearances, the struggle for justice is, in many ways, a continued battle between memory and forgetfulness. They insist they will not give up their fight, they will not forget and they will not forgive.

Among the serious crimes committed in J&K, government forces are accused of 8,000–10,000 Kashmiris' enforced custodial disappearances since the eruption of armed uprising twenty-nine years ago.[4] There are also credible reports about the discoveries of over 6,000 unmarked and mass graves.[5] At a press conference in 2008, the state government headed by the then CM Omar Abdullah had admitted that the number of those who have disappeared in J&K was about 4,000. The government also claimed that many of those listed as 'disappeared' may have crossed the LoC to receive 'arms training' to fight India. Abdullah, after formally announcing the rehabilitation policy for ex-rebels on 23 November 2010, had informed the J&K Legislative Assembly in 2013 that at least 3,974 militants from the Kashmir Valley had crossed the LoC for arms training. Currently, there are 4,088 persons listed as 'missing' in government records, many of whom are believed to be stationed in Pakistan and PaK.

The Association of Parents of Disappeared Persons (APDP) is an organization that seeks justice for those whose relatives have disappeared in custody. It is headed by the 'Iron Lady of Kashmir', Parveena Ahanger, a mother whose sixteen-year-old son, Javed, disappeared in custody in January 1990. Despite her personal tragedy, or perhaps because of it, Parveena is determined in her quest for justice. Members of APDP are mostly women who have lost their husbands, or mothers who await the return of their sons.

Parveena continues to wait for a miracle that would return her son, Javed, to her. Javed was picked up by government forces from his home in the early 1990s. In several of my interviews with Parveena, at her home in Narkura Budgam and at the APDP's office in Srinagar, I have seen a spark in her eyes that betrays her never-say-die attitude. Apart from her personal crusade, she looks after the families of women whose husbands have disappeared and who are known by the poignant term, 'half-widows'. A 'half-widow' is a woman whose husband has either 'disappeared' in custody by government forces or non-State actors like pro-India counter-insurgency bands in the mid-1990s. No one knows the exact number of women living their life as 'half-widows' since the outbreak of anti-State armed rebellion in the Kashmir Valley. It is an expression that has become part of Kashmir's narrative and lexicon post-1989. On the 10th of every month, Parveena leads a peaceful sit-in along with other women at Srinagar's city centre. They quietly assemble in a small circle, holding placards and pictures of disappeared husbands, sons and family members. Not a single angry slogan is raised.

Parveena, along with other members of the APDP, organizes this monthly symbolic sit-in protest with the aim of impressing upon local authorities the need to provide answers. Unfortunately, in Kashmir, the regime does not like the idea of being questioned. There exists a wide chasm between the rights that citizens should have and what they actually enjoy in a place hit by a long-standing conflict. Human rights activists—those committed to preserving dignity and honour, and those interested in documenting people's tragedies—have found the going incredibly tough. Some have died in the course of their work, some survived miraculously in deadly attacks and others are just about managing to survive in an atmosphere of persistent fear and uncertainty.

Parveena has told me time and again that she won't give up her struggle and would continue to seek justice for her son and others. 'Is law only for people like Burhan? What about ordinary people like me and my son, Javed? Are these forces not governed by any law?' she said to me when I last met her in August 2016 in Budgam. In the latest civilian uprising, another son of hers was injured by pellets. She said that neither the then CM Mehbooba Mufti nor the former CM Omar Abdullah could understand the pain and agony of Kashmir's mothers because they have not lost their children to the conflict.

Over the last fifteen years that I have known Parveena, I have never seen her lose faith in her struggle even once. She appears as strong today as she was years ago. Government forces might have killed one Burhan, she says, but a thousand Burhans will rise to fight the State aggression and violence in Kashmir—a sentiment that is often echoed in the Valley after Burhan Wani's killing.

On 30 August, the International Day for the Disappeared, programmes are organized in the Kashmir Valley. Poems are recited, plays are staged and paintings exhibited to highlight Kashmir's pain with an objective to remember those who perhaps exist but are missing, or might have been killed but their bodies not handed over to their families. The Parveena Ahanger-led faction of the APDP also participates in these programmes to raise the demand for justice.

On 30 August 2014, JKCCS, a human rights body, staged a play, 'Be te Chus Shahid' ('I'm also a witness'), by a young theatre director, Arshad Mushtaq, on the theme of enforced custodial disappearances.

'Be te Chus Shahid' begins with an elderly man carrying a red box full of letters. He looks at an electric pole nearby. He is tired and says that much time has passed; he has been on this journey for a long time. He is unaware of his destination and how much more time it would take to reach it. The going is often tough. While the journey is tedious and wearisome, the old man says, it is important to apply one's mind and continue the process of thinking. Thinking is critical—he repeats several times. Had everyone cared to think before acting, there would not have been a problem. The journey would have been much easier.

Somewhere down the line, continues the old man, we find someone who reminds us to think. Otherwise, Satan is omnipresent with his honey tongue to deviate us from our main journey, our primary objective. He goes to sit by a stone. Once again, he emphasizes the importance of thinking. A voice from the audience rings out, 'Who has time for thinking? Come to the point. Say what you actually want to say'.

The old man responds that the burden of thinking is not mandatory for everyone, only for those who are prepared to think.

He says that he knows the audience might be wondering who he is, where he has come from and what exactly he is carrying with him. 'I'm the one who I always have been. I'm a Kashmiri. And obviously when I'm a Kashmiri, I would have come from some corner of Kashmir, and I belong to Kashmir.'

Before the old man can clarify what he is carrying in his box, we hear the sound of someone approaching. It is a young boy who is looking for someone, whom he calls out loudly. There is no one there other than the old man. He spots the boy and asks him to come closer. Annoyed, the young boy refuses, saying that the old man isn't even an acquaintance. A poignant conversation between the old man and the young boy (two generations of Kashmiris) becomes the main plot of the play.

The young boy gets irritated when the old man talks about 'knowing, thinking and identity'. He arrogantly asks the old man to mind his own business and not meddle in his affairs. In the next scene, the boy is waiting for a friend to play a cricket match. The old man does not seem to mind the boy's haughtiness and impatience. He repeats to himself that he has been on a tiresome journey. The boy is intrigued and asks the old man about his journey. Given his age, the old man should have stayed at home trying to discover God, the boy cheekily advises him. If he wanted to undertake a long journey, he should have done it when he was young.

The old man smiles. He was awake and aware when he was young, he says, and it is because of his wakefulness that he has set out on this all-important journey. 'What journey?' asks the boy again. 'Would you care to explain? What is in the box you're carrying?' the boy asks.

After a pause, the old man replies, 'It contains my identity. Not only mine, but yours too. Also of many others. There are many messages in this.'

Someone calls out to the old man from off the stage. He responds.

The old man hands his box of letters to the young boy, who takes it rather reluctantly. The old man rushes offstage after insisting the boy take good care of the 'amaanat' (entrustment). After hesitating a bit, the boy starts reading the letters one by one. He is astounded and overwhelmed. The first letter is about Hilal, whose mother is calling out to him and hoping for his miraculous return. The young boy picks up another letter. This story is even more painful. It is from a son to his father, who disappeared in custody. The son had passed his examination and been promoted to the fifth standard. All he wants is for his father to know that he had passed his exams. The boy takes out a third letter from the box. This one is about a man who has lowered seven unidentified bodies into the grave. He marks the bodies in his own way, with the hope that if ever someone comes to enquire about them, they would be able to ascertain the identities of the dead.

As he reads the letters, tears trickle down the young boy's cheeks. He begins to understand the importance of the old man's journey, and what he has been entrusted with. Meanwhile, the old man reappears on stage and asks the young boy to return the box of letters.

'I hope I didn't take too long to return,' he says. The young boy shakes his head and says that he won't give the letters back. 'Are you sure; are you aware, and ready, for this long journey?' asks the old man. Confident, the boy says that he is prepared and aware that the box contains more than just letters. It contains his existence, his identity, his story and the story of his fellow Kashmiris, the collective journey of their existence. 'And like you, I'm also a witness,' the boy says. *'Be te Chus Shahid.'*

As the old man turns to leave, the boy calls him back to ask one last question. 'Tell me where had you gone? Who called you?'

'I was called by the one who entrusted me with this responsibility,' he replies. He says he is convinced that the young boy is the right person to carry on the journey and mission of remembrance as a conscious witness.

'Yes, I'm a witness. *Be te Chus Shahid*', the boy reiterates. Both the old man and the young boy look towards the sky. The sun rises.

★

Apart from the splendour of its landscape, the beauty of its freshwater lakes and Mughal gardens, its people's hospitality and its Sufi culture of tolerance and transcendental spirituality, Kashmir is also known for its humour, satire and creativity. Through the years of oppression and suffering, Kashmiris have learned to laugh and poke fun at themselves and their perceived oppressors. In the new culture of resistance, hidden forms of expression are as relevant as the visible forms, displayed through slogans, graffiti, cartoons, music, protests, sit-ins, hunger strikes, candlelight vigils, and even stone pelting. How effective are the different forms of resistance? And what exactly constitutes creative forms of resistance?

As touched upon before, there is a widespread perception among the people that the narratives of India and Pakistan on Kashmir are written from hegemonic positions with monolithic projections that gloss over the realities and complexities of the conflict. These contentious perceptions have induced creative responses and endeavours, which go beyond prose, to investigate and study in order to challenge representations seen as 'propagandist' and 'rhetorical.' That is why Kashmir has witnessed the emergence of new indigenous voices that not only offer fresh perspectives but also give us a sense of how Kashmiris have lived and experienced their conflict. Cartoonists like Suhail H. Naqshbandi and Mir Suhail Qadri, rap artists like Mohammad Muneem and MC Kash, and musicians like Ali Saffudin are some of those who are employing creative forms to tell Kashmir's story. Kashmir's new literature of resistance cannot be brushed aside as merely a literature of propaganda or of protest. Rather, this new culture of writing and documentation offers an outlet to suppressed aspirations and an articulation of collective memories of pain and resilience.

Kashmir's award-winning artist and sculptor, Masood Hussain, came up with an artistic portrayal of the civilian uprising after Burhan Wani's killing. He told Barkha Dutt on NDTV 24x7, in a programme aired on 18 August 2016, that he remained a silent spectator for a month, but once he saw pellet-hit children lying on hospital beds in distress and pain, something stirred within him. He saw the future of the young steeped in darkness and their dreams crushed.[7] As a result, Hussain decided to protest through his artwork. His most striking artwork includes a Kashmiri child holding a schoolbag full of stones; two boys, who have been blinded by pellets, walking together, a long shadow cast ahead of them; and a boy and a girl with pellet-marked faces, wearing oversized sunglasses. His images are self-explanatory, and he calls them 'silent images'. These have replaced the beautiful landscape, social life and culture of his earlier paintings.

Generally, Kashmiri women used to frequently visit shrines, which are located at every nook and cranny of the Valley and also act as cathartic spaces apart from being places of spirituality and meditation. Dr Arshad Hussain, one of Kashmir's leading psychiatrists, often tells me that in Kashmir, 'God is a doctor', meaning that faith in God and the practice of visiting shrines in Kashmir has actually been a liberating, cathartic and therapeutic experience for many. Women used to visit yarbals where they would wash their clothes and talk. Many Kashmiris would also visit famous alcoves of almonds like Badamwari in Srinagar to spend time with their spouses, kids, parents and grandparents. Because of the conflict, uncertainty, urbanization, environmental degradation and modern lifestyles, some of these spaces have been lost in the last three decades. That's why people in Kashmir now employ various means to vent their inner feelings to stay sane.

Kashmir today has many cafés and other public spaces where the young and assertive generation can be seen writing their stories, creating pieces of art, making cartoons, reciting poetry and discussing contemporary politics passionately. Before the outbreak of the current conflict, there were many spaces, like Srinagar downtown's waane pyaend, which would act both as an intellectual and a cathartic space during the continued battle for existence and identity. Many attempts are now being made to reclaim these lost social and intellectual spaces. There are many who are making efforts to create such spaces for discussions and debates, and conducting talks and workshops on important sociopolitical and cultural themes. Yet, it is difficult to foretell what this new phase of resistance might bring about.

Among the creative chroniclers of Kashmir's contemporary history, one name stands out—the late Agha Shahid Ali, who inspired many with his poetry collections like *The Country Without a Post Office*. He is often credited for narrating the Kashmir story to the wider world.

Mushtaq Kashmiri is another poet whose name immediately comes to mind when one thinks of Kashmir. Born in a middle-class family in Srinagar, Mushtaq migrated to Pakistan with his wife and four daughters. Named Ghulam Mohammad Bhat, he shot to literary fame as 'Mushtaq Kashmiri'. After his poems and writings in Kashmiri and Urdu upset the powers-that-be, he went into a self-imposed exile. As per reports, the Jammu and Kashmir Cultural Academy has not kept records of his work for obvious reasons.

Poetry, it is widely believed, speaks unpalatable truths and unravels many a knot. And it unveils secrets, too. Prose might make people think about what is happening around them, but poetry gives them ways of understanding and interpreting. I remember several evocative conversations with a widely respected humourist-poet, Zareef Ahmad Zareef, at his ancestral home in downtown Srinagar, very close to the famous shrine of Sheikh Hamzah Makhdoom Saheb (also known as Hazrat 'Sultan-ul-Arifeen') on the southern side of Hari Parbat Hill. Zareef is renowned for his wisecracks and witticisms in Kashmiri. It doesn't take the old man long to have his audiences in stitches with his witty remarks and satirical one-liners. He delivers amazing dialogues with utmost ease, especially in the language he knows the best—Kashmiri. One of his collections, titled *Taaran Garee* (Trickery), covers the complexities of the Kashmir conflict in a satirical manner and was well received.

Once, Zareef imparted an unforgettable lesson about driving on Kashmir's roads to me. 'Look, whenever you see an autorickshaw in front of you indicating it is turning right, please bear in mind that it will inevitably turn left.' His advice has stood me in good stead! Though the audience bursts into laughter whenever Zareef is on stage, he manages to keep a straight face. He hurls his sharp remarks at an impressive speed. But, the circumstances in Kashmir have led to the emergence of many speed breakers even on the 'highways of poetry'. During an interview, Zareef told me that he no longer enjoys writing satire and humour. 'How can I even make (an) attempt to think of making the people laugh with humour and satire, when many of them are being killed, tortured, tormented, raped, maimed and disappeared in custody?'

Besides the above, dramas are also staged with themes that are relevant to the Kashmir discourse, for instance, an I-card becoming the most important document in one's life. Stepping out without one can mean a severe thrashing by government troops; in some cases, it might even lead to detention, interrogation, arrest and sometimes death. During the 1990s, during what became routine frisking in private and public buses, government forces personnel would ask for identity proofs. If someone had forgotten to carry their I-card, it meant a catastrophe.

Mohammad Amin Bhat, a well-known theatre personality in Kashmir, had written a play about the importance of this document in Kashmir and how a piece of paper came to be valued more than an individual's life. 'Shanaakhti Card, Kashmir Aur Drama' (Identity Card, Kashmir and Drama) was screened at Srinagar's Tagore Hall in 2006.

Shareef-ud-Din Shehri, the lead character, is a middle-class state government employee who makes ends meet with great difficulty. One day, while on his way to office, Shareef-ud-Din's pocket is picked and he loses his wallet, which had his I-card along with some money and other documents. As fate would have it, the pickpocket meets with a road accident and dies on the spot. His face is disfigured beyond recognition. After finding the I-card, wallet and other things in his possession, the police personnel investigating the case conclude that the deceased is Shareef-ud-Din. His family is informed and the body handed over to them.

Despondent about his lost wallet, Shareef-ud-Din reaches home. He is shocked to find his family, friends and relatives mourning his 'death'. He tries to convince them that he's alive, but no one believes him. 'We've seen your I-card and dead body, why should we believe you, you impostor!' Disappointed, Shareef-ud-Din decides to arrange for his own burial despite being alive.

✱

As the curfew and killings continued in Kashmir after Burhan Wani's death, the united APHC camp decided to use new modes of expression to intensify their protest campaign. Syed Ali Geelani himself launched a graffiti campaign by painting 'Go India Go Back' on a wall outside his Hyderpora residence-cum-office. Many youth, some masked and some not, followed Geelani's example to paint walls with pro-independence and pro-Burhan graffiti across the Valley. Senior Indian journalist and columnist, Prem Shankar Jha, on his visit to Kashmir in August 2016 mentioned that he had never before witnessed such unanimity of the azadi sentiment since the first outbreak of armed revolt many years ago. He noted that there was a wall of support for the basic demand of azadi from New Delhi that stretched across every stratum of Kashmir society.[8]

> What India is facing is not, therefore, another bout of unrest to be managed and then forgotten, but an uprising. The last such upsurge had followed the Gowkadal massacre of January 1990, when the Kashmir police* had opened fire on a large, unarmed procession from both ends of a street, killing between twenty-four and fifty-five unarmed civilians. This had instantly converted what had till then been a simmering revolt into a general uprising.

A week before 8 July 2016, I met JKLF chief, Mohammad Yasin Malik, at his office in Abi Guzar, Srinagar, for an interview. It was Ramzan, and Eid-ul-Fitr was a few days away. After unprecedented restrictions on Kashmir's resistance leaders, which had been imposed by the PDP-BJP government since March 2015, pro-azadi

---

*Mr Jha wrongly mentions the Kashmir police here; it was actually the CRPF.

leaders were enjoying some respite in the sacred month of fasting. Malik blamed the state government for targeting him in particular, because of an increasing perception that he was becoming the most visible face of the resistance. And so, he was being arrested, detained and placed under house arrest—at times, without much of a reason. Another theory was that since the JKLF was involved in the kidnapping of Rubaiya Sayeed, Mehbooba Mufti's sister, in the 1990s, the government was, therefore, especially vengeful towards Malik. Despite the tightening of restrictions, the JKLF was allowed to organize an iftar party to break the daily fast on 2 July, for which invitations were also extended to prominent members of Sikh and Pandit communities. Participants at JKLF's iftar party numbered about 4,000.

Talking about political dissent, choking of spaces and creative forms of protest, Malik told me about his marathon signature campaign in 2003. He told me how his party had collected signatures and thumb impressions of more than 1.5 million (15 lakh) people across the length and breadth of the state, all of whom expressed a desire to have a say in the resolution of the Kashmir dispute. Malik claimed that his campaign was the only transparent democratic exercise to have happened in J&K. Under his leadership, the JKLF launched its campaign on a massive scale, which lasted for over three-and-a-half years, to ascertain the wishes and aspirations of the people of the state. It was hailed as a peaceful, democratic and creative exercise.

The JKLF had presented copies of the campaign in a compact disc to the then PM, Dr Manmohan Singh, and Pakistan's then president, Pervez Musharraf, in 2006. Malik also said that he sent copies of the campaign to over 150 embassies of the world. My interview with Malik happened in the backdrop of the united pro-azadi camp's ten-point resolution, which, according to both factions of the APHC and the JKLF, was endorsed by a large number of people across the Valley on 1 July 2016. The resolution was aimed at fighting the then PDP-BJP government's alleged anti-Kashmir policies.

'Dialogue is the first and last hope in any conflict-resolution process, but it is unfortunate that New Delhi's undemocratic policies have forced the people of Kashmir to lose faith in the institution of dialogue,' Malik said. New Delhi had even held talks with the military generals of Pakistan (in an obvious reference to Musharraf), but it was shying away from holding talks with a democratically elected government in Pakistan, which was then headed by Nawaz Sharif (and is currently headed by Imran Khan). He insisted that Kashmir is the principal party in the Kashmir dispute.

After its signature campaign, JKLF also launched Safar-e-Azadi (Journey to Freedom), a campaign which included holding public rallies and meeting people in different pockets of Kashmir. The government of the time did not allow Malik the space to complete his campaign.

Days after my exclusive interview with him and his successful iftar, Burhan Wani was killed and another cycle of Kashmir's summer uprising began. Malik's freedom was short-lived. He was arrested again and lodged in jail. His jail journeys have become a new normal for him. On 22 February 2019, Yasin Malik was arrested and kept under detention at police station Kothibagh Srinagar. Fifteen days after his detention, he was booked under PSA and shifted to Kot Balwal Jail.

★

Times are changing and so are the dynamics of resistance in Kashmir. However, one expression of anti-Delhi that has remained consistent over the years is Kashmiris' overt and vocal support of Pakistan's cricket team. When India and Pakistan battle it out in a cricket field, the hearts of a majority of Kashmiris beat for Pakistan. Though there's no research on this, I can make a claim that more than 85 per cent of Kashmiris want Pakistan to win against India in cricket matches. However, this should not be seen as an expression of their desire to merge with Pakistan.

Since early childhood, I have witnessed the extraordinary support from Kashmiris—young and old, boys and girls, men and women—for Pakistan's national cricket team. Walls in homes are often adorned with posters and framed pictures of the legendary cricketer-turned-politician Imran Khan, who led Pakistan to World Cup victory in 1992; left-arm paceman Wasim Akram, known as the 'Sultan of Swing'; 'Boom Boom' Shahid Afridi, renowned for his big hitting and crafty leg-spin bowling and Waqar Younis, the former captain known worldwide for his toe-crushing yorkers. I distinctly remember a close relative jumping in joy and hitting his head on iron hooks suspended from the ceiling, as soon as Javed Miandad hit a famous last ball six off Chetan Sharma at Sharjah in the mid-1980s. Similar scenes are routine whenever the Indian and Pakistani cricket teams clash. I also remember many teary-eyed older people sitting on their prayer mats and raising their hands in prayer for the success of the Pakistani cricket team whenever there was an India-Pakistan match. For many Kashmiris, India-Pakistan cricket matches are like 'war minus the shooting'—the mother of all encounters!

In 1983 and 1986, the Indian national cricket team played two international games, against the West Indies and Australia, at Srinagar's SKCS. Like everyone else, I too was glued to the television screen at a friend's place on 9 September 1986 as a young child. Steve Waugh, one of my all-time favourite cricketers, was playing in the match. Allan Border, the former Aussie skipper, was judged 'Man of the Match' for scoring a match-winning knock of ninety. The Indian team did not find many supporters at the stadium cheering for them. Rather, they were treated as 'foreigners' and 'unwelcome guests' and booed. India was humbled by three wickets. I remember feeling happy and satisfied over their debacle on Kashmir's soil. History books and the memoirs by some cricketers inform us that this was the second international match that India hosted at Srinagar's SKCS. The anti-State armed revolt in Kashmir began three years after the India-Australia cricket encounter.

In his book, *Runs'n Ruins*, Sunil Gavaskar reminisces about a match in 1983, when the reception that the Indian team got wasn't all that different from 1986. India was the surprise world champion in 1983, beating the great West Indies. The Indians hosted West Indies in a five-match one day international (ODI) series in October 1983. The first match was played at SKCS in Srinagar. Gavaskar rated the Kashmiri crowd as amongst the 'worst he has seen in his life'. He notes in his book:

> ...we were stunned by the change. As the Indian players came into the arena to loosen up and do their physical exercises, they were booed by some sections of the crowd. This was unbelievable. Here we were in India and being hooted even before a ball had been bowled. Being hooted at after a defeat is understandable, but this was incredible. Moreover, there were many in the crowd shouting pro-Pakistan slogans which confounded us, because we were playing the West Indies and not Pakistan. The West Indians were as surprised as we were but were obviously delighted to find support in their first big encounter against us after their defeat in the Prudential Cup finals.

The Indian team eventually lost that game by a margin of twenty-eight runs, a revised target in a match reduced to twenty-two overs in the second innings when the West Indians batted. Chasing a modest target set by the Indians, the visitors didn't lose even a single wicket. Sadly for the Indian team, their players had to witness the same scenes during their clash with the Aussies, in September 1986. International cricket games eventually stopped being played in Kashmir, partly because of the lack of support for India and partly due to the armed movement that began in 1989.

There are some Kashmiris, especially those who play and understand sports beyond ideologies and politics, who do admire Indian cricket stars like Sachin Tendulkar, Mohammad Azharuddin, Sourav Ganguly, Virat Kohli, Mahendra Singh Dhoni and Rohit Sharma, among others, but there is no doubt that most Kashmiris want Pakistan to prevail over India in a cricket game. I'm sure that India's 0-4 whitewash in 2011, and 4-1 in 2018, at the hands of England; its successive defeats in the test series Down Under in 2012; and its test series defeats in South Africa, would have at least healed some of the 'wounds' that were inflicted on my cousin Rafiq Geelani and many other Kashmiris like him, who had found it difficult to digest it when India was crowned 'World Champion' in the fifty-over format in 2011. Unpredictable victories in tests by the Pakistani team over the #1-ranked English side in the United Arab Emirates and then drawing a four-match test series in England to be ranked as the #1 test team in the world in 2016 (in August 2016, Pakistan also became the #1 International Cricket Council-ranked test side after levelling their four-match test series against England) brought smiles back on the faces of many Kashmiris. Kashmir erupted in joy when a weak Pakistani team led by Sarfaraz Ahmed thrashed a stronger Team India under Virat Kohli in the Champions Trophy finals in England in 2017. It was almost a replica of Pakistan's World Cup triumph under Imran Khan in 1992.

Anyway, I had mixed feelings when India and Sri Lanka were battling it out during the 2011 World Cup final at the Wankhede Stadium in Mumbai. I was in Digha in West Bengal at the time. The mood inside the hotel room was somewhat gloomy. I had gone there with my cousins for a break, but India's victory had spoiled the party. I wanted the Lankans to lift the trophy, but the cricketer in me said 'Well played!' to India. Team India deserved to win. Yuvraj Singh had batted and bowled splendidly throughout the tournament and left-arm pacer Zaheer Khan too had been magnificent with the ball in his hand.

Being older, I delivered what I thought was an impressive and mature lecture on sportsmanship and the sportsman spirit. It seemed to work, and soon, we were outside the hotel where overjoyed crowds were celebrating, drinking, dancing and smearing colours on each other.

Even though much is said in modern times about not mixing sports and politics, it really doesn't work that way. After the terror attacks in Mumbai in 2008, not a single Pakistani cricketer featured in the lucrative Indian Premier League (IPL). These are the sad realities of the times we live in.

'Politics should not be mixed with sports.'

'Cricket is just a game.'

'After all, it is just sports.'

These are worn-out phrases that are often repeated when our favourite cricket team loses; and the team we don't want to see on top, wins. Cricket is a sport. Sport is politics. Politics is sport. Cricket is politics. You can't separate the two. If you think you can, you're simply being delusional. And those who proudly claim to have graduated to another level and learnt the art of detaching cricket from the debate of 'freedom' are simply lying.

'I am always amazed when I hear people saying that sport creates goodwill between the nations, and that if only the common peoples of the world could meet one another at football or cricket, they would have no inclination to meet on the battlefield,' George Orwell wrote in his famous essay, 'The Sporting Spirit'.

When India defeated Pakistan in the semi-finals of the coveted Cricket World Cup at Mohali in 2011, many Kashmiris felt dejected and defeated. India celebrated; Kashmir mourned Pakistan's loss. India and Pakistan met again in the Asia Cup in 2012. India won again. Kashmir's streets, I'm told, wore a deserted look. India celebrated; Kashmiris felt a pang in their hearts. When Pakistan was finally crowned Asian Champions in 2012, there were celebrations in Kashmir. It was as if Eid and Diwali had arrived together. This happens every time Pakistan wins, and India loses. Or when India's early exit from any big tournament is guaranteed.

An India-Pakistan encounter in the middle of that twenty-two-yard strip is not just a cricket match in Kashmir. Kashmiris, more often than not, find some rationale to 'politicize' this game of glorious uncertainties. A friend argues, 'When the Indian media sells an influx of tourists in Kashmir as an "indicator of normalcy" and a "goodbye to the freedom struggle", why should Kashmiris not want India to lose a cricket match, even if they are playing a minnow?'

In his mid-thirties, Faheem Gundroo is a trained engineer who feels proud of his 'bond with green'. His unconditional love for Pakistani cricket has a history. 'Nothing unites the Kashmiri nation more than Pakistan's victory in cricket,' he writes in his blog. 'During the '71 war, my father and a friend would stand atop the terrace in Jammu and shout slogans while waving green flags whenever a Pakistani jet flew by, unmindful of the wrath from neighbours belonging to other faiths,' he argues. 'The love and affection for Pakistan comes naturally to us (Kashmiris); we are fed upon it. Our stories are entwined with it—and the Stoics wouldn't know why!'

Kashmiris praise Pakistan's team primarily to hurt India's 'ego' and, in some way, retaliate for all the times when the hawkish sections of the Noida- and Mumbai-based media wickedly mixes up issues of routine administration and matters of day-to-day governance with the larger dynamics of the Kashmir dispute, and sell tourism, winter sports and civic polls in Kashmir as an alternative to the promised 'plebiscite'.

If an Indian fan boasts about Sachin Tendulkar's world record of hundred international tons, a Kashmiri argues about the fastest ball being bowled by the 'Rawalpindi Express', Shoaib Akhtar; a hundred scored by Afridi in thirty-seven balls and Akram and Younis being in the all-time highest wicket-takers list (#2 and #3, respectively[9]) in limited overs' cricket. An India fan reminds Kashmiris about Pakistan's defeats at the hands of India in the World Cup quarter-finals (1996), semis (2011) and the T20 final (2007), while Kashmiris brag about the overall edge Pakistan holds over India by having won seventy-three out of 131 ODIs played against India.

Kashmiris also remind Team India's fans about the series victories by Pakistan in India under Imran Khan's leadership in the 1980s, which included Javed Miandad's sixer off Chetan Sharma's last ball at Sharjah (1986); Aaqib Javed's hat-trick and seven-wicket haul against India at Sharjah (1991); Saeed Anwar's mammoth innings of 194 against India in Chennai (1997); the famous victories in the Chennai test in January 1999; Shoaib Akhtar 'disturbing the furniture' of Dravid and Tendulkar in two successive deliveries at the Eden Gardens (1999); the 2-1 victory in a three-match series when the Misbah-ul-Haq-led ODI side toured India and played three matches at Chennai, Kolkata and Delhi, in which Pakistan won the first two matches comfortably while

India won the third match at Delhi by a slim margin (2012–13); and Pakistan's victory in the Champions Trophy finals against India (2017).

On 22 March 2012, the day when Pakistan was crowned the Asia Cup champion, top-ranking police officer S.M. Sahai chose to update his Facebook status with this cheeky message, 'Sometimes Pakistan also should be happy.' Cricket isn't apolitical as such in Kashmir. Mr Sahai got some befitting replies in the comments that followed his post.[10]

> I am the 1992 world cup winner. I am the 2009 T20 world champion. I am the last ball sixer at Sharjah. I ended the career of Kris Srikanth with that ferocious bouncer. I am the "Sultan of Swing". I invented the reverse swing and the "Doosra". I mastered multiple hat-tricks. I am the "Cornered Tiger". I am the fastest ball, the longest six, the shattered stumps at Eden Gardens, the highest individual score of 194 at Chennai, the 37-ball century, the 40-ball century at Kanpur. Now I am the Asian Champion 2012. I am the aggression. I am the passion. I am the unpredictable. I am Pakistan.

In February 2014, a university in Meerut in Uttar Pradesh suspended at least sixty-seven Kashmiri students for cheering for the Pakistani cricket team after it beat India in a tense Asia Cup contest. These students were suspended from the Swami Vivekanand Subharti University and the vice chancellor had described their behaviour 'unacceptable.'

Cricket is a sport in Kashmir. Cricket is politics in Kashmir. Cricket is one of the many symbols of resistance. It gives a reason to Kashmiris to hit back at New Delhi in whatever small way they can. So, while I wish that politics and sports remain separate and weren't mixed, conflicts do have their own dynamics, challenges and compulsions.

As a school boy, I grew up listening to exciting cricket commentary (in chaste Urdu) on Radio Pakistan.

Aasman par halke halke badal chaye huwe hain, aur maidan par iss waqt Pakistan ki team chayi huyi hai. Bharat ki wicktein aisi girti gayien jaise khizaan ke mousam main paidoun se patte gira karte hain!

(The sky has been taken over by light clouds, and the cricket ground has been taken over by the Pakistani team. India's wickets have been falling like trees shedding their leaves in autumn).

I immediately fell in love with this language of elegance and grace. And I continue to nurture a strong passion for Urdu. Kashmiri children born in the 1990s—also described by some as 'children of conflict'—have heard countless bedtime stories from their grandparents about how older Kashmiris loved Pakistan. They also loved Pakistan's cricket and hockey teams, radio commentary in 'adab ki zubaan' (the literary language) Urdu, thought-provoking television serials, as well as Pakistan's 'sahar angez mouseeqi' (magical music) in 'dil gudaaz aawaz' (heart-breaking voice). Kashmiris' love for Pakistan is not just limited to its language or its cricket team, it goes beyond that. Iconic Pakistani tele-serials *Ankahi, Tanhaiyaan, Dhoop Kinarey* and recent ones such as *Zindagi Gulzar Hai* and *Humsafar* are household names in Kashmir. It is no secret that many Kashmiri brides prefer Pakistani bridal apparel on their weddings. In Kashmir, one comes across people whose unconditional love for Pakistan will surpass the proudest and most patriotic Pakistanis. A few Pakistanis may even end up doubting their 'quom parasti' (nationalism) and 'hubul watni' (patriotism) on encountering such Kashmiris.

The fact is that a substantial pro-Pakistan political constituency does exist in the Kashmir Valley. This constituency has existed in the Himalayan Valley since the day Pakistan came into being as an independent nation state on 14 August 1947. During the current phase of rebellion in Kashmir, we have seen numerous images of young Kashmiris' lifeless bodies wrapped in Pakistani flags, in place of the customary white shrouds, being lowered into graves by their old and fragile fathers. Such images are enough to give us an idea of how deep-rooted the pro-Pakistan sentiment is in Kashmir. Even the former head of the Northern Command of the Indian Army, Lieutenant General (Retired) D.S. Hooda, in an interview with BBC Urdu, acknowledged that Pakistan enjoys widespread support in the Kashmir Valley. Lt. Gen. Hooda said, 'There is a lot of support for Pakistan. The Indian Army's role is to bring the security situation at a level that encourages political activity within the state of Jammu and Kashmir.' The former Army officer also asserted that Kashmir can't be resolved militarily. 'If we say that the Kashmir issue has a martial solution, it will be false. The issue is an internal and multifaceted issue.'

That said, some Kashmiris do question the role of Pakistan in Kashmir, especially after the outbreak of the armed struggle. They do say that Pakistan's hands are not clean either. They are of the view that Pakistan replicated the Afghan model of resistance against Soviet occupation in Kashmir with the aim to either avenge the Fall of Dhaka in 1971 or to gain control of the territory. Some, in private interactions, express dissatisfaction over Pakistan's oft-repeated rhetorical claim that 'Pakistan will continue to extend moral, diplomatic and political support to the people of Kashmir' in their political struggle. Some also question Pakistan's official policy regarding Kashmir, which they feel keeps wavering from time to time. They feel frustrated over what they describe as 'Islamabad's inconsistent Kashmir policy'. A few voices from Kashmir's new and assertive generation are also worried about how the extremist jihadi elements, such as the LeT, have hijacked the Kashmir solidarity movement in Pakistan. They are concerned about why more and more voices from Pakistan's vibrant civil society and liberal circles don't speak up enough about Kashmir. Furthermore, there is also a concern over why the Pakistani electronic media is not holding prime-time television debates on Kashmir to counter the Delhi-based media's Kashmir narrative largely based on propaganda, falsehoods and vitriol, to raise global awareness about the genesis of the Kashmiri dispute and to hold government forces accountable for the alleged atrocities committed on the people of Kashmir.

There is anger against the State and ruling dispensations in Delhi when it comes to the treatment of Kashmiris. However, to assume that Pakistan's role in Kashmir cannot be questioned, evaluated, critiqued, commented upon or rationally analysed is also naïve. Many say that the daily killings of Kashmiris are mere statistics for New Delhi and perhaps important to punish a dissenting populace. Kashmir's funerals are good pictures for many accomplished and aspiring photojournalists. For journalists, writers and political commentators, the killings and funerals are news stories and features. People's painful accounts are 'good quotes'. These are brief news updates for the world community. It is a mere law-and-order issue and a matter of easy money, promotion and citation for erring personnel of government forces. It is perhaps significant for Islamabad to keep the intensity of the conflict in Kashmir at a certain pace. For stakeholders of various ideologies within Kashmir, these act as fuel for driving their respective political vehicles. Some genuinely do feel the pain and agree in private that killings shouldn't happen, but they do not muster the courage to say the same thing in public. Others are only anxious to know whether there would be a 'hartal' after the killings. Some audaciously say that killings 'keep the political sentiment alive' but believe someone *else* should die. As if Kashmiri lives do not matter.

I am reminded of a comment by a young man from south Kashmir who once nonchalantly told a group of journalists in Srinagar: *'Hum qurbani daite hain, aap hamari qurbani aur mazalim ka tajziya karte hain'* ('We offer sacrifices and you analyse our sufferings and sacrifices'). At that time, we all had a hearty laugh. Later, I realized how true his words were.

No doubt, there is a stronger sentiment for Azadi, but the pro-Pakistan constituency in Kashmir is also an undeniable reality. Kashmir bleeds every single day. Kashmir suffers every single day. Kashmir mourns every single day. Given the love Kashmiris have for Pakistan, can Pakistan now move beyond rhetoric and try to know and understand what it means for Kashmiri fathers to bury the lifeless bodies of their young sons on an almost daily basis? Can Pakistan do a rethink on its Kashmir policy? Can Islamabad divorce rhetoric and embrace statesmanship? Can

Delhi reciprocate and come to the negotiating table to discuss and resolve Kashmir?

Pakistan and India have fought two full-fledged wars over their dispute on Kashmir in 1947–48 and 1965, and engaged in the Kargil conflict in 1999. As Kashmiris take to creative forms of resistance, there is a need for imaginative leadership and courageous political will in both countries to think out of the box and come up with a durable, people-centric solution for permanent peace in the region. There is no point in dehumanizing or demonizing Kashmiris. Two generations of Kashmiris have been brought up in an atmosphere in which they were coerced into adopting a different vocabulary. Their minds have been roiled by fake encounters, custodial killings, disappearances, cordon and search operations, human rights abuses, migration of Kashmiri Pandits, grenade blasts, ambushes, rapes, humiliation, curfews, civil curfews, and many other impressions that should ideally have no place in the lives of people, especially children, anywhere.

Words and narratives are important. Words are weapons. So is memory. What is not written is not remembered. Words, like justice, should flow like a mighty stream.

As goes the German proverb: '*Wir sollen die hoffnung niemals aufgeben*' ('We should never abandon hope')!

NOTES, SOURCES AND REFERENCES

1. Source 1: Varadarajan, S. (2005, February 01). My Foreword to Iftikhar Gilani's My Days in Prison. Retrieved from https://svaradarajan.com/2005/02/01/my-foreword-to-iftikhar-gilanis-my-days-in-prison/
   Source 2: Mannika. (2003, January 3). Iftikhar Gilani: No safeguards in the Official Secrets Act. Retrieved from http://www.thehoot.org/media-watch/law-and-policy/iftikhar-gilani-no-safeguards-in-the-official-secrets-act-651
2. Geelani, G. (2017, May 28). Poets and Rebels. Retrieved from http://www.kashmirink.in/news/coverstory/poets-and-rebels/361.html
3. Shahid, G. N. (2016). *Eelan Jaari Hai.*
4. Data by leading human rights body, JKCCS.
5. Scott-Clark, C. (2012, July 09). The mass graves of Kashmir. Retrieved from https://www.theguardian.com/world/2012/jul/09/mass-graves-of-kashmir
6. Kashmir Ground Zero: 3765 Cartridges, 1.3 Million Pellets - Lack Of Vision? (2016, August 18). Retrieved from http://www.ndtv.com/video/news/the-buck-

stops-here/kashmir-ground-zero-3765-cartridges-1-3-million-pellets-lack-of-vision-427893

7. Jha, P. S. (2016, August 23). The Rise of Kashmir's Second 'Intifada'. Retrieved from https://thewire.in/politics/kashmir-uprising

8. Roy, N. (2018, April 03). 10 players with the most wickets in ODI Cricket. Retrieved   from   https://cricket.yahoo.net/news/10-players-most-wickets-odi-104948349

9. Geelani, G. (2012, December 20). For Kashmiris Indo-Pak cricket isn't just a sport. Retrieved from https://www.dawn.com/news/772736

7

HELL IN PARADISE

My memories of growing up in Srinagar are a mixed recollection of school picnics, freedom songs, crackdowns, civilian killings, torture and the painful migration of Pandits. I cannot forget the fact that my teachers, whether Muslims or Pandits, never discriminated against pupils on the basis of their faith, colour or ideology. I consider myself fortunate to have been under the guidance of teachers whose humanity taught us so much, so early on.

During the late 1980s, I would stand upright in the first row at the morning assembly along with my classmates, including my Pandit classmate, Rahul, singing 'Hum Honge Kamyaab' ('We Shall Overcome') and other such songs as loudly as I could. Those were peaceful times. Muslims, Hindus and Sikhs studied in the same schools, played together, shared their lunches, attended each other's weddings and birthday parties, and offered condolences when someone in the neighbourhood passed away, of natural causes mostly and as yet not by bullets fired by government troops or in grenade and IED (improvized explosive device) attacks by militants. We sympathized with each other and even engaged in casual verbal brawls, as classmates normally do.

Then, all of a sudden, that tranquility seemed to vanish into thin air. My beautiful memories of Angels Public School, Abhay Public School, Light Public School and Shaheen Public School in Srinagar soon began turning into nightmares. Massive paintings of philosopher-poet Allama Iqbal, educationist Sir Syed Ahmed Khan and poet Rabindranath Tagore, that adorned the walls of my school, became pockmarked with stray bullets that would hit them on a regular basis. The sound of bullets replaced the music of bells at school. Instead of paint and colours on walls, there were bullet marks and holes. Every single bullet mark had a story to tell. Every single bullet hole was a grim reminder that the times had changed. Our paradise had disappeared before our eyes, and had been replaced with what we could only think of as hell.

For the outside world, Kashmir appears like a paradise, because of its beauty, its snow-clad mountains, the valleys of Gulmarg and Pahalgam, the glaciers of Sonmarg, Chenab and Jhelum rivers, the Mughal gardens Shalimar and Nishat, the mesmerizing Dal (now polluted and filthy), the Nigeen and Wular lakes, the Verinag and Kokernag springs, and the Aharbal waterfall.

Unfortunately, not many tourists are aware that since the late 1980s, people in the Kashmir Valley have witnessed, first-hand, the horrors of violence. This beautiful land has been ravaged by conflict for nearly seven decades now. Caught in a tug of war between two nuclear powers, the Kashmir Valley is today riven by conflicts of ethnicity, religion, national and political identity, and by rival claims to its territory. Kashmir is a story of bloodshed and betrayals and a string of broken promises.

Though the current phase of dispute began in 1947 and soon transformed into a violent conflict, it was in 1989 that life as Kashmiris knew it changed irrevocably. Suddenly, we were surrounded by hostile government soldiers. I remember everything: how I was slapped after I'd read, at their orders, an HM poster pasted in our locality; how they stared at me, hurled abuses and threatened me for no fault of mine as I walked down my streets; and how they forced me to bend down on my knees and walk on my elbows on an undeclared curfew day when I was to appear for my Class X examinations.

That HM poster was in Urdu and obviously anti-State and anti-Delhi. It was the 1990s, and I was about thirteen. I remember trying to balance out the content while reading it, but the officer in charge of the patrol party figured out what I was trying to do and shouted, '*Hamein bewaqoof banata hai kya?*' ('Are you trying to fool us?'). I was forced to read it as it was, word by word, syllable by syllable. The HM had made a passionate appeal to the locals to continue their support for the azadi movement and observe complete shutdown on India's Republic Day (26 January), Independence Day (15 August), and the day Indian Army personnel were airlifted to Srinagar in 1947 (27 October). India's Independence and Republic Days were even referred to as 'Youm-e-Siyah' (Black Days).

I vividly remember the Army's crackdowns. Through announcements from local mosques, a particular area would be cordoned off. All the people of that area, especially the men, would be forcibly assembled in an open ground for identification parades, in order to flush out militants, the mujahideen. I remember the operations that we, as school children, referred to as 'catch and kill'. Men, especially the youth, who were taken into custody, would possibly end up dead as a result of third degree in custody. I remember firings, cross-firings, grenade blasts, mine blasts and deadly encounters between armed militants and the government forces. Sometimes, crackdowns and search operations would last for three consecutive days. The elderly men would often be ridiculed and the young ones kicked, beaten, thrashed and abused. I remember violent and deafening grenade blasts, engineered by suspected militants to target government soliders, sometimes right outside private English-medium schools in Srinagar, in which civilians would be injured. Such 'unsuccessful' attacks would not be claimed by any militant outfit.

I remember massive anti-State demonstrations in which tens of thousands of Kashmiris participated, chanting slogans of freedom from New Delhi, and slogans in support of gun-wielding Kashmiri and foreign militants. Yes, I also remember the Pandits leaving the Valley that is known as Pir Waer. All these add to the swollen cache of painful memories.

Many squarely blame Jagmohan Malhotra, who had been hastily summoned for a second stint as governor of J&K on 19 January 1990, for the departure of the Pandit community. Everyone in Kashmir knows Jagmohan by his first name only. He was the state's most controversial governor, and his second spell the most contentious. Pandits represent less than 5 per cent of J&K's total population. Representatives of the majority community, the Kashmiri Muslims, accuse Jagmohan of having misused his power, position and authority in facilitating the migration of Pandits with the objective of launching a full-scale attack on the Muslim community. Jagmohan is also accused of helping remove Pandits from the scene so they would not suffer during counter-militancy operations conducted by government forces.

Mehboob Makhdoomi, who has studied International Business and Economy at Harvard University and done his MBA from Pennsylvania University, in his piece, 'We're sorry; We betrayed you', published in *Greater Kashmir* writes about an old letter, dated 22 September 1990, which was written by twenty-three prominent Kashmiri Pandits, who had migrated from the Valley in January 1990, to Kashmiri Muslims.[1] The letter, Mehboob Makhdoomi reveals, was addressed to the 'Muslims of Kashmir' and sent to the editor of one of Kashmir's largest dailies at the time. The signatories included Brij Nath Bhan, M.L. Dhar, K.L. Kaw, Chuni Lal Raina, Moti Lal Mam, Ashok Koul, M.L. Munshi, B.N. Gunjoo, Pushkar Nath Koul and Kamal Raina, besides others.

According to Makhdoomi, the letter begins by admitting that the Pandit community was made 'a scapegoat' by Jagmohan, self-styled leaders of their community and other vested interests. The writers, as per the letter quoted by Makhdoomi, describe their migration 'a drama' enacted by the 'BJP, RSS and Shiv Sena'. The signatories confess their migration was 'very vital for preserving and protecting Dharm and the unity and integrity of India', as they were promised 'rehabilitation as soon as the people of (the) Valley were silenced and made to surrender'. It says they felt 'ashamed to have become tools in the hands of enemies of our nation' and 'for not participating in the freedom struggle of our motherland from the alien rule'. Makhdoomi claims that anybody who wants a copy of the letter in his possession can get it from him.

A contrarian point of view is of those Pandits who accuse the majority community, and also Pakistan-backed armed militants, of 'ethnic cleansing' in the Valley. At the time of their departure from the Valley, Pandits were estimated to be between 1,50,000 and 1,90,000 in number.[2]

These statistics have been hotly debated ever since, as has the terminology—whether 'exodus' should be the appropriate term or 'migration'—used to describe their flight.

Perhaps a fundamental question is, whether there's a political truth, beyond the Hindu-Muslim binary choice and beneath the multipolarity of conflicting and competing narratives. Sadly, much of the scholarship on Kashmir has failed to check this tendency of looking at issues only in terms of 'for' or 'against'. In between this sharply etched binary lies another perspective that sees human beings as human beings, not just as Kashmiri Muslims or Kashmiri Hindus. The problem is that very few Pandits or Muslims acknowledge the pain and suffering the other has endured in the last twenty-nine years. Voices that have dared to rise above ideological and religious differences to acknowledge pain as pain, without making any attempt to quantify or reduce it to a mere number game, are rare. There are ultra-radical voices from both communities and they are also loud.

The larger truth is that Kashmiri Muslims have suffered immensely at the hands of the government's Armed Forces, and Kashmiri Pandits too have suffered because of the loss of their homeland. Sometimes, I tend to blame myself, too. Yes, I know I was very young then, and could not have exerted any influence to either cause—the Pandit migration or prevent it. But I do strongly feel that we could have lived together in communal harmony, in the spirit of Kashmir's composite culture. As proud Kashmiris, we could have fought the circumstances that led to the migration. Perhaps it is my idealism. I'm aware that those were not ideal times; neither are these.

The Kashmir I knew was a garden whose beauty was enhanced by the varied flowers that blossomed there. It belonged to me; my classmate Rahul; my father's Pandit friend, Upender Uncle; my teachers, Madam Bharti Koul, Anita, Teja and Usha; and tens of thousands of people who belonged to different faiths and backgrounds. Our garden stands diminished for the loss of diversity. We stand separated because of the circumstances, not choice. Sadly, Kashmir is being used as a laboratory for various experiments, including that of Otherness.

★

Who was responsible for the Pandit migration?

There are often shrill debates on Indian television channels about 'Kashmiriyat', a term used to describe the centuries-old communal harmony in J&K. Many Pandits blame their Muslim brethren; some blame militants, the pro-freedom forces and the religious forces active in the state; and yet others blame the unfortunate circumstances of 1989. Many Muslims blame Jagmohan, some say the Pandits shouldn't have left Kashmir, and a few maintain that what happened was unfortunate and should have never been allowed.

I have a slightly different take on this issue. I believe that the Muslim community in the Valley is partly responsible as a whole. I also believe that the Pandit community is partly responsible for their own departure, for the simple reason that the two communities had, till then, shared an enviable history of harmony, communal confluence and elegant bonds of friendship despite political and ideological divergences. Dealing with sensitive topics such as the Kashmiri Pandit and the Kashmiri Muslim narratives—whether with regard to communal harmony vs. communal tensions, or conflict vs. confluence—requires both literary sensibility and intellectual nuance. We should not have allowed unfortunate circumstances to dictate our decisions, our lives, our history and our present, and above all, sunder our cultural and emotional bond.

Unfortunately, we did.

Was it possible for Pandits not to have left Kashmir at that time? In my several articles and columns, I might have criticized the politics of Mirwaiz Umar Farooq, the chairman of a faction of the APHC; or Sajad Gani Lone, now a pro-India politician backed by the BJP and a former minister in the PDP-BJP coalition government; but credit must be given where it is due. Both men lost their fathers in violent attacks. Mirwaiz Moulvi Farooq was killed on 21 May 1990, and Abdul Gani Lone on 21 May 2002, which happened to be the twelfth death anniversary of Moulvi Farooq. Mirwaiz Umar, Sajad Lone and his brother, Bilal Lone, too, had the option of settling somewhere far away from the hell of Kashmir, but they didn't leave. They chose to face the challenges before them. Whatever anyone's opinion of Sajad Lone's politics might be, he did not leave Kashmir after his father's assassination. Mirwaiz, too, could easily have settled abroad, but he decided to brave it in Kashmir.

To give a personal example, my mother was seriously wounded in a blast in the late 1990s, when unidentified attackers hurled a grenade at a bunker at Safa Kadal in Srinagar. The grenade missed the intended target, as often happened, and like many pedestrians, my mother too was injured. Her left foot was badly wounded and never healed completely. We could have left then, especially since we had a successful shawl business in Kolkata. But, we chose to stay.

The quantum of time that the governments of India and Pakistan waste in not paying attention to the aspirations of the people of Kashmir is directly proportional to the suffering that Kashmiris have to endure. Time translates into increased misery. Time, for Kashmiris, is a reminder that freedom is elusive and justice is delayed, and therefore denied as well.

According to JKCCS, from 1989 till December 2018, over 70,000 state subjects, i.e. permanent residents of J&K including civilians, armed rebels, Armed Forces from Kashmir (J&K Police, CRPF, JAK Light Infantry, informers, renegades, SPOs, etc.) have been killed.[3] Casualty figures provided by the Government of India and MHA are contradictory. According to official figures, between January 1990 and April 2011, 43,460 people have been killed in Kashmir. Of these, according to official data, 16,868 are civilians; 21,323 are militants; and 5,369 are armed forces.[4] According to the Union Home Ministry, only 13,000 civilians have been killed in J&K during the last twenty-nine years, which means they are fewer than they were eight years ago in 2011. The MHA figures are in total contrast to the claims of human rights groups, which put the civilian deaths at a higher value.[5] In response to an RTI application, the Union Home Ministry divulged that since the start of militancy in 1990 in J&K, 13,491 civilians and 5,055 security force personnel were killed in various incidents, apart from 21,965 militants. The data, which puts the total number of killed persons at 40,961, puts statistics of the injured force personnel at 13,000.

Unofficially, the death toll stands close to 100,000,[6] most of whom are civilians, militants and political workers espousing different ideologies. The families of civilians killed in the conflict did not leave Kashmir. In 2008, more than sixty civilians, mostly boys in their teens, were killed after government forces fired upon peaceful anti-State demonstrations. Their families did not leave Kashmir. In the summer of 2010, at least 120 persons[7], mostly teenagers and school-going boys, fell to the bullets fired by the state forces. Their families did not leave Kashmir. In 2016, following Burhan Wani's killing, at least a hundred persons were killed in government forces' action against civilian protesters[8], over 1,100 youth were partially or completely blinded with pellets[9] and over 15,000 people were injured.[10] Many civilians were killed in 2017–18 near the encounter sites during protest demonstrations and clashes with government forces. Their families did not leave Kashmir.

Should the Pandits have braved whatever might have come their way and avoided leaving their homeland? It is debatable. Maybe it wasn't possible. Or, maybe it was. Life hasn't been the same for those Pandits who had to take refuge in migrant camps in Jammu, or for those who left for other parts of India. Their narrative is as important. It can neither be ignored nor sidelined.

Sameer Bhat, a former colleague at Eenadu Television (ETV), would tell me painful stories of his community's migration. I met him in 2004 in Hyderabad. Sameer, his wife, his ailing mother and children would bear the scorching heat and humidity of Jammu in a temporary shed that, according to him, consisted of one small room. His stories would often make me feel a pang in my heart. His was just one family among hundreds who had to survive in similar conditions.

A close Pandit friend of my father, who lived in Rainawari in Srinagar, left Kashmir along with his entire family when his house was burnt down, allegedly by suspected militants. He used to buy shawls from us. At the time of their migration, he owed my father a large sum of money. The cheque he had given to make the payment, bounced. After apologizing, he promised to repay every single penny once he settled down in Kolkata. My father offered all possible help and told the family they did not need to pay us back, because we understood what they had gone through. As an honest businessman, he kept his word and repaid everything he owed in small installments over the years. That is Pandit pride and honour.

Leaving one's homeland, where one's ancestors lived for hundreds of years, is painful. Staying there in tragic times is perhaps even more dreadful. The social fabric of Kashmir and the centuries-old bond between Muslims and Pandits was severely rent following the migration.

In 2006, sixteen years after the Pandit migration, I was working as a journalist and contributing features to BBC Urdu and radio stories to Deutsche Welle (Voice of Germany). I would often write about Kashmir. At the time, the PDP-Congress coalition government in the state had made arrangements for some Pandit families to temporarily return to Kashmir to celebrate Kheer Bhawani, a popular festival. I, as a budding journalist, accompanied some of the families who had returned for the festival. It was an opportunity to know their perspective on their 'temporary' return to their homeland.

As they went about religious rituals at the temple of Mata Ragnya in the Tulmula area of Ganderbal, some 30 km away from Srinagar, I spoke to the various participants. Santosh Bhat, a Pandit woman born in downtown Srinagar in Haba Kadal, who had left after 1989, said, 'Everything changed. With migration, our entire world changed. It's really very painful to leave as beautiful a homeland as Kashmir.' She was critical of the authorities and politicians. 'All their talk about our return to our homeland and the improvement in the security situation in Kashmir is a hoax.

They (the politicians) are deceiving us, all the people, for their own political gains.' B.J. Takra, another Pandit, told me that little had changed on the ground in Kashmir. 'I know for sure that the majority community in Kashmir—the Muslims—never supports anything unfavourable to Kashmiri Hindus. We have lived and survived for centuries together. But unfortunately, the security situation post-1989 left us with no option. And we decided to migrate from Kashmir.' Raj Kumar told me that despite the overwhelming desire of Kashmiri Muslims and Hindus to live together once again, the return of Pandits to their homeland was not viable in the present circumstances. Bhushan Lal Bhat, a former activist of the NC, said that a just political resolution was required for the Kashmir conflict so that everyone might live in peace again.

Shabir Shah, a pro-independence leader and chairman of the Jammu and Kashmir Democratic Freedom Party, was at Ganderbal to interact with the visiting Pandit families. 'I come here every year so that I can meet my Pandit brethren to impress upon them that the time has come for their safe return to their cherished homeland,' he said. He lauded the courage of those who had stayed back in Kashmir despite the troubles. 'I salute their valour and hugely value their emotion and grit. It's time that everyone comes back now.'

As a matter of fact, some Pandit families never left Kashmir. An acquaintance, Amit Wanchoo, stayed despite the fact that his grandfather, late Hirdai Nath Wanchoo, a human rights monitor and activist, was assassinated on 5 December 1992. HRW dedicated one of its reports to him.[11] Another Pandit I know, Sanjay Tickoo, who heads the Kashmiri Pandit Sangharsh Samiti, continues to live in downtown Srinagar.

Why are Pandits scared of returning to their homeland? Some say that the presence of people like Farooq Ahmad Dar, alias Bita Karate, in Kashmir, frightens them. After his arrest in 1990, Dar had confessed on Indian television that, as a member of the JKLF, he was entrusted with the job of twenty targeted killings, most of them from the Pandit community. He spent sixteen years in jail before his release. Later, he said he was coerced into making a confessional statement in prison under duress. He is currently back in prison in an alleged 'terror funding' case, after being arrested by the National Investigation Agency (NIA) sleuths.

★

On the other side of the coin are the concerns of more than 8.5 million Kashmiri Muslims living in the Valley, parts of Jammu, Chenab, Pir Panjal and Ladakh, which also need to be acknowledged and understood in their context and historicity. In August 1992, government forces launched a brutal offensive in Kashmir called 'Operation Tiger'. It involved surprise raids and search operations designed to capture and kill militants.[12] This marked the ugly beginning of extrajudicial executions of detainees, notoriously known to Kashmiris as 'catch and kill'. Another offensive code-named 'Operation Shiva' soon followed in October 1992.[13]

There are several examples, as explained in the previous chapter, of young men being picked up by government forces on suspicion of their being connected with militants and made to disappear in custody. Some 8,000–10,000 are listed as disappeared. As a young journalist, I had visited one such family in Srinagar in 2006. The family's search has unfortunately still not ended. Abdul Rasheed Beigh and his wife, hapless parents in Nowshara, Srinagar, await the return of their son, Fayaz Ahmad Beigh. They have done everything they could to secure their son's release, but all their efforts, money, hopes and tears, have not borne fruit. Thousands of parents and half-widows in Kashmir desperately await the return of their sons and husbands, hoping against hope that one day they will be reunited with their loved ones. Beigh has been fighting a 'lost' battle since Fayaz was picked up on 6 September 1997. 'We looked in every corner, explored every single possibility, knocked on every single door, visited shrines and saints, paid money to government-sponsored gunmen, renegades, and made several requests to the APHC, but we achieved nothing at all,' he told me while his wife, Maryam Bano, broke down again.

Beigh's struggle might be tragically replicated many times over in Kashmir, but he compiled it into a booklet, *Hiraastee Gumshudgee Aur Be Parvaah Hukumraan* (Custodial Disappearances and Callous Authorities). Whenever he is overwhelmed by sadness, he takes out his pen and writes about his son, his disappearance and the struggle to find him. 'Eventually, I found a heap of paper and decided to compile it into a forty-four-page booklet,' he said.

Rasheed Beigh and Maryam Bano have met many ministers, senior police and security officials and top militant commanders, and prayed endlessly. Hope has remained elusive as ever. Beigh has quietly resigned himself to destiny and pragmatism, and perhaps, accepted the harsh reality that his son may never come home again. But Fayaz's mother refuses to surrender hope.

Fayaz worked as a cameraman in the department of Central Asian Studies at the University of Kashmir. On 6 September 1997, a Saturday, he started for the university on his motorcycle. According to a typed notice provided by the University of Kashmir, he was taken into custody by the Special Task Force from the Lethpora, Awantipora camp of the J&K Police at 12.30 p.m. on the same day. He was whisked away from the southern gate of the university, never to be seen since.

Beigh told me that the Division Bench of the state high court gave a verdict in their favour. The custodial disappearance of their son was confirmed by the State Human Rights Commission (SHRC). And still no action was taken against either the state police or its Task Force. The police's version mentions that Fayaz gave them the slip and ran away under the cover of darkness. No one believed the report.

While rejecting it outright and terming it 'concocted and fabricated', the SHRC recommended strong action against the erring cops and a compensation of ₹5 lakh to be given to Fayaz's family.

Maryam Bano said, 'Had this gloom not descended on us, we wouldn't have had to spend our hard-earned money on saints and renegades. If my son is not alive anymore, let the authorities make an announcement so that we can perform Fayaz's last rites as per religious rituals and have closure.' She still hopes for a 'maybe'. This story is replicated in thousands of other cases, across Kashmir. A couplet by poet Malikzada Manzoor Ahmed aptly sums up this tragedy:

'Darwaaze par aahat sun kar uss kee taraf kyoun dhyaan gaya
Aaney waali sirf hawa ho aisa bhi ho sakta hai.'

('Why did a noise at the door nudge my thoughts towards him;
It's quite possible that it is just the wind.')

Apart from widespread custodial disappearances, a series of well-documented civilian massacres have occurred in Kashmir at the hands of the Armed Forces, especially in the early 1990s. On 21 January 1990, the CRPF opened indiscriminate fire on peaceful protestors at Srinagar's Gowkadal bridge. People had defied curfew to protest against atrocities during search operations the previous night. The historian, William Dalrymple, who was in Srinagar at the time as a foreign correspondent, wrote in *The Guardian* that several thousand Kashmiris marched peacefully out of the old city to protest.[14] When the crowd was halfway across the Gowkadal bridge, CRPF soldiers opened fire with automatic rifles, from three directions. At least fifty Kashmiris, all of them civilians, were brutally killed. Several poets have also captured the tragedy of Gowkadal in their stirring and moving poems.

On 21 May 1990, Kashmir's popular socio-religious leader, Mirwaiz Moulvi Mohammad Farooq, was assassinated by unknown assailants, possibly from a pro-Pakistan militant organization, at his Nigeen residence in Srinagar. His bullet-ridden body was rushed to SKIMS, Soura, where he breathed his last. I have faint memories of this incident. I heard women in our neighbourhood wailing and beating their chests in the traditional gesture of mourning. '*Khodayo! Moulvi Saeb ha korukh shaheed*' ('Oh God! The Mirwaiz has been martyred'), they wailed. Thousands of mourners took part in the funeral procession from Soura to Nowshera. An acquaintance took me along, holding my hand tightly. People carried the coffin on their shoulders.

Hours later, we heard that the CRPF opened fire indiscriminately on a peaceful assembly of people, who were part of the funeral procession, once they reached Hawal near the Islamia College of Science and Commerce, in Srinagar. At least sixty civilians were brutally killed.[15] Mourners were fired upon with automatic rifles and machine guns. At home, we heard relentless sirens of ambulances carrying the injured mourners to SKIMS. Eyewitnesses have recounted the horrors of that day. A memorial erected in Hawal has the names of all those killed on that ill-fated day, including a distant relative of ours.

On 6 January 1993, forty-three people were killed in another civilian massacre in north Kashmir's apple town, Sopore. HRW mentions in a report that the civilians were shot or burned to death when paramilitary forces stormed through a neighbourhood, probably in retaliation for an attack by militants in which two government soldiers were killed.[16] The report quotes a local police officer, who was present at the scene, saying that the security forces 'ran amok'. I remember people in Srinagar discussing this massacre with moist eyes. It was a chilling January—quite literally. For Kashmiris, the month of January means a month of civilian massacres.

Around the end of that same year, on 22 October, Bijbehara in south Kashmir's Anantnag district witnessed yet another civilian massacre. BSF personnel opened fire on a peaceful rally. More than forty civilians, including a thirteen-year-old member of the Pandit community named Kamal Ji Koul, were killed, while more than 150 were injured. After Koul's death in the massacre, his family migrated from Kashmir.[17] Most of the dead are buried in the martyrs' graveyard there. A detailed list of the victims, with their names, ages and addresses, is inscribed on a stone at the graveyard.

The rally at Bijbehara was to protest the Hazratbal siege. After offering Friday prayers in Bijbehara's Jamia Masjid, the people of the town, in a form of a peaceful procession, marched through the streets. When they reached the main road, the personnel of the 74 BSF Battalion allowed them to assemble at the highway and then allegedly fired indiscriminately at the protesters from all sides. According to some political analysts, the carnage, allegedly committed and orchestrated by the 74th Battalion, was planned. According to eyewitnesses, 10,000 to 15,000 people had first gathered in the courtyard of the central mosque. The protestors chanted slogans against the siege and in support of Kashmir's resolution. As soon as they reached the highway that connects Srinagar with Jammu, the BSF troops stationed there started firing indiscriminately, killing thirty-seven on the spot while leaving around 150 or more seriously injured.

These civilian massacres sent out the message that even peaceful assemblies would not be entertained. Every single attempt made by the people to voice their aspirations and grievances was met with force. Kashmiris have likened the bloodbaths in Gowkadal, Hawal, Sopore and Bijbehara to the Jallianwala Bagh massacre, which took place in Amritsar in 1919, when unarmed civilians were fired upon by British troops.

I was too young to remember the intricate details of these massacres, but I vividly remember the panic they caused among the people. They further fueled anti-State anger in the people, and also became new issues of hatred.

At the time of these massacres, several members of the minority Pandit community were also under attack from suspected militants of the LeT. In one such attack on 25 January 1998, at least twenty-three Pandits were killed at Wandhama in Ganderbal district. On 20 March 2000, thirty-five members of the minority Sikh community were mercilessly killed in Chattisinghpora, in south Kashmir's Anantnag district, by fifteen unknown gunmen who had ordered them to assemble at the village gurudwara. Prior to this massacre, the Sikhs had never been targeted in Kashmir, neither by the government forces nor the militants. In yet another incident, on 23 March, twenty-four Hindus were killed by suspected militants in Nadimarg hamlet of south Kashmir's Pulwama district.

The Chattisinghpora massacre occurred at a time when the then US President, Bill Clinton, was on a visit to India. Allegations have been made that Delhi's intelligence agencies had orchestrated the massacre to malign Kashmir's struggle as 'communal'. The APHC and HM blamed Delhi for this bloodbath. It was followed by an ugly incident at Pathribal village in Anantnag where Army personnel killed five local labourers and dubbed them 'foreign mercenaries', falsely claiming that they were responsible for the Chattisinghpora massacre. The innocent labourers were killed on 25 March, only five days after the Chattisinghpora massacre. In official press handouts, the government forces claimed to have blown up a hut where the men were hiding after a brief gunfight, from which five bodies were retrieved. These were charred beyond recognition.

After villagers in Pathribal found seven men missing, they protested the official claim about the encounter. Succumbing to intense public pressure, the authorities agreed to exhume the bodies of the 'foreign militants'. An investigation conducted by the Central Bureau of Investigation (CBI) established that the Army had killed five innocent people in a fake encounter. On 19 March 2012, the CBI informed the Supreme Court of India that the fake encounter at Pathribal 'were cold-blooded murders and the accused officials deserve to be meted out exemplary punishment.' Not a single soldier found guilty has been punished till date.

At least seventeen persons were detained by local police and made to disappear between 21–24 March, soon after the Chattisinghpora massacre. The London-based Amnesty International said in its report that the five bodies were buried separately in Pathribal without any postmortem examination.[18] The report also stated that it was unclear if armed militant groups, renegades or State agents were responsible for the unlawful killings at Chattisinghpora.

★

Some Kashmiri Pandits maintain that slogans like '*Azadi ka matlab kya—La'illaha Ilallah*' ('What does freedom mean—there is no God, except Allah') keep them from returning to Kashmir. But what is so frightening about this slogan, which is an article of faith for all Muslims? Rahul Pandita, a Kashmiri Pandit author-journalist, in his book, *Our Moon Has Blood Clots*, refers to another controversial slogan, '*Asey banawun yete Pakistan—Batav rostuy batneiv saan*' ('We have to turn Kashmir into Pakistan—Without Pandit men, but with Pandit women'). This slogan is seriously contested in Kashmir. Even if such a slogan would have been raised, it can in no way be attributed to the 'freedom movement'. It could well be the handiwork of some hardline elements, which in no way represent the majority community in the state.

The dynamics of protest demonstrations and rallies are complex in Kashmir. Usually, a majority of participants remain disciplined and do not resort to provocations, but there is always the presence of smaller groups that sometimes create indiscipline and raise slogans that are not in harmony with the majority. This fragmentation is rare but cannot be ruled out or denied.

However, many Kashmiris ask this question—what about the many members of Right-wing Hindu parties chanting provocative and objectionable slogans in mainland India? For instance,

'Bharat main jo rehna hai, Ram Ram hee kehna hai'

('To live in India, you must only chant "Ram Ram"')

'Musalmanoun ke do hi sthan: Pakistan ya qabristan'[19]

('There are only two places for Muslims:
Pakistan or the graveyard')

Aren't these slogans scary?

They also question several incidents of mob lynchings in other parts of India in which members of the minority community have been at the receiving end. For instance, they talk about a disturbing trend of mob lynchings: Mohammad Akhlaq of Dadri, Uttar Pradesh (September 2015), Pehlu Khan of Alwar, Rajasthan (April 2017), Hafiz Junaid of Haryana (June 2017), Mohammad Afrazul Khan of Rajasmand, Rajasthan (December 2017), Mohammad Qasim of Hapur, Uttar Pradesh (June 2018) and many others. Sadly, some of them were even killed on suspicion of either eating or storing beef.

This whataboutery does not help anyone. The unpalatable truth, however, is that since the ascendancy of Narendra Modi to power in New Delhi in May 2014, the insecurities of the minority communities in India have increased manifold. At an event in Thiruvananthapuram in July 2018, Shashi Tharoor, a well-known Congress leader and former minister in the UPA regime, warned that if the BJP wins the 2019 elections, it will lead to the creation of a 'Hindu Pakistan.'[20] 'If they (BJP) win a repeat in the Lok Sabha, our democratic constitution as we understand it will not survive as they will have all the elements they need to tear apart the constitution of India and write a new one'. That 'new one', Tharoor argued, will pave the way for establishing a 'Hindu Rashtra' that will remove equality for minorities. 'Rajnath Singh has made it clear that secularism and socialism, which were added (to the Preamble) as an amendment, should be removed. And then they (BJP) have to prepare ground to establish RSS' Hindu Rashtra in place of the constitutional system. This is their main aim,' Sitaram Yechury of the CPI(M) told reporters.[21] Similarly, broadcast journalist Barkha Dutt, in one of her pieces in *The Washington Post,* asked 'Will Modi stop India's cow terrorists from killing Muslims?'[22] She described the use of 'cow vigilantes' as repugnant euphemism and argued that the use of the word '"vigilantism" to describe hate crimes against India's Muslims is nothing more than the hideous normalization of bigotry.'

★

If one goes by the Muslim-Hindu binary and vitriolic commentary by radical voices from both communities, one might perhaps arrive at the discomforting conclusion that Muslims and Hindus are at war with one another. There is no denying that the cracks between Kashmiri Muslims and Kashmiri Pandits have widened in the last three decades. But beyond this is another world of Kashmiri Muslim and Kashmiri Pandit harmony and cultural confluence. Because of their history of togetherness, despite political and ideological variances, they perhaps continue to have expectations from one another. A section of Kashmiri Muslims might see the Pandit community as rabid Hindus, extensions of the State and Delhi's informers and agents or 'fifth columnists'. Similarly, a section of Pandits might also see Muslims as proxies of Pakistan. But these are extremist and polarized narratives. And mentioned earlier, historian Khalid Bashir had noted that the transformation of Kashmir from a Hindu to a Muslim society had given birth to the 'forcible coversion' narrative. The author opined that this was 'a fairy tale' based mostly on the observations of Jonaraja. In his view, 'this narrative became the hallmark of a miniscule minority of Brahmans, who refused to convert to Islam, and continued playing a victim card.'

There is no denying that in the absence of first-hand experience of multiculturalism, the present generation of both Kashmiri Muslim and Kashmiri Pandit communities have drifted apart from one another. There is a serious ideological difference between the two communities as well. But there is a possibility of reversing the clock to the times when the two lived together in harmony.

There is a view that Kashmiri Muslims and Pandits have grievances against each other. They might indeed have serious political differences, but surely they can live together like they had for decades and centuries. They're throwing tantrums and seeking attention from one another, and perhaps expecting a lot from the opposite side. To some, it seems that what the Pandits are saying is, 'If we left Kashmir, why didn't you call us back? Were just one or two calls and invitations enough? Shouldn't you be doing more and calling us back more earnestly and receiving us with open arms?' And the Muslims are saying, 'Why did you leave us when things were tough? You shouldn't have abandoned us and left us all alone in the first place. Shouldn't you have faced the challenges and tough circumstances like us? Shouldn't you have stayed here and never left?'

Despite the inflexibility and hardening of positions from both sides, many Kashmiri Muslim families, including ours, continue to send walnuts and nadrus from Kashmir to friends from the Pandit community now scattered across various parts of India, on the occasion of Maha Shivratri. It was routine for Muslims and Pandits to have friends from the other community and invite each other to their homes. Many women from both the communities would visit popular 'astaans' (shrines) to tie ritualistic threads and pray together for their children's success in examinations and for the good health of their families. Children studied and attended tuition classes together. Why can't that Kashmir be recreated? While asking questions like 'How welcoming is the Valley?' we must also ask, 'How enthusiastic are the Pandits to return to their homeland?' Can't the two communities laugh together, mourn together and live together, as they had done for centuries? Is it really impossible?

NOTES, SOURCES AND REFERENCES

1. Makhdoomi, M. (2016, September 27). We're Sorry; We betrayed you. Retrieved from http://www.greaterkashmir.com/news/opinion/story/229355.html
2. Source 1: Exodus of Kashmiri Pandits: What happened on January 19, 26 years ago? (2016, January 19). Retrieved from http://indiatoday.intoday.in/story/exodus-of-kashmiri-pandits-january-19-jammu-and-kashmir/1/574071.html
    Source 2: Irfan, H. (2016, June 11). Kashmiri Pandits slam migration figures; reject state government figures. Retrieved from http://economictimes. indiatimes.com/articleshow/52696691.cms?utm_source=contentofinterest&utm_medium=text&utm_campaign=cppst
3. *ANNUAL HUMAN RIGHTS REVIEW 2018* (Rep.). (2018). Srinagar, J&K: Jammu Kashmir Coalition of Civil Society & Association of Parents of Disappeared Persons. Retrieved from http://jkccs.net/wp-content/uploads/2018/12/Annual-Report-2018.pdf
4. Nandal, R. S. (2011, June 19). State data refutes claim of 1 lakh killed in Kashmir | India News—Times of India. Retrieved from https://timesofindia. indiatimes.com/india/State-data-refutes-claim-of-1-lakh-killed-in-Kashmir/articleshow/8918214.cms
5. Rashid, D. A. (2017, April 30). 13000 civilians, 22000 militants killed in Kashmir since 1989: MHA. Retrieved from https://www.greaterkashmir.com/news/kashmir/13000-civilians-22000-militants-killed-inkashmir-since-1989-mha/247921.html
6. India revises Kashmir death toll to 47,000. (2008, November 21). Retrieved from https://in.reuters.com/article/idINIndia- 36624520081121
7. 2010 KILLING| SHRC seeks appearance of victim families. (2016, December 22). Retrieved from https://www.greaterkashmir.com/news/kashmir/2010-killing-shrc-seeks-appearance-of-victim-families/236780.html
8. Ahmad, M. (2017, October 20). 'This Blindness Is a Constant Reminder of the Brutality We Have Faced'. Retrieved from https://thewire.in/government/pellet-guns-kashmir
9. Saha, A. (2017, March 08). Six youth face partial blindness: Why Kashmir's pellet woes are far from over. Retrieved from https://www.hindustantimes.

com/india-news/why-kashmir-s-pelletwoes-are-far-from-over/story-beLuuCuyrRVRo5h0otAE8M.html
10. Zia, A. (2017, April 26). Resistance is a way of life for Kashmiri youth. Retrieved from https://www.aljazeera.com/indepth/opinion/2017/04/resistance-life-kashmiri-youth-170425081937812.html
11. *Threats against Human Rights Defenders* (Rep.). (1999). Human Rights Watch. Retrieved from https://www.hrw.org/legacy/reports/1999/kashmir/defenders.htm
12. *The Human Rights Crisis in Kashmir* (Rep.). (1999). Asia Watch (HRW) & Physicians for Human Rights. Retrieved from https://www.hrw.org/sites/default/files/reports/INDIA937.PDF, p. 37
13. Ibid.
14. Dalrymple, W. (2010, June 19). Curfewed Night | Book review. Retrieved from https://www.theguardian.com/books/2010/jun/20/curfewed-night-basharat-peer-dalrymple
15. Wani, A. S. (2015, May 21). Hawal massacre anniversary: 'It was hell; saw paramilitary men firing with machine guns on civilians'. Retrieved from http://www.greaterkashmir.com/news/kashmir/hawal-massacre-anniversary-it-was-hell-saw-paramilitary-men-firing-with-machine-guns-on-civilians/186931.html
16. *The Human Rights Crisis in Kashmir* (Rep.). (1999). Asia Watch (HRW) & Physicians for Human Rights. Retrieved from https://www.hrw.org/sites/default/files/reports/INDIA937.PDF, p. 38
17. Bijbehara Massacre: A survivor remembers. (2018, October 23). Retrieved from https://kashmirlife.net/bijbehara-massacre-a-survivor-remembers-154014/
18. *India: A Trail of Unlawful Killings in Jammu and Kashmir: Chithisinghpora and its Aftermath* (Rep.). (2000). London, UK. Amnesty International. Retrieved from https://www.amnesty.org/en/library/asset/ASA20/024/2000/en/dom-ASA200242000en.html
19. Hameed, S. (2014, August 23). A harvest of horror and shame. Retrieved from http://www.thehindu.com/todays-paper/tp-opinion/a-harvest-of-horror-and-shame/article6343606.ece
20. India will become 'Hindu Pakistan' if BJP wins in 2019: Shashi Tharoor. (2018, July 12). Retrieved from https://economictimes.indiatimes.com/news/politics-and-nation/india-will-become-hindu-pakistan-if-bjp-wins-in-2019-shashi-tharoor/articleshow/64956946.cms
21. BJP wants to establish Hindu Rashtra: Opposition. (2015, November 26). Retrieved from https://economictimes.indiatimes.com/?utm_expid=.tZsN_qORRO-NwGsScGpIUA.0&utm_referrer=https://economictimes.indiatimes.com/news/politics-and-nation/bjp-wants-to-establish-hindu-rashtra-opposition/articleshow/49939384.cms?from=mdr
22. Dutt, B. (2018, July 24). Will Modi stop India's cow terrorists from killing Muslims? Retrieved from https://www.washingtonpost.com/news/global-opinions/wp/2018/07/24/will-modi-stop-indias-cow-terrorists-from-killing-muslims/?utm_term=.6d872e1035d5

8

MEDIA WARS

In war, they say, truth is often the first casualty. In a conflict zone like Kashmir, where the conflict has extended to close to three decades, truth is not just a casualty; it is often overlaid with competing narratives and interpretations. As a result, working as a journalist in Kashmir is not a cakewalk. As the armed struggle erupted in 1989, journalists were often caught in the crossfire—literally, at times. They became 'soft' targets for the government's Armed Forces, paramilitary personnel, policemen, government-sponsored counterinsurgents (renegades) and militants fighting for Kashmir's Azadi. Since then, journalists have been killed, intimidated, assaulted, kidnapped and coerced into toeing the line. They have been caught between the Armed Forces and the militants, often as sitting ducks for both, especially in the 1990s.

At times, in the early stages of the conflict, threats of violence and kidnappings made news of journalists themselves. At other times, journalists had to agonize over what to write: highlighting militants' remarks made them guilty of 'glorifying' or 'romanticizing' them, while carrying official statements meant they would be branded 'government agents'.

The practice of withholding advertisements by the government started after the 2008 summer agitation. In 2016, this became widespread, depriving newspapers of income. Recently, the J&K government headed by governor Satya Pal Malik stopped advertisements to *Greater Kashmir* and *Kashmir Reader*. Officially, no reason was given. The ban was imposed nevertheless, prompting Kashmir Editors' Guild to carry blank front pages on 10 March 2019, to protest denial of state advertisements.[1]

After breaking the record of enforcing the longest-ever curfew in the Kashmir Valley in the aftermath of Burhan's killing, the PDP-BJP government, in an unprecedented move, also banned a vibrant English daily, *Kashmir Reader,* on the evening of 3 October 2016. Farooq Ahmad Lone, the then deputy commissioner of Srinagar, issued the order to stop the publication of *Kashmir Reader* forthwith. The government order described the newspaper as 'a threat to the public tranquility': '...on the basis of credible inputs it has been observed that the daily News Paper namely *Kashmir Reader* published within the territorial jurisdiction of District Srinagar contains such material and content which leads to incite acts of violence and disturb public peace and tranquility.'[2]

Successive governments have curtailed the number of advertisements to newspapers that carry any kind of allegedly separatist content. After the 2010 street protests, the MHA issued an advisory to cut back or place a blanket ban on government advertisements to the Jammu-based English daily *Kashmir Times,* and Srinagar-based *Rising Kashmir* and *Greater Kashmir.* 'They just do it. They want newspaper editors to "behave", said a prominent journalist. All government advertisements were stopped to *Rising Kashmir* between 2010 and 2012. *Kashmir Times* continues to suffer because of the 2010 ban. Anuradha Bhasin, executive editor, *Kashmir Times,* says that the politics of controlling the media began in 2010. 'The continued ban on our advertisement since 2010 has affected our circulation, quality and staff members.' She points out that in other Indian states, the media is corporate-owned, but in J&K, the Army and intelligence agencies often play the role of the corporation. 'There is no uniform or standard advertisement policy based on a newspaper's credibility or circulation. The policy is whimsical. The government releases or stops advertisements to a newspaper based on its whims,' she adds.

While everyone struggles with the effects of this lost income, reporters and subeditors have to cope with another burden, that of editors telling them in subtly coded language what kind of terminology and nomenclature to follow to avoid losing government advertisements.

Along the way, another incremental casualty has been the absence of women journalists in the field. Conservative attitudes, the risks, and a combination of poor wages and a dangerous working environment militated against women choosing journalism as a career. At one point, some top rebel commanders of various guerrilla outfits like the HM and the JKLF wrote weekly columns in Urdu newspapers published from Srinagar, especially the popular weekly, *Chattan*. Some wrote under their own names; others used pseudonyms. Muhammad Farooq Rehmani, chairman of the Jammu and Kashmir People's Freedom League, and the late Amanullah Khan, co-founder of JKLF, were regular contributors. Rehmani propounded his pro-Pakistan ideology while Khan would make a case for Kashmir's independence. 'Their columns would generate a lot of debate in the early 1990s,' says Bashir Manzar, formerly associated with the militant organization, Muslim Janbaz Force in the 1990s and currently a staunch pro-India editor at Srinagar-based English daily, *Kashmir Images*. He would write for *Chattan*, too, under the nom de plume, Vikas Gul. 'Those were difficult years for journalists. There were no English newspapers then. *Chattan* was the most popular Urdu weekly. Those days, it was the militant's "darling" newspaper. And believe me, it used to sell like hot cakes.'

A journalist is considered to be adventurous, one who enjoys the challenges that his/her profession throws up. Indeed, I'm thrilled to be one. I always wanted to tell stories. The art of storytelling would always attract me. Hearing cricket commentators like Geoffrey Boycott, Richie Benaud and Ian Chappell, and watching presenters on television channels would interest me. As a child, clandestinely imitating them before a mirror had become a hobby for me. Every word that went on the airwaves seemed sacred to me, as if it was the gospel truth.

I began my career by writing snippets for a Srinagar-based English daily and soon switched to reporting events concerning common Kashmiris. I soon realized that in Kashmir, reporting events means walking a tightrope. The fundamentals of journalism—the five Ws (who, what, where, when, why) and one H (how), written objectively and with balance—began to fade away from my mind, not because of amnesia, but because of the ground realities in Kashmir.

No journalist in the world can understand the need behind using the word 'allegedly' in a news report better than those working in conflict zones. This word can mean the difference between life and death. For a journalist reporting on death and disaster, the word 'allegedly' is a recipe for survival. You learn quickly that even if you have seen with your own eyes a person in uniform firing a volley of bullets at a civilian on a street, you have to use the word 'allegedly' in your news story.

A few months as a trainee journalist made me realize that the 'third casualty' in times of conflict could be reporting all shades of opinion fearlessly. It is never easy for a human rights defender or a journalist to document and report the facts in Kashmir.

In 2002, I saw Zaffar Iqbal, a former colleague at an English newspaper, lying in a pool of blood, battling for his life. Unidentified assailants had shot several rounds of bullets at him from close range. He survived miraculously, though he still bears prominent scars on his nose and neck. I spent several hours while he was in the intensive care unit and later the post-operative ward at SKIMS. I was amazed to see him smile despite being in great pain. I vividly remember him being carried away on a stretcher when he signalled to me for a piece of paper and pen. He wanted to communicate something but couldn't speak. Blood was oozing from his nose and ears. 'I want to urinate,' he wrote.

There were conflicting reports about how and why Iqbal was targeted. We could never get to the bottom of the story. Living in a conflict zone often means relying on versions presented by the local police, public relations officers of the Army and the paramilitary, and the numerous spokespersons of guerrilla outfits like the HM and LeT. 'Journalists are sitting ducks,' says Zaffar. 'When perpetrators can't beat mediapersons, they get angry and in their frustration, use them as soft targets. Scribes working in a conflict zone are expected to please everyone, but one can't really make everybody happy.'

Soon after this horrific incident, close relatives and friends suggested that it might be better if I were to switch to some other profession. I politely refused. I don't know why. For obvious reasons, journalistic mediocrity is patronized in Kashmir and professionalism is discouraged. As far as non-State actors are concerned, any journalist who might consider a militant outfit's press note unfit for publication would invite its wrath. Newspaper offices have been routinely attacked in Kashmir. The offices of widely circulated English dailies like *Greater Kashmir* and several other publications have been attacked either by rebels or their sympathizers.

In the early years of armed militancy, journalists found themselves caught between the brutal State and equally brutal non-State actors. In 1996, Bashir Manzar, who worked as an associate editor with *Greater Kashmir* at the time, was kidnapped by the government-sponsored group, Ikhwan. He told me that the gunmen asked what his last wish was. He said it was to eat fish. After eating vast amounts of it, he vomited. Thankfully, he was let go.

Zafar Meraj, veteran journalist and editor of the English daily, *Kashmir Monitor*, was abducted by government-sponsored renegades in the late 1990s and shot on the Srinagar-Muzaffarabad road. They left him for dead. Despite multiple bullet injuries, he survived. In 2014, he unsuccessfully fought the assembly elections on the PDP ticket from Srinagar's Habba Kadal constituency. After losing in the elections, he became bitter and turned into one of the fiercest critics of the party he had once sympathized with.

On 7 September 1995, Yusuf Jameel, the BBC's correspondent in Srinagar at the time, survived a parcel bomb explosion at his Srinagar office when his colleague, Mushtaq Ali, opened a package addressed to Jameel. Ali, who was a photojournalist at Agence France-Presse, was seriously wounded in the blast and died a few days later. A memorial dedicated to him stands at the entrance of the Press Enclave in Srinagar.

'It was a letter bomb addressed to me,' says Jameel, who now works with *The Asian Age*. 'Fortunately, I survived. Unfortunately, Mushtaq Ali had to pay a heavy price for opening the parcel. After their threats to shut me up had failed, the army tried to kill me through the notorious renegade leader, Kuka Parray.' He says it is not unusual to face intimidation. 'In a conflict zone, this is but natural. Violence has become part of our daily life. I, for one, decided to face it and take things in my stride.'

All journalists would receive more than a dozen press statements from political parties and militant outfits on a daily basis. A journalist was then dubbed 'pro-militant' or 'pro-government', depending on who the aggrieved party was. Everyone expected coverage of their statements on BBC radio's popular evening broadcast. 'It was a Catch-22 situation. A double-edged sword,' Jameel remembers. The BBC advised him against taking undue risks. 'My organization knew that the army had been threatening me for some time. They advised caution. I did take precautions and curtailed my movements. I wouldn't go out alone. But who knew that the perpetrators would target me with a parcel bomb inside my office?'

In June 2006, unidentified gunmen assaulted and attempted to shoot Shujaat Bukhari, former special correspondent of the Chennai-based *The Hindu*, who later became editor-in-chief of *Rising Kashmir*. A man accosted Bukhari near Lal Chowk in the evening, pulled out a pistol and directed him to get into a waiting autorickshaw, in which another man was already sitting. 'At one point, one of the men received a call on his mobile phone. The autorickshaw abruptly changed direction. It stopped near Saidhpora, Eidgah, about 7 km from Lal Chowk, and I was pushed out and kicked. One of them took aim and pulled the trigger, but the pistol failed to fire. Then they fled,' he had told me three years ago. Unfortunately, he was not as lucky the next time. Twelve years later, in the month of Ramzan, he was killed outside his office in the Press Enclave in Srinagar.

On the evening of 14 June 2018, the devastating news about Bukhari's death came first through worried whispers, and then via an official confirmation. On TV, broadcast journalist Nazir

Masoodi said in a choked voice, '[The] editor-in-chief of the English daily *Rising Kashmir* has been killed by unidentified gunmen [...] just outside his office in the Press Enclave in the heart of Srinagar at around 7:20pm (IST) [...].'[3]

Professionally, I had known the slain editor for fourteen years. The last time I spoke to him was on his 50th birthday to wish him. He died the same year. Bukhari was a widely travelled, full-of-life journalist. He is survived by his parents, wife Dr Tehmeena, and two children. In the profession, he was my senior by over a decade, having cut his teeth as a reporter for the Jammu-based English daily *Kashmir Times* in the early 1990s. Later, he worked as a special correspondent for *The Hindu* for over a decade. For about two years, we worked together for Deutsche Welle as foreign contributors from Srinagar, before he started his own newspaper, *Rising Kashmir*, in 2008. Bukhari was also a promoter of his mother tongue, and one of the important cogs in the wheels of north Kashmir's literary organization, Adbi Markaz Kamraz. Additionally, he was editor of the daily *Buland Kashmir* and weekly *Parcham* in Urdu, and *Sangarmal* in Kashmiri.

In Kashmir, there are multiple narratives with regards to Bukhari's killing. One view is that apart from being an influential editor, he was also actively involved in Track-II dialogues and various peace initiatives. He had organized several conferences in Delhi, Dubai and Bangkok on Kashmir as a representative of the UK-based Conciliation Resources, an independent non-profit organization working towards peace-building. This stirred debate in Kashmir as to whether a journalist should become involved in such initiatives as a peacenik.

'Shujaat Bukhari occupied a dangerous space where his stature upset many in Pakistan, India and Kashmir,' said a key Kashmir observer who preferred to remain anonymous.

Khurram Parvez, a leading human rights activist and programme coordinator at JKCCS, was arrested in September 2016 after being detained under the notorious PSA. Parvez was charged with 'inciting protesters' a day after he was barred from travelling to Geneva to attend the UN Human Rights Council on

15 September 2016. Five days later, a court ordered his release, citing violations of procedure in his arrest and detention. He was first lodged at Kothibagh police station in Srinagar, taken to a sub-jail in frontier district Kupwara in north Kashmir to deny him legal aid, and subsequently shifted to Kot Bhalwal Jail in Jammu. In its hard-hitting editorial titled 'Rising Tensions in Kashmir', *The New York Times* demanded his release: 'Mr Parvez, who was subsequently detained on spurious charges, should be released and allowed to travel.'[4]

The two banned armed outfits, LeT and HM, had expressed discontent after the Dubai conference held in July 2017. In an interview, HM chief Syed Salahuddin had said that all participants of the Dubai conference were on 'India's payroll'.

Through a newspaper column, Ershad Mahmud, a Pakistani peace activist and one of Bukhari's many friends, had conveyed the message that there was a threat to the editor's life, after which Mahmud had found someone to contact Salahuddin. According to Mahmud, the HM chief had telegraphed that 'Salahuddin is not so low as to order the assassination of journalists'.

'Minutes before his [Bukhari's] death, he called me from Srinagar and advised me to take care as the campaign against us from fake social media accounts was getting shriller. His voice was wobbly, so I asked him to call later in the night to discuss in detail. Barely twenty minutes later, news of his cold-blooded murder started flashing,' wrote Iftikhar Gilani, a Kashmiri journalist based in Turkey and one of Bukhari's closest friends.[5]

'If Bukhari's closest friends knew that the threat to his life was so real, all they needed to do was to give a sound counsel [...] Shujaat could have stayed in either Delhi or Jammu for some months [...],' a prominent political analyst said on condition of anonymity.

Rabid members of a particular community, which included Ashoke Pandit and Aditya Raj Kaul, had been after Bukhari on the social media space, accusing him of being 'a pro-jihadi journalist'. Pro-Hindutva journalists such as Jagruti Shukla had said that 'Bukhari was killed by the same jihadi forces he sympathized with', while Indian political scientist Madhu Kishwar had accused Bukhari of taking crores of rupees from 'agencies' without ever substantiating her claim. This had forced Bukhari to file a defamation case against Kishwar.

On Kashmir's home turf, a section of people accused Bukhari of being an 'Indian collaborator' who, in their perception, was 'on a mission to sabotage the Tehreek-i-Azadi' and of receiving funds from the Indian Army to sustain his newspaper. Ironically, Delhi's federal government had curtailed advertisements to his newspaper, accusing it of propagating a 'secessionist agenda'. This is how blurred and dangerous the lines are in Kashmir.

On 21 June, the entire Kashmir Valley observed a complete shutdown to protest Bukhari's assassination on the call given by Kashmir's Joint Resistance Leadership comprising Syed Ali Geelani, Mirwaiz Umar Farooq and Mohammad Yasin Malik. All militant groups and political parties from across the ideological divide condemned his killing.

However, soon after Bukhari's murder, the J&K police registered an FIR number 51/2018 in the Kothibagh police station in Srinagar and suspected that a group comprising three militants were behind the editor's killing.[6] During the course of the investigations, police suspected the role of a top LeT militant Naveed Jatt—who, according to the police, was a Pakistani national from Multan—in Bukhari's killing, along with two local militants identified as Azad Ahmad Malik alias Azad Dada, and Muzaffar, a resident of Sopat in south Kashmir's Qazigund. Police claimed 'huge success' after killing Jatt alias Abu Hanzullah in a gunfight in central Kashmir's Budgam district on 28 November 2018. Azad, who was also suspected by the police to have played a role in Bukhari's killing, was killed five days before Jatt in south Kashmir's Anantnag district in a deadly encounter. 'Muzaffar is still alive,' a top police officer, who was privy to the investigations, revealed to me. In police records, Jatt had entered Kashmir in 2012 and was arrested in 2014. In February 2018, he gave the police a slip when he was being taken to a hospital in Srinagar for treatment.

'He (Naveed Jatt) was wanted by law for his complicity in a

series of terror crimes including (the) killing of noted journalist Shujaat Bukhari, attacks on security establishments and many other civilian atrocities,' said a statement issued by the J&K police on the evening of 28 November 2018.

However, many in Kashmir refused to buy the police's version and continued to ask: 'Who killed Shujaat Bukhari?' Some also suspected that Jatt was arrested from the site of an encounter in south Kashmir on 23 November 2018 in which six militants, including Azad Dada, had been killed. Their suspicion was that Jatt had been allegedly killed in a staged gunfight in central Kashmir a few days after his arrest and torture.

Riyaz Masroor, BBC's correspondent in Srinagar, was severely beaten by policemen outside his residence in July 2010, when a wave of pro-independence rallies rocked Kashmir. At the time, the Omar Abdullah-led coalition government had announced that curfew passes would be issued to journalists. 'Kashmir had turned into a virtual prison because of severe restrictions in long curfews in 2010. People were living as prisoners. As soon as I stepped out of my house, a policeman started beating me without giving me a fair chance to explain anything,' Masroor says.

On the second Friday of Ramzan, 26 June 2015, a group of young men mercilessly thrashed photojournalist Bilal Bahadur, who was covering clashes between the police and young men in downtown Nowhatta, outside the central mosque. 'I was taking pictures in Nowhatta Chowk. All of a sudden, a group of boys attacked me without any reason,' Bahadur recounts.

Newspaper terminology in Kashmir has also changed over the years. At the peak of militancy, Urdu newspapers would use the term 'mujahideen' for the militants. It changed, from 'guerrilla' to 'askariyat pasand' (gun-wielding rebels), to 'baagi' (rebel), and finally to 'shidat pasand' (extremists/militants). In the early 1990s, all leading newspapers in the Valley would publish news and views that reflected the dominant public discourse about the Kashmir problem and the human rights abuses, and the coverage of the pro-azadi movement and anti-State demonstrations. Naseer Ganai, a journalist, says,

In the initial years of the anti-India armed rebellion, the front page, edit page, and op-ed pages of newspapers would reflect the dominant political opinion of Kashmir. The focus was on enforced custodial disappearances, human rights excesses by the army and paramilitary, and the opinion pages would talk about the resolution of the Kashmir issue.

'Journalism is literature in a hurry,' Matthew Arnold had famously proclaimed. Journalists act as watchdogs of society and as conduits between the people and the government. But sometimes, the devil lies in the message and the messenger becomes the victim. Journalists in Kashmir have lived through a war-like situation, literally and figuratively. While the conflict might have abated, there are still landmines they have to watch out for. In this chapter, it is difficult to document all the hardships that journalists working in Kashmir have faced, but I do want to focus on one aspect, which is how vast sections of the media channels based in Noida, New Delhi and Mumbai have distorted Kashmir's ground realities.

Robert Fisk, noted British author and journalist, in an article published in *The Independent* on 21 June 2010, writes how journalists covering a conflict zone often become 'partners in crime.'[7] 'Most of all, it's about the terror of power and the power of terror. Power and terror have become interchangeable. We journalists have let this happen. Our language has become not just a debased ally, but a full verbal partner in the language of governments and armies and generals and weapons.'

Noam Chomsky, the well-known American public intellectual and linguist, in *Manufacturing Consent: The Political Economy of the Mass Media*, talks about how 'propaganda is to democracy what violence is to a dictatorship.' Economist Edward S. Herman and Chomsky together put forward a 'propaganda model' as a framework for analysing and understanding how the mainstream US media work and depend heavily and uncritically on elite information sources, and participate in propaganda campaigns obliging elite interests.[8]

Chomsky also talks about 'ten strategies of manipulation' by the media:[9]

- The strategy of distraction
- Create problems, then offer solutions
- The gradual strategy
- The strategy of deferring
- Go to the public as a little child
- Use the emotional side more than the reflection
- Keep the public in ignorance and mediocrity
- Encourage the public to be complacent with mediocrity
- Strengthen self-blame
- Get to know the individuals better than they know themselves

A journalist should, under no circumstances, become a government's stenographer or an activist for a cause. The job of a scribe is to constantly critique those in power, challenge people at the helm and ask tough questions. In the last hot and humid week of July 2015, some of the big names in Indian journalism converged on the banks of the Dal Lake to share their perspectives on themes like 'Kashmir's Portrayal in Indian Media' and 'Indian Electronic Media and Idea of Nationalism'. I was a panelist in several rounds of discussions.

The journalistic community in the Valley was divided over attending the inaugural Srinagar Media Summit in 2015, organized by *Lehar*, a lesser-known non-governmental organization. Top Indian journalists, columnists and commentators included late Kuldip Nayar, Saeed Naqvi, Siddharth Varadarajan, Humra Quraishi, Jayanta Ghosal, Shahid Siddiqui, Saba Naqvi, Rana Ayyub and Madhu Kishwar, among others. With notable exceptions, most of the invited journalists chose to use the platform to 'sermonize' and offer unsolicited suggestions to the Kashmiri audience, rather than listen to what the Kashmiris had to say.

In his inaugural speech, the late Nayar, instead of speaking on the subject, chose to talk about Pakistan-India relations and said it was impossible for Kashmiris to change the political status quo. He urged Kashmiris to be aware of geopolitical realities and reconcile with India. The idea of independent Kashmir threatens India, he said, adding that granting independence to the state was out of question. Granting maximum autonomy within the Indian Constitution could, however, be a solution. Nayar, who was born in Sialkot (now in Pakistan), said, quoting Pakistan's former PM Nawaz Sharif:

> My friendship with Nawaz Sharif goes back a long way. I met him in Jeddah (Saudi Arabia) during his wilderness years... He told me 'Neither we can take Kashmir from you, nor you can give Kashmir (to us)'... Kashmiris must realize that India will never let go of Kashmir, because secularism and democracy form the very spirit of India. We can offer all kinds of sacrifices to protect India's secular and democratic fabric.

Nayar's remarks had made the audience, which had comprised mostly young students and aspiring journalists, uncomfortable and tense. Some of them asked the panelists tough questions, and some students had got up in protest and shouted azadi slogans.

In tune with the remarks made by Nayar, Saeed Naqvi had said that the 'status quo will not be altered so far as the Kashmir issue is concerned, certain adjustments have to be made, as Kuldip has made it clear... In Kashmir, people's hearts are affected.' Naqvi did agree that a large section of the Delhi-based media is brought up on a diet of nationalism, jingoism and patriotism. 'It is not evolved yet and can trigger a riot by exaggerating one incident and downplaying another... There are certain sins which are common across the media,' he said.

Siddharth Varadarajan, Humra Quraishi and Rana Ayyub had adopted an approach that was more balanced and admitted that there have been attempts to 'kill stories in Kashmir for protecting (the) national interest.' Varadarajan, co-founder of *The Wire*, said that the decade of the 1990s was not a time Indian journalism could be proud of vis-à-vis Kashmir. 'Coverage of human rights abuses in Kashmir from 1989 to 2001 in the Indian media was pretty bad—virtually non-existent. The Press Council of India also did a shoddy job.' He acknowledged that there was blatant manipulation of the media in the early 1990s, but many journalists tried to do fair and balanced reporting even then, sometimes at their own risk. He, however, cautioned that one should not mistake the opinions of a journalist for the position of the Indian State, because there is a tendency in a conflict zone to pin the entire blame of collective failure of the state institutions on the media. On the Pathribal killings of March 2000, Varadarajan had said that some print journalists had played a key role in highlighting the cold-blooded murder of five civilians, but justice had not been served because of the systemic failures of State institutions. Be that as it may, it would be unfair to claim that all Indian newspapers, television channels and journalists are partners in crime. But misplaced nationalism and jingoism does blur perspectives. Why don't more journalists attempt to present the entire range of competing and conflicting narratives in Kashmir?

On 31 August 2016, Naseer Ahmad, a veteran broadcast journalist, quit his job at a news channel, alleging that he was being 'forced' to prepare 'fabricated anti-Kashmir' reports.[10] Naseer was affiliated with the Zee News Network for sixteen long years and joined IBN7 Hindi in November 2014. He also alleged that his channel had refused to air a news story about Riyaz Ahmad, an ATM guard who was purportedly killed by CRPF soldiers as he was returning home from work in 2016.

The problem is not as much about not covering Kashmir, but how it is covered and the language that is employed, which often criminalizes the legitimate political opinions and aspirations of Kashmiris. The attempts to stereotype Kashmiris as 'Pakistan proxies' and demonize their struggle with superficial coverage not only misleads the people in mainland India but also drives a wedge between them and Kashmiris.

In their coverage of the protests in 2016, some electronic media channels used old footage from 2008 and 2010. In July 2016, Zee News, Aaj Tak and India Today aired two videos to support the case that the crisis was sponsored by Pakistan and that Kashmiri mobs had been attacking government forces. In the first video, a young boy in his undershirt, surrounded by a group of CRPF personnel, was seen crying and saying, 'Geelani is paying ₹500 for throwing stones at Indian soldiers.' The video, from 2008, was run as an 'exclusive' report. In another attempt to distort reality, a pheran-clad Kashmiri man was shown throwing a petrol bomb at CRPF personnel. A woollen pheran in the heat of July? This was obviously false reportage.

Using old videos to tell a new story is unethical on multiple counts. The boy shown making a 'confession' in the first video later narrated his ordeal of being allegedly coerced by CRPF men in 2008 to make the statement. In any case, why was it shown as an 'exclusive' in 2016? By airing these videos, the channels in question only lend credence to the Kashmiri argument that vast sections of India's hypernationalist media cash in on falsehoods, propaganda and provocation, and feed on a daily diet of anti-Pakistan and anti-Kashmir rhetoric.

Appallingly, as the civilian death toll escalated in 2016, *Times Now* ran a ticker saying, '32 die in Kashmir in Pakistan-sponsored violence'. There can be no better example of the Delhi-based media's Pakistan paranoia. Afterwards, the same channel ran a campaign saying that Pakistan had sent ₹100 crore to encourage stone pelting in Kashmir through Syed Ali Geelani, who has been under house arrest for the last eight years. It must be said that those mediapersons who consider every word of the Army and police as the gospel truth, willingly become partners in the propaganda. They try to blame Pakistan for everything that happens or does not happen in Kashmir. True, Pakistan will always want to take advantage of a particular situation that is unfavourable for India, but the azadi sentiment is indigenous and deep-rooted in Kashmir. This reality of what Kashmir feels and wants is undeniable.

In the aftermath of India's air strike inside Pakistan territory on 26 February 2019 in 'retaliation' to the 14 February attack on a CRPF convoy in south Kashmir's Pulwama district, even somewhat moderate voices in Indian television seem to have forgotten the fundamental lessons of journalism. To say that the role played by overwhelming sections of the Indian media—even by celebrated television anchors—during the recent escalation of violence between Pakistan and India, was provocative, propagandist and irresponsible would be an understatement.

It doesn't help that a crisis invariably means that journalists from outside the state are airdropped into Kashmir. Many television journalists, who can hardly tell whether the APHC is a conglomerate or a single party or what exactly is the difference between the APHC led by Geelani and the one headed by Mirwaiz Umar Farooq, or how many districts there are in the Kashmir Valley and how their names are pronounced, can hardly do justice to the Kashmir story. They are parachuted in to parrot the government's lines on Kashmir. They do not come to Kashmir to report facts. They come to distort them, and act as extensions of the State.

They often do the job of firefighting and think of themselves as conflict managers rather than journalists reporting and analysing the facts on the ground, as they are. Whenever Kashmir is on edge, this 'army in civvies' on 'Mission Kashmir' with the aim to 'douse flames' will tell you that Kashmir is angry, and that Kashmiris are feeling more alienated than before. But they won't tell you the truth: that Kashmiris are raising azadi slogans and demanding a just political solution to the Kashmir dispute.

These propagandists in the guise of journalists try and equate State-sponsored violence with young protesters hurling stones. They show pictures of fourteen members of the paramilitary and the police being treated for minor scratches at an Army hospital in Srinagar to draw unfair parallels with the violence perpetrated by government forces in which hundreds are killed and thousands wounded. They try to stoke nationalistic passions in various parts of India by erroneously showing that brave soldiers are exercising maximum restraint while dealing with Kashmir's 'agitational terrorism' and 'terrorist sympathizers'. These terms are often used to demonize Kashmiris and criminalize and delegitimize their political aspirations and demands.

Large sections of the Delhi-based media wear their patriotism on their sleeves and behave as if they are defending their borders from their air-conditioned studios and OB (outside broadcasting) vans. They could be described as 'fidayeen in television studios'. India and its corporate-owned media and propagandists must wake up to the reality that it is not merely anger or alienation that they witness in Kashmir but the unambiguous political demand of the people of the state for a just political resolution.

Having said that, there are sections of the Indian print and online media that have done an excellent job in telling various aspects of the Kashmir story in an impartial and balanced manner. Many journalists, columnists and academics have written excellent pieces on Kashmir.

I have been witness to how some journalists frame their questions to shikarawallahs near the Dal Lake. They ask questions like whether they want tourists to visit the Valley. Naturally, the shikarawallahs say 'yes'. In their piece to the camera, the journalists weave a narrative that the shikarawallahs in Kashmir have nothing to do with the azadi movement because all they aspire for is a good tourist season. I remember an Indian journalist advising Kashmiris to be 'happy' in 2012, to forget the scars of the past, move on and enjoy life.[11] Because tourists were flooding the Valley at the time and a million visitors were expected that season, the birds were singing again, the tulips of Kashmir were better than Amsterdam's, the hoardings in Pampore proclaimed that the 'world's best saffron grows here', tourist huts in Gulmarg were full, no rooms were vacant at hotels, and houseboats too were fully occupied. Tourist activity was portrayed as a 'normalcy indicator' and erroneously juxtaposed with Kashmir's political narrative. The journalist argued that only the Kashmiri elite who enjoyed a life of luxury in America and Europe were desperate to preserve the 'sentiment for freedom'. He wrote that those wearing jeans and sipping cappuccino at cafés had nothing to do with Azadi. The Kashmir in salwar-kameez is orthodox and sad, he seemed to imply, while the Kashmir in jeans is liberal and happy. Kashmir at dastarkhwan is extremist; Kashmir at a café or fast-food joint is moderate. Kashmir watching PTV and QTV* doesn't want to forget; the Kashmir watching MTV, Sony, and IPL on Set Max is willing to forget, forgive and move on. If Kashmiris are updating their statuses on Facebook, they are a danger to peace, security

---

*PTV and QTV are Pakistani channels.

and stability. If the state's former CM (Omar Abdullah) is on Twitter, it means that peace has returned.

Till then, Kashmir was a 'nuclear flashpoint', the 'world's highest militarized zone', and a 'beautiful prison'. But all of a sudden, we were told that Kashmir is happy. Kashmir wants to forget. Kashmir wants to forgive. Kashmir wants to move on. Below is an excerpt from the article:

> Trauma in Kashmir is like a heritage building—the elite fight to preserve it. 'Don't forget', is their predominant message, 'Don't forget to be traumatised... Is it obscene to search for happiness in Kashmir, is it obscene for a writer from the south of India to wander around Kashmir interviewing people who will tell him that they want to get on with their lives despite the presence of the Indian Army? What is the stake of an outsider in Kashmir? The fact is that Kashmir, too, has occupied India. Kashmir is the reason why India is one of the worst victims of terrorism. All Indians have a stake in Kashmir's state of mind.

Writers with such a mindset seem to suggest something along the lines of, 'If rape becomes unavoidable, enjoy it'. Has Washington 'moved on' and forgotten 9/11? Has Delhi 'moved on' from the 26/11 Mumbai attacks and decided to make peace with Pakistan? Have Muslims in India 'moved on' from the Babri Masjid demolition and the 2002 Gujarat pogrom, and are they happy with their poor social, political and economic status? Have Palestinians 'moved on' to forget the atrocities of the Israeli State and its Army, and accepted the occupation of its land as its fate?

Kashmir is an 'inseparable limb', we hear from Delhi. Kashmir is our 'jugular vein', we hear from Islamabad. They decide whether Kashmir is happy or sad, what Kashmir should get or not, and what Kashmir deserves or not. They decide what is good for Kashmir or not. They decide whether independence is viable or not. They decide whether the calm is 'deceptive, temporary or permanent'. They decide whether 'common sense is finally prevailing and winning' or 'missing', may be forced into a 'custodial disappearance', or possibly, killed in a 'fake encounter', buried in 'mass graves'. They decide. They sermonize. Kashmir listens.

If a skullcap-wearing shikarawallah rows his boat in the Dal Lake to earn his livelihood, it means he wants to get on with his life. It does not mean that he has no political opinion. The same holds true for the hotelier who wants rooms occupied, and the travel agent who wants tourists to visit the Valley. If a student sips a cappuccino or eats a burger, does it mean he or she is happy with the current state of affairs and wants to support Delhi? If a couple listens to romantic ghazals at a restaurant, does it mean they have given up their basic political, economic and human rights?

In 2016, Kashmir's shikarawallahs unanimously declared that New Delhi-based journalists had distorted their narrative.[12] Lending their backing to the 2016 uprising, they said their aspirations were no different from those of their fellow Kashmiris. The Shikarawallah Association of Kashmir said that it was more concerned about the loss of precious human lives than the 'tourist season'.

In 2016, several star anchors and scribes came rushing to Kashmir to cover why Kashmir's school toppers were joining rebel groups. There was a time when it was said that only rich expatriate 'Facebook assassins' were instigating violence. Then, it was said that only 5 per cent of the dissenting population who allegedly came from below-poverty-line families were involved in protests. Both these claims have been falsified.

On 9 August 2016, Narendra Modi first broke his silence on the unrest that had gripped Kashmir following the killing of Burhan Wani. Unfortunately, he also ended up stereotyping Kashmiri youth as stone pelters. He described tens of thousands of common Kashmiris protesting on the streets of Kashmir as a 'handful of people who have been misled' to cause trouble. He made an appeal to the young, saying that those who should be holding laptops, bats and balls in their hands and those who should be having dreams in their hearts are the ones carrying stones. I wanted to ask him if there were indeed a 'handful of people' out on the streets, why did the CRPF need to use 1.3 million pellets in just thirty-two days[13]? This was stated by the CRPF in an affidavit, in response to a public interest litigation seeking a ban on the use of pellet-firing shotguns. As mentioned before, in November 2018, a nineteen-month baby named Hiba from south Kashmir became the youngest pellet victim of Kashmir. Doctors performing surgery on Hiba's eye feared that she might permanently lose vision in that eye. Hiba was at home with her mother when clashes broke out outside between government forces and young protesters in Shopian district.

On 17 August 2016, Kashmiri journalist Sumaiya Yousuf was abused, beaten, heckled and threatened by a senior sub-divisional police officer in Srinagar on her way home from work. She was carrying a curfew pass and a press card with her. But, it didn't matter. Yousuf later wrote a first-person account to describe her ordeal.[14] She was not interviewed by any news channel based in Noida or Mumbai because perhaps her story did not fit in with the Indian media's dominant Kashmir narrative. The Noida- and Mumbai-based media houses did not conduct any prime-time debates on the custodial murders of lecturer Shabir and school principal Rizwan either.

During the 2016 agitation, most of the leaders who espouse the cause of self-determination were either in jail or under house arrest. Those who were not in prison were not allowed free movement to propagate their viewpoint. A blanket ban was placed on Internet, cellular and SMS services, and data connectivity.[15] After Burhan's killing, all cellular services, barring those provided by the State-owned Bharat Sanchar Nigam Limited, were rendered dysfunctional for many weeks. A clear attempt was made to kill the Kashmir story through a communication blockade.[16] The population was kept under constant vigil and strict surveillance by troops who patrolled the streets. That was how peace was arrived at on the battleground of ideas.

On 18 April 2016, an official press release by the office of Kashmir's then divisional commissioner said, 'The Divisional Commissioner, Kashmir, Dr Asgar Hassan Samoon, Monday directed the operators of social media news agencies to obtain proper permission from the concerned Deputy Commissioners for posting news on social media news groups along with sources.' This was not just a routine statement from the divisional commissioner's office. A warning for those who would not comply soon followed. It said strict action would be taken against 'violators'. The then PDP-BJP government's official crackdown on social media platforms like WhatsApp gave the state the distinction of being the first place in the world where a registration certificate was needed to form a WhatsApp group. The state government's directive for WhatsApp groups and the close monitoring of social media activity on Facebook and Twitter took everyone by surprise. Many started questioning such restrictions on the Internet in an age when the world is moving towards increased privacy and encryption.

Ahmed Ali Fayyaz, senior Kashmiri journalist, has been running a news portal on Whatsapp called First Post. He received a strict warning from the police, and an FIR was registered against him for allegedly defaming the J&K police's SOG. 'Intolerance touching its zenith in J&K. To gag media, Mehboobaji's Police filed FIR and sought my imprisonment for 3 yrs for "defaming" SOG,' he wrote on Twitter.

After Burhan Wani's killing, the government shut down local media outlets for more than four days. A near-total blackout on news was ensured after the then PDP-BJP government's chief spokesperson and senior cabinet minister, Naeem Akhtar, 'conveyed' the coalition government's decision to enforce restrictions on the media on 15 July to the editors and publishers of Srinagar-based newspapers.[17] Successive governments in J&K have gagged local media and imposed curbs, like the complete blackout of the Internet and the General Packet Radio Service.

Police personnel raided the offices of Kashmir's leading English dailies, *Greater Kashmir*, *Rising Kashmir*, *Kashmir Reader*, *Kashmir Observer*, and others. 'Authorities on Saturday midnight gagged *Greater Kashmir* by raiding its corporate office at Rangreth on city outskirts. Police arrested printing press foreman, Biju Chaudary, and two other employees,' the newspaper's website said. The policemen seized the plates of *Greater Kashmir* along with more than 50,000 printed copies of its sister publication,

Kashmir Uzma, and closed down its printing press.

A police party from Budgam police station raided *Rising Kashmir*'s press and seized copies of the newspaper. It reported on its website that the police took into custody all its employees, including foreman Mohammad Yousuf, and asked him to identify the distribution site. 'They later reached Press Enclave in Srinagar and seized the vehicle along with the driver,' *Rising Kashmir* said on its webpage.

The role played by a majority of journalists from India, especially those working for television channels (barring rare exceptions), has dented their credibility in Kashmir. The partisan, biased, unfair, one-sided and often provocative coverage of Kashmir by a large section of the electronic media has played a detrimental role in misguiding the general masses in India about the real problem in Kashmir. Not only does this erode the credibility of the media, it further estranges the common Kashmiri from New Delhi.

Most Indian journalists, barring reasonable exceptions, cover Kashmir only during a crisis, and often from air-conditioned studios in Noida and Mumbai, and, therefore, are not interested in the nuances of the Kashmir story. That's why we seldom hear that Burhan represents the fifth generation of Kashmiris since 1931 to have fought for fundamental human and political rights.

The Dal Lake freezes over only during harsh winter, but when it comes to reporting about Kashmir, the mindset of the Indian media and the political dispensations in New Delhi remain frozen through all seasons.

NOTES, SOURCES AND REFERENCES

1. Kashmir dailies carry blank front pages to protest denial of state ads. (2019, March 10). Retrieved from https://www.telegraphindia.com/india/kashmirdailies-carry-blank-front-pages-to-protest-denial-of-state-ads/cid/1686547
2. Masood, B. (2016, October 03). J&K govt bans Kashmir Reader, calls it a threat to 'public tranquility'. Retrieved from http://indianexpress.com/article/india/india-news-india/j-k-govt-bans-kashmir-reader-calls-it-a-threat-to-public-tranquility-3063128/
3. Geelani, G. (2018, June 24). Footprints: What Weapons Can't Kill. Retrieved

from https://www.dawn.com/news/1415727

4. Rising Tensions in Kashmir [Editorial]. (2016, September 23). The New York Times. Retrieved from https://www.nytimes.com/2016/09/24/opinion/rising-tensions-in-kashmir.html

5. Gilani, I. (2018, June 20). Shujaat Bukhari: A profile in courage. Retrieved from https://www.dnaindia.com/analysis/column-shujaat-bukhari-a-profile-in-courage-2627372

6. An off-the record conversation with a top J&K Police officer.

7. Fighting talk: The new propaganda. (2010, June 21). Retrieved from http://www.independent.co.uk/voices/commentators/fisk/fighting-talk-the-new-propaganda-2006001.html

8. Herman, E. S., & Chomsky, N. (1988). Manufacturing consent: A propaganda model. *Manufacturing Consent.*

9. Chomsky, N. (2011). 10 strategies of manipulation by the media. Retrieved from https://parisis.files.wordpress.com/2011/01/noam-chomsky.pdf

10. Qazi, S. (2016, September 03). Kashmiri journalist on why he left IBN7: 'Blind nationalism can't be news'. Retrieved from http://www.catchnews.com/india-news/kashmiri-journalist-on-why-he-left-ibn7-blind-nationalism-can-t-be-news-1472835437.html

11. Joseph, M. (2012, April 21). Sorry, Kashmir Is Happy. Retrieved from http://www.openthemagazine.com/article/india/sorry-kashmir-is-happy

12. Shikarawalas Say They Now Long For Azadi, Not Tourists. (2017, April 03). Retrieved from https://kashmirobserver.net/2016/business/shikarawalas-say-they-now-long-azadi-not-tourists-9145

13. Ashiq, P. (2016, August 19). 1.3 million pellets used in 32 days, CRPF tells HC. Retrieved from http://www.thehindu.com/todays-paper/13-million-pellets-used-in-32-days-crpf-tells-hc/article9005202.ece

14. Yousuf, S. (2019, June 10). Woman Reporter Attacked: Isn. Retrieved from http://www.thecitizen.in/index.php/NewsDetail/index/3/8527/Woman-Reporter-Attacked-Isnt-This-Your-Police-Ms-Mufti

15. Hassan, A. (2019, March 25). Forced to Log Off: Why the Global Internet Shutdown Score is Not Good News for Kashmir. Retrieved from https://www.news18.com/news/india/forced-to-log-off-why-the-global-internetshutdown-score-is-not-good-news-for-kashmir-2076721.html

16. Jan Rydzak (言睿择). (2019, March 23). 1/ NEW WORKING PAPER on #InternetShutdown-s and protest in #India based on thousands of data points from 2016. Bottom line: shutdowns are followed by a clear *increase* in violent protest & have very ambiguous effects on peaceful demonstrations. #KeepItOn papers.ssrn.com/sol3/papers.cf... pic.twitter.com/B6kfZUmGVF. Retrieved from https://twitter.com/ElCalavero/status/1109599815824887808

17. Ganai, N. (2019, March 20). India's Chanakyas | Meet Naeem Akhtar, Former J&K CM Mehbooba Mufti's 'Chanakya'. Retrieved from https://www.outlookindia.com/magazine/story/india-news-mehbooba-mufti-advisorswaheed-ur-rehman-parra-and-naeem-akhtar/301356

9

THE PATH AHEAD

Though atrocities like the Holocaust and the Palestinian crisis are rightly memorialized for their horror, the world is yet to take cognizance of the conflict in Kashmir despite its close to 100,000* dead, over 6,000 mass and unmarked graves in three districts of the Kashmir Valley, the Rajouri and Poonch districts in the Pir Panjal region, and the thousands of disappeared youth since 1989.

In 2014, I visited the Holocaust Memorial in Berlin. The Bundestag (the German parliament) had approved the Memorial's construction on 25 June 1999. The visit to the 'Memorial to the Murdered Jews of Europe' at the centre of the German capital, was heart-wrenching and a chilling reminder of the shattered dreams and lives of the estimated 6 million Jews who were mercilessly murdered by Nazi Germany. Such memorials keep alive the memory of the horrific crimes.

Passing through a seemingly endless sea of rectangular stone slabs and blocks, one is overwhelmed by deep distress and anxiety. I felt as if I was walking through the graveyards of Kashmir. There are numerous 'martyrs' graveyards' in almost every district of Kashmir and in Pir Panjal, but the state does not allow any formal memorials to honour victims of State-sponsored violence. At the Information Centre underneath Berlin's Memorial, the Holocaust victims have names and faces. In Kashmir, many victims' graves are unmarked. A guide at the Holocaust Memorial asked for my

---

*As mentioned is Chapter 7, there are various estimates regarding the death toll. This is an unofficial estimate.

opinion about the Memorial's architecture. 'What do you think of these rectangular slabs?' she asked. 'A chilling reminder of the worst times and horrible crimes in German history,' I replied. What has happened before can happen again.[1] The challenge, therefore, is to ensure that the worst is not repeated. In the modern world, where economic and strategic relations are decisive and paramount, human rights and freedoms often take a back seat. I was reminded of this sad reality again, when, as a 'Munich Young Leader,' I participated in the historic 50th Müncher Sicherheitskonferenz (Munich Security Conference) in February 2014. At this high-profile three-day world event, strategies to manage and resolve global conflicts were discussed exhaustively. The conflicts in Syria, Ukraine and Afghanistan topped the list. The Israel-Palestine dispute also found a detailed mention. Issues like cybercrime, data abuse and surveillance were discussed. The controversial nuclear programme of Iran was deliberated upon at some length. There was, however, no mention of the Kashmir conflict. Not a single statement was made on critical human rights issues in the region. I witnessed the same indifference (or ignorance, perhaps) at the Berlin Foreign Policy Forum in November 2015 and also at the annual Munich Young Leaders' meeting in Madrid, Spain, in September 2018.

The silence on Kashmir I encountered at these international forums angered me. Why does the world ignore Kashmir? Is this deliberate, to please New Delhi? Is this 'ignorance' an attempt to strengthen economic ties with a major emerging market? Or is it simply because Kashmir has no strategic importance for either the US or Europe?

International relations are largely built on quid pro quo. Pakistan and China granted each other the Most Favoured Nation (MFN) status in 1963, after China attacked India in 1962. It was a reconfirmation of sorts that China and Pakistan treated India as their common enemy. Noted South Asia experts have also argued that Pakistan-China relations are inspired by their mutual rivalry with India. In Pakistan, the perception of China is that of an unfaltering 'all-weather friend' and a reliable ally, regardless of regional and global stances.[2] 'In 1962, Saudi Arabia did not support

Pakistan when a resolution on Kashmir came up for discussion in the United Nations, so as to not alienate India,' writes Christophe Jaffrelot in *Pakistan at The Crossroads: Domestic Dynamics and External Pressures.*

Apart from the hundreds of martyrs' graveyards that dot the Valley, I have also been witness to thousands of ugly military bunkers. In 2008, I got a chance to see a huge Cold War-era nuclear bunker in Germany that had been thrown open to the public. I, along with friends and colleagues in Bonn, paid a visit to the bunker that was situated beneath the vine-covered hills of the Ahr Valley. The experience forced me to think about the repercussions, if India and Pakistan were to ever indulge in a nuclear war. As mentioned earlier, both countries came close to fighting one after the suicide bomb attack in Pulwama in February 2019. The IAF claimed to have launched an air strike in Balakot, Pakistan, at a JeM target, to which the Pakistan Air Force responded with its air strike while crossing over the LoC.

Inside the bunker, the local guide explained some interesting facts about the Cold War and the need for constructing such a huge bunker at the time. Its construction started in 1960 and was completed twelve years later, in 1972. It was designed to house some 3,000 German officials, all important men and women—including the chancellor, the president, cabinet members, members of the Constitutional Court (the highest court in Deutschland) and other key officials.

After the end of the communist regime in East Germany in 1989, the fall of the Berlin Wall, the historic reunification of East and West Germany in October 1990, and finally the transfer of the reunified German government and political institutions from Bonn to Berlin in 1991, the German government decided to close the nuclear bunker in 1997. It was, our guide told us, one of West Germany's best-kept secrets. It was stocked with oxygen tanks, gas masks and a sufficient quantity of food for 3,000 people for one month. The bunker is now a museum.

West Germany's nuclear bunker made me think of Kashmir. The ugly security bunkers of government forces dot every corner of Kashmir. Every Kashmiri child knows what a 'bunker' is. While planning visits to relatives, friends or doctors, or going to tuition classes during times of unrest, we always discussed which routes had fewer bunkers and were relatively safer to take. Apart from making the region look like a battlefield, these bunkers made of piled-up sandbags, evoked an atmosphere of fear. At many places, sand bunkers were replaced by concrete ones—a signal that the troops would stay on in Kashmir.

In 2006, there was an attempt to 'beautify' the bunkers. It was to make them appear 'people-friendly' and 'presentable' to tourists, said government officials. The old structures were replaced by new ones, which had exteriors that looked like wooden huts, with sandbags or concrete structures on the inside, from where they were not easily visible. In the first phase, the bunkers from Airport Road to Shalimar Garden in Srinagar were 'modernized'. The construction of each unit would cost the state exchequer over ₹20,000, taking the first phase investment to nearly ₹300,000. At that time, pro-independence parties and the APHC accused the government of 'camouflaging the prevailing situation in restive Kashmir'.

Saleem Beg, the then director general of the state's tourism department, believed that the place would be better off without the bunkers in the first place. 'There should be no bunkers; the question of ugly or beautiful does not arise,' he told me. The government said that the aim of the drive was to attract more tourists to the state. At the time, though the police believed that the state was returning to normalcy, it maintained that 'bunkers can't be removed'. The then inspector general of police (Kashmir Zone), K. Rajendra Kumar, told me that the construction wing of the J&K police was building new bunkers to make them 'visually people-friendly'. 'We don't want to make tourists think of Kashmir as a battlefield,' said Kumar, who retired as the director general of the J&K Police.

Regardless of the official line, Kashmir remains a battlefield for a variety of reasons. In 2012, there was one government armed person for every seventeen Kashmiris.[3] This was so during the post-Burhan agitation that erupted in July 2016. Despite official claims made by the Army and police chiefs that militancy has declined and there were only a few hundred present in the Valley at the time, why was such a huge Army presence required to fight 250-odd armed rebels? Ironically, in other parts of the globe, amusement parks, gardens, playgrounds, stadiums, roads, buildings, bridges, airports, railway stations, shopping malls, museums, circuses, theatres, cinemas, bowling alleys, bars and pubs are given a facelift to attract tourists, but in Kashmir, it was the bunkers!

Meanwhile, on a visit to Amsterdam in early 2010, I had a chance to see the house where Holocaust victim Anne Frank sought refuge along with her family to escape the persecution of Jews. She wrote a diary in which she recorded painful accounts about her hiding and atrocities of Hitler's Nazi troops. It was first published in 1947, two years after her death in a Nazi concentration camp at age fifteen.

I have often wondered why Germany, which favours 'free speech', considers it necessary to ban Adolf Hitler's autobiography *Mein Kampf* (My Struggle). In Germany, there are few other bans or restrictions in place. Nazi symbols such as the salute have been deemed illegal in the country since the end of World War II. The denial of the Holocaust is unlawful. Germany's parliament passed a law in 1985 making it a crime to deny the mass killings (extermination) of the Jews. Nine years later, in 1994, the law was tightened further. Now, anyone who publicly endorses, denies or plays down the genocide of Jews faces a maximum penalty of five years in jail and a fine. In 2010, a German court convicted Richard Williamson, a British Bishop, of incitement and imposed a fine of €10,000 after he was accused of denying the Holocaust.

In late 2008, I visited various cities in Poland, Gdynia, Gdańsk and Sopot, where I was also able to see the Holocaust Memorial. In April 2015, I visited the Imperial War Museum in London. Each visit was a rewarding experience and a reminder that it is in the world's best interest to resolve conflicts for durable peace. In this context, several international relations experts, academics and political scientists have written volumes about 'the role of negotiations as a means to understand and reform the conflict, thereby strengthening its viability as the main tool of conflict resolution.'[4] There is every chance that unresolved conflicts will escalate and give rise to violence and threaten regional stability and peace.

In the years following the World War II, many recalled and recorded stories of horror in Nazi concentration camps, where inmates were subjected to unimaginable torture. They were treated as slaves, abused and humiliated until they gave up and died of exhaustion, disease or physical pain, or were exterminated. Many Germans I spoke to feel ashamed of their country's tainted history.

Kashmir is full of painful stories, too. In the traumatized Valley, civilians have been killed, arrested, tormented, tortured, harassed, paraded naked and subjected to humiliation and physical harm. Since 1989, there has been no end to stories of horror and pain. JKCCS and APDP published a report regarding the same in February 2019, using 432 case studies.[5] Perhaps not at the scale of the Nazi pogrom in Europe, but Kashmir too has had its share of 'concentration camps'. Interrogation centres like Papa-II, Cargo and Tattoo Ground, were established to subject civilians to sustained torture. People still get goosebumps when they pass any of these centres. Though Papa-II, which overlooks the Dal Lake, has been converted to 'Fairview', former CM Mehbooba Mufti's official residence, Tattoo Ground and Cargo are intact.

Fifty years down the line, the geopolitical situation might alter. There could be a new world order. The power balance in South Asia could shift. Maybe, by that time, the people of India might realize how they were misled by sections of the media about the ground realities of Kashmir, and the inhuman treatment meted out to Kashmiris. What then?

Ramachandra Guha, in one of his pieces in *Hindustan Times*, in October 2016, argued:[6]

> While elsewhere in the country, Virat Kohli scores double hundreds, and R. Ashwin claims his 200th wicket, records of

another sort are being broken in Kashmir. Here the curfew has reached its century of days, the death toll is close to a century too, while bullet injuries and blindings now number in the thousands rather than hundreds. The records set by Kohli, Ashwin and company bring credit to Indian cricket. The records being set in Kashmir bring shame to India and Indian democracy.

In modern Germany, most Germans strongly condemn Adolf Hitler's acts and there is little or no sympathy for him. They refuse to acknowledge any good Hitler might have done, because his evil deeds are so overwhelming. A majority of Germans don't even want to hear his name or talk about him.

Today, the questions before the New Delhi establishment, its political leadership, and its people are: Would you like to address and resolve the Kashmir issue today, or let it linger for years? Would you want your future generations to feel apologetic about the civilian killings in Kashmir, the choking of democratic spaces and the widespread crackdown on common people?

Kashmir's struggle is essentially a political struggle that involves identity, ethnicity, religion and nationalism. Kashmir has had its versions of 'concentration camps', where people were tortured, mutilated and humiliated, and subjected to sexual atrocities and terrible physical pain.[7] This one-time 'paradise on earth' seems synonymous with pain, abuse, violation and the denial of basic human and political rights. How can Kashmir's paradise be regained?

Negotiation is a non-violent technique. Inflexible political stances have seldom allowed Delhi and Islamabad to continue negotiations or composite dialogue processes for a long time. It is in the interest of Islamabad, Delhi and Srinagar to take lessons from German history, the Holocaust and the fall of the Berlin Wall. Kashmir may not have Berlin-style memorials or 'Anne Frank' kind of diaries yet, but its present generation is keeping the memory alive in many creative ways.

How can the leadership in India, Pakistan and Kashmir arrive at a 'win-win' situation and resolve the dispute forever so that future generations do not suffer? Is such a solution at all possible, which can satisfy all the stakeholders? What are the solutions and formulae that have been proposed thus far? Precisely speaking, what is the ideal Kashmir solution, if there is one at all?

Fundamentally, there are three stated positions. New Delhi considers J&K as its 'atoot ang' (inseparable limb) and through a Parliamentary Resolution of 22 February 1994, also lays claim to the part of J&K that had been administered by Pakistan since 1947.[8] Islamabad lays claim to the part of J&K administered by India and calls it its 'shah rag' (jugular vein). In J&K, the dominant sentiment is for complete independence from both Pakistan and India, though there are sections that favour a merger with Pakistan or are happy with the status quo. Some experts and Kashmir watchers have been arguing that there are no 'magic bullet solutions' to Kashmir; some have termed it intractable, while others claim that only a statesman-like leadership in the involved nation states, backed by strong political will, can actually resolve it once and for all. In this scenario, what could be the ideal solution? Does such a leadership exist, which is prepared to think 'out of the box'? Will the people of Kashmir accept anything short of Azadi?

One of J&K's oldest regional political parties, the NC, favours greater autonomy. The NC also passed a resolution in the state's legislative assembly on 26 June 2000, after accepting the report and recommendations of the State Autonomy Committee (SAC).[9] The greater autonomy that the NC seeks will be a constitutional position that the state enjoyed before 1953, when New Delhi only controlled defence, communications, foreign affairs and currency.

Ramachandra Guha in another one of the columns he wrote for *Hindustan Times* in 2016, titled 'Why We Must Listen to Jayaprakash Narayan on Kashmir', quoted the latter, saying that 'it will be a suicide of the soul of India, if India tried to suppress the Kashmiri people by force'.[10] Rather than rely on repression, Guha, quoting Narayan, wrote, what 'the Government of India can do is go back to the 1947–53 days, that is, go back to the time when the state had acceded to India only in three subjects [i.e. Defence, Foreign Affairs and Communications]. This would mean providing for the fullest possible autonomy.'

The state of J&K has its own constitution and flag. Also, by virtue of its 'permanent residence' (state subject) law and Article 370, it enjoys a special status within the Union of India. No resident from any other state can buy land or property in the state. Though the NC does not challenge the region's constitutional relationship with the Union of India, it refuses to accept the status quo either and insists that J&K has only acceded to India, and not merged with it.

In his autobiography, *My Country, My Life*, L.K. Advani, former deputy PM of India, while talking about the NC's autonomy resolution in a chapter titled 'Dealing with the Kashmir Issue', writes:[11]

> The nation was shocked on 26 June 2000, during the Vajpayee government's rule in New Delhi, when the Jammu and Kashmir Assembly adopted a report of the State Autonomy Committee (SAC) and asked the Centre to immediately implement it. The SAC recommended return of the constitutional situation in J&K to its pre-1953 status by restoring to the state all subjects for governance except defence, foreign affairs, currency and communication.

Advani minces no words while explaining how the NC chewed up its demand. He writes: 'This was one occasion when both Atalji and I had to be very firm with the state's chief minister, Dr Farooq Abdullah, whose National Conference was in fact a part of the ruling NDA at the Centre. We advised him not to press for the implementation of the SAC report.' When Abdullah was told to 'bend', he 'crawled'. Advani writes that 'Indeed, Atalji told Dr Abdullah to decide whether to continue in the NDA at the Centre following the Union Cabinet's rejection of the state assembly's autonomy resolution. To his credit, Dr Abdullah allowed the issue to lapse.'

The BJP-led NDA government's Union cabinet, in its meeting in New Delhi on 4 July that year, rejected the NC's autonomy resolution. On the same day, Advani adopted a hawkish stand on the issue and told the media that accepting the assembly's autonomy resolution will 'set the clock back'. However, to find a meaningful and long-lasting solution, New Delhi, as a confidence-building measure, has to set the clock back at some stage, something that has been accepted by senior Indian politicians like P. Chidambaram, Sitaram Yechury and Dr Karan Singh (I have alluded to this in earlier chapters).

The PDP also favours a solution within the ambit of the Indian Constitution and bats for self-rule in both parts of Kashmir with a possible joint control (India-Pakistan) mechanism. 'Achievable Nationhood' is another model floated by Sajad Lone, who heads a faction of the Peoples' Conference and is considered to be a poster boy of the BJP. Lone's model talks of a state of affairs where 'the long-term objective would be to convert the entire territory of the state of J&K into a neutral, peace zone.' It includes demilitarization, decommissioning of weapons of non-State armed groups and hopes that a new security paradigm would emerge once peace has been established. Subject to the principle that foreign affairs are the responsibility of India, J&K will have the right to engage on its own with the State of Pakistan and the state of J&K within the parameters of the respectively 'defined relationships'. Lone takes inspiration from the 'Hong Kong model' in terms of independence and powers of the government of Hong Kong, as well as the evolution of an irreversible, interdependent relationship between the British, the Irish Republic and Northern Ireland in the Good Friday Agreement. He feels a blend of these could provide an inspiring and stimulating setting for resolution and peace in J&K. However, his detractors in Kashmir have joked about his model and dismissed it as 'Chewable Nationhood'. The speed with which he has switched sides and loyalties and gone from one political ideology to another has made many in Kashmir look at his politics with deep suspicion, but he continues to be a darling of New Delhi—more so of the BJP. Former spymaster A.S. Dulat, in his memoir, calls Sajad a 'wild card.'[12] 'He has many qualities, but he's a little unpredictable.' Dulat further writes,

'Though Sajad was a borderline separatist—remember, he learned from his father (Khwaja Abdul Ghani Lone) that his separatism wasn't going to last very long—he was Delhi's favoured separatist. But he has looked for extraordinary favours from Delhi, and because of his temperament, Delhi has not been able to handle him properly.'

In his personal capacity, Saifuddin Soz, veteran Congress leader and a former Union minister during the UPA government's rule in New Delhi, believes that Pervez Musharraf's four-point Kashmir formula could well be merged with the 1952 Delhi Agreement, which, according to him, could lead to a permanent solution of Kashmir within the Indian Constitution. In my several interactions with Soz in Srinagar, he reiterated that 'history does not give opportunity time and again.' He describes his solution within the realm of possibility and which, he believes, could give Kashmiris a sense of achievement. He is also a votary of opening channels of communication with all stakeholders, including the APHC. His press conference in Srinagar in late August 2016, in which he supported Musharraf's four-point Kashmir formula stirred a political hornet's nest and ruffled feathers in New Delhi. But all these proposed solutions, like autonomy and self-rule, are largely termed as demands of the political elite of the Kashmir Valley, especially those who are either State beneficiaries or enjoy Delhi's blessings.

On the contrary, both factions of the APHC demand a referendum under the auspices of the UN, and also favour tripartite talks, while the JKLF led by Yasin Malik demands complete independence for the whole of J&K, including PaK. The BJP, however, favours Kashmir's complete integration with the Union of India and wants to scrap Article 370. Overall, every single political party based in Srinagar, irrespective of ideology and stated position, is pro-resolution, whether inside or outside the ambit of the Indian Constitution. Almost everyone feels suffocated with the current status quo in one or the other way.

Let me explain a few propositions, proposals and formulae that have been floated thus far. What is the 1952 Delhi Agreement?

It is considered a follow-up to Article 370, which grants special status to J&K.

Dr Nyla Ali Khan, a Kashmiri academic based in Oklahoma, USA, and who is also the granddaughter of Sheikh Abdullah, explains the Delhi Agreement thus:[13]

> Broadly, in October 1949, the Constituent Assembly of India reinforced the stipulation that New Delhi's jurisdiction in the state would remain limited to the categories of defence, foreign affairs, and communications, which had been underlined in the Instrument of Accession. Subsequent to India acquiring the status of a republic in 1950, this constitutional provision enabled the incorporation of Article 370 into the Indian constitution, which ratified the autonomous status of Jammu and Kashmir within the Indian Union. Article 370 stipulates that New Delhi can legislate on the subjects of defence, foreign affairs, and communications only in just and equitable consultation with the Government of Jammu and Kashmir State, and can intervene in other subjects only with the consent of the Jammu and Kashmir Assembly... The subsequent negotiations in June and July 1952 between a delegation of the J&K government led by Sheikh Mohammad Abdullah and Mirza Afzal Beg, and a delegation of the Indian government led by Nehru, resulted in the Delhi Agreement, which reinforced the autonomous status of J&K.

At these talks, Dr Khan says that the Kashmiri delegation relented on just one issue: it conceded the extension of the Indian Supreme Court's arbitrating jurisdiction to the state in case of disputes between the federal government and the state government, or between J&K and another state of the Indian Union. But the Kashmiri delegation shrewdly disallowed an extension of the Indian Supreme Court's purview to the state as the ultimate arbitrator in all civil and criminal cases before J&K's courts.

The delegation, Dr Khan says, was also careful to prevent the financial and fiscal integration of the state with the Indian

Union. They ruled out any modifications to their land reform programme, which had dispossessed the feudal class without any right to compensation. It was also agreed that, as opposed to the other units in the Union, the residual powers of legislation would be vested in the state assembly instead of the Centre. The 1952 Delhi Agreement resulted in what could be interpreted as a 'dual citizenship' for the people of J&K.

Let me briefly explain Musharraf's four-point formula and the major players in Kashmir who oppose or support it. From Islamabad's perspective, Delhi has successfully contained the Kashmir story with its sheer military might and economic strength. There is a realization in Pakistan that the Kashmir dispute cannot be resolved through military means. Despite rigid official stances and emotional rhetoric, both nations are fully aware of the dominant aspirations of the majority of people in both parts of Kashmir. Many policymakers in Pakistan reckon that after 9/11, an armed rebellion, even in the context of a freedom struggle, is no longer tenable. They also believe that the environment in Pakistan is not conducive to forcing any fresh Kashmir resolution on India. But this realization might also be a strategic pause. It has rightly been observed that it does not take long for both countries to harden their positions on Kashmir, seemingly beyond repair, or engage in unprecedented bonhomie in a jiffy, to the surprise of many.

Academic Dr Shaheen Showket Dar, in his book *Role of Negotiations in Conflict Resolution: A Way out of Kashmir Conflict*, argues that 'India and Pakistan together can be strategically more powerful than China's One Belt One Road (OBOR) project of the China-Pakistan Economic Corridor (CPEC). But they fail to explore the geopolitical opportunities and are living as adversaries in South Asia region.'[14] Factors, which include the baggage of history for both India and Pakistan, their ideological egos, their hegemonic ambitions and their strategic interests, act as impediments in the conflict-resolution process. Because of the unresolved Kashmir dispute, the two nuclear neighbours had been dragged into the Cold War rivalry as well. Additionally, Delhi is allergic to any third-party intervention on Kashmir, which does not help matters.

In several Track-II dialogues that I have been a part of, former diplomats from Pakistan have been candid enough to admit that the LoC could actually be made irrelevant, reduced to just a line on the map, to resolve Kashmir permanently. In his memoir, *Neither A Hawk Nor A Dove*, Khurshid Mahmud Kasuri, Pakistan's foreign minister from 2002–07, argues that no solution of the Kashmir dispute can be 'perfect' from the point of view of Pakistan, India or the Kashmiris.[15] 'It would have to be the best possible under the circumstances.'

The moot point is: does such a solution exist, which is honorable, implementable, palatable and politically acceptable to all stakeholders? How far can India go? How much will Delhi concede? How much flexibility will Islamabad exhibit? Will it satisfy the Kashmiris?

Kasuri writes that India and Pakistan have recognized that there are 'forces' in both countries that do not like the normalization of relations between them, and there are also people who wouldn't settle for less than a 'maximalist solution'. But the broad contours of a feasible agreement on Kashmir, according to Kasuri, are demilitarization and reduction in violence, self-governance, a joint control mechanism for both parts of the state and rendering the LoC immaterial. In other words, this is the four-point formula proposed by Musharraf.

Such a solution might well be palatable to Islamabad and Delhi, as both appear more or less convinced that 'the boundaries can't be redrawn' and territorial sovereignties should not be challenged. Both countries are fully aware of the dominant political aspirations of the people in J&K and know that a significant number of Kashmiris are in favour of independence from both. However, the two nations appear unified in their antagonism to the idea of an independent state of J&K.

But will it be acceptable to the Kashmiris? While the four-point formula does provide a certain 'sense of achievement' to Kashmiris, it falls way short of satisfying their larger political aspirations. Most people in the Kashmir Valley, Chenab, Pir Panjal and Kargil would, therefore, see demilitarization, self-governance, joint control, cross-LoC travel and trade, only as steps and confidence-building measures towards a settlement, and not the final solution. They obviously want more.

If New Delhi were to display its 'willingness' to reverse time to find a solution in Kashmir, it will make for a good beginning by reducing the existing trust deficit. After A.B. Vajpayee made some headway in 2003 in Srinagar, the next Indian PM, Dr Manmohan Singh, famously said on 8 January 2007, 'I dream of a day, while retaining our respective national identities, one can have breakfast in Amritsar, lunch in Lahore, and dinner in Kabul.' With the commencement of the Srinagar-Muzaffarabad bus service in April 2005, this did not seem terribly improbable.

One of the contours of the broad agreement on Kashmir that was agreed upon between India and Pakistan, according to Kasuri's book, was demilitarization. To Pakistan's demand that the footprint of Indian Armed Forces be substantially reduced from the civilian areas of J&K, New Delhi in its counter-proposal had made a similar demand with respect to PaK. In the absence of a quid pro quo, Indians told Pakistanis that their proposal was undoable. Eventually, Pakistan too had agreed to withdraw its troops from its side of Kashmir in the interest of a settlement.

During backchannel negotiations, another important point discussed was about the reduction of violence in J&K. Pakistan had quietly conceded that militancy in Kashmir was not in its own long-term interest. It believed that Kashmir made a strong moral, legal and political case, anyway. There was also a broad consensus on weaning armed militants off violence and impart skills to them with the aim to help them integrate back into the society. Self-governance and a joint mechanism for both parts of Kashmir were important elements in this framework.

In backchannel diplomacy and Track-II dialogues on Kashmir, the four-point formula was widely described as an 'ideal solution under the circumstances' in India and Pakistan. In Kashmir, however, it drew scathing criticism from veteran APHC leader,

Syed Ali Geelani. In a chapter, 'Musharraf Ka Chaar Nikati Formula' (Musharraf's four-point formula) in the third volume of his autobiography, *Wular Kinaray-III*, Geelani writes that the proposal was a result of Musharraf's 'change of heart'.[16] 'Going against Pakistan's long-adopted policy on Kashmir, Jenab Pervez Musharraf offered his four-point formula to satisfy his own desire.' Geelani ridicules Musharraf by saying that he had 'lost his self-confidence' and was suffering from 'acute mental depression' while proposing his 'K-formula'. Geelani also blames Pakistan's former military dictator for 'undermining Pakistan's age-old stance on Kashmir and official policy to lend support to the just struggle of Kashmiris on moral, political and diplomatic fronts'.

Musharraf had said in December 2006 that he was willing to give up his country's claim on Kashmir if India agreed to a self-government plan and backed wide-ranging autonomy or self-rule for Kashmir, with both countries jointly supervising the disputed Himalayan region. He also suggested that the borders and the LoC would remain unchanged but could be made 'irrelevant' by allowing hassle-free trade, travel and tourism between the two parts of Kashmir.

Historically speaking, Pakistan's foreign policy in relation to Kashmir has largely remained steady for the past sixty-nine years. Many rightly argue that Pakistan's foreign policy vis-a-vis Kashmir only witnessed some divergence when Musharraf had proposed his four-point formula.

In January 2004, Musharraf had said in an interview that the governments of Pakistan and India needed to approach the Kashmir issue with flexibility.[17] It was a typical quid pro quo offer. In *Neither A Hawk Nor A Dove*, Khurshid Mahmud Kasuri quotes Musharraf as saying that '...when parties come to a negotiating table, they cannot afford to hold on to maximalist positions and "no unilateral action can be taken. I have been saying that we must go beyond stated positions and show flexibility. But it can't be done unilaterally by Pakistan. So, there is reciprocity involved."'[18]

Mirwaiz Umar Farooq favoured the formula as a 'good beginning' for a lasting solution. In several interviews, he reiterated his support for dialogue and Musharraf's K-formula. Dr Nyla Ali Khan overtly supports Musharraf's K-formula and told me in a telephonic interview in 2015 that the proposal about phased demilitarization and regional autonomy for both parts of Kashmir, trans-Kashmir travel and trade, and people-to-people contact, would have definitely made a 'good beginning'. She argued that the formula would not have been an end in itself. But it certainly would have helped build bridges of friendship and confidence in J&K, and between India and Pakistan to move forward.

What are the prospects of this formula in post-Burhan Kashmir? Since Narendra Modi took over as India's PM in May 2014, official positions on Kashmir in both India and Pakistan have hardened again. Foreign secretary-level talks were cancelled in August 2014, after New Delhi objected to the meeting between APHC leaders and Pakistan's then high commissioner, Abdul Basit. In August 2015, national security advisor-level talks were cancelled after both countries accused each other of sabotaging the process. Pakistan said that India was setting preconditions for the talks, a charge denied by India. Abdul Basit said that Pakistan was not subservient to India and declared that the APHC was an important stakeholder in Kashmir. Interestingly, the Agenda of Alliance agreed upon between the BJP and PDP in 2015 also explicitly talked about reconciliation with Pakistan and advocated talks with the APHC as a stakeholder. As of now, after the 2019 Pulwama attack, Delhi has even withdrawn the MFN status to Pakistan, on 15 February 2019.[19]

With the hardening of the position on Kashmir by the BJP government in New Delhi, a tectonic shift in its foreign policy and Narendra Modi raising the issue of Balochistan from the ramparts of Red Fort in his 15 August speech, Pakistan responded in equal measure. That's perhaps why Nawaz Sharif hailed the slain HM commander Burhan Wani as a 'martyr', 'freedom fighter' and 'a symbol of the Kashmiri Intifada' in his speech at the UN General Assembly in New York and reiterated Pakistan's official position that 'it will continue to lend moral, diplomatic and political support to the freedom struggle of the people of Kashmir.'[20]

After his success in the general elections in Pakistan held in July 2018, the legendary cricketer-turned-politician and PM-elect Imran Khan rang up his old friend Navjot Singh Sidhu, former Indian cricket player, to extend the invitation to his oath-taking ceremony in Islamabad. The invitations were also extended to former Indian captains and cricketing legends Sunil Gavaskar and Kapil Dev. Sidhu attended the ceremony while Gavaskar and Dev could not travel to Pakistan, citing professional or personal reasons. The Pakistani Army Chief General Qamar Javed Bajwa, Sidhu, cricketer-turned-commentator Rameez Raja and celebrated paceman Wasim Akram were among the special guests present at the swearing-in ceremony.[21] Khan talked peace and said 'If India moves one step forward, we will move two.' Khan also said that he wants to fix the India-Pakistan ties through dialogue but maintained that the bone of contention between India and Pakistan was Kashmir.

On 28 November 2018, in a groundbreaking move, Imran Khan also opened the 4-km-long Kartarpur Corridor to allow members of the Sikh community living in the Indian state of Punjab to pay obeisance at the final resting place of Guru Nanak Dev situated in the Pakistani part of Punjab. Like Khan, Sidhu too won many a heart in both countries, especially the peaceniks, by attending the stone-laying foundation for the Kartarpur Corridor. Pakistan called Kartarpur a 'corridor of peace' while Sidhu, in his inimitable style, described it as a 'corridor of infinite possibilities.'[22] The Pakistani premier reiterated his peace overtures. In his address to the Sikh pilgrims from India, he likened the happiness that he saw on the faces of devotees to the feeling that Muslims get on reaching Medina or Mecca. Khan cited the example of the present-day cordial relationship between Germany and France after both these European countries had fought wars and been bitter rivals in the past. 'If France and Germany can move forward, why can't we?' he asked. He assured India that all the political parties, government and the Army in Pakistan were on the same page. 'We want civilized relationship. Kashmir is the only problem. Are not we capable of solving a dispute? We need will to resolve the issue.'[23] He said that Pakistan aspires to have a good relationship with India so that more and more border-crossing points are opened for trade, commerce, people-to-people contact and pilgrimage tourism. He also mentioned how China alleviated poverty through trade.

The very act of Imran Khan mentioning Kashmir at Kartarpur angered New Delhi. In Srinagar though, many expressed happiness over the opening of the Kartarpur Corridor, hoping that people in both parts of Kashmir were also allowed hassle-free travel, trade, pilgrimage tourism and uninterrupted cultural and academic exchanges. Many invoked the fall of the Berlin Wall. However, India's Ministry of External Affairs (MEA) issued a hard-hitting statement: 'Pakistan is reminded that it must fulfil its international obligations and take effective and credible action to stop providing shelter and all kind of support to cross-border terrorism from territories under its control.'[24] The MEA statement slammed Khan for politicizing the 'pious occasion' and said that 'Kashmir was an integral and inalienable part of India.'

That has been the India-Pakistan story for nearly seven decades—blowing hot and cold. Under such circumstances, how is one expected to muster the courage to sound optimistic about a possible solution of Kashmir? But pessimism is not an option either. What's the solution then? What's the way forward? What's the path ahead?

Apart from the *Outlook* survey, in the Chatham House study mentioned in an earlier chapter, an overwhelming 74–95 per cent of respondents in Kashmir (even without the inclusion of important districts like Pulwama and Kupwara) had favoured independence.[25] Chatham House claims that its poll was the first of its kind to be conducted on both sides of the LoC that has separated India- and Pakistan-controlled Kashmir since the UN brokered a ceasefire on 1 January 1949. The project was directed by Robert W. Bradnock, a visiting senior research fellow at King's College London and associate fellow at Chatham House, and Richard Schofield, King's College London. It was sponsored by Dr Saif al-Islam Gaddafi, son of the deposed Libyan dictator, Muammar Gaddafi.

As noted earlier, an overwhelming 80 per cent of Kashmiris, according to the poll, had felt that the dispute was important for them personally. Only 2 per cent had said that they would vote to join Pakistan. Similarly, in PaK, 50 per cent had said that they would vote for the whole of J&K to join Pakistan, while only 1 per cent had said that they would favour joining India. At least 28 per cent, mostly from districts like Jammu, Udhampur and Kathua, had said that they would vote for India.

Keeping J&K with it gives Delhi a chance at the global stage to showcase itself as a plural and multicultural democracy with a Muslim-majority region as its part. For rhetorical purposes, Delhi also says that Kashmir under Pakistan's administration is also India's integral part. A resolution to this effect, passed by the Indian Parliament on 22 February 1994, says, 'J&K was an integral part of India, and that Pakistan must vacate parts of the State under its occupation.'[26] The resolution declares that the state of J&K has been, is, and shall be, an 'integral part of India' and any attempt to separate it from the rest of the country will be resisted by necessary means and that all attempts to interfere in India's internal matters will be met resolutely. Pakistan, on its part, calls the part of Kashmir under India's administration as 'India-held Kashmir' or 'India-occupied Kashmir'.

As noted earlier, after the killing of Burhan Wani, the then Pakistani PM Nawaz Sharif declared him a 'martyr' and a 'freedom fighter' while addressing a special cabinet meeting in Lahore on 15 July to discuss the situation in Kashmir. Five days later, Pakistan observed a nationwide 'Black Day', on 20 July 2016, to protest the 'brutalities of Indian forces in Kashmir'. In his speech at the UN General Assembly in New York on 21 September 2016, Nawaz Sharif described Burhan as a 'young leader' of Kashmir and reiterated his country's support to the political struggle of Kashmiris.

Pakistan even observes 19 July as the day of the 'renewal of the historical resolution of Kashmir's accession to Pakistan passed by the people of the state. It is pertinent to recall that the AJKMC, on 19 July 1947, in Srinagar, had demanded the then Dogra rulers to materialize the accession of the state to Pakistan, honouring the decision and point of view of the Muslim-majority population in the state. Besides this, on 5 February, Pakistan observes a national holiday on account of 'Kashmir Solidarity Day'.

The aforementioned observations prove that the official positions of both India and Pakistan appear to be unbending. The way forward is not easy by any stretch of the imagination. Officially, both countries seem hell-bent on killing nuances and sticking to rigidity. However, both show some flexibility during Track-II dialogues and backchannel diplomacy where rhetoric is usually absent or toned down.

Like Kasuri, India's well-respected legal luminary and commentator, A.G. Noorani, in *The Kashmir Dispute, 1947–2012*, says, 'A settlement requires concessions on both sides'.[27] He writes that neither India nor Pakistan support the idea of Kashmir's independence. Musharraf's four-point formula and self-rule fit like a glove, since self-rule is an integral part of those points. According to Noorani, the four points on which an India-Pakistan consensus exists are, 'Self-governance or self-rule for both parts of the state; the opening of the LoC so that it becomes, as the prime minister [then Dr Manmohan Singh] said on 24 March 2006 "just lines on a map"; a joint management mechanism for both parts; and demilitarization'. In Noorani's view, it's a 'win-win situation' for both India and Pakistan. He warns that populism or jockeying for position to brand the conciliation a sell-out would be destructive.

In one of his pieces in *Dawn*, Noorani reiterated that 'The Kashmir dispute has three parties—India, Pakistan and the people of Kashmir. All three must concur in the terms of its settlement, which will have to be a compromise. Force has clearly failed...'[28] He concluded by saying that 'Pakistan is not only a party to the

Kashmir dispute but a party within Kashmir as well. No accord will succeed unless all the three sides concur—and compromise.'

During my long stay in Germany as editor at Deutsche Welle in Bonn, I had colleagues from various countries, which included China, India, Afghanistan, Russia, Pakistan, Palestine, Iran, Bangladesh and Kenya, among others. It was an opportunity for me to learn about the perspective of young Pakistanis from different parts of the country, like Lahore, Peshawar, Karachi, Islamabad and Multan. What I found was contrary to the belief of Kashmiris that all Pakistanis can go to any extent to help them achieve their cherished goal of freedom. While there is hardly any doubt that most Pakistanis do have a soft corner for Kashmiris and support their political struggle, it is not true that all are willing to pay a cost. They have their own dreams, aspirations and ambitions to fulfil, too.

Some young, ambitious and aspirational Pakistanis do not necessarily relate to the Kashmir problem in the manner of the old generation, or the Army, ISI and political elite. Many Kashmiris would want to believe in the routine statements, word by word, coming from officials in Islamabad, which would, more often than not, go like this: 'Pakistan will continue to provide moral, diplomatic and political support to Kashmiris in their just struggle for freedom from India.'

When lawyers in Pakistan were registering their protest against Pervez Musharraf for deposing the then Chief Justice, Iftikhar Chaudhary, and other Supreme Court judges, one of my colleagues said she was extremely happy. I asked her why. So, she told me a joke she claimed had become popular in Pakistan. 'Mr Bush to Mr Mush: "Behave yourself and support my 'war against terror' or else, I'll be forced to bring democracy to your country, too... in the way I brought it to Afghanistan and Iraq."' I had also read an interesting placard posted on a social networking site. It read, 'I'm a Muslim, kill me and call it "Collateral Damage"; imprison me and call it "Security Measure"; exile my people en masse and call it the "New Middle East"; rob my resources, invade my land, alter my leadership and call it "Democracy". This message reminded me of Kashmir.

The European Union and the US voiced serious concerns over the human rights abuses in China-controlled Tibet before the 2008 Beijing Olympic Games. George W. Bush, then the US president, was 'worried' about the loss of human lives in Lhasa during protest demonstrations. The Chinese authorities confirmed at least twenty-two deaths,[29] but the Tibetan government-in-exile, headquartered in Dharamsala in India, put the death toll at more than hundred.[30] People are being killed at the hands of Israeli troops in Palestine almost on a daily basis. People are being killed in Syria, Iraq and Afghanistan. The US drone attacks are killing people in the tribal areas of Pakistan. Government forces are killing people in Kashmir. Protests in Kashmir, which are held for just reasons and genuine problems, are normally 'solved' with bullets and pellets. Pakistan's armed forces are killing dissenters in Balochistan. Human rights are human rights, and abuses are abuses. Even if a single innocent life is lost, it is a violation and should be condemned in the strongest possible manner. But seldom do we see strong statements of denunciation from the European Union or the US administration against these countries. There is selective condemnation. There is selective appeasement.

After the wave of protests in the summer of 2008 in Kashmir, authorities in Pakistan had again woken up from their slumber. Pakistan's Foreign Minister, Shah Mehmood Qureshi, issued a routine statement, which had the content Kashmiris are so familiar with. 'Pakistan will continue to provide moral, diplomatic and political support to Kashmiris in their just struggle against India.' I called up the Pakistani colleague who had shared the 'Bush to Mush' joke with me, and narrated this statement to her. 'A good joke,' she said.

Irfan, a young computer professional from Karachi, has been living in Germany since 2004. He candidly admits that the 'wild passion' for Kashmir in Pakistan has actually been detrimental to the growth and development of Pakistan. 'For the past sixty or seventy years, we have been held hostage to the official slogan, "Kashmir is our jugular vein", but it has only created problems for Pakistan, especially the present generation, which is more worried about its security, future and Pakistan's image worldwide.' Many in Kashmir, who feel close to Pakistan and favour the two-nation theory, will certainly be surprised if not shocked to know such views. Some of the young Pakistanis I had interacted with believed that Kashmir should automatically become a part of Pakistan for its geographical proximity and cultural and religious affiliation. But many of them were categorical that Pakistan has only invited trouble by investing immensely in Kashmir and Kashmiris. 'Kashmiris should fight for their rights on their own; it is their war, not ours,' said one of them.

But Atif Tauqeer had other views. Tauqeer is a wonderful poet whose father had served in the Pakistan Army. As a result, his views are in tune with the Pakistani Army's stand. 'Kashmir is a natural part of Pakistan. We fully support Kashmir's fight against India because we want Kashmir to be our part,' Tauqeer would often tell me. But he would make it clear that Kashmir has to fight on its own and stop relying on Pakistan for support. I could see a reflection of Syed Ali Geelani's views in Tauqeer. Not surprisingly, Tauqeer is Geelani's fan. He would make references off and on to Geelani's political speeches. He would also narrate interesting stories of his father who had served in the Pakistani Army. He is still in Germany and travels across Europe to give talks on current affairs and recite poetry.

Shamil Shams, a poet and a liberal, would always be forthright while expressing his views on politics and political disputes around the globe. 'I'm quite open even to the idea of Balochistan seceding from Pakistan, if that be the desire of the people of that province. Kashmiris too have their rights and they should fight for these.' In his heart, though, Shamil looked at India, Pakistan and Bangladesh as one entity and would quite often say that the Partition of the Indian subcontinent didn't serve any purpose. About the creation of Bangladesh, he would openly say that it was high time that Pakistan apologized to Bangladeshis for the human rights abuses that took place during the 1971 war that eventually led to its creation. Another friend reminded him of

India's role in the creation of Bangladesh as a separate nation and recommended a book, *The Blood Telegram*, written by Gary J. Bass, to know how India under Indira Gandhi's leadership helped create Mukti Bahini, the Bangladeshi armed group that fought against Pakistan.

I would thoroughly enjoy these conversations with a cross-section of young Pakistanis at our favourite bistro in Bonn, near the Hauptbahnhof (city centre). We would organize weekly or fortnightly Urdu poetry sessions. We would celebrate the anniversaries of popular Urdu poets Faiz Ahmad Faiz, Ahmed Faraz, Habib Jalib, Jaun Elia and Munir Niazi, among others. Tauqeer would always be ready with a new ghazal, Shamil would come with his poems and couplets, and I would give them both company. We would debate how hostilities between India and Pakistan could end and how the Kashmir dispute could be resolved amicably without a war and bloodshed.

This is young Pakistan. In Kashmir, there is a sizeable population that passionately relates to the idea of Pakistan as an Islamic Republic and proudly chants slogans like *'Jeevay Jeevay, Pakistan'*.

Interestingly, poet Faiz Ahmad Faiz too had proposed a unique Kashmir solution. Journalist-turned-politician, the late Shamim Ahmad Shamim, a Member of the Indian Parliament from Kashmir and editor of the Urdu weekly, *Aina*, had called on Faiz in Lahore in 1969. In the interview, Shamim asked Faiz what he thought might be the best solution for Kashmir. 'The best solution for Kashmir is that both countries should leave Kashmir alone and, as a khudmukhtar (self-governing) state, Kashmir should establish friendly relations with both countries. Eventually this is what will happen; but after suffering much harm and damage. People like you on both sides should jointly propose such a proposal.' The interview was first published in *Aina* and reprinted in the Srinagar-based Urdu weekly, *Chattan*, on 18 April 2011.[31]

The influential Left-wing intellectual and revolutionary poet, Faiz, had a strong Kashmir connection. Faiz's nikah was performed in Srinagar in October 1941. In his book *The Kashmir Dispute, 1947–2012*, historian Abdul Gafoor Noorani writes that Kashmir's then most popular political leader Sheikh Mohammed Abdullah performed Faiz's nikah at Srinagar where the well-known poet married a young English girl, Alys George (she took the name Kulsoom after converting to Islam). 'The nikahnama (deed of marriage) was signed by G.M. Sadiq, Bakshi Ghulam Mohammed [both former PMs of Jammu and Kashmir] and Dr Noor Husain as witnesses,' Noorani writes.[32]

In several programmes and seminars, Pakistan's well-known romantic and revolutionary poet, Ahmed Faraz, had also overtly lent his support to Kashmir's political movement. According to Pakistan's renowned columnist and humourist Ata ul Haq Qasmi, Faraz once had a verbal spat with a certain Indian minister in a live programme on television. Once it was raining cats and dogs, and Faraz, along with several other poets and intellectuals of his country, participated in a march by foot to the Indian High Commission in Pakistan with a memorandum related to Kashmir.

Another famous Pakistani poet, Syed Zameer Jafri, writes that Faraz was more patriotic than him. Jafri records that in November 1993, a group of celebrated poets and intellectuals had gathered in Pakistan's capital city, Islamabad, to participate in a literary event. Faraz was one of the participants. 'We were collecting signatures of writers on a resolution in relation to human rights abuses... The resolution while deploring the human rights excesses in Kashmir had urged upon India to abide by the United Nations' Security Council resolutions on Kashmir for Kashmir's just solution,' Jafri writes. According to him, some of his friends were unsure how the great poet would react on the contents of the resolution on Kashmir. They were in a quandary. As soon as Jafri went close to Faraz, the poet got infuriated and while looking him in the eye, said angrily: 'What have you written, Baba? Resolutions will serve no purpose; I am not signing this.'[33] Jafri goes on to write that everyone thought that the inevitable had happened. But they were proven wrong when Faraz continued to say this: 'This resolution lacks teeth. It has an apologetic tone. We must assert on Kashmir with vigour and vitality.'

★

One ought to keep in mind that Kashmir is an issue that involves politics, territory, borders, religion, nationalism, democracy, ethnicity, identity and various other factors. It comprises more than the Kashmir Valley itself and the identity politics in different regions is varied. For instance, in Jammu, the situation is different, as Hindu nationalist parties are in favour of J&K's complete integration with the Indian Union. Hindus largely identify with the idea of India while Muslims of other regions in Jammu Province, like Rajouri, Poonch, Doda, Kishtwar and Bhaderwah, do not. This division was brought to the fore during the infamous 'Praja Parishad' agitation in the winter of 1952–53 in Jammu, over the demand for the full integration of J&K with India on the basis of 'ek vidhan, ek nishan, ek pradhan' (one constitution, one flag, one president). Mountainous Ladakh is another region where Muslims and Buddhists live in Kargil and Leh respectively. Hindus and Buddhists are a minority while Muslims are in a majority in the entire state of J&K.

Religion, nationalism, and cultural and other identities are salient to understanding the evolution of conflict in Kashmir. Yet, much of the academic scholarship has ignored or underplayed the role of identity by reducing the conflict to a territorial dispute. By identifying the key forms of identity that shape political mobilization, and interrogating the different ways in which they facilitate or hinder mobilization, one can generate interest in an ethnographically rich account of the Kashmir conflict and assess why no resolution has occurred thus far. Along with an analysis of the conflict, one may also try looking for alternative models from different parts of the world that might be applicable to Kashmir.

Some parallels can be drawn between Northern Ireland and Kashmir, both of which took place within electoral democracies (UK and India, respectively). First, like the violent guerrilla warfare between the Irish Republican Army and the British, there is an ongoing armed militancy against Delhi's rule in Kashmir since 1989. Though the levels of violence have significantly dropped over the years, the encounters between armed Kashmiri rebels and government forces have not completely ended. Second, just as the Special Powers Act, a stringent law, gave the authorities exceptional powers to arrest, detain without trial, and suppress political dissent in Northern Ireland, the Indian Army also enjoys immunity from prosecution in J&K under the shield of the AFSPA, in force since June 1990.

There are various other comparisons between Northern Ireland and Kashmir that include backchannel diplomacy and offers of third-party mediations, and also the instances of categorical reluctance by the US to interfere in Kashmir at different junctures. Are there any lessons that can be drawn from the Northern Ireland example to resolve the Kashmir conflict, which involves Kashmiri nationalism, ethnicity, religion and geopolitics? Is the leadership in Pakistan, India and Kashmir prepared to think out of the box to ensure the conflict does not linger on? Can Delhi, Islamabad and Srinagar produce statesmen who believe in the power of peaceful negotiation as an effective tool of conflict resolution with a vision for peace and prosperity for future generations?

NOTES, SOURCES AND REFERENCES

1. Source 1: Masoodi, H. (2016, October 26). Terezin Ghetto And Man of Two Parables. Retrieved from http://www.greaterkashmir.com/news/opinion/terezin-ghetto-and-man-of-two-parables/231795.html
    Source 2: Vijayan, S. (2016, October 25). Curfew is the Camp. Retrieved from http://warscapes.com/opinion/curfew-camp
2. Jaffrelot, C. (2016). *Pakistan at the Crossroads: Domestic Dynamics and External Pressures*. Random House India, Chapter 'Pakistan–China Symbiotic Relations' by Farah Jan and Serge Granger
3. Scott-Clark, C. (2012, July 09). The mass graves of Kashmir. Retrieved from https://www.theguardian.com/world/2012/jul/09/mass-graves-of-kashmir
4. Dar, S. S. (2019). *Role of Negotiations in Conflict Resolution: A Way out of Kashmir Conflict*, G. B. Books, Chapter 5, p. 100
5. *Torture: Indian State's Instrument of Control in Indian administered Jammu and Kashmir* (Rep.). (2019). Srinagar, J&K: APDP & JKCCS.)
6. Guha, R. (2016, October 22). Valley on the Boil: Why No One Has Clean Hands

in Kashmir. Retrieved from http://www.hindustantimes.com/columns/why-no-one-has-clean-hands-in-kashmir/story-cQpbbwprW19kmE4vtaBPiP.html
7. McGirk, T. (2011, October 22). Kashmiri student tells of torture: Tim McGirk in Srinagar reports on. Retrieved from http://www.independent.co.uk/news/world/kashmiri-student-tells-of-torture-tim-mcgirk-in-srinagar-reports-on-the-increasing-evidence-of-2325054.html
8. Parliament Resolution on Jammu and Kashmir. (1994, February 22). Retrieved from http://www.satp.org/satporgtp/countries/india/document/papers/parliament_resolution_on_Jammu_and_Kashmir.htm
9. Bukhari, S. (2000, June 27). J&K Assembly passes autonomy resolution amid protest. Retrieved from http://www.thehindu.com/2000/06/27/stories/01270001.htm
10. Guha, R. (2016, September 24). Why we must listen to Jayaprakash Narayan on Kashmir. Retrieved from https://www.hindustantimes.com/columns/why-we-must-listen-to-jayaprakash-narayan-on-kashmir/story-1ESKtjC4GSm0kzrGumhcYO.html
11. Advani, L. K. (2008). *My Country, My Life*. Rupa Publications.
12. Dulat, A. S., & Sinha, A. (2015). *Kashmir: The Vajpayee Years*. Noida, Uttar Pradesh, India: HarperCollins India., p. 321
13. The US-based Kashmiri academic Dr Nyla Ali Khan's e-mailed response to the author.
14. Dar, S.S. (2019). *Role of Negotiations in Conflict Resolution: A Way out of Kashmir Conflict*. G B Books, p. 104
15 Kasuri, K. M. (2015). *Neither a Hawk nor a Dove: An Insider's Account of Pakistan's Foreign Policy*. Penguin UK.
16. Geelani, S.A. (2015). *Wular Kinaray-III*, p. 407
17. Reddy, B. M. (2004, December 25). Pakistan for mutual flexibility on Kashmir, says Musharraf. Retrieved from https://www.thehindu.com/2004/12/25/stories/2004122504701200.htm
18. Kasuri, K. M. (2015). *Neither a Hawk nor a Dove: An Insider's Account of Pakistan's Foreign Policy*. Penguin UK.
19. India revokes Most Favoured Nation status granted to Pakistan. (2019, February 15). Retrieved from https://www.thehindu.com/news/national/india-revokes-most-favoured-nation-status-topakistan/article26278480.ece
20. Full text of Nawaz Sharif's speech at UN general assembly. (2016, September 21). Retrieved from https://www.hindustantimes.com/india-news/full-text-of-nawaz-sharif-s-speech-at-un-general-assembly/story-bdlcijC6NbfJgnjYupBBhN.html
21. Imran Khan takes oath as Pakistan's 22nd Prime Minister. (2018, August 18). Retrieved from https://economictimes.indiatimes.com/news/international/world-news/imran-khan-takes-oath-as-pakistan-pm/articleshow/65448725.cms
22. Kartarpur Sahib corridor will erase 'enmity' between India and Pakistan: Navjot Singh Sidhu | India News - Times of India. (2018, November 27). Retrieved from https://timesofindia.indiatimes.com/india/kartarpur-corridor-will-erase-enmity-between-india-and-pakistan-sidhu/articleshow/66826688.cms
23. PM Imran Khan performs ground-breaking of Kartarpur Corridor. (2018, November 28). Retrieved from https://www.thenews.com.pk/latest/399393-live-updates-kartarpur-corridor-inauguration

24. India, Ministry of External Affairs. (2018). *Official Spokesperson's response to queries regarding a reference to "Kashmir" by Pakistan Prime Minister today.* Retrieved from https://www.mea.gov.in/media-briefings.htm?dtl/30657/Official +Spokespersons+response+to+queries+regarding+a+reference+to+Kashmir+by +Pakistan+Prime+Minister+today

25. Bradnock, R. W., & Schofield, R. (2010). *Kashmir: Paths to Peace.* London: Chatham House.

26. Parliament Resolution on Jammu and Kashmir. (1994, February 22). Retrieved from http://www.satp.org/satporgtp/countries/india/document/papers/ parliament_resolution_on_Jammu_and_Kashmir.htm

27. Noorani, A.G.A.M. (2013). *The Kashmir Dispute, 1947-2012.* Tulika Books.

28. Noorani, A. G. (2018, November 17). Kashmir Solution. Retrieved from https:// www.dawn.com/news/1446101/kashmir-solution

29. Weaver, M., & Branigan, T. (2008, March 25). Two killed at pro-Tibet rally in China. Retrieved from https://www.theguardian.com/world/2008/mar/25/tibet. china

30. Spencer, R. (2008, March 15). China unleashes guns and tear gas as Tibet protests turn violent. Retrieved from https://www.telegraph.co.uk/news/ worldnews/1581798/China-unleashes-guns-and-tear-gas-as-Tibet-protests-turn-violent.html

31. Noorani, A.G.A.M. (2013). *The Kashmir Dispute, 1947-2012.* Tulika Books. The interview was first published in *Aina*, was and reprinted in the Srinagar-based Urdu weekly, *Chattan*, on 18 April 2011.

32. Noorani, A.G.A.M. (2013). *The Kashmir Dispute, 1947-2012.* Tulika Books.

33. Geelani, G. (2016, May 05). Iqbal, Faiz & Faraz and Kashmir Connection. Retrieved from http://www.risingkashmir.in/article/iqbal-faiz--faraz-and-kashmir-connection/

10

A LEADERSHIP CRISIS

Mera rehbar mere jaisa,
main bhi apne rehbar jaisa.
Usse wafa say bair hai,
main makr-o-faraib ka shaidaiee.

(My leader is a reflection of me,
I'm as good or bad as him.
For he's not a fan of loyalty,
I too am fond of deceit and fraud.)

M any in Kashmir are convinced that the 'baton of freedom' has passed on to the fifth generation. Many Kashmiris say their children also want to fight the perceived 'oppressor' with whatever they have: a sigh, a word, a poem, a song, a cartoon, a graffiti, a pen, a stone or a gun. Burhan Wani represents this new generation of Kashmiris. They say with pride that Delhi is losing Kashmir psychologically, emotionally and morally, even if it may be territorially secure in terms of Delhi's military control over the region. It is also losing a battle for a narrative. Shekhar Gupta, editor-in-chief of The Print, in one of the columns that he wrote for Rediff, argued: 'That is why it might be an arguable point that while Kashmir is territorially secure, we are fast losing it emotionally and psychologically.'[1]

P. Chidambaram, India's former minister for home affairs and finance during the Congress-led federal government in New Delhi, echoed the same view in February 2017, that he had 'a sinking feeling that Kashmir was nearly lost for India because the

Central government used brute force to quell dissent there (in Kashmir).'[2] Chidambaram said this while addressing a meeting organized by Manthan, a public discourse platform, in Hyderabad. In one of the many pieces on Kashmir that he wrote for *The Indian Express*, he argued: 'The alienation of the people of the Kashmir Valley is nearly complete. We are on the brink of losing Kashmir. We cannot retrieve the situation through a "muscular" policy—tough talk by ministers, dire warnings from the Army Chief, deploying more troops or killing more protesters.'[3] He, however, maintained: 'Among the people, a very small number wants the Valley to become part of Pakistan. A number of persons have turned militants and taken to violence but, at the worst of times, that number did not exceed a few hundred. The overwhelming majority, though, demands azadi.'[4] Chidambaram also feels that when people of the Kashmir Valley ask for 'Azadi', most want autonomy.[5] He has been a strong votary of granting or restoring autonomy to the state of J&K.

However, not many in Kashmir would concur with Chidambaram's definition of Azadi. The people of Kashmir define azadi as a genuine political demand for a separate homeland for all regions of the erstwhile state of J&K that existed before the partition in 1947—the Kashmir Valley, the Jammu province, Ladakh, Gilgit-Baltistan and 'Azad Kashmir'. An overwhelming majority, as is evident by the *Outlook* poll and Chatham House survey, asserts its political and ethnic identity and also unique culture. The idea of a separate homeland is that of an independent, sovereign and secular J&K, which is self-governing and not controlled or administered either by Pakistan or India.

Though there are sections that favour the region's complete merger with Pakistan, some in parts of Jammu province (barring Muslim-dominated areas of the Chenab Valley and Pir Panjal) and Leh in Ladakh prefer integration with New Delhi over independence, merger with Pakistan or autonomy, while a few are convinced that the status quo cannot be altered. There is also a section that sees the Kashmir conflict in the larger global paradigm and the Kashmir region as a victim of The Great Game*. They argue that Kashmiris should perhaps adopt a wait-and-watch policy until the geopolitical situation turns favourable. Dr Siddiq Wahid, a noted academic, historian and former vice chancellor of the Islamic University of Science and Technology, believes that the people of Kashmir are on the 'right side of history': 'The "moderate" versus "radical" binary is a divisive affliction that those who have resisted subjugation in the State of J&K on both sides of the Line of Control have suffered since the beginning... We need to stop being moderate and be unconventional, be radical.'[6] Many are hopeful that Kashmir's 'Tungsten Moment'** will arrive.

Unfortunately—or, perhaps, deliberately—many policymakers, politicians and analysts in Delhi love to see the Kashmir dispute either as a plain law-and-order problem or view the many layers of Kashmir's struggle for political, economic and human rights only through the prism of the armed militancy. The new age of armed rebellion in Kashmir, many argue, is rather a symbolic, romantic and emotional act, especially at a time when the institution of dialogue in Kashmir remains discredited for a variety of reasons, primarily because of Delhi's new policy of four Ds: 'Deny there is a problem; Defend your territory; and Defeat and Destroy the enemies.'[7] This frozen mindset needs to change. Instead, the policy should be 2As and 2Rs: Acknowledge there is a problem; Accept that the people want a peaceful political resolution; Respect the verdict of the people; and Resolve the dispute. Do not live in a permanent denial. Denialism is no solution. You cannot ignore the big fat elephant in the room by closing your eyes. It's the fifth generation of Kashmiris on the streets. Will people subject their eyes to pellet injuries because somebody has paid them ₹500?

Some political scientists also describe Kashmir's renewed

---

*The Great Game was a political and diplomatic confrontation regarding Afghanistan and the neighbouring areas of Central and South Asia, between the British and Russian Empires in the nineteenth century.
**Thomas Alva Edison performed many experiments before he developed devices in fields such as electric power generation. The 'Tungsten Moment' is a reference to the moment when he invented the bulb after many failed attempts.

militancy as a radical and desperate political act in the absence of any meaningful political engagement amongst representatives of Delhi, Islamabad and Srinagar. Experts on guerrilla warfare articulate that when damage is inflicted on the rebels by the State forces in terms of targeted strikes, say for instance in Afghanistan or Syria, they immediately retaliate in equal measure, or even more fiercely, to cause hurt to their adversary. But in Kashmir, the local militants, who are neither battle-hardened nor fully trained in combat, wait for their turns in residential houses they consider as 'safe houses' to get killed by government forces. Their act of picking up a gun is a desperate act to challenge the status quo.

Once killed in a gunfight, there are grand funerals in which thousands of local people participate to express condolence, show empathy, raise passionate anti-State slogans, and give vent to their political aspirations. Many say that in Kashmir, one can express his/her political sentiment without the fear of reprisal, only at the funerals. Sadly, such congregations have become spaces for dissent as normal spaces for dissent stand choked. At the funerals, a tiny group of armed rebels usually makes an appearance to offer a symbolic gun salute to honour their fallen comrades. One can see civilians, both men and women, forming a human chain to protect those militants. At times, the police believes that such emotional congregations also act as recruitment centres. Young boys of an impressionable age present in the funerals see their fallen friends and acquaintances as 'martyrs'. Some take a life-turning decision there and then, joining the ranks of militants, often in solidarity. This cycle repeats itself.

According to reliable sources in the J&K police, government forces have killed at least 595 armed rebels, most of them local Kashmiris, from January 2016 till 30 November 2018.[8]

In the first eleven months in 2018, 227 militants were killed,[9] which included highly educated Kashmiri youth and PhD scholars like Manan Wani, university assistant professor Mohammad Rafi Bhat and MPhil researcher Sabzar[10]. According to the South Asia Terrorism Portal (SATP), from 2014 to 15 February 2019, government forces have killed 913 militants.[11] During this time period, the number of civilians that have been killed in State forces' action during protests and also near the encounter sites when civilian protesters gather with the aim to save the rebels from state forces, is 203.[12]

On the other hand, according to government records, in 2014–18, 339 government forces personnel—mostly J&K policemen, paramilitary CRPF and Army troopers—have been killed in militant attacks,[13] while SATP data (till 15 February 2019) shows it to be 397.[14] They also include those killed in border skirmishes or attacks near the LoC, working boundary and international border. The militants who infiltrate Kashmir from Pakistan are well-trained and it is generally them who plan and supervise attacks on State forces.

Because of daily killings and the psychological pain that these inflict on the populace, there are also sections that are worried and deeply concerned that Kashmir's fifth generation has to be brought up in the same uncertain and violent political atmosphere that they have endured. Some blame the leadership across the ideological spectrum—or lack of it—for the continuing crisis in the lives of common Kashmiris.

Since I was quite young, I have been listening to poems carefully and trying to understand their meaning from men of letters. Though some are unambiguous, many have messages hidden between the lines. My father and I would often discuss Urdu and Kashmiri poetry, and also debate the Kashmir issue at home. He had experience on his side. I had passion and books. After the armed struggle began, such discussions had become the order of the day in every Kashmiri household, at every single marriage party or social get-together—and at almost every condolence meeting.

At times, these debates would end on an acrimonious note, creating bad blood between relatives and neighbours. Most of the times, however, they would lay bare the democratic political behaviour of the Kashmiri populace, as most Kashmiris believe in a battle of ideas (not the 'battle of ideas' that the PDP believes in, though![15]). I recall one of the most gratifying experiences of such a political discourse at a relative's home, with a common Kashmiri aged seventy or thereabouts, whom I didn't even know by name. In a conversation with a group of people, I put forth my view that nothing would happen for Kashmiris unless they maintained discipline in their political struggle for a safe, secure and dignified future. Everyone, except for the elderly man, nodded in agreement. Visibly upset by my remark, he argued that Kashmiris have offered supreme sacrifices for a cause that is dear to them, but history stands witness to the fact that their leaders have always stabbed them in the back.

Taking me back to the struggle of 1931 against Maharaja Hari Singh's regime, he said that ordinary people came out on the streets, willingly faced bullets, offered sacrifices, languished in jails, preferred death over materialistic gains, didn't compromise, and offered whatever they had. But what happened thereafter? Who betrayed the nation? The people or their leaders?

The gentleman went on to talk about the Plebiscite struggle from 1953 till 1975. People again came out on the streets and gave full support to the leaders, who were apparently espousing their cause. People sacrificed and their leaders breached their trust. In a supposed reference to Sheikh Mohammad Abdullah's infamous accord in 1975, he called it a brazen display of crushing the sentiment and aspirations of the people of Kashmir at the altar of power politics. What options have the leaders—of all shades, opinions and colours—left for the people to choose from? Sheikh Abdullah had been an immensely popular leader among Kashmiris until the infamous accord he signed with Indira Gandhi. Many Kashmiris believe that the Sheikh compromised and collaborated with the establishment in New Delhi for personal and political gains, but the 'dictatorial' decision in the garb of a 'democratically' chosen leader proved detrimental to the future of Kashmir.

Unravelling the historical knots of Kashmiri politics and the seasons of betrayal, he said, 'What could people do except support leaders who they believed advocated their cause?' He finally came to the subject of 1989—the year of the inception of armed resistance, when people in their thousands came out on the streets, openly staged anti-State protest demonstrations and raised high-pitched slogans in favour of Kashmir's freedom. But nearly three decades down the line, the 'results are the same.'

'Is there a single house in Kashmir that did not provide shelter to armed guerrillas, about whom people thought they were warriors fighting for a just cause—saviours; men who could take people out of the quagmire they were caught in?' he questioned. 'What did some of them (mujahideen) do in return?' he asked. The armed groups in the 1990s ended up fighting amongst themselves over trivia, against their own brethren and rival groups, started resolving petty land disputes, and in some rare cases, got married to the daughters of families who had provided them with shelter and supported them unconditionally, he said. Some became counter-insurgents and renegades, fighting elections under the Indian Constitution. Some of these even emerged victorious and started ruling people like the Army and police do. Some lost the elections and started committing injustices against the already oppressed people. To lend credibility to his argument, he cited examples of the notorious militant-turned-counter-insurgents like Kuka Parray, Usman Majeed, Javed Shah and Papa Kishtwari, besides others.

He still wasn't done. No leader or party escaped his ire. He took a dig at the pro-freedom APHC leadership, some of whom he accused of being sell-outs to New Delhi. They considered the 'job done' after issuing statements to the press from their posh homes, which were as ineffective as 'paper missiles.' Kashmiri leaders, like Sheikh Abdullah, Bakshi Ghulam Mohammad, G.M. Sadiq, Mir Qasim, Mufti Sayeed and the APHC leaders, have played spoilsport, he said. He refused to comment much on the current breed of young pro-India politicians like Omar Abdullah, Mehbooba Mufti or Sajad Lone. All of them have no option but to carry on with the petty dynastic politics, he said. In his view, the freedom movement was intact, and the azadi sentiment alive, only because of people's sacrifices and their overwhelming desire to alter the existing state of affairs.

Concluding his argument, he said that New Delhi might have betrayed Kashmiris, but many Kashmiri leaders have betrayed their own people as well. New Delhi will always attempt to corrupt Kashmiri leaders, but the question is—who will fall into the trap? The people of Kashmir have felt betrayed by their leaders time and again, and the elderly man's view might easily be one that is echoed by many others in the Valley. The PDP leaders are a case in point. Mehbooba Mufti, for instance, built her political career on the popular sentiment of Azadi. She would visit families of slain militants and mourn their death along with their mothers and sisters. Senior journalist, Muzamil Jaleel, said in an article in *The Indian Express*, 'Mourning was her politics.'[16] In 2015, her party stitched a partnership with the BJP against the popular mood in the Kashmir Valley.

First, as an Opposition leader in 2009 and 2010, when Omar Abdullah was the CM, Mehbooba Mufti would stage protests and demand an end to civilian killings at the hands of government forces. She would vociferously advocate the revocation of AFSPA and refer to disaffected youth and teenagers as 'our children'. After taking oath as the CM in March 2016, though, she justified the killing of teenagers by government forces in a press conference in Srinagar on 25 August 2016. Flanked by Rajnath Singh, who was on his second visit to the Valley after Burhan Wani's killing, Mehbooba Mufti lost her cool while responding to a reporter's question, saying, '*Kya Damhal Hanjipora main woh pandrah saal ka baccha, jis ne police station pe hamla kiya tha, toffee khareedne gaya tha, doodh lane gaya tha?*' ('Did the fifteen-year-old boy, who attacked the police station at Damhal Hanjipora (in south Kashmir), go there to buy toffee or milk?').[17]

During their Opposition days, senior PDP leader Naeem Akhtar, known as 'PDP's Chanakya', would often say things like, 'The government forces are killing innocent Kashmiri people for sport', but the language, tone and tenour obviously changed once the PDP came to power in March 2015. The same leader would then defend the pellet horror in 2016, which *The New York Times* described as 'An Epidemic of "Dead Eyes."'[18]

During her election campaign in 2014, Mehbooba Mufti said on record that the PDP was the only party to stop the BJP's 'Mission 44+', referring to the BJP's election campaign and desire to win forty-four assembly seats in J&K. She also claimed that Kashmiris will never 'sell their zameer' to join hands with the BJP, which she did a volte face on. The PDP also lost the plot by arresting prominent APHC and JKLF leaders and not allowing them any breathing space. Its slogan, '*Goli se nahin, boli se*' ('Not with bullets, but with words') seemed meaningless when over 15,000 civilians had been injured with pellets, bullets and tear gas shells in the crackdown on protesters; and when more than 6,000 had been arrested and cases under the controversial PSA had been filed against 400 civilians and political activists in the aftermath of Burhan Wani's killing in 2016.

Pro-Delhi politics in Kashmir is often seen as indulging in doublespeak. On the one hand, regional parties like the NC and PDP keep the 'resistance pot' boiling, and on the other, they work overtime to be on the right side of New Delhi. The Abdullah family's record has been no different from the Mufti family's. When 120 boys were killed in government forces' action during the 2010 summer uprising in the Valley, Omar Abdullah was the CM. I was in Bonn at the time and deeply distressed by the daily killings of Kashmir's teenagers. I decided to write an open letter to Abdullah and thank him for how he was condoning action against unarmed teenagers and, hence, defending the indefensible. These were published in *Greater Kashmir*. Below is the first letter:[19]

2 August 2010

In less than two months, Mr Omar Abdullah's most disciplined police force and India's extremely tolerant paramilitary, CRPF, have only claimed 44 innocent lives in the hapless Kashmir Valley. Did we ever have such a humane, tolerant and competitive Chief Minister in recent history? I salute you, Sir.

Thank you, our most tolerant leader in recent times. Thank you for your zero tolerance on human rights abuses.

Thank you for keeping all the promises that you had made before becoming India's youngest Chief Minister. Thank you for silencing all your critics, all those voices you didn't or don't want to hear. All those speaking against your 'idea of democracy' are anyway miscreants, few in number. Thank you for putting all those leaders behind bars that you'd promised to initiate a peace dialogue with. Thank you for labelling all those young people as Lashkar-e-Toiba (LeT) operatives that you'd promised to give jobs to, whose bright future you had alluded to in your election promises.

Thank you for marginalizing your own people and pushing your own youth to the wall. Thank you for not listening to anyone, because there is no one who can advise Your Highness!

Thank you for creating a 1990-like situation again, when almost every street in Kashmir was filled with common people chanting passionate slogans for freedom and facing (the) state's wrath.

Thank you for seeking the army's help to cool down tempers and for giving a licence to spill blood on Kashmir's streets. Thank you for refusing to read the writing on the wall, which only shows how brave and defiant you are, Mr Abdullah.

Thank you for not taking the people of Kashmir seriously, for not listening to them, for listening to New Delhi only, and for uniting the people of the state again despite their ideological and other differences.

Thank you for achieving something that few have so far managed in Kashmir. Thank you for bringing tens of thousands of Kashmiris to fight for the same idea, the same goal and the same target, even though that idea might be opposed to yours.

Thank you for letting the people of this sacred land realize their own strength. Thank you for making a common man understand that 'the size of the dog in the fight doesn't matter, what matters is the size of the fight in the dog'.

What an incredible record you've maintained thus far. Not a single violation of human rights, not a single fake encounter, not a single innocent killed, not a single arrest, not even a house arrest, not a single restriction on the media, not a single violent incident. A clean record, I must say.

Thank you for not imposing indefinite curfews as often as you could have. Thank you for not gagging the media and journalists as often as you could have. Thank you for exercising maximum restraint.

Thank you for making a desperate appeal for peace to all those parties, individuals and elements you'd until yesterday (called) 'enemies of peace and tranquillity'.

I want to thank you in the same manner as the Brazilian author, Paulo Coelho, thanked the former President of the United States, George W. Bush, for all his achievements before and after his hugely unpopular invasion of Iraq.

Thank you, our popular and great leader, Mr Omar Abdullah. Thank you very much!

The second letter was published in *Greater Kashmir* on 17 August 2010:

I had thanked you, our worthy Chief Minister, for your various achievements in my last letter. Today, I believe it is an appropriate time to thank you again, for your list of achievements is getting bigger and more impressive with each passing day.

The last time I thanked you, the death toll of innocent civilians in Kashmir stood at 44. It has now gone up to 120. What an achievement at an amazingly brisk pace, to kill and muzzle all those voices you don't like or want to hear. Mr Omar Abdullah, you're not alone at all. The establishment at New Delhi, the Army, CRPF, J&K Police, your cabinet colleagues and party members, are all with you, rallying behind you. Only the people of Kashmir, who elected you, aren't. It is only that the opposition PDP that is not with you, the pro-freedom APHC, a majority of Kashmiri lawyers and journalists, and some eight million miscreant inhabitants of the Kashmir Valley. Other than these, everyone else is with you, for you, of you, by you!

This is not a big challenge for you, as long as you continue to issue shoot-at-sight orders to silence these miscreants, few in number. It is only the common people who are against you and might raise slogans against you, but hats off to your power of concentration, your courage, tolerance and resilience that you did not feel compelled to give up power. You're so powerless while in power, what will happen when you are out of power?

I wonder if we ever had such a humane, tolerant and competitive Chief Minister in recent memory.

Thank you, our great, popular and tolerant leader, Mr Omar Abdullah!

Be that as it may, credit is due to Omar Abdullah for accepting on the record that he had made mistakes as the CM and for advising Mehbooba Mufti not to repeat them. After Burhan Wani's killing, Abdullah said in one of his tweets on 8 July 2016: 'Alas Burhan isn't the 1st to pick up the gun & won't be the last. @JKNC_ has always maintained that a political problem needs pol. Solution.' A day after, he wrote that Burhan's ability to recruit young people into militancy from his grave will far outstrip anything he could have done while alive. On 16 July, he confessed that he had learnt from his mistakes, and would ensure they weren't repeated. He accused Mehbooba Mufti of not only repeating them but multiplying them many times over.

In all fairness, and as mentioned before, Mehbooba Mufti in an exclusive interview with me in August 2018 did admit that forging an alliance with BJP 'was an unpopular decision'. She also regretted making certain statements against civilians that hurt the sentiment of the people. 'I was more angry than frustrated... All I can say is, please forgive me...if you can. I was the chief minister when the killings happened, and it does not matter why and how it happened.'

In June 2018, when the BJP walked out of its alliance with the PDP after a little over three years, the J&K Legislative Assembly was kept in suspended animation. In November 2018, BJP's top leader, Ram Madhav, and several spokespersons of his party described the PDP and NC as 'terrorist-friendly' parties. The Hindu nationalist party feared that the two regional parties, the PDP and NC, could unite with the Congress to form a government in J&K and keep the BJP out of power. Governor Satya Pal Malik, who was allegedly sent to Kashmir on 'Amit Shah's ticket'[20] in August 2018, in a controversial decision, hurriedly dissolved the J&K Legislative Assembly on 21 November after political rivals— PDP led by Mehbooba Mufti, and People's Conference led by Sajad Lone—staked claims to form the government. First, Mufti posted a letter on Twitter in which she claimed support of fifty-six MLAs, including those from the NC and the Congress party. She said that her faxed letter to Raj Bhawan in Jammu was not received. Minutes later, in a dramatic move, Sajad Lone too posted a Whatsapp message that showed him sending his letter in the form of a message to the governor's personal assistant. He claimed he too had numbers to form the government. Immediately, Governor Malik dissolved the Assembly to put all speculations to rest. The governor said his office was closed for the Eid Milad-un-Nabi holidays and there was no one to receive any fax there. The news about a 'snag' in the fax machine at Raj Bhawan became a joke in Kashmir and elsewhere. *The Telegraph* wrote a catchy headline on the fiasco: 'Operation fax pas.'[21]

The credibility of pro-India politics in J&K has been severely eroded, especially after the civilian uprising in 2016. Many 'mainstream' politicians have acknowledged that their politics is on the precipice of irrelevance in Kashmir. The APHC leaders too have been blamed for their brand of politics, passion play and 'lack of vision' and strategy, and for not having a blueprint for the resolution of the dispute. The conglomerate's infighting and cliquishness has also been criticized. A faction of the APHC has been blamed for not being democratic and run by the all-powerful executive council members. In the past, fissures in the

APHC camp led by the popular head priest, Mirwaiz Umar Farooq, had surfaced.

The APHC, it may well be recalled, was formed on 10 March 1993 as the political face of Kashmir's resistance movement to find a political solution to Kashmir when armed militancy had internationalized the dispute. Its aim was to achieve the 'right to self-determination' for Kashmiris in accordance with the UNSC resolutions on Kashmir. Since its inception, the APHC has seen many ups and downs. The biggest setback to it was the split it suffered after the 2002 Assembly elections in the state.

The widely admired pro-resistance leader, Syed Ali Geelani, accused some APHC leaders of violating the conglomerate's constitution by remaining silent over the fielding of 'proxies' by Sajad Lone in the elections. After serious disagreements over why the APHC did not launch a vigorous boycott campaign before the elections, Geelani parted ways with Mirwaiz Umar Farooq's APHC. Soon after his release from prison at the time, Geelani formed his own Tehreek-i-Hurriyat and Hurriyat Conference (now known as APHC-G) calling it a 'purification process'. From then on, the two factions of the APHC have been led by Syed Ali Geelani (APHC-G) and by Mirwaiz Umar Farooq (APHC-M).

Soon after the split, many smaller parties joined Geelani's Hurriyat. Within no time, most of them deserted Geelani, alleging they were not being heard and had little say in the decision-making process. On many occasions, Geelani has been accused by some of having a 'dictatorial attitude' and being a 'one-man show'.

All was not well with the APHC-M either. The controversy began when one of its prominent leaders, Professor Abdul Gani Bhat, defied the APHC's constitution by declaring that the UNSC resolutions on Kashmir had become 'irrelevant' and 'impracticable', and that the APHC needed to explore the option of forging an alliance with pro-India mainstream politicians to give shape to a 'common minimum programme'. Mirwaiz Umar Farooq—who is a strong votary of the UN resolutions and also favours tripartite talks—was accused of maintaining silence over Bhat's remarks. There have been times when Geelani, too, has made controversial remarks like 'They have left no option for youth than to take up arms'[22] or that 'the people of Kashmir have failed the leadership.'[23] In fact, Mirwaiz and Yasin Malik too have made such statements about the youth and the gun. The trio has also been accused of maintaining silence when any act of human rights violation is committed by armed rebels.

I am not sure whether Kashmir's responsible leaders realize the impact that their press statements have on the impressionable minds of youngsters and teenagers.

In the autumn of 2017 I had visited Hajin, a town in north Kashmir's Bandipore district situated some 40 km from Srinagar. Hajin was infamous for being the hub of a controversial State-sponsored militia known as Ikhwan in the mid-1990s. To reach Hajin, one must drive through picturesque roads lined with poplar and Kashmir's distinctive chinar trees. But fear seems to have settled on this place, which is obviously no stranger to violence. This small market town has become a new flashpoint, as today it has found itself in the news for being used as a transit route and base camp for foreign militants belonging to the outlawed Pakistan-based group, LeT. From here, the armed rebels divide into splinter groups to launch attacks on government forces. The authorities believe that it has been chosen as a transit route because of its topography.

Residents of Hajin allege that government forces routinely carry out so-called 'cordon and search operations', locally called 'crackdowns', to 'harass us for no fault of ours.'[24] Anti-State feelings are running high among the locals. 'The army and police personnel beat us, seize our bikes and cars and ransack our houses during these operations,' a local chemist told me while wishing to remain anonymous.

Fear of a different kind has gripped Hajin after a gap of over a decade. In the town, I met the forty-six-year-old Abdul Hamid Mir, father of slain nineteen-year-old militant Abid alias Arhan. I asked Mir about the news of the dramatic homecoming of Majid Khan, a star footballer from south Kashmir who had briefly joined the LeT in November 2017. 'I thought my son Abid had returned home,' he said. Tears rolled down Mir's face as he talked about his son. He recounted fond memories of Abid as an 'obedient, dazzling and polite boy'. Mir, a reasonably successful businessman dealing in pharmaceuticals in the town, lost his son, a commerce student, in an encounter with government forces in August 2017. Abid was killed along with his two associates, namely Javed Dar and Danish Dar, in Amargarh Sopore, a town 50 km north of Srinagar. Abid joined the ranks of LeT in May without his father getting a whiff of it. Between 12 May and 5 August, he remained active as a Lashkar militant for eighty-six days before being killed.

But how did a bright student like him end up joining the ranks of the armed rebels?

'The rest of the Kashmir Valley has not witnessed the kind of brutalities that Hajin has,' Mir said, adding that 'young and impressionable minds often discuss the past in their homes'. Abid would also discuss Kashmir's political question, and its present and past, at home. For Abid, according to his father, 'the situation of being a slave in one's own land was stifling'. Life, said Mir, was going smoothly for Abid until early 2013, when he was in Class IX. 'He (Abid) was very fond of Bollywood. Then, Afzal Guru was hanged in February 2013. Everything changed.' After Guru's execution there was a visible change in his behaviour. Abid also attended the funeral of popular HM commander Burhan Wani in July 2016, his father informed. 'From a bubbly character, Abid suddenly became a quiet person,' Mir said.

Apart from Guru's execution and Wani's killing, there was something more that drastically changed Abid's personality.

Ironically, he received his primary education from Indian Army's Goodwill School in Bandipore district and then studied at Jawahar Navodaya Vidyalaya in the frontier town of Uri in north Kashmir's Baramulla district. Abid's father is himself an alumnus of Sainik School Manasbal while his younger son, Zakir, studies at the same school. He recalled that once his son was selected for a tour to Jawahar Navodaya Vidyalaya in Uttar Pradesh where he and his classmates were allegedly coerced to sing the Indian national anthem. According to Mir, Abid had flatly refused to do so, thus inviting the wrath of his teachers. 'The teachers beat my son ruthlessly. A bone in his leg was severely injured and it took almost a year to heal. That incident also changed him as a person,' the father said. Only after a written apology, Mir said, was his son allowed to attend his school in Uri again. Soon after, Abid stopped watching Delhi-based news channels, as he developed a strong dislike for what was being said. Instead, he began offering regular prayers at a mosque nearby. The father further stated that after seeing a visible change in his son, he would often talk to him to impress upon him that Kashmir's problem would be resolved only through political means. 'My son would never argue with me. He was very polite,' he said, adding that he was totally unaware as to when Abid had joined the Lashkar.

Prior to his joining the LeT, Abid had registered himself as a BCom student at Islamia College of Science and Commerce in Hawal, Srinagar. 'I believe my son could have contributed more to Kashmir because he was a genius,' Mir said.

Of the notorious government-sponsored renegades, the Ikhwanis/Nawabadis, Mir said, 'They were looters. They looted our wealth and robbed us of our honour. Government forces pull us out and search our houses against our will. We are never free in our own land.'

No one seems to care about the loss of Kashmir's human resource—its young boys—to violence. On one of my recent visits to south Kashmir, I met the old and ailing Ghulam Hassan Sheikh, father of Aatif Hassan Sheikh aka Babloo, the young man from Anantnag district who has the distinction of being named in more than fifty FIRs—a record of sorts. From 2007–10 and then again in 2016, the Sheikh family alleges that their son Aatif has more than fifty cases registered against him. He stands accused of participating in stone pelting incidents and professing pro-Pakistan ideology on social media. According to the family, the story of Aatif's long arrests, detentions and short releases began in 2007. At the time I had visited Aatif's home, he was lodged in Srinagar's Central Jail after being booked under the PSA in July for 'promoting secessionist ideology' and refusing to 'join the mainstream' politics. It was the third PSA detention that he was facing at the time. Before being brought to Central Jail Srinagar, he was put in the Kot Bhalwal and Kathua jails in Jammu. Intriguingly, the PSA dossier, under which the thirty-one-year-old Aatif was arrested in July, had been prepared and signed in August 2015. He was arrested outside Anantnag district court where he had gone for a hearing in an old case. His lawyer Mir Shafqat Hussain believes that at the time of his client's arrest, the period of his detention was technically over. 'It is ironic that someone is arrested a year after the case is registered,' he said.

Ghulam Hassan Sheikh, Aatif's seventy-one-year-old father, is a retired government employee. Aatif's mother, who retired as a nursing supervisor, is currently bedridden due to various ailments that include diabetes and arthritis. In 2009, the senior Sheikh, after having witnessed his son being put behind bars every now and then, decided to get him married when he was only twenty-three. 'Unfortunately, the police did not allow him (Aatif) to lead a normal life,' the old and broken father told me at his residence in Deva Colony, in old Anantnag. Aatif, according to his father, was also picked up by the police when he was a three-day-old groom. He was accused of participating in pro-freedom protests and stone throwing incidents. He remained inside the Anantnag police station for about three weeks before being released. In 2010, Aatif's young wife, Sami Jan, delivered a baby girl, but the father was again in jail. The baby died soon after but Aatif was not allowed to see his daughter even then. 'Aatif never met his baby girl. Never saw her. Neither alive nor dead,' Sheikh said.

Before being arrested during the 2010 summer agitation, Aatif was working with Bharti Airtel and then also secured a job with HDFC bank. However, owing to the adverse reports from the local police, he lost his job, first with the cellular company and later with the bank, too. After his release in 2011, the father persuaded his son to open a hosiery shop in the neighbourhood. Due to regular summons by the police and routine court hearings, Aatif's newly started business did not pick up as desired. Aatif's parents persuaded their son to lead a normal life after his marriage and the death of his daughter. 'Yes, my son espouses a political aspiration, but he does not participate in any violent activities. Why is my son being imprisoned for having a view on Kashmir's political question?' Sheikh asked. Meanwhile, after some time, the Sheikh family was blessed with a baby boy. The grandfather named him 'Ahrar'. Five-year-old Ahrar does not get to meet his father often. It is now getting increasingly tougher for the family to evade uncomfortable queries from Ahrar about Aatif. 'It is not easy to face him (Ahrar). And it is painful to answer Ahrar's questions about Babloo (Aatif),' Sheikh said. Recently, a picture of the father-son duo hugging each other outside the district court Anantnag went viral. In the picture, a chained Aatif can be seen taking Ahrar in his arms and kissing him.

The Sheikh family is hoping that their son, now a pharmaceutical dealer, will be released soon so that he is allowed to settle down with his wife and son like a normal family. *'Mera beta Aatif sangbaz nahin hai, pathar baz nahin hai. Uska sirf ek siyasi nazariya hai'* ('My son is not a stone pelter, he does not throw stones. He just has a political view'), the senior Sheikh said.

Altaf Khan, senior superintendent of police, Anantnag, told me that most of the cases registered against Aatif are regarding his alleged participation in stone pelting incidents. Khan, however, denied that over fifty cases are registered against Aatif. 'Not more than five or six FIRs,' he said, though the family and friends of Aatif insist otherwise.

Aatif was later released.

There are several cases in which police harassment becomes one of the many reasons for youngsters to pick up the gun after the options of peaceful assembly, participation in a protest demonstration or speaking freely on Kashmir in educational institutions is denied to them.

Coming back to the leadership, there was a time when Professor Bhat had remarked in a passionate speech in a mosque in Srinagar, during the early 1990s, that 'the dawn of freedom has arrived' and that 'only the formal announcement was awaited': '*Azadi ka sooraj tulu ho chuka hai, ab sirf ee'laan karna baqi hai*'.

As a schoolboy, I had listened to that speech with keen interest. Almost two decades later, the volte face by the same leader at a public rally in 2012, in his native hamlet, Botengo, in Sopore in north Kashmir, was intriguing. With his speech in the early 1990s, he had inspired a new generation in Kashmir, and with his remark in 2012, he had crushed their dreams and hopes. Contrary to expectations, this controversial statement made by the learned APHC leader did not shock many. It invited little reaction from columnists and lukewarm responses from some lesser-known leaders.

This is perhaps because the people of Kashmir are inured to such theatrics. Political leaders from both camps—mainstream (pro-Delhi) and pro-freedom—have said many things in Kashmir, contradicted themselves time and again, then said many things again, only to renege on their promises yet again. After all, politicians tend to thrive on controversies and convenient statements that project their versions. People do not expect their politicians to be in the mould of Plato's 'philosopher-kings', 'those who love the sight of truth'. They are aware that those at the helm of affairs and those espousing the cause of freedom are ordinary politicians, who have deliberately left the doors open for temptations of all kinds, and who, at any given stage, are liable to change their colours with the ease of chameleons. In politics, they say, rats marry snakes, and there are no untouchables.

In 2012, the APHC led by the Mirwaiz found itself at a crossroads. A seminar that concluded on 20 May 2012 at the APHC headquarters in Srinagar reflected where the party was headed. Things turned ugly when supporters of the Mirwaiz began chanting slogans in his support and reportedly tried to physically assault another prominent APHC leader, Nayeem Khan. Soon, followers of Nayeem Khan and Shabir Shah confronted the Mirwaiz's supporters, which resulted in an exchange of blows. For a brief moment, the APHC headquarters at Rajbagh in Srinagar turned into a wrestling ring. That this happened at a seminar titled 'Blood of Martyrs: Our Role' was a clear indicator of how deep the fissures were.

Interestingly, Mirwaiz Umar Farooq, Bilal Gani Lone and Prof. Bhat did not attend the seminar as they were reportedly under house arrest. As per local media reports, trouble began when Nayeem Khan explicitly challenged the Mirwaiz's silence over Prof. Bhat's controversial remarks at the public rally in his native place, Botengo. 'I have every right to ask my chairman to take action against a person who has violated and challenged the APHC constitution,' Nayeem Khan, chief of National Front, was quoted as having said.[25] 'If Shabir Shah could be expelled from the APHC for meeting the US Ambassador in 1993, and Moulana Abbas Ansari ousted for meeting interlocutors appointed by the Indian Home Ministry, why couldn't Prof. Bhat be shown the door for his remarks violating the Hurriyat constitution?' Khan reportedly asked.

Shabir Shah, chief of the Democratic Freedom Party, also voiced his concern over Mirwaiz Umar Farooq's alleged inaction on the issue. 'We will not accept double standards. Prof. Bhat has spoken against the aspirations of Kashmiri people, and against the APHC's constitution. By creating a fuss, they (a reference to Prof. Bhat and the Mirwaiz) are trying to weaken the freedom movement,' Shah said.[26] Ironically, leaders like Shabir Shah and Nayeem Khan are no strangers to controversy. Khan came under fire for his alleged 'willingness' to participate in the 2008 assembly elections'.[27] Both Shah and Khan are currently under the custody of the NIA for their alleged role in a 'terror funding case and fuelling the unrest in the Kashmir Valley in 2016'. In January 2018, the NIA filed its 1,279-page charge sheet before the Delhi court to seek permission 'to continue its probe in alleged funding of terror and secessionist activities in the Kashmir Valley.'[28]

However, political groups in Kashmir allege that the BJP government is using all powerful State institutions to 'suppress the sentiment of freedom of the people of Kashmir'. Analysts argue that the current government in Delhi is wiping away the middle ground in Kashmir by imposing bans on sociopolitical and religious organizations (JeI and JKLF), arresting political dissidents, and stifling dissent, which leaves a vacuum and actually makes hardliners relevant.

A difference of opinion in any amalgam, conglomerate, group or party is understandable, and its expression is, in fact, the foundation of democracy. It requires tolerance to respect a view one doesn't agree with. But somewhere, a line has to be drawn. When someone challenges the very foundation of an alliance and overtly shifts the goalpost, he or she should either be asked to withdraw the controversial remarks or apologize to the people. If the goal remains the same, different means to achieve it can be employed. But when the goal changes, it calls for introspection. Ironically, Prof. Bhat has said on record that he was accountable to none.

However, Mirwaiz Umar Farooq did serve show cause notices to Prof. Bhat, Nayeem Khan and Azam Inquilabi, asking them why action should not be initiated against them. Shabir Shah was asked to refrain from going public on critical issues. This happened at a gap of some weeks after the contentious seminar. Nothing substantial happened thereafter. Another criticism of the APHC amalgams is that they do not have a vision document on the political future of J&K.

In her essay, 'Shall We Leave It to the Experts', Arundhati Roy remarks:[29]

> Cynics say that real life is a choice between the failed revolution and the shabby deal. I don't know...maybe they're right. But even they should know that there's no limit to just how shabby that shabby deal can be. What we need to search for and find, what we need to hone and perfect into a magnificent, shining thing, is a new kind of politics. Not the politics of governance, but the politics of resistance. The politics of opposition. The politics of forcing accountability... In the present circumstances, I'd say the only thing worth globalizing is dissent...

At this stage, Kashmiris are not sure how 'shabby' that 'shabby deal' actually is. Some leaders have been candid to say that the top brass of the APHC seldom bothers to seek opinions from the general council. This is also indicative of the fact that the amalgam is perhaps not run in a democratic manner.

JKLF chief Yasin Malik has been instrumental in forging some unity between the two factions of the APHC. Even before Burhan's killing, Malik made efforts to get the resistance leadership on a common platform. After Burhan's killing, the people of Kashmir followed the protest calendar of the united resistance leadership in letter and spirit. Another positive change as far as the APHC leaders are concerned is their willingness to engage with different civil society groups and Indian audiences by participating in seminars and conferences organized outside Kashmir. This has helped in some ways to take the voice of Kashmir to those in mainland India who are interested in hearing something beyond the State's narrative.

One may not agree with Syed Ali Geelani's political ideology that Kashmir is a 'natural part' of Pakistan. One may have other major or minor disagreements with some of his past and present strategies as a political and religious leader and his brand of politics, too. But he is revered in Kashmir for what he is and what he stands for. He commands tremendous respect in the Valley for his perceived steadfastness and incorruptibility. Geelani is the calendar and currency in Kashmir's resistance politics. He is a living symbol of anti-State resistance.

★

Many of my friends in various parts of India and abroad (though Indians, too, are considered 'foreigners' in Kashmir) often mention how Kashmir's warmth, generosity and family values leave an indelible impression on their minds. A majority of them leave Kashmir with a pledge to visit this 'beautiful prison' again. But when some Kashmiri leaders and students studying in various colleges and universities in India are attacked, harassed, detained or arrested as a result of anti-Kashmir prejudice, it leaves a bad taste in the mouth.[30] Post the Pulwama attack, there were many attacks on Kashmiri traders, students and academics in several parts of India, most notably in Bihar, Uttarakhand, West Bengal, Karnataka and Maharashtra. This is not to say that the entire Indian population, or the journalist fraternity as a whole, is hostile to Kashmiris. There are many who do not approve of the State's policy on Kashmir. They also challenge the State's monopoly over violence.

The problem with New Delhi vis-a-vis Kashmir is that it only manages the conflict and hopes that tempers will cool down. This serves no purpose because after every period of relative calm, Kashmir is on the boil again and Delhi repeats the same exercise of sending interlocutors during the crisis time, asking them to prepare detailed reports and then throwing their reports into the dustbin. While more Kashmiris die on streets, 'experts' sitting in television studios in New Delhi come up with weird theories and suggest remedies to cool tempers. None of this makes any difference on the ground.

There is another side to Kashmir, which leaders from both camps either ignore completely or do not pay the kind of attention it deserves. In the early 2000s, rumours about a young cricketer of a rival team in our locality, who disappeared all of sudden, were doing the rounds. He did not feature in local tournaments anymore. A skilful medium-pacer, Tanvir (name changed) could also be handy with his bat down the order. As a young boy, he would play cricket with others his age. We enquired about him: 'Why isn't Tanvir around, playing cricket?' Some of his teammates revealed that he had joined the Mujahid Tanzeem, an organization of 'holy warriors' fighting Delhi's rule in Kashmir. He had left the playground forever, and gone underground.

From an amateur cricketer, Tanvir had metamorphosed into an active militant. During his playing days, he had come into contact with a respected local militant commander. Under his influence, Tanvir had decided to join the armed movement. Though he had joined miltancy, he had not crossed over the LoC to receive arms training in PaK. Some years passed by, and

Tanvir was arrested by government forces. As a journalist, I got a chance to meet him soon after his release from jail. For obvious reasons, he did not want to be named. I can't, therefore, refer to him by his real name. For more than three years, he had done all that he was supposed to do. As an obedient guerrilla, Tanvir obeyed the orders—both good and bad—that he received from his seniors. He did what his section, platoon, company, battalion, district and divisional commanders ordered him to, which was mostly aimed at strengthening their position and planning attacks on government forces. Then, one day, as was inevitable, he was arrested.

He considered himself fortunate that he wasn't shot dead in a 'fake encounter' at the time of his arrest. After customary interrogation, he was severely tortured. He was given electric shocks, heavy rollers were rolled over his thin legs, his genitals were pierced with thin knitting pins and there were burn marks all over his body. He was behind bars for nearly three-and-a-half years without trial under the draconian PSA. Tanvir had lost all hope of surviving within the dark concrete walls of his prison, the interrogation centre. After his health condition deteriorated, counter-insurgency officers feared he would die in custody. Therefore, the prospect of his release became possible upon signing a bond that he won't join any militant group again. Fortnightly attendance at a local police station was made mandatory for him. After his release, he needed to be treated for the injuries he had received during his incarceration for four years.

Tanvir was from a poor family. He could not even think of continuing on the same path that he had deliberately chosen for himself as an impressionable young boy. The militant commanders who had earlier showered praises on his tremendous abilities as a guerrilla, and his loyalty towards the cause, didn't want him back in their ranks. Tanvir could no longer lob grenades on military vehicles and run away like a hare, as he would do before he was arrested and tortured.

Tanvir thought that perhaps his poor family didn't want him as a burden in the house, and perhaps society might also not want him as a good-for-nothing rebel. He had committed many unknown 'crimes'—released militants are often mistrusted. Some people detest them for being a bhagoda (runaway), or suspect them of being a mukhbir. And those suspected of being the latter for the police or the Army are often shot dead. In early November 2018, a top commander of the HM, purportedly Riyaz Naikoo, released a 'confession' video of an eighteen-year-old called Nadeem Manzoor. Manzoor was accused of being an Army informer and suspected to have played a role in getting two militants in Shopian district killed. He was shot dead. Several Kashmiris criticized the act of killing a teenager and argued that he should have only been given a warning. In their audio message, the militants reprimanded those raising questions about Manzoor's killing and, in fact, dubbed as 'Indian agents' all those who criticized the killing on social media. The militants also released video recordings of another execution, which was filmed and circulated on social media—of a nineteen-year-old Huzaif Ashraf, who was abducted and slaughtered in an orchard.[31] Masked men flaunting a blood-soaked knife and an AK-47 assualt rifle threatened more such executions of Army and police informers.

Kashmiri militants enjoy public sympathy and support because the perception is that the ill-trained rebels have a high moral compass, for they are fighting a very powerful adversary with limited resources with the aim to alter the status quo. However, when they are seen involved in a civilian killing, people do raise tough questions, especially on social media or in private chatter. The anger was visible when two foreign militants of LeT in north Kashmir allegedly used a twelve-year-old boy, Atif, as a human shield. Many Kashmiris took to social media to deplore the act. The Indian Army was also criticized for blowing up the house in which the militants had taken shelter. People argued that government forces should have suspended their operation to save the life of the child.[32]

I am reminded of another meeting with a militant when I was in my early teens—a commander actually (a fact I did not know at the time). Shaheen (name changed) was introduced to me as a wealthy businessman from Kishtwar. He was a regular visitor at a relative's home. I would often go there to play cricket with boys of my age. He would stay for a couple of days or more at a time, only to return after a fortnight, sometimes after a gap of a month or so. But his visits were always a surprise.

Handsome, well-built, with a neatly trimmed beard and a perennial smile on his face, Shaheen had somewhat of a grasp, if not a complete hold, over the Urdu language. He was rather fond of poets like Allama Iqbal, Mirza Ghalib and Faiz. Though I was young, I realized that something was off about this businessman who never talked about his 'business'. Whoever I asked seemed to deflect the question. My curiosity, therefore, grew with each passing day.

Finally, my question was answered. His morning began with scanning all the major Urdu and English dailies published from Srinagar. Often, he would make notes and encircle columns and news items of interest. 'Why are you reading so many newspapers?' I asked him once, casually. 'Reading is important', was Shaheen's short and sweet response. My curiosity slowly began to turn into suspicion. It was only when something untoward happened in the neighbourhood that I got to know who Shaheen actually was. There was an exchange of fire between militants and government troops a few hundred metres outside my relative's home. Everyone began panicking. I caught sight of Shaheen's face—it was ashen. He left hastily, riding his red-and-black motorbike.

As he hurried away, I noticed he was carrying an AK-47 rifle. Until then, I had seen pictures of this rifle in newspapers and videos on television channels. Some more facts about Shaheen were gradually revealed. Shaheen wasn't his real name. He was from Srinagar, and the son of a retired professor of statistics. And he was actually the district commander of the HM!

Many days, weeks and months passed before I saw Shaheen again. Now that I knew who he was, my questions were pointed and specific. He'd make it a point to answer all of them with a smile on his face, and when I'd be emotionally charged, he knew how to calm me down, the smile ever-present on his face.

From Urdu poetry to the genesis of the Kashmir dispute, he'd be willing to discuss anything I was up for. Most of his answers seemed convincing, or perhaps I was too young to know the art of providing a counterargument. Once, someone asked him why he was not married. 'I'm already married to the cause of our land's freedom,' he said.

Soft-spoken as he was, Shaheen was also charismatic. It was from him that I heard these lines by the legendary Mirza Ghalib for the first time:

'Ashiqi sabr talab aur taman'na betaab,
dil ka kya rang karoun khoon e jigar honay tak?'

(Love matures slowly, but it is difficult to control desire.
What should one do get peace while the process of love is going on?)

Shaheen didn't teach me how to fire bullets or lob grenades, but he did explain why he had chosen that path for himself. I didn't say anything. Perhaps I didn't know what to say to him. Once again, he disappeared without prior warning. And I never saw him again. Many years later, in the late 1990s, we got to know that Shaheen had been killed in a fierce encounter on the outskirts of Srinagar. Front-page pictures in newspapers confirmed his death. In the eyes of a vast majority, he had achieved 'martyrdom'.

★

Ordinary Kashmiris do not suffer only because of political uncertainty and conflict but also because of lack of good governance—underdevelopment, dilapidated roads, lack of healthcare and education, and corruption. One way in which some have attempted to get some basic changes to the infrastructure is through the electoral process that would bring in elected representatives who might address their grievances. Taking part in the political process conducted by Delhi is viewed with deep suspicion, however. Those who do so are often ridiculed and labelled 'traitors' or 'collaborators'. Government representatives are seen as New Delhi's stooges or nodding goats. The dilemma 'to vote or not' lies not so much in the boycott calls by resistance leaders as in the deeply rooted endemic mistrust of Kashmiris towards the government. Some voices in Kashmir want issues like healthcare, education and development to be declared 'conflict neutral', but others argue that nothing is conflict or politics neutral in a conflict zone like Kashmir and, therefore, prefer a political resolution first; everything else later. Even pro-India political leaders of the NC, PDP and the Congress make it clear to voters that their vote only concerns local governance issues and administrative purposes; it is not a vote *for* India.

Now if a common Kashmiri casts his/her vote in the assembly elections for local governance, he/she is largely seen as a beneficiary of military siege and occupation. But if the ordinary person boycotts the elections, he/she suffers the lack of development, clean drinking water, healthcare, good roads, availability of power and jobs. It is a Catch-22 situation, as resistance groups call for a boycott of elections while pro-Delhi political outfits appeal for votes for better governance. Resistance leaders believe that elections under Delhi's rule in Kashmir, and in the presence of government troops, are a sham. Some also say that Delhi's stranglehold on Kashmir is largely executed through puppet regimes with little legitimacy. Hardly anyone addresses the plight of the common people.

In an interview with NDTV's Barkha Dutt on the programme, *The Buck Stops Here*, in September 2016, historian Ramachandra Guha said that the government under PM Narendra Modi was the 'most anti-intellectual' the country had ever had.[33] Guha referred to India as a '50-50 democracy'. According to him, the BJP-led government is also 'hostile' to the writers' community.

Speaking on the politics of identity in the same interview, Guha drew parallels between the Kashmir issue and Sri Lanka:

The Sri Lanka treatment of Tamils is like the Indian treatment of Kashmiris—harsh, arbitrary, involving the excessive use of force and denying local autonomy. At the same time, those who are protesting against discrimination, while they have legitimate grievances, have expressed these grievances too much through the vehicle of armed struggle and the assassination of rivals and the purging of minorities. The Tamil Tigers purged Muslims and Kashmiri Muslims purged Kashmiri Pandits. It is a complex problem. The large party of the blame lies with the states, the Indian state and Sri Lankan state. The rebels are not blameless either. Dignified autonomy is the solution.

On 27 Novermber 2018, addressing a monthly provincial committee meeting for Kashmir Province at NC's headquarters at Nawa-e-Subha in Srinagar, the party's vice president and former CM, Omar Abdullah, voiced concern over the 'unbridled civilian killings and human rights violations in the state.'[34] 'The never-ending vicious circle of killings in Kashmir which gained momentum since the PDP-BJP alliance came in being continues to devour our young and old. People especially the youth of the state stand disenchanted due to wrong policies being implemented by BJP led central government,' he said. Omar solicited an earnest effort from the New Delhi government 'to instil confidence in the people. The ironist strategy should pave (the) way for reconciliation and rapprochement.'

The problem appears to be a lack of political will and statesmanship in New Delhi, Islamabad and Srinagar. It seems unlikely that Modi and his Pakistani counterpart will seize the moment and script history by coming to the negotiating table to resolve Kashmir, especially when Modi has won a second term in May 2019. It is easier to be a war-monger; it involves much greater work to broker peace. I am reminded of Faraz's verses from a poem about Pakistan-India friendship:

'Tumhein bhi zo'm Mahabharata ladee tum ne
Hamein bhi fakhr ki hum Karbala ke aadi hain
Tumhare Des main aaya houn dosto ab ki
Na saz-o-naghma ki mehfil na shayri ke liye
Agar tumhari ana hi ka hai sawal

Chalo main haath badhata houn dosti ke liye'

(You're proud to have fought the Mahabharata,
We're elated to have endured the Karbala.
Friends, I've arrived in your country,
Neither for musical concerts nor poetry recitals.
If it is all about your ego,
Let me extend the hand of friendship.)

Friendship between India and Pakistan has always benefited Kashmiris the most. The ceasefire on the LoC saves lives, quite literally. Hostility between the two nations pushes Kashmiris to the wall. Can India and Pakistan find leaders who can rise above empty rhetoric meant to appease domestic constituencies, and sit together to make a sincere attempt to resolve Kashmir? Can all the stakeholders involved show maturity to bring permanent peace in South Asia and employ negotiations as a peaceful and meaningful tool to resolve the Kashmir conflict? Can Srinagar become a bridge of friendship between Islamabad and Delhi, and not a bone of contention? Can someone make it happen, instead of waiting for things to happen?

Who will extend the hand of friendship? Who will reciprocate? Will Srinagar produce such a statesman?

NOTES, SOURCES AND REFERENCES

1. Has India lost Kashmir? (2017, May 10). Retrieved from https://www.rediff.com/news/column/has-india-lost-kashmir/20170510.htm
2. Kashmir is nearly lost, says Chidambaram. (2017, February 25). Retrieved from https://www.thehindu.com/news/cities/Hyderabad/kashmir-is-nearly-lost-says-chidambaram/article17365791.ece
3. Chidambaram, P. (2017, April 15). Across the aisle: Kashmir is sliding into disaster. Retrieved from https://indianexpress.com/article/opinion/columns/kashmir-is-sliding-into-disaster-4614675/
4. Ibid.
5. When People Of Kashmir Ask For 'Azadi', Most Want Autonomy: Chidambaram. (2017, October 28). Retrieved from https://www.ndtv.com/india-news/when-people-of-kashmir-ask-for-azadi-most-want-autonomy-chidambaram-1768316
6. Siddiq, W. (2018, June 10). Let us stop being "moderate" and be "radical". Retrieved from https://www.greaterkashmir.com/news/opinion/let-us-stop-

being-moderate-and-be-radical/287693.html

7. Banerjee, R. (2018, July 04). The Human on The K-Table. Retrieved from https://www.outlookindia.com/magazine/story/the-human-on-the-k-table-time-for-a-new-narrative-to-break-logjam-in-kashmir/300355

8. Source 1: 150 militants killed, 81 security personnel lost lives in 2016: Mehbooba Mufti. (2018, July 13). Retrieved from https://economictimes.indiatimes.com/news/defence/150-militants-killed-81-security-personnel-lost-lives-in-2016-mehbooba-mufti/articleshow/56313632.cms
    Source 2: 213 militants killed in 2017: J-K govt. (2018, January 18). Retrieved from https://www.thehindu.com/news/national/213-militantskilled-in-2017-j-k-govt/article22465415.ece
    Source 3: Roshangar, R. A. (2018, November 28). At least 413 killed in 2018 due to violence in Kashmir. Retrieved from https://www.indiatoday.in/india/jammu-and-kashmir/story/at-least-413-killed-in-2018-due-to-violence-in-kashmir-1397684-2018-11-28

9. Army uses winter offensive against militants in Kashmir. (2018, December 02). Retrieved from https://www.deccanherald.com/national/infiltration-down-security-706045.html

10. Geelani, G. (2018, December 04). The rise of educated young Kashmir militants: Propaganda or unpalatable truth? Retrieved from https://thedefensepost.com/2018/11/30/kashmir-educated-young-militants-propaganda-unpalatable-truth/

11. Yearly Fatalities. (2019, June 08). Retrieved from https://www.satp.org/datasheet-terrorist-attack/fatalities/india-jammu-kashmir

12. Ibid.

13. Rawat, M. (2019, May 18). Pulwama terror attack: In last 5 years, J&K saw 93% rise in death of security personnel in terror attacks. Retrieved from https://www.indiatoday.in/india/story/pulwama-terror-attack-jammu-kashmir-terrorism-data-last-5-years-soldiers-killed-1456427-2019-02-14

14. Yearly Fatalities. (2019, June 08). Retrieved from https://www.satp.org/datasheet-terrorist-attack/fatalities/india-jammu-kashmir

15. Ganai, N. (2015, June 27). How J&K's caught in PDP's battle of ideas. Retrieved from https://www.dailyo.in/politics/jammu-kashmir-pdp-bjp-mehbooba-mufti-mohammad-sayeed-separatists-kashmir-university-jamia-mosque/story/1/4628.html

16. Jaleel, M. (2016, July 31). Mehbooba's dark hour: As Kashmir erupts, Mufti walking the tightrope with her hands tied as CM. Retrieved from http://indianexpress.com/article/india/india-news-india/kashmir-protest-burhan-wani-killing-mehbooba-mufti-pdp-bjp-alliance-5113/

17. Kashmir unrest: CM Mehbooba loses cool, walks out of press conference. (2016, August 25). Retrieved from http://indiatoday.intoday.in/story/kashmir-unrest-mehbooba-press-conference-rajnath-singh/1/748853.html

18. Barry, E. (2016, August 28). An Epidemic of 'Dead Eyes' in Kashmir as India Uses Pellet Guns on Protesters. Retrieved from https://www.nytimes.com/2016/08/29/world/asia/pellet-guns-used-in-kashmir-protests-cause-dead-eyes-epidemic.html

19. Source 1: Geelani, G. (2015, March 13). Shoes are thrown at great leaders.

Retrieved from http://www.greaterkashmir.com/news/opinion/shoes-are-thrown-at-great-leaders/81035.html

Source 2: Geelani, G. (2010, August 02). Thank you, [C]hief [M]inister Mr. Omar [Web log post]. Retrieved from http://gemwrites.blogspot.com/2010/08/thank-you-chief-minister-mr-omar.html?view=flipcard

20. Thakur, S. (2018, August 22). To Kashmir, on Shah ticket. Retrieved from https://www.telegraphindia.com/india/to-kashmir-on-shah-ticket/cid/1311556

21. Thakur, S. (2018, November 22). Operation fax pas. Retrieved from https://epaper.telegraphindia.com/index.php?pagedate=2018-11-22&edcode=71&subcode=79&mod=1&pgnum=1&type=a

22. Wani, A. S. (2018, November 02). Repression forcing Kashmir youth to pick up arms: Geelani. Retrieved from https://www.greaterkashmir.com/news/kashmir/repression-forcing-kashmir-youth-to-pick-up-arms-geelani/

23. Bukhari, S. (2015, November 28). People have failed leadership: Geelani. Retrieved from http://www.risingkashmir.com/news/people-have-failed-leadership-geelani

24. Hajin: The Kashmir town that is a 'militant hub'. (2017, November 28). Retrieved from http://www.bbc.com/news/world-asia-india-42062192

25. Maqbool, Z. (2015, March 14). Expel Prof Bhat, demand Hurriyat (M) leaders. Retrieved from http://m.greaterkashmir.com/news/kashmir/expel-prof-bhat-demand-hurriyat-m-leaders/121077.html

26. Dulat, A. S. (2015). Kashmir's Mandela or Delhi's Agent: Shabir Shah. In *Kashmir: The Vajpayee Years*. Noida, U.P.: HarperCollins India.

27. Ibid.

28. Terror funding case: NIA files chargesheet against LeT chief Hafeez Saeed, Hizbul's Syed Salahuddin. (2018, January 18). Retrieved from http://www.livemint.com/Politics/OuYQiApyzuU0VxGsJh5emI/Terror-funding-case-NIA-files-chargesheet-against-LeT-chief.html

29. Roy, A. (2002, January 13). Shall We Leave It to the Experts? Retrieved from https://www.outlookindia.com/magazine/story/shall-we-leave-it-to-the-experts/214223

30. Source 1: Ghose, D. (2016, August 05). Kashmiri man 'liked, shared anti-India' Facebook posts, arrested. Retrieved from http://indianexpress.com/article/india/india-news-india/kashmiri-held-on-train-for-liking-anti-india-web-posts-2954534/

Source 2: Chaturvedi, A. (2014, March 10). 67 Kashmiri students, suspended for cheering for Pakistan, to return to UP college. Retrieved from http://www.ndtv.com/meerut-news/67-kashmiri-students-suspended-for-cheering-for-pakistan-to-return-to-up-college-553431

Source 3: Three Kashmiri students beaten over 'minor argument' in Haryana college. (2016, September 28). Retrieved from http://www.hindustantimes.com/india-news/three-kashmiri-students-beaten-over-minor-argument-in-haryana-college/story-msks09JoWlocHiWBJWS1pO.html

Source 4: Rajasthan: Four Kashmiri students allegedly 'beaten up' over beef rumours. (2016, March 16). Retrieved from http://indianexpress.com/article/cities/jaipur/mewar-university-four-kashmiri-students-allegedly-beaten-up-over-beef-rumours/

31. Masoodi, N. (2018, November 23). Blog: The ISIS-Style Executions In Kashmir Are Backfiring For Militants. Retrieved from https://www.ndtv.com/blog/the-filmed-execution-of-teens-in-kashmir-1952167

32. Zargar, S. (2019, March 25). The killing of a 12-year-old boy in Kashmir has prompted local voices to decry militant tactics. Retrieved from https://scroll.in/article/917743/the-killing-of-a-12-year-old-boy-in-kashmir-has-prompted-local-voices-to-decry-militant-tactics

33. Source 1: NDTV. (2016, September, 15). Modi government anti-intellectual, Congress finished as political force: Ram Guha. Retrieved from https://www.youtube.com/watch?v=V8Pun7pB4Gk

    Source 2: Guha also makes similar argument in his book *Democrats and Dissenters*

34. A press statement issued by the NC, dated 27 November 2018.

ACKNOWLEDGEMENTS

Without a whisker of a doubt, I would first love to thank someone who can smell the sentiment on the Kashmir streets and understands the importance of the narratives and chronicles—Tashakur!

Moreover, I cannot forget to thank my friend, a wonderful colleague and former senior editor at Deutsche Welle in Bonn, Amjad Ali. He introduced me to the wider literary world and made me fall in unconditional love with Urdu poetry, as never before. His birthday gifts were amazing. I owe a lot to him for believing in me.

A big thank you is due to the entire Rupa Publications team, especially to my indefatigable editor Debangana Banerjee, cool-as-a-cucumber Rudra Narayan Sharma, and the smiling Vasundhara. All of them have been a wonderful support. Thank you to Kapish with whom I have held several rounds of fruitful discussions to make everything work smoothly.

Thanks to Swati, whose editing skills I truly appreciate. Her attention to detail is something I can neither ignore nor forget.

I also express my gratitude to the late Barbara Harlow, who believed in the content as well as the intent of me as the author, and saw a book in me. Equally, I feel indebted to Professor Mridu Rai, who was among the first ones to have gone through the initial draft of my manuscript and taken pains to give her detailed feedback for progress.

Besides, it is only fair to thank acclaimed authors and historians Andrew Whitehead, Christopher Snedden and Victoria Schofield for being kind to read the manuscript with professionalism and humility, and for being gracious enough to endorse the book.

And how can I not mention Burhaan Kinu for his amazing

picture, which we used on the cover for the book, with his permission!

Thank you Muneer, Samiullah, Majid, Faisul, Khurram, Suhail, Faheem, Ejaz, Waheed, Hina, Parveena Ahanger, Tamanna Baji, G.N. Shahid, IF and WQ for all your support and encouragement, and to the many unsung heroes who I cannot identify by name for obvious reasons.

At the end of the day, I am a storyteller. And I come from a place where funerals of the young are political events, mourning is permanent politics, and the people are in a constant battle between memory and forgetfulness. Therefore, I must not forget to thank all those people whose stories I have narrated while trying my best to act as a conduit and to present their stories with honesty of purpose. I thank all the women heroes who play a leading role in the politics of protest and resistance in Kashmir and yet remain unsung, and to all the Kashmiri children who deserve to live with dignity, dream, aspire, have an opinion, and do not deserve to face bullets and pellets, an uncertain political future and the crisis of identity!

Last but not the least, I thank Sabu for reading the chapters with great dedication in the harsh winters of Jammu and Kashmir.